THE

MOST

WONDERFUL

TIME

ALSO BY JAYNE ALLEN

Black Girls Must Die Exhausted

Black Girls Must Be Magic

Black Girls Must Have It All

THE MOST WONDERFUL TIME

A Novel

JAYNE ALLEN

HARPER PERENNIAL

NEW YORK • LONDON • TORONTO • SYDNEY • NEW DELHI • AUCKLAND

HARPER ● PERENNIAL

THE MOST WONDERFUL TIME. Copyright © 2024 by Jaunique Sealey. All rights reserved. Printed in the United States of America. No part of this book may be used or reproduced in any manner whatsoever without written permission except in the case of brief quotations embodied in critical articles and reviews. For information, address HarperCollins Publishers, 195 Broadway, New York, NY 10007.

HarperCollins books may be purchased for educational, business, or sales promotional use. For information, please email the Special Markets Department at SPsales@harpercollins.com.

FIRST EDITION

Designed by Jamie Lynn Kerner

Library of Congress Cataloging-in-Publication Data has been applied for.

ISBN 978-0-06-313796-7 (pbk.)
ISBN 978-0-06-339287-8 (library edition)

24 25 26 27 28 LBC 5 4 3 2 1

This book is for you, but, truly, for who you'll be after you read it. And for you now, I hope that *this* you will enjoy the journey and all the characters you'll meet along the way—and that you'll have the most wonderful time.

THE
MOST
WONDERFUL
TIME

DECEMBER 10

• ● •

CHELSEA FLINT ON AN OTHERWISE LOVELY MORNING IN MALIBU, CALIFORNIA

In Southern California, sunlight simply *is*. From majestic daybreaks until orange sherbet sunsets wash the sky, the sun is everywhere. Its warmth kisses the tops of the swaying palm trees and lays a blanket across the sable-colored beach sand. Its light tickles the rippling surface of the ocean and makes it writhe in sparkling delight. And in Malibu, a sleepy beach town just up the Pacific coast from the bustling metropolis of Hollywoodland, the sun makes a glorious daily procession to each of the 10,500 residents. That's why they're there—for the sun and the sea. But where our story begins, at *this* daybreak, the sun was having a very hard time finding its way to Chelsea Flint.

Flanked by modern coastal mansions, a modest beachside cottage sat, stuck in time like a weathered shipwreck. At its bedroom window, the sun's rays wiggled through thin gaps in closed shutters to create their soft strokes on a still-sleeping Chelsea Flint's freckled face. Outside, the Pacific roared gently, with white-capped waves lapping the sand at low tide. A lovely morning it was, but Chelsea remained blissfully unaware of the obvious: from her ocean-facing bedroom, the developing splendor outdoors made a view so remarkable that it should never, absolutely never, ever be covered. But her shutters were shut as tightly as her eyes, while she was bundled cozily—red hair extending like a fountain of lava—into an avalanche of bedding, piles of comforter and pillows engulfing her slight-bodied frame like a bath of meringue. She was deep, deep in a forgetful slumber, far away from the realities that would shortly come to call with the sudden shriek of her cell phone.

The blaring sound of the ringing phone made a stark contrast with the calm and rhythmic whoosh of the ocean. The phone was rude and insistent and would not be ignored. Chelsea awoke with a start, fumbled around to find the device, and eventually stopped its cacophonous assault. She finally croaked a groggy "Hi, Helena" into the closest end, which she hoped contained the microphone. For Chelsea, it was much too early for any reasonable conversation, but that was when Helena, Chelsea's art gallerist and agent, most liked to call. Helena was a Londoner and respected absolutely no other time zone than the one that she herself was currently in. And that was to be expected, because Helena's time was literally money, and she had little of the former to spare, unless you happened to be a member of such and such royal family, lately rumored to be her biggest clients. She was also one of the absolute best at what she did, and if you were lucky enough to fall into a coveted spot in her tightly curated client list, you would certainly tolerate this minor disruption. Because when Helena called, money followed, or at least it was supposed to. What artist with even an inkling of ambition wouldn't want a direct line to the director of the Guggenheim or the Tate Modern? Helena had the sort of enviable Rolodex that could only be built through decades of experience and a healthy dose of *Je ne sais quoi* and *Je m'en fous*. Once, Helena was even able to convince the notoriously crabby curator of the Centre Pompidou to house her *American* client's neon-light '80s retrospective with full-on repeated reruns of *Family Ties*.

For Helena, however, Chelsea was no ordinary client. She was family, or at least considered so, as much as a person like Helena would ever acknowledge. But unlike Helena's regular clients, Chelsea was far from the top of her career. In almost every regard, it was much more like the bottom. A bottomless bottom. Nonetheless, she was given special attention on this morning, addressed by the brusque staccato tone coming through the phone that was only very slightly softened with the sporadic melodic highs of Helena's British accent.

"Darling, darling, you must wake up. Can you hear me?" Helena shouted over sounds of the blaring horns of traffic in London, or wherever on earth she happened to be that day. Helena certainly had her choice of locales.

Chelsea, still in a state of half sleep, managed to coax her mouth to utter raspy words into the hyperactive phone at her ear. "You . . . sold the painting?" Bracing herself for what response might come, her hand came up to cover her eyes. The money from a sale was money that Chelsea urgently needed, a fact with which Helena was intimately familiar.

"See, darling, that's just it. I haven't sold *any* of your paintings. None. They simply won't sell. Frankly, it's quite frustrating. I'm not even sure I could give them away at this point . . ."

At these words, Chelsea felt the pang of panic begin to build in her gut, bubbling right next to a familiar shock of rumbling hunger coming from her empty stomach. Over the phone speaker, Chelsea heard Helena say to someone else, "You can leave me just there." She wasted no opportunity for efficiency and had clearly called Chelsea while in transit.

Chelsea, more awake now, managed to feign an awkward disbelief. "None? Not any of the oceanscapes?" Of course, not the drab brown landscapes she'd painted in the style of Georgia O'Keefe but with the absence of the same level of color mastery. "I worked *so* hard on those!" (Actually, she had not.)

"Not the Endangered Wildlife series? You said you loved those paintings."

"I cannot say I share that recollection, dear. Of the latest collection, *love* as a word was certainly *not* used."

"Maybe it's just the season?" Chelsea made her weak offer of an excuse even though several seasons had already passed, all with the same outcome. It wasn't the season; it was her work. And it wasn't her talent—it was her mood. To put it lightly, she was in a funk.

"I've no doubt of your talent, Chelsea. I just hate to mention it, because it's distasteful to discuss . . . but, oh dear, given the amounts outstanding, it's best to be honest. And not just as your gallerist, love. Your parents, may their souls rest peacefully, were such dear friends, and I certainly realize how difficult it's been—even after *all* this time. But as of now, I've made quite an investment to cover costs for the Malibu house. And . . . well, I should just get on with saying it, the winter taxes are due."

Chelsea groaned. "How much time do we have?"

"None, I'm afraid. As of exactly today, the first installment, which came due in November, is officially delinquent. And the second installment is due in February."

The house that Chelsea occupied wasn't quite hers. On paper, it was, but the responsibility it had come with was unwelcome and chaotic. Seven years ago, when her parents died suddenly in a boating accident during their last "field trip" to Costa Rica, Chelsea simultaneously became both an adult orphan and a homeowner with the mounting problem of a heap of poorly managed debt. And as she'd been an only child, there was no one to share the burden or the grief.

Chelsea's parents were the quintessential "fun" parents, never the model of responsibility. And they didn't need to be the latter. They'd left a rather posh life in stodgy, aristocratic

London for a much livelier time on the West Coast of America, fueled by the remnants of crusted and aged-over family wealth. Such wealth, after generations of spending rather than earning, and of comforts rather than constraints, had dissipated by the time it reached Chelsea. Still, she'd been raised for adventure. Her mother told her that she could always come home. Her father always had strong arms to hold her when she fell too far or made too big of a mistake. And now, before she'd learned enough, before she'd painted enough, before she'd paid enough attention, they were gone. She was in trouble, and whereas before, she could always return home if she needed to, she already *was* home.

Chelsea sat up in the bed to think more clearly, pulling the sheets up around her with her free hand. In her other hand was her phone and her ongoing call with Helena. Feeling pressure to offer a solution, but entirely empty of even the slightest idea, she sighed loudly. The house had become more like a confinement at this point, the only place she could afford to live. At one time, her earnings as an artist were plentiful enough to fund an independent life in a much more dynamic part of town. Now, the cost of property taxes had come to outpace her earnings, even without a mortgage. And this was because, despite the denial, she was still making but no longer selling her works.

"And there's *nothing* you can sell?" Chelsea asked, although she knew before the start of a careful and measured response what Helena's reply would be.

"Chelsea . . . your work lately . . . you must realize it's uninspired, bland, dare I say it . . . *dystopian* is perhaps the right word. You may be going for Georgia O'Keefe, but you are coming dangerously close to Beksiński. Well, there now, I think I did say it quite *clearly*."

"*Dystopian*, really?"

"Yes, dear, *quite*. I'm so sorry to say."

Chelsea let her bare arm flop down on the bed, resting in the froth of mangled comforter. If not for the sun trying to reach her through the covered windows, without the clear sensation of its warmth on her bare shoulder, she'd think that this was another vivid anxiety dream, the bad sort of dreaming that she'd tried to push away with everything from Ambien to ketamine. The fitful dreaming led to the latest bout of oversleeping. *A phase*, Chelsea thought to herself and tried to shake it off and make sense of it to Helena.

"It's only been a few months. This will pass. It's just . . . temporary."

Chelsea squeezed her eyes shut tightly, hoping that she could somehow escape back into trouble-free sleep, even if just momentarily. Helena's next words were unrecognizably garbled in a moment of static, until the voice over the phone line returned as clear and insistent as ever, but this time leaving Chelsea struck with disbelief.

"Darling, listen to me. I've decided to let the house, just for a bit, until we can get things sorted with selling your work."

"Let the house? Helena. You cannot rent out my house. I live here."

"But you *won't*, dear, if you can't pay the taxes. Just for a short while, let the house earn the money that . . . unfortunately, your art cannot. The rental value for just one week is all you'll need. And for one week, you can stay literally anywhere else. Chelsea, I've been sparing you, certainly, but we had an arrangement. You were supposed to be paying me back in earnings. You were also supposed to be supporting yourself in earnings. Earnings that—as I need not remind you—you currently aren't making. Perhaps you have a better idea?"

But Chelsea did not. The money supporting her was the dwindling remains of a prior sale and a generous advance of funds from Helena. The amount of delinquent property taxes couldn't be made up in weeks or even months of gig work. But it probably could be made up in just one week of rental income. Helena had a point. Letting the house go, even if just for a week, was really the best option for keeping it.

"I'm all out of ideas," Chelsea admitted.

"Very well, then. My assistant will set it up on a site, and perhaps quickly someone will come calling . . . even though it's offseason. I should hope so."

Chelsea fought the urge to protest. It seemed so sudden, so unfair, so overwhelming. And yet, renting was an obvious solution, considering the circumstance. And if she was perfectly honest, even with more time, she simply wasn't in the problem-solving state of mind. For years now, she'd been grappling with the consequences of decisions she hadn't participated in. The worry of it all was enough of a distraction that she could never find herself on the upward side of grief. There was always something new to try to get over. And Helena seemed to pick up on the thought.

"We'll tackle just one thing at a time. Taxes first and then the debt. I do wish your parents had . . . Well, there's no point to that, is there? Misfortune can't be the ruin of everything you've worked for. You're so talented it literally makes me ache, and to see it waste away in that little box on the beach, it's unbearable, really."

At this, Chelsea rolled over, taking a wad of the bed coverings with her in an expanding cocoon.

"Are you there, dear?" Helena's voice crackled in her ear, sounding more like *ah* (crackle) . . . *yah* (crackle) . . . *th* (crackle) . . . *deee*, fading off into complete distortion and ending with the disconnection of the call, abruptly silencing the phone. Chelsea struggled forward to a seated position in her bed and listened for a moment to the waves of the ocean making sounds like static against the sand. *Deep breath in . . . 1 . . . 2 . . . 3 . . . 4 . . . 5 . . .* She practiced the breathing exercises that her last therapist taught her. A technique for the overwhelm of her more intense moments of anxiety.

Chelsea had told no one, not even Helena, about the therapy or the years of anxiety that precipitated it. Anxiety wasn't even a name Chelsea had available for the feelings that followed her back from Scotland, having spent the funeral rites in a complete blur. At first, she had no idea what was wrong, shaking like she was nervous in public, a dwindling appetite that caused her to lose so much weight that it actually changed her appearance. Not feeling herself, she gradually dropped out of social settings, removing herself from the stimuli that also fueled her creative inspiration. The house in Malibu became a retreat at first, and then, when her work stopped selling and she couldn't afford to live elsewhere, it became home. A forty-minute drive from LA, Malibu wasn't just a commute, however—it was a commitment . . . to stay. Eventually, frustration led her to an internet search of her symptoms, and then to a therapist who finally stated the obvious for Chelsea, that she'd endured too much trauma all at once. The breathing tools so far were the only thing that worked to calm her body, those and the smallness of a familiar place, maybe the proximity to the ocean, maybe holding on to what she could of the past.

With the exercises completed, a calmer Chelsea decided that it was time to meet the day. It was the earliest she'd been awake in weeks, but there wasn't a chance of falling back to sleep. Questions bubbled inexorably into her thoughts. *Who would come to sleep in this bed? Who would look out from this window at the ocean? And if they were here, where would she go?* Even if Helena managed to reconnect the call, whether they spoke now or later, with blooming trepidation Chelsea understood that change was already on its way.

RAMONA TUCKER ON AN ESPECIALLY COLD AND PARTICULARLY DREARY MORNING IN CHICAGO, ILLINOIS . . .

LEANING AGAINST FLOOR-TO-CEILING WINDOWS IN HER OFFICE on the twenty-ninth floor, Ramona Tucker wrapped brightly manicured brown fingers around her Santa Claus coffee mug as she stood viewing the downtown winter skyline. At Denton, Lord, and Orwell—Chicago's largest architecture firm—it was easy enough to look out over the city and find at least one of their projects. But although Ramona was at work, that wasn't the focus of her thinking. And although she was looking at the window, she wasn't looking through it. Ramona was seeing her own reflection and thinking about escape. In that reflection, she saw a woman in her earliest thirties, conservatively dressed, with the silhouette of a well-defined twist-out hairstyle on naturally textured hair. She saw cheekbones and full, plum-tinted lips. She saw the curves of her shape, round up top and down below her waist, curves that she'd been trying to tame for what was supposed to be the biggest event of her life. On the fourth finger of her left hand that steadied her mug sat an engagement ring, a tiny disco ball reflecting the light of the room. The wedding planning had gotten out of hand. And it had gotten out of hand because, as things currently stood with her now "ex" fiancé, there wasn't going to be a wedding.

No escape from here, she thought, while simultaneously calculating the December wind's velocity along the length of the company high-rise. On the ground, the same wind would whip strongly enough to bring tears to her eyes. This far up, it would send her all the way to Kansas. And maybe Kansas wasn't so bad of an idea. The glistening of her engagement ring caught her eye again as she brought her hand up for a zip of energy from the fragrant dark roast. It was surely time to wake up. The vapor from the mug flushed her face with warmth, and she blinked away sentimental tears. It was the cusp of the holidays, and there was no such thing as a holiday with her family without Malik. And there was no such thing as a holiday with Malik so long as they were broken up.

A sound at her door commanded Ramona's attention. Startled, she drew in a quick, deep breath. It was still the middle of the workday, and final review of the company's end-of-the-year financial reports was her responsibility. Every comma, figure, and dollar sign needed to be perfectly placed before they went to the CFO for signature. She looked up quickly and smoothed her skirt, hoping with these minor adjustments she could discreetly swipe away any sign of sadness or disorder before her visitor noticed. Emotion was certainly not their office culture.

"Hey, Moe!"

Ramona's eyes traced the voice back to bright red lips underneath a wide round fluff of hair. Ramona's colleague Latrice stood positioned in the middle of the doorframe, with sparkling brown eyes and a disposition much sunnier than the day called for.

"I was looking for a coffee accomplice," she said. "But I see you beat me to it."

Latrice was an architect. A *dope* one. She was so dope she could be fearless at work in ways that Ramona couldn't fathom. Where Ramona was all curves, Latrice was all lines and proportion—lean, angled, and perfectly tailored. With her slim-cut slacks, she wore Jordans. Under her blazers, on the days she chose to wear one, was a hoodie when she felt like it, and other times a bow tie, and sometimes a T-shirt. Already promoted to a project manager, she managed a team and still outworked everyone. But excellence didn't stand between her and coffee or the time she decided was hers for a break.

Things for Ramona were much more steady in all respects as an accounting director, but with steadiness came a certain lack of flexibility. She'd translated her studies into a more certain and immediately lucrative take on her passion for buildings and design. After six months of art school and mounting bills, Ramona decided that she'd be better off utilizing her undergraduate minor in finance as the surest way to pay her school loans. Ramona's career in finance placed her in a world away from what the creatives did, on different floors, on different schedules, but most important, at a higher starting salary. It wasn't living her dreams, but it was stability. Her family was from Chicago's South Side, working class with no room for generational missteps. Nonetheless, despite their dissimilar roles and penchants for uncertainty, Ramona and Latrice became fast friends in the way that so often happens between friendly brown faces in a company when diversity is slim. This was especially so at Denton, where the two ladies were the *only* chocolate-brown faces to be seen at their workplace in the executive hallways.

"Sorry, girl." Ramona sighed. "I needed a pick-me-up. The mornings are still rough."

Latrice's eyes widened. "*Still?* Please tell me that S-T-I-L-L doesn't mean M-A-L-I-K." Latrice punctuated it with an eye roll so brief and so smooth, it seemed like a part of his name. Appropriately, the eye roll landed her gaze on Ramona's left hand. "And we're not even going to discuss why you're still wearing—"

Ramona raised a warning eyebrow with a tilt of her head. "There is *no* need to talk about the ring . . . or Malik, or whatever is going on at his new place . . . or even that he *has* a *new place*."

Latrice squinted back at her with the expert examination of a close friend. Suddenly, she seemed to find what she was looking for.

"Okay. Then, why is your cheek wet?" Latrice launched a dramatized whisper while moving farther into the office, closing the door behind her. "Is that a tear?" She continued her approach with the care shown toward a wounded animal. "You and Malik broke up almost a *month* ago. What happened now that has you crying *at work?*"

"First of all, Latrice, I am *not* crying."

"Yes, Ramona, yes, you are. I can see the streak on your cheek."

Ramona quickly reached her hand up to swipe against her face and confirmed Latrice's observation. Even after the flush of warmth in her cheeks, however, she wasn't ready to concede. "For the record, a single tear is an *almost* cry. I refuse to give him the satisfaction." Ramona walks back to her desk.

"If you say so. And then if not Malik, what has you *almost* crying in your good clothes . . . at your desk?"

Ramona looked down at her outfit: well put together, but all black like she'd been wearing every day for the past two weeks. She drained the last of her coffee and set the mug down between two stacks of number-filled papers on her desk.

"Just that . . . You know how my family is . . . Melba Tucker is the queen of Christmas. And Christmas Eve? Everyone comes, everyone."

"Am I invited this year? 'Cause I didn't get the memo."

Ramona looked down at her phone on her desk. "You would have if she had your phone number. You know my mother is technology challenged. She sent another reminder today . . . in a massive group text."

"Keep me off the group text . . . but forward the details— last year was epic." Latrice patted her entirely flat stomach. "I had to pop the top button on my pants." Christmas was an institution in the Tucker household, as Latrice had observed first-hand at the family's enormous once-a-year gathering.

"Sending it now, a Melba Tucker Holiday Spectacular . . ." Ramona picked up her phone to navigate the screen with her fingertip. "And, of course, she'll expect Malik at Christmas Eve. If I show up solo, she'll be devastated. Everyone will." Ramona flopped into her desk chair. "My brother, my sister-in-law, my cousins will be there, and of course Carlos will bring a date . . ." Ramona watched Latrice's screw-face start to soften, and so continued layering her much-deserved self-pity. "What if this is just a temporary breakup? Couldn't be at a worse time. And this ring . . ." Ramona pulled her hand up between her and Latrice. "If it was *really* over, wouldn't he ask for it back?"

Ramona's friend shifted on her high-top tie-ups and placed a hand of perfectly manicured, unpainted fingertips on the clean lines of her narrow hip. Her fingers tapped a slow cascade, one at a time. Meanwhile, Ramona turned toward the window to look at the snow that had started to fall. "Now all I can think of is how to escape this Christmas," she mused. "I wish I could just disappear now and reappear on December twenty-sixth."

Latrice positioned herself in Ramona's guest chair and brought her hand to her chin, turning her eyes to the ceiling for a long pause.

"Well . . ." Latrice said finally, her voice full of mischief. "Why don't you?" She stood up and crossed the remaining distance to Ramona and took a seat in one of the few open spaces on top of the desk. She leaned in to touch Ramona's shoulder, squaring their eyes. "When's the last time you took a vacation?"

"And *miss* the holidays with my family?" Ramona punctuated with her best "come on, now" look. "I've never missed a Christmas Eve. No matter where I went, they'd be sending search and rescue."

"They can't come get you if they don't know where you are . . ." Latrice looked particularly pleased with her brilliance.

"Girl. As much time as you've spent with them, you clearly don't know my family!" Ramona threw her hands up. "And even if I could *somehow* escape, this is the most expensive time possible to travel! I'm not trying to spend my entire bonus on a hotel stay and airfare."

"Moe, haven't you ever heard of Airbnb? Or what about people who do that . . . what's it called, *home swap*? You have a fabulous downtown condo in the heart of Chicago, right in the center of *everything*. I'm sure some lovely couple would want to spend a little holiday time making memories in front of your exposed brick fireplace."

"Latrice, the Hawk is out and it's cold as a witch's titty. What earthly stranger would want to come here from what would have to be their *warmer* place, to come stay in mine during Chicago winter?"

"Oh, Moe, that's easy—someone who wants to see some real snow for a change. This isn't just Chicago, it's a magical winter wonderland! It's the warm, sweet and salty, buttery crunch of Garrett's cheese and caramel popcorn and the tinsel of the State Street Macy's holiday windows. It's shopping on Michigan Avenue. It's ice skating next to the Bean."

Ramona sighed. "Latrice, you missed your calling as a marketer."

"Let us not forget that I design *dreams* that people can inhabit," Latrice corrected. "And even if I have to set it up myself, you're going."

Latrice is crazy, Ramona thought. But the idea of escape was starting to creep into her doubt and nestle into the realm of possibilities.

"Wait, but what if Malik changes his mind? We lived together; we were engaged. Maybe all it'll take is a little more time for him to realize he made a mistake. What if—"

Latrice ticked her tongue against her teeth.

"Ramona, I hate to be the one to say it, but it's a real possibility that Malik's not coming back. Maybe he *is* exploring his options. Maybe he *has* moved on. And maybe you need to do the same. Girl, live you some life."

Even if Latrice was right, Ramona wasn't ready to accept her take. So, instead, she thought about Malik. In all the preparations for the wedding, they'd both discovered that they weren't as ready for marriage, at least to each other, as they each originally thought. Ramona was a saver, focused on the inevitable rainy day. By the end of the month, Malik had spent very close to his last dime. Ramona owned her condo and sweated every dollar of her HOA fees. Malik felt fine renting. Ramona had a sweet tooth. Malik was a personal trainer and a strict vegan. Ramona liked her evenings in with a glass of wine and the fireplace. Malik would rather be in a sports bar. But still, they'd made plans together for the future. She told herself that together they made one whole, each compensating for what the other was missing. But Malik didn't see it that way. After one particularly contentious counseling session and two days of brooding, he told Ramona that he didn't think that love was enough. And then, by the fifth session, he said he didn't think he wanted to get married before he stabilized his life on his own. Ramona didn't believe him until two weeks later and only after he walked out of the door of the condo with the last box of his things.

In time, she just knew he'd come to his senses and miss the life they'd had together. She had to admit that it didn't bode well that she'd hardly heard from him beyond logistics and that they hadn't seen each other at all. Maybe Latrice was right, about leaving at least, but how could she sneak out of town under the nose of her very own family? And what would she tell her mother?

"It's a good idea," Ramona said finally, with considerable hesitation. "But . . ."

By now, Latrice had turned her attention to her phone, alternating between aggressive scrolling and frantic tapping on the screen. Seeming to have found what she was looking for, she turned back to Ramona.

"You may not know it now, but you're going. Just leave the details up to me."

Ramona settled deeper into her office chair and made a thinking steeple with her fingers. Latrice looked at her expectantly. She hesitated before responding, knowing that Latrice would interpret anything that wasn't an absolute no as a yes.

"Latrice," Ramona said with a semi-defeated sigh, "I have no idea how this could possibly work. It's a nice idea, but I can't just go missing for a week. What would I tell my family?"

At this, Latrice jumped to her feet, waving her arms excitedly, knowing that somehow, she had won. "How about you tell them *nothing*! Try that for once! Everything about your life isn't family business!"

"Ha! Try telling *that* to my mother."

CHELSEA IN MALIBU . . .

CHELSEA'S EARLY-MORNING CALL WITH HELENA SENT HER INTO a restlessness that persisted into the evening. With the bubbling energy building within her, it was impossible to sit and focus on painting, and even harder to sit with the truth. Chelsea had never told Helena about her anxiety, and she never told the whole story about the core of her artistic inspiration. She painted moments of her childhood at the beach, the bright colors of her memory, a redheaded child in the surf kicking up a spray of water, laughing with smiling cheeks covered with freckles. She painted what she remembered of her mother's hands in the kitchen with tomatoes and hard pasta strewn on the counter. She managed the reds of the tomatoes and the exact yellow-tinged color of the noodle pieces so realistically, but also made them so much more beautiful and vibrant than in life. That was her expertise. She captured her first *first kiss*, two people in the height of new passion, and called the painting *Heartbreak*, just for knowing that it would end, that it did end. She'd painted love as its loss. So, what could she paint when her heart was already broken? When it hurt too much to remember, and when it felt like everything there was to lose was already gone?

Chelsea's answer was a retreat to her formal training, inspiration from artists she studied. She tried landscapes, colors that were less bold, more classic. She tried channeling the passion of other people's interests, hence the Endangered Wildlife series. All because she no longer had access to her heart.

"You're living in some sort of a shell." Helena had said this to her when she phoned back.

Although Chelsea responded with a knee-jerk "What shell?" she'd been reflecting on Helena's sentiment all day. Chelsea knew that Helena was trying to push her, to pull out of her the Chelsea that she used to be, but it was no help to be confronted by the old you when the new you was faring so poorly.

"You *used* to live in Los Angeles. Downtown in the heart of things," Helena said. "You were once in the movement of all that was happening, all that was changing. You made the world come to you, and you never hid from anything." Helena also said, which struck Chelsea particularly deeply, "Malibu is not the rest of the world." Chelsea had tasted the rest of the world and knew how much this was true. And although she insisted again that it was just a phase, she worried that she actually might have changed, and that growth for her was perhaps wisely looking for security. What if the risk of adventure was the risk of erasure? Adventure hadn't fared so well for her parents, after all. So, why trust a world that can't be controlled when you can stick to what you know? That was Chelsea's plan, and she'd just been focusing on the "what you know" part in particular.

But Helena had called her work *dystopian*. To Chelsea, that meant a world that didn't work. A world that was falling apart. *Dystopian?* She looked down at her drafting table at her latest piece, dark colors in sharp contrast to the stark white of the surface she'd taped the watercolor paper to. Her colors used to pop off the page like Technicolor. *Uninspired, maybe?* Chelsea thought. But still, Helena's word haunted her like a ghost as she walked out of her studio into the hallway in quick steps to the back of her house. She slid open the glass door and stepped out to pace the wood slats of her deck. It was her place to commune with the ocean, especially when the tide was high and swept all the way around the piles underneath her, as if she were on the bow of a ship. She loved to hear the wind and the roar, the sound of the birds, to feel the energy of the ions in the air. There was an electricity here that she could plug into just by being present. It delivered a calm that she could access just by walking along the creaking planks. 5...4...3...2...1... She counted her breaths and reached inside for stillness and for answers. And the only place available was to reach back in time.

Chelsea had at one time built an enviable career for herself, and remarkably early on. At only twenty-three, she'd happened upon the right collective of young contrarians, some of them graduates like her, and some dropouts of her fine arts program at USC. In pre-gentrification Downtown LA, the entire city center was a canvas, with so many available building walls, empty warehouses, and retail spaces. What others had abandoned made way for opportunity, a place for creativity to nestle and for youthful energy to be directed. Chelsea and her crew converted a cheap loft into home. There they lived together when it was still too dangerous to walk the darkened streets alone at night.

Chelsea and her friends began to produce a series of "secret shows" that did everything that conventional galleries weren't. Anywhere could become a venue. They used deserted auto-repair shops, with rusted car parts hanging on the walls; an old barbershop once, with the chairs still in place and mirrors on the wall. They took advantage of warehouses and unused floors of office buildings. Anything and any place could be put to use, especially when they brought people together with the perfect combination of the hottest DJs, the city's best drugs, and a well-curated guest list. Once, a particularly reclusive rock star was spotted at one of the shows, and then everyone wanted to go. The artists reclaimed downtown, made it better. And as they did so, developers started to make it more expensive. Just as downtown Los Angeles was becoming an international destination, Chelsea was becoming a darling rebel of the burgeoning international art scene.

Just out of art school, her piece *Heartbreak* scored a rare and entirely unexpected feature on *ARTnews*. From there, her career exploded. The entire underground show, including Chelsea's work, was featured in the *Los Angeles Times*. Then, the blog of a top young fashion designer picked up the hashtag #HeARTbreak, which became the It phrase of the spring/summer season. All of a sudden, the influential crowd was all over it with viral fervor. Love was heartbreak, heartbreak was art—a first kiss was a tragic reminder of the end of youth and beauty, and Chelsea's art piece *Heartbreak* had started it all. Patrons, brands, and collectors couldn't get enough of her. Helena jumped in to manage the swarm of new business opportunities, and it seemed like Chelsea was destined for her own solo show at Gagosian.

As more pieces sold, Chelsea moved from the heart of the city into her new loft without roommates. More and more, she began to live her life as a series of blurred moments—unfocused, just like her work was becoming as well. She partied, air-kissed, and slept with famous men whose faces she'd sometimes forget but whose names everyone else used frequently. And being grounded didn't matter, because she was on an adventure. But that was all before Malibu.

Chelsea's parents had lived in Malibu all her remembered life, as artists and bohemians. From diapers to high school, she grew up there. She felt secure and protected in that small world, the tiny community where it seemed like there were no strangers. It was so safe, it was almost stagnant, and it gave the illusion that not only would it never change, but also that it shouldn't. And in part that was why everything fell apart so chaotically. After the sudden passing of her parents, grief became a wall between her and the details of her prior life, a lost connection between the old Chelsea—the fierce and fearless one—and any aspect of how she presently lived, ensconced in a . . . *What had Helena called it? A shell?*

Once she moved to Malibu, her world shrank, as did the demand for her work. Art buyers aren't particularly motivated by sympathy, and with absence and distance, the tethers were stretched so far on her social connections that eventually they snapped, one by one by one. Her "new" place now, in Malibu, which was the oldest one she'd ever had, was a long drive and a world away from the downtown energy where the pack of wolves she used to run with ran on along without her.

After a mess of insurance and paperwork and debt, she was left with Helena, a house, and enough self-doubt to fill the entirety of the Pacific Ocean. And of course, the panic attacks. They were frequent and unpredictable at first, until Chelsea finally learned how to regain some sense of control, over her body at least. But those tools hadn't been tested in the broader world, in challenging places and new circumstances. And she didn't have any tools to recapture the lightning in a bottle that launched her work.

For two years she languished until she tried again to pick up her paintbrush. After three sketches and four painted studies, Chelsea thought she'd produced a Munch-esque piece of just enough sorrow that it was beautiful. To her it was so moving, it brought her to tears. Chelsea congratulated herself for the effort. It felt momentous, like she had finally re-created *Heartbreak*. Helena flew in personally to view it and promised she'd present it to all of her most important buyers. But it never sold. After that, what felt like giving her all, Chelsea stopped trusting her instincts and started trusting structure instead. She'd spent the last two years after that sinking deeper and deeper into a routine, convinced that would be life enough. She slept as long as possible, woke up begrudgingly, made her coffee, and spent her days watching the waves of the ocean, something that never changed and always changed. And she stayed the same.

On this day, Helena's call sparked the rattling engine of Chelsea's imagination. Helena was right that this couldn't be her forever. Financially, she couldn't afford it, and the only way she'd ever learned to earn a living was broken at best. Outside, on the deck, the breeze of the ocean ran invisible fingers through her hair, soothing her, calming the rising panic as she considered it: the idea of leaving and all the accompanying fear. But even after hours of staring, the fear persisted, of where she would go, and would she make it back, and would the sameness she'd come to rely upon still last.

RAMONA IN CHICAGO DURING THE FIRST-GLASS-OF-WINE TIME OF THE EVENING . . .

IN THE EVENING, RAMONA SAT IN HER CONDO, DOING SOMEthing that she would die from embarrassment over if anyone knew about it. As the snow came down in gentle flurries outside her window, across from the gaslit fireplace ensconced in a faux-salvaged exposed-brick wall, she reclined in her most comfortable chair, scrolling through pictures in her phone. She and Malik on the waterfront two summers ago. She and Malik at their one-year-anniversary dinner that he took her to before a surprise jazz concert. Malik flexing his carefully hewn muscles at the new gym where he took the trainer job. Malik . . . shirtless on the sofa . . . and another one that made her blush so deeply that she scrolled past it in a blur. Ramona felt like these were more than just memories, they were meant to be promises. She believed the good times that were shared meant of course they should continue. An instilled sense of Midwestern values weighed heavily toward marriage in that regard. Some part of Ramona, a very small part, did wonder what else there was other than marriage for a couple. Her parents had been married over three decades. Her brother was married, as were many of her friends from high school and college. It felt like something she was just supposed to do if she loved someone, and the rest was worked on, together.

Malik's retreat made no clear sense to Ramona, and sometimes looking at the pictures, the smiles as captured proof of happiness, she scoured them for any clue there that things weren't meant to work out. But there was nothing more she could see. Ramona clicked away from her photos and checked just one more time, first for any work emails, and then with more hope, for any text messages that perhaps she'd missed. Beside her, Wookiee licked her hand, the usual signal for food or more affection, and then sat and looked at her, tilting his irresistible face. Wookiee, a five-year-old caramel-colored shih-poo, was her constant companion and much more predictable than any human. Unable to resist the face of her own four-legged *Star Wars*–esque alien, Ramona freed one hand to bury it in his silky fur as he nuzzled his nose into her thigh. With her other hand, she shifted her scrolling screen navigation to her thumb, looking for treasure. Most noticeably absent was any ongoing communication from her ex, not even for something forgotten or left behind in the home they once shared together. Not even to ask about the dog. The extremely thin line that remained between her and what was likely complete insanity was the sole fact that he hadn't asked for the ring back. To Ramona, that meant that somehow, at least in some small way, he was still holding on as well.

Disillusioned by the phone, she stood to make her way to the kitchen, imagining some other happy couple spending the holidays at her place. She pulled down a wineglass and grabbed the bottle nearest to her on the counter. The cork stood up from the neck at attention, a reminder of prior glasses during nights past. Her shih-poo made himself known at her feet, snuggling close for more attention.

"You don't want me to leave, do you, Wookiee?" Ramona reached down to pet her dog as she spoke. "You think Latrice is crazy and Mommy should stay here with you, right?" Wookiee cocked his head to the side and looked at her as if she had a treat. The text message ping from her phone startled both of them, but it sent Ramona scrambling back to her still-warm seat.

Hope rushed through her body, and her fingers fumbled through the unlock code. Her stomach dropped as she saw the message waiting for her.

MA: SHALL WE GO LOOK AT MORE DRESSES ON SAT?
Looking FORwaRd to your TIME OFF!

Ramona's mother somehow always managed to trip the caps lock, and all her messages came as a ransom note. Ramona sighed, let the lids of her eyes drop closed, and felt her head turning back and forth involuntarily as if her neck were trying to get her to change her mind. *Just go ahead and cancel the wedding,* her conscience dared. But as had happened so many times since Malik left, Ramona looked down and saw the ring on her finger, the ring she still had, and opted for hope. *Just give him a little more time,* she told herself. But Ramona knew still, at some point, she'd have to face the bigger truth and ask herself the deeper questions—like, how could she be so sure about a man who was so unsure about her? And for the ring that she wore, what of herself was she trading away? But for now, she'd let hope sparkle on, and the disco ball on her finger glistened as if on cue. After thinking a bit and swallowing down the swell of guilt, Ramona typed her reply to her mother.

RAMONA: Saturday is perfect.

DECEMBER 14

•●°

CHELSEA ON ANOTHER LOVELY MORNING
IN MALIBU . . .

Chelsea held a small, weathered metal tube between her thumb and forefinger and squeezed just a little more cerulean blue onto her paint palette to adjust the gray she'd been mixing for the past half hour. She normally painted from memory, inside her modest studio, converted out of what used to be the second bedroom and away from the all-consuming view of the ocean. She had a simple setup—a drafting table, an easel, a set of drawers for basic organization of her many tubes of paint. And half-painted canvases plus sketches littered themselves around the floor, settling into all the available spaces like members of a social club. Her studio was her sanctuary, and the ocean was her inspiration. She was trying to render the brilliant gloom of a Malibu morning overcast in the winter. She found the ceiling of low-lying clouds to be quite captivating; the feeling of being outdoors in it captured all of her senses and brought the ocean mist up to cover her like a blanket needing just five more minutes in the dryer. It was a communion with nature and her surroundings. The experience reminded her of life in the Arts District in Los Angeles, where everything around her felt alive and so distinctively unbeautiful.

Breaking through the cracks in her concentration was the distant but still very audible sound of music coming from the beach outside. It was time for Jay to start his morning Surf Yoga class. Why he picked the space in front of her place, she couldn't figure out. The beach in California was public land, all the way up to the high tide line. And most days, in the spirit of community, Chelsea just considered it part of the charm. Sometimes, she'd wave with a closed-mouth smile and try to telepathically shame him into turning the sound down. And, usually, that didn't work. So, when it was truly important to her, on a day like today, trying to capture a fleeting bit of inspiration, she'd be much more direct. Unlike many of her neighbors, especially those in the much larger houses that flanked the beachfront, Chelsea was used to the compromises made to share resources. But as much as it was known for surfing or ocean breezes, Malibu had a complicated relationship with access to those things and a reputation for its residents continually trying to expand their property lines to keep so-called "others" off "their" beaches. The beach behind Chelsea's cottage was a particularly nice stretch, probably nicer than what her modest little home deserved. It seemed more fitting for her next-door neighbor Joan's home, a three-story modern showplace with decks on two levels. And meticulous Joan was never one to let anything slide. Chelsea had either heard or passively witnessed Joan and Jay's fair share of run-ins, which she stayed fully out of, but Jay was undaunted just the same.

Hoping to finish at least a good section of painting, Chelsea decided it was worth a break to see if Jay might oblige at least a minor reduction in decibels. She dipped her brush into her water container and sloshed it around until the water ran clear enough from the bristles she squeezed between her fingers. She stood up, straightened her overalls, and flip-flopped her way through the short distance of the hallway, across the kitchen alcove and compact living room, out to the deck, and down the stairs to the sand.

"Jay!" she yelled, walking closer. He didn't hear her. The music was louder down there, but so was the ocean in its rhythmic roar. "Jay!" she yelled again, louder this time. He finally looked up.

"Oh, hey, Chelsea," he said. His tone was casual, without a care in the universe. She knew that he knew what she wanted, but he was going to make her ask. Jay maintained his boyish charm and a sun-kissed aura of vitality that glowed through his flawless brown skin, although Chelsea thought he was older than the age of "surfer bro" culture, maybe in his early forties, even. She had no question about the appeal he held for the many women in his classes. In fact, he was ruggedly handsome, in a way, with salt-and-pepper accents in the hair at the sides of his head, dark eyes and attractive facial features, the square shoulders of a strong swimmer, and a body that seemed to fill out his wetsuit respectably. If not for the blaring music and overall difficulty she had taking him seriously, maybe she too would let her glances linger as long as the ladies who flocked him did. But this was not her mission.

"Could ya just turn it down a bit?" Chelsea pointed to the speaker. Despite the familiar nature of this exchange, Jay still managed to look genuinely surprised.

"Really, it's that loud?" He pulled his hand up against his eyebrows like a shield.

"Yes, *that* loud. I'm trying to paint a mood that's definitely not *this*." Chelsea air-canvased the scene before her with her hands. The "this" that Chelsea referred to was far too upbeat for what she was hoping to express. The well-toned class attendees, in a mix of brightly colored spandex separates, alongside some half-zipped wetsuits, shifted a bit, looking to their leader. Chelsea felt a tinge of self-consciousness as she hoped that she hadn't come off as too harsh. In the days since Helena's call, maybe she'd been on edge.

"Good morning!" The woman's voice was coming from behind her, to her left. She recognized it without having to look, twisting slightly in that direction.

"Hey, Joan." She ended the obligatory greeting to her neighbor with a small wave. Jay looked up and did so as well, although Chelsea had the sense that Joan likely wasn't directing her greeting to both of them. Joan waved back casually with the hand that was free of coffee and went about situating herself on the deck. This morning, Joan's carefully highlighted hair was pulled back into a ponytail with a tied Hermès scarf, standard issue for her. If Jay was sun-kissed brown, then for a white woman, Joan's skin was a true product of Malibu and her age—sun-consumed and the color of caramel, with freckles and sunspots you could only see up close. Her tasteful cream cotton tank was tucked neatly into her denim jeans of the same color, making a stick-lean silhouette of a perfect letter *P* from the neck down.

On many other mornings, Joan would make a regular ritual of dusting her deck pillows and making busy before she angled herself just perfectly toward the ocean. After her occasional less-friendly scuffle with Jay about the noise, she'd settle into her spot that didn't take her any farther away from it. In fact, she'd appear to be looking at the horizon but was positioned exactly so that behind her large-frame Chloé (or Chanel) sunglasses, she could also watch every second of Jay's class. Not that Joan seemed to have any particular interest in Jay, just that she was interested in everyone's everything and never let a happening pass without some kind of assessment.

Joan was a weathered beauty and quintessential Malibu divorcée. As Chelsea understood it, she was discarded remains of a so-called successful life, a midlife crisis casualty when her famous movie producer husband started sleeping with his second assistant-turned-live-in-girlfriend, now fiancée. This was a story Chelsea gleaned not so much from Joan but mainly from paragraphs and paragraphs of the articles written about the scandal. Joan didn't need to tell her because *everybody* knew. From her marriage she walked away with a (very) large bank account, an empty nest, and a restless heart, broken and dysfunctional, but still beating in its own quirky way. She would bend over backwards if you asked her for help, and when you didn't, she'd bend *you* over backwards to accept her assistance. With neither of her grown children around to helicopter, Joan was unrelenting at best toward the people whose lives she still had the ability to affect. She seemed like a hummingbird whose entire life might stop if she stopped moving. If you looked at her closely enough, in rarer moments you might catch a glimpse of the hours of nonspecific worry that crisscrossed her face, even when hidden by her unusually large designer sunglasses and beach hats. Some nights, she'd bring Chelsea whole gourmet dinners, poached salmon and grilled asparagus, perfectly tender pearls of couscous, and once after Chelsea had sneezed too loudly near a window, she found a still-warm jar of homemade chicken noodle soup against her door. Joan would often say the meals were so she'd have fewer leftovers, but Chelsea suspected that, more often than not, she was the only intended recipient.

"Joan. Come join us!" Jay called out from his spot on the beach and then turned back to Chelsea. "You too, ya might like it." As he spoke, he made a large gesture of pushing the volume button on his speaker. The music quieted.

"Next time!" Chelsea waved as she turned back to her bungalow, trying to add some friendly sparkle to her show of gratitude. She had absolutely no intention of ever joining. *Maybe her houseguest would enjoy it.* The thought made Chelsea groan. Walking back inside, she waited for Jay to echo his usual reply, *Life's too short for next time, Chelsea!*, sounding like a bride's uncle two beers in at a wedding. But he didn't and thus saved her from an awkward closing of the screen door in his smiling face.

Twenty minutes of relative quiet later, she was back in her studio, returned to her painting, when she heard her phone ringing in the kitchen. Morning calls were usually from one person, and having made quick haste to answer it, even before the phone properly reached her ear, she could hear the buzz of Helena's surroundings.

"Chelsea, darling, can you hear me?" Helena's voice resounded loudly through Chelsea's earpiece. Chelsea caught her breath before responding. There had been a time when she loved hearing from Helena. It meant good news, a buyer, an idea, or money coming in that could sustain her just a bit longer. But not this call. She already knew that this call was going to change her world, no matter what was said.

"Oh, hi, Helena, yes, yes, I can hear you," Chelsea shouted above the noise.

"I'm so sorry, dear, it's quite noisy. I decided to take a brisk walk to dinner. A lovely restaurant you should try when you're next here."

Chelsea wondered if Helena was telling her that she'd be hosting Londoners.

"And on the topic of travel, I have good news for you," Helena continued in her proper staccato. "You're quite the lucky one at the start of things. I never imagined it would happen so quickly, especially during Malibu's offseason. But I've got someone interested. It seems you've been saved by some dear woman in Chicago."

"Chicago? I . . . I thought you were about to say London." Chelsea tried to envision Christmas in London with the toffee pudding and the old-time traditions, if she were to join Helena there. But Helena holidayed in the Canary Islands, Chelsea remembered, and she wondered if Helena would insist. "So, I guess it's the Canary Islands for me, then?" Chelsea mused aloud.

"Oh, no . . . dear, no. I wouldn't ask you to come all the way across the pond. You'll be going to Chicago . . . I negotiated a swap for you."

Chelsea's breath caught in her throat. She felt her heart start to quicken and a coldness build. It was the onset of panic, the trigger of anxiety. She closed her eyes and pulled in a long, staggered inhale. For a moment, her breathing was all she heard, everything else became a more distant echo. By the time she felt the whoosh of her lungs emptying, she had more control. It was the change she anticipated, but knowledge was insufficient preparation for an overwhelming confrontation with the reality of it.

"*I'm* going to *Chicago*?"

"Yes, dear!" Helena said as brightly as if she'd sold a painting. "Isn't that lovely? It's all arranged, and perfectly so. Your guest will come there, you'll go to Chicago to stay at her fabulous condo right on the lakefront. Well, likely *frozen*, but . . ." Helena muttered the last bit to herself, but then regained the cheery sales disposition that came so naturally to her. "I heard she works in architecture, so I'm sure the accommodations will be quite lovely."

Chicago? Chelsea thought again. She'd never been to Chicago, not even for her art, and other than Burning Man and skiing, she couldn't recall being anywhere in the US that wasn't on an ocean coast.

Helena filled Chelsea's silence with even-louder-than-needed forced cheer.

"She was a tough negotiator, that one, but in the end, it turned out perfectly, I think. Now, just the last item, for hospitality's sake, you'll make her feel welcome, yes? Perhaps a nice note? A little sprucing? We'll want to make a good impression."

"Helena, I—"

"Well, that's it, then, isn't it? We owe money, we'll make money. Chelsea, if this doesn't work out . . . If we can't afford to pay the taxes, we *will* have to sell the house. That's how this works. And perhaps you'll find something there, dear, that you seem to have lost where you are."

Chelsea brought a hand up to her temple, rubbing it to release the tension. *The taxes . . . a swap? Chicago?* And she was still supposed to produce in the meantime? And write a note? It was all too much. After hanging up with Helena she made her way into her bedroom and lay down with a mind to restart the day, pretending the conversation with Helena was a distant memory, perhaps just a bad dream. She drew the shutters, buried herself in a familiar position in her bedding, and let herself be lulled to sleep by the sounds of the ocean, a rhythmic roar advancing and subsiding that she could just manage to hear above the still-too-loud thumping of Jay's speakers across the sand.

RAMONA ON A COLD AND DREARY WINTER AFTERNOON IN CHICAGO . . .

RAMONA SAT AT A TABLE FOR TWO INSIDE THE FRENCH SANDwich café down the block from work, waiting for Latrice to join her for lunch. She shifted in the chair to look at the time on her phone. Latrice was late enough to notice, and Ramona wondered what the holdup could be. Ramona rarely left her office for lunchtime excursions, but Latrice insisted that they meet up for the break in the day. In the middle of the server's third stop to fill her water glass, asking if she was ready to order, she spotted Latrice rushing through the door in a bundle of winter parka, gloves, and giant scarf. She stomped the remnants of slush away on the floor mat as the door closed behind her. Ramona waved frantically. Latrice looked excited.

"Girl, let me tell you, he made a way out of no way for you today!"

"A way for me? Latrice, you know I only had an hour."

Latrice waved her hand across her face as if to shoo Ramona's words away.

"Listen, Moe, I figured it out. You're going on a trip, just like I said. No oceans to cross, no family to confront, no Malik to worry about, just you and peace and tranquility." At this, Latrice threw her arms in the air and almost hit a server passing by. A precision hip swerve avoided a likely disastrous collision.

"Latrice, I *told you*, I can't go. I . . ."

"Moe, before you go there, hear me out, mm 'k?"

Ramona's mouth opened to protest, but nothing came out before Latrice continued.

"So, there's this house on the beach in California—in Malibu, you know, where all the celebrities go, but it's so cute and kinda shabby chic. It's perfect and literally *right* on the sand." Latrice gave Ramona a gigantic grin. "I reached out and because it's offseason, got you a discount . . . a *big* discount, really, and there's just one thing . . ."

"Latrice, if this is some swinger's colony or room share or something, I'm not interested. Not even if I was inclined to be interested, which for the record, I'm not."

"Come on, Moe! You know me better than that. I'd never send you somewhere that I'd rather go myself." Latrice gave a big mischievous smile.

Ramona picked up the menu. "You're wasting your time and mine—we need to order."

Latrice pushed her hand back down to the table. "Not until I tell you the rest. Look, the catch is that it's offseason, but that just means less hours of sun."

"And? That's it?"

"Well, there's one more thing. The owner of the house is this super-fancy British woman and evidently her niece or goddaughter or something like that is an artist who lives there and . . . well, she'd be coming to stay at your place, while you stay in hers."

Ramona began to choke on her water. With what breath she could suck in, she started her sputtering protest. "Who's staying in my place? A stranger? So they can steal all my stuff? Latrice, you have got to be kidding me."

"Ramona, it's not a stranger. *Malik* is a stranger. He lived with you for a year and stole your heart. At least this lady is offering something. You're staying in her otherwise unaffordable beach house, and for a *nice* discount. During that time, she's staying in your place. Come on," Latrice's voice sang out to Ramona. "It's a good deal . . ."

"This . . ." Ramona gestured in a circle with her hands. "This is *not* a good idea. I . . . I can't. It's too much." Ramona shook her head and signaled for the server who Latrice had shooed away again at the beginning of their conversation. He looked relieved to be finally heading over. "Time to order." Ramona shoved the menu toward her friend and pretended to scour her own copy, hoping to end the conversation.

"We're going to eat, but I'm going to finish. And before we leave, you're going to be excited."

Ramona could only shake her head because deep down within, she knew Latrice was right.

After their food arrived and following a few needed moments of the relative silence of eating, crunching, and sipping through their selections, Latrice, geared up for convincing, made her final pitch.

"Moe, let's be honest. You're on the verge of a breakdown. Not only are you still wearing an engagement ring when there's no engagement, but you're still going actual dress shopping with your mother. You need this."

Ramona looked down into her soup. With the mention of dress shopping, Latrice had landed a blow. She could justify it, but just barely. Malik hadn't asked her to return the ring. That was it. And other than that small detail, there was no reason to move forward with a frilly and pointless wedding gown purchase. Most of all, she hated lying to her mother, her father, and ostensibly to herself, but currently, she had no imagination for the alternative and no will to disappoint. A deposit had been placed on the venue; a date had been set. Malik already made his first investment, and it was sitting on her finger. All she needed was a little more time. *Maybe just after the holiday*, Ramona thought, watching staggered uneaten croutons float across a bowl-size tomato lake. Latrice's voice brought her attention back.

"There's no way you can fake it through this holiday, Ramona. You need to go, get yourself together, and come back a new woman. And with any luck, you'll lose that engagement ring in the ocean somewhere."

Although the thought of losing the ring delivered a strike of panic to Ramona's gut, Ramona knew she couldn't argue with Latrice. She was undeniably spiraling out of balance—the evidence was mounting daily. And the ring was the loose thread holding the fragile shambles all together. She was, in fact, holding her grilled cheese sandwich with the hand that still hosted the modestly mounted diamond solitaire Malik gave her on her birthday, but it had been weeks since they'd exchanged two words. In her purse was an unanswered text message from her mother asking what dress store she wanted to visit the following day. And in her heart was a growing urge to be away from it all.

"What about my dog?" she managed to finally say.

"Leave your dog with Carlos," Latrice offered quickly.

"Okay, well, what about my mom and the rest of my family?"

"Well, the best way to tell a lie is to tell a half-truth." Latrice punctuated it with a crunch, as she polished off the last fry on her plate.

DECEMBER 15

* ● *

RAMONA IN CHICAGO IN THE MIDDLE OF AN ORGASM OF TAFFETA, TULLE, BEADING, AND LACE . . .

RAMONA STOOD ON THE PEDESTAL UPON WHICH SHE'D BEEN DI-rected to stand by a well-appointed and extremely attentive sales attendant. In front of the elaborate three-way mirror gilded in rose gold, her own image was admittedly breathtaking.

"Oh my, Ramona, that one is just gorgeous." Ramona's mother, Melba Tucker, brought her hand up to cover her mouth. The other hand held a delicate stem of champagne. On this Saturday, the first one that followed Latrice's very specific plan of a Christmas escape to Malibu, Ramona and her mother were in L'Atelier Elegant Bridal, a gorgeous boutique in the South Loop that seemed intent on making you believe you were a lucky guest in the boudoir of a very wealthy woman who had more money than you—*much* more, and no expense to spare. The gathered satin curtains that hung from ceiling to floor ac-cented the sides of large shop windows. The windows allowed in perfect streams of light that bounced through the cream-colored shop interior, twinkled through the prismatic crystals of the hanging chandeliers, and danced in kaleidoscopic colors on the exquisite hardwood floors.

This exact location had been a dream of Ramona's, as it was for many brides-to-be in Chicago—it was one of the most well-known and exclusive purveyors of bridal couture. L'Atelier only allowed one bride per appointment, and so for Ramona, it was extra uncomfortable to pretend on this particular Saturday that the thousands of dollars reflected on the price tag attached to her was even remotely within her realm of consideration. Behind her in her reflection, the long display of wedding dresses lining the walls stood like witnesses to her embarrassment. And unfortunately for Ramona, there was no style of dress that couldn't be found in this perfectly curated bridal fantasy of a wedding apparel boutique. In another circumstance, this visit would certainly be the epitome of a girlhood dream—visiting with her mother, delighting in the designs, worried only about alterations, soothed by the bubbles in endless glasses of champagne.

This was not today's occasion.

Melba Tucker and the sales attendant awaited Ramona's response, which, based on how incredibly perfect she looked, surely was expected to be an enthusiastic "This is the one . . ." Given the circumstances, however, as this was obviously *not* something she could say, this was the exact moment that Ramona realized the lie she'd been living could possibly be worse than the lie she was about to tell. There was nobody who, wearing this particular dress, wouldn't envision themselves getting married, whether there was a wedding to be had or not.

While the dress was fortunately still a spared expense, the wedding planning had otherwise been moving forward and, even before the breakup, had begun to run up quite a tab. Ramona's father, a proud man of quiet tradition, was happy to take the background, like the bass line in the groove of her family dynamic. He had dipped into his retirement account to put the deposit down on her reception at the DuSable Museum of African American History, an opportunity to combine class and culture with a notable destination for their guests.

Such a popular venue as it was, the date needed to be reserved well in advance, with a *nonrefundable* deposit. Ramona hated, absolutely *hated* wasting money, and the only thing she hated more than wasting her own was the idea of wasting the hard-earned money of her working-class parents. This wedding was not just for Ramona, it was for the family. And so, it was the tipping point, standing there in the perfect dress, in the perfect boutique, that became the perfect moment to open the hatch. But first, she needed to escape the dress, which started to feel heavy and constraining, causing Ramona to shift in it, fumbling at the latches and closures.

The sales attendant looked instantly horrified. "Oh dear, let me help you," she said.

"Do you not like it?" Ramona's mother's face dropped.

Ramona's eyes scanned wildly; she was feeling suddenly too hot, and too tightly bound, and perhaps even too beautiful, just wanting to be regular again, with her own two feet on the ground.

"I . . . it's . . . too tight . . ." Ramona said. It was the best she could come up with and, in the moment, close to the truth. "I . . . feel like I can't breathe." She fanned herself for emphasis as the sales attendant worked with fast fingers to free her from the innumerable latches and clasps. Finally, she felt a rush of cooler air at her back, and the weight of the gown loosened around her. The now very flustered sales attendant held the gown open for Ramona to step out of it.

"Would you like me to bring you—"

"—I just need a moment." Ramona stood in her shaper garments and placed one hand on her hip. The other she used to try to wave away the growing concern.

Melba stepped toward her daughter with a crinkled brow and a strong shadow of worry across her face. Ramona felt doubly guilty.

"I think the . . . um . . . stress of . . . this wedding is—"

"It's too much, isn't it?" Her mother smoothed a tuft of hair away from Ramona's forehead.

Her stomach in knots, Ramona figured that it was now or never. And still, it was near impossible to get the words to meet her tongue. She hated lying. But, before she ruined anything else, it was necessary. She took a deep breath and, before she could change her mind, pushed the words out. "I think . . . um, I think that Malik is going to want to do a getaway for this Christmas."

Instantly a stab of guilt struck Ramona so deeply she almost cringed. Melba examined her and brought her eyes to meet her daughter's. She pushed back her own fluff of black-dyed curls and put her hands on her rounded hips.

"What do you mean 'a getaway'?" Melba's eyes narrowed with something that looked to Ramona like suspicion. "How do you *get away* from Christmas? From your family? From the wedding? Chile, maybe he was just talkin'."

Ramona felt her heartbeat all the way in her ears and started to doubt the possibility that she could get away with this. To escape the gravitational pull of a Melba Tucker Christmas? Still, she tried again.

"No, it was a serious conversation. A good idea maybe. Just this year . . . to take a break from planning, and . . . maybe start our own traditions."

Instantly, Ramona knew that she'd made a mistake. If anyone loved Christmas, it was Melba Tucker. If anyone loved her family, it was Melba Tucker. If anyone loved Christmas with her family, it was most certainly, absolutely, one hundred percent Melba Tucker, and she had the traditions to prove it.

"Ramona Tucker, what is wrong with *our* traditions?" Melba scolded. "You always loved the seven fishes on Christmas Eve, and you know Carlos is going to bring the coquito, and the costumes . . . the dancing. I don't understand!" With theatrical-quality indignation and a dramatic flip of her hands, Ramona's mother turned back to the dresses in front of her and seemed to be homing in on another selection's intricate beading detail.

Ramona stepped forward to pretend to sort through dresses herself. In the air between them, Melba had clearly claimed victory and considered the matter settled. Circling now in a lie within a lie, Ramona had to choose the true path of least resistance. Tell her mother the whole truth now and ruin Christmas for everyone or find a way to stretch time just a little longer to give her a chance to make her lie much less lie-ish. Finding the slimmest thread of morality, holding on to a dress with way too much lace at the collar, Ramona found enough courage to push her point yet again. She had one more card to play, her mother's own spirit of adventure, the calling of the larger world, of bigger dreams, a life she wanted for her daughter more than anything else.

"I was just thinking that next year might be . . . so *different*, with marriage and all. What if we never get the chance again? You've always told me that life is about taking chances." Ramona studied her mother for a response. She hoped that the appeal to adventure would stir something in the woman who'd flown millions of miles in her career as a flight attendant. Melba Tucker was one of the first people in their neighborhood to have a passport filled with stamps. She'd bring back the most delightful artifacts, souvenirs, and traditions from her trips, proudly displayed in their home. If Melba Tucker loved Christmas, she lived for adventure. As much as Melba wished for Ramona to have this trait in common, her daughter the saver was much more like her father.

"Oooh! Look at this one!" Melba pulled a dress off the rack, holding it as high as her arms could reach so that she and Ramona could admire it together. "Why don't you try this one on?" Ramona felt sick. The smiling sales attendant reappeared to shift the dress out of her mother's hands.

"Lovely choice!" the sales attendant said. "I'll just hang this by the mirror for you while you browse. Would you ladies care for more champagne?"

This has gone too far, Ramona thought to herself as she raised her palm to her forehead. Her mother nodded yes excitedly.

"Very well, shall I make that two glasses?" The saleslady smiled at them in sunlight beams.

"Sure," Ramona said resignedly.

"I'm just so excited!" Ramona's mother proclaimed her delight to nobody in particular. "We've never had a big wedding in the family."

Ramona felt her face flush. Her last and best attempt hadn't worked. And the one thing she hadn't tried, was the truth . . . at least, *some* of it.

"The stress of planning for this, even though we haven't gotten very far, has really taken a toll. Both Malik and I need a break from it." Ramona took her mother's hands. "Ma, we *need* this. I need this. It's just one Christmas. Say you won't mind."

Melba's face softened, and she reached up to gently tend to the spiraled strands of Ramona's twist out.

"I can't say I won't mind, Ramona, because family is family. But I can say I understand. If you and Malik want to go off on your trip *this* year . . ." Melba raised an eyebrow and paused for a beat. "Then . . . don't consider me trying to stop you."

Ramona sighed in relief just as the grinning sales attendant came back with two slender flutes of bubbling effervescence.

Ramona's mother patted her arm. "Don't worry, if you don't want yours, I'll drink it."

"Oh no, I *definitely* want it." Ramona gave her best smile. She grabbed the champagne to swallow as much as she could in a single gulp.

•●

IT WASN'T UNTIL EARLY EVENING THAT RAMONA'S WOOZY HAZE began to subside from the three whole champagne flutes it took to get through a try-on of the remaining dresses chosen by her mother at the bridal boutique. At home and comfortable, Ramona was grateful for the arrival of Carlos. For most of her life, since elementary school, even in the absence of a biological relationship, she knew him as her *play brother*. A non-relation fixture, Carlos was a permanent bolt-on. Ramona's family was Carlos's family, and Ramona was closer to Carlos than even her actual brother, who also called Carlos his sibling. Other than Latrice, Carlos was her closest person—he knew her character. And when push came to shove, very purely, he always aligned his interests with her happiness. Guilt prompted her to call him for an emergency intervention before her soul completely slipped out of her body. Reluctantly, she updated him on the disaster of a dress-shopping debacle.

"You told Ma what?!" Seated at the kitchen island, Carlos erupted from his goblet chair like a geyser. Carlos was six feet of all-boyish charm, dark-brown curls on his head, deep brown eyes, and long lashes that brushed cheeks of café au lait skin. Typically, in any conversation with Ramona, he brought the energy of a sports announcer. He took interest as if her stories were a spectator match, an active listener who never missed a detail—a delight for Ramona in normal confidence. But this reaction made for an extra shot of face-burning guilt as she elaborated.

"I told her Malik and I were going to go away for Christmas, Carlos. Honestly, I just can't do this anymore. If she ever found out I'd been lying to her this whole time, my God, I can't even imagine."

Carlos raised a thick eyebrow, and his hand rose to rub the set of crinkles in his forehead. "Ramona, I can't believe you made me cancel a date for this. Why can't you just tell her—"

Ramona pleaded with her hands. "She's so excited about the wedding, and—" At the word *wedding*, Carlos immediately raised both eyebrows, widening his eyes even further. Ramona felt the correction as sharply as if he'd physically poked her in her belly button. "—What was *supposed* to be a wedding. What could *still be* a wedding! Malik could come back, and then everything would just go back to the way it was supposed to be. It's Christmas . . . so why take everyone through a breakup that might not be fully broken?"

Carlos looked around Ramona's living room. "Moe, the man took all his clothes, his PlayStation, even his do-rags from the bathroom. I would say it's broken. Broke down. Finito."

Ramona interrupted him with a wave. "I get it, Carlos. It looks bad. But can't you understand why *just for* Christmas, it's *me* who needs to disappear?"

Carlos's large grin widened. "Oh, for sure, I get it. At this point, you really have no choice. A ring and no Malik on Christmas Eve? Man, no one misses Ma's Christmas Eve. You'd be busted anyway."

"Thanks . . . for making me feel *worse*." Ramona turned and pulled two wineglasses out of the cabinet. She tugged the loose cork out of the bottle on the counter, poured two glasses of a fragrant red blend, and walked one over to Carlos. He put a generous hand on her back. Holding her glass at her hip, she eased into the brotherly gesture and placed her head on his shoulder.

"Look," Carlos said into her hair, "I'll do what I can to help."

At this, Ramona perked up.

"You will?" she asked eagerly, eyes and spirits lifted, surprised he hadn't needed more convincing, especially given what she'd be needing.

Carlos cut his sip short, almost spilling the wine from his glass.

"Wait, what does that mean to you?" Almost as if on cue, an ambling Wookiee came up to Carlos's knee, sniffing his hand for a petting. Ramona gave a wide grin, the same one she'd used thousands of times with Carlos when he was teetering on the edge of a much-wanted *yes*.

"Oh no. Moe. The dog?" Carlos let out a big sigh but reached down to pet Wookiee on top of his irresistible head, dipping his fingers in the curved tufts of caramel-colored fur. Wookiee gave a panting smile, all sparkling eyes and open mouth with his tongue hanging out.

"Carlos, you love Wookiee," Ramona cajoled.

"No, *you* love Wookiee, and I love you," Carlos corrected.

"You need some companionship."

"I have plenty of companionship."

"You go on plenty of dates." Ramona made her own correction. "What's wrong with doting attachment?"

"You know I have trust issues . . . and allergies . . ."

"You are *not* allergic to Wookiee."

"Who said I was talking about Wookiee?"

Ramona resorted to doe eyes and batted her lashes. "Please?"

When Carlos groaned, Ramona knew she was close. "For how long?" he asked.

"Just a week," she said blithely. "I'll be back on the twenty-sixth of December."

Carlos sighed away the rest of his remaining resistance. "One week, huh?"

"Yep, all I need is one week in sunny Malibu, California."

DECEMBER 19

· • ·

RAMONA ON A SUNNY AFTERNOON IN
SOUTHERN CALIFORNIA . . .

RUMBLING WHEELS TOUCHED DOWN AT LOS ANGELES INTERNAtional Airport, delivering Ramona to her new home and quickly hatched escape for the week of Christmas. From the window as the plane approached the landing strip, she could see tall, swaying palm trees standing right next to low-lying buildings in the flight path. And everything seemed kissed by the sunshine. Somewhere in the distance, the ocean waved its welcome along the shoreline.

I'll take it, Ramona thought, still nestled in her seat. She exhaled a deep breath and pulled out her phone to arrange a rideshare to Chelsea's address, which had been front and center in a confirmation forwarded by Latrice. Latrice offered to absorb some of the cost as an early Christmas present, but once she committed to going, Ramona insisted on paying her friend the full amount of the reservation, plus a little extra for handling the administration, and . . . her stubbornness. As the chime sounded signaling for the removal of seat belts, Ramona started to feel an actual sense of excitement, almost guiltless, almost giddy. She'd never had cause to travel to California before, other than a stopover on a family trip to Hawaii. But a new place wasn't the rumbling engine of her burgeoning happiness, nor was the fact of her very first solo vacation. It was the freedom, the first true feeling of freedom she'd felt since the moment Malik left. Right there in her seat, she slid the engagement ring off her finger and placed it in a small black pouch back in the zippered part of her purse. And with that single action, she took a deep breath that was so deep she accidentally sang a note on her exhale.

The drive to Malibu was lengthy but eventually became scenic, alongside seemingly unending miles of coastline along the Pacific Coast Highway. After a sign signaling a welcome to Santa Monica, she passed a festive pier that looked like a permanent carnival, complete with giant Ferris wheel slowly turning its occupants. She passed golden sand and volleyball nets, campers, clubhouses, garages, and gates, but she never once lost complete sight of the ocean beside her. It was magnificent. Its sheer magnitude extended so far that the expanse of the water and the sky combined into a delightful blue promise of paradise and tranquility. Ramona made a mental note to thank Latrice before the night was over.

"I could get used to this." Ramona sighed.

"I'm sorry, I couldn't hear you. Could you say that again?" the car's driver called back, startling her.

"Oh, sorry!" she said with a laugh. "I didn't mean to say that out loud."

"Don't worry, I get it," the driver said, looking at her through the rearview mirror. "It's a beautiful view that never gets old. Where're you visiting from?"

"Cold and snowy Chicago," said Ramona, as if the answer were the punch line to a joke.

"Ooh, Chicago! Been there once for a baseball game. Some great food in that place. I wish I could find even one good deep-dish pizza anywhere in this city."

Ramona laughed. "So . . . Lou Malnati's or Giordano's?" she gave the driver a big smile alongside a small test of his taste.

"Oh man, I tried them both, but it's hard to top that butter crust, right?"

Ramona laughed again, feeling an immediate sense of familiarity. "You must have some favorites here too, right?"

The driver dipped his head to the side as if Ramona had proposed a new idea.

"See, that's the thing about Los Angeles. So many transplants from all over, coming and going so often, I mean sure, we've got some great restaurants, but I don't know that we're known for anything great other than of course north-of-the-border Mexican food, sushi, and maybe a pretty good burger." At his last idea, Ramona's ears perked up. Diet be dammed, she'd been wanting a burger ever since she'd watched Latrice devour that plate of fries over lunch.

"A burger?" she asked, hoping he hadn't heard her stomach growl. "You're speaking my language."

"Oh man, we passed a great spot right by the airport, but a really good one, you can find it almost anywhere. My favorite is Round and Out. They even have a secret menu. Trust me, if you make it there, order your burger 'wild style.' Your mouth will thank you later."

"'Wild style,' I like that . . ." Ramona mused, turning to look at the ocean again.

By the time Ramona pulled up in front of a relatively unassuming garage, her driver had filled her mind with ideas of a new kind of Christmas in LA, one replete with sunshine, the lighted decorations in the streets of Beverly Hills, timed "snowfalls" next to the giant Christmas tree at the open-air shopping center. A place that evidently had some form of warm-weather snow you had to see to believe, and enough food recommendations to fill a trip of several months. She thanked him with a large tip and made her way to look for the lockbox to retrieve the key to Chelsea's bungalow.

Malibu was impressive, a secret paradise that was so idyllically beautiful, if someone described it to you, you'd think they were exaggerating. The blue of the ocean was *so* blue, it was the visual definition of what blue was always supposed to be. But then, that was before you turned your gaze up to the sky. The sky was not just a ubiquitous background to the sea, but an ever-changing backdrop to the hillside, shifting noticeably with every mile of roadway along the PCH. Ramona's vacation destination was a quaint little box of a cottage, dipped down in low profile below the edge of the roadway, so low that she could really only see the slated roof before the ocean behind it. It looked like half the house was missing, perhaps, until she reached it and realized that, in fact, what she saw was all there was to it. In complete contrast was an imposing structure next door, a home of multiple levels, all windows and burnished concrete, a wall-enclosed fortress by the sea. *I can't even image how much that one costs . . . or who lives there*, Ramona thought. She'd barely managed to afford even her relatively meager accommodations. Nonetheless, she was here, in her own small way, with her very own slice of beachfront.

The lockbox opening was a clumsy ordeal, the one hiccup in the otherwise dreamlike arrival that had Ramona floating on air. She managed to figure the thing out, a mechanical puzzle of numbers and switches that took enough tries so as to instill some doubt she'd be able to gain entry. After a fifth attempt, having reread the instructions on the confirmation email, she heard a satisfying click, and the box released its treasure of a key. Once inside, Ramona was overwhelmed by the brightness of the efficient but open space. It was small, but tidy, and as small as it seemed on the outside, especially in relation to its neighbor, the inside was perfect and wrapped around Ramona almost instantly like a glove. But what was absolutely breathtaking, what elicited an audible gasp that surprised Ramona to hear her own voice, was the view of the ocean. She hadn't expected it to be so close. She hadn't expected to see it unfold before her so majestically. It was a postcard come to life, nothing but the sparkling expanse of ocean stretching in a glistening carpet all the way out to the horizon beyond. "Wow . . ." Ramona breathed the word until her breath ran out, awestruck as she was. From a wall of windows, there was the full extension of that bluest blue, the dancing ripples, all shimmering light in a way that was very much alive. She wasn't just on the ocean, she was in the ocean, as if on a boat, with the view from the living room leaving no trace of the sand or anything below. Just an expanse of water from here to eternity. To take it all in was hypnotic; she could stay there forever, standing stunned and still holding the handle of her roller bag.

Ramona's eyes were greedy with the view. When she'd finally gotten her fill of it, reminding herself that it was real, that *this* was really where she was staying, that she didn't have to hoard images into her memory, she was finally able to pull her gaze to the rest of the surroundings. The living area cascaded inward from the door in ripples of sunlight across the wooden ceiling beams all the way into the delightful kitchen area that reminded her of a country cottage. She was thrilled to see the ocean blue in the room also, the white of the clouds and the warm beige of sand repeated throughout the space she entered. More than just direct access, she felt like she had her own version of the beach inside this place, all to herself.

She rolled her bag across the planks of the floors, winding her way past an outdated but quaint bathroom into a hallway with a room at each end. Taking a peek into the room to her left, she opened the cracked door to reveal an artist's studio, full of paintings and supplies, with an easel holding a gloomy painting half done, but with a cornucopia of much brighter colors represented elsewhere. There were paintings on the floor and against the walls, hanging on the walls, with very little of the otherwise white walls showing at all. It added to the charm of the place. Ramona could imagine what it would be like to be an artist there and wondered how one would manage to not be overwhelmed by all the inspiration to behold. Backing her way out of the room, she pulled the door closed and turned to the room to her right, which was a bedroom facing the ocean. Neat and seemingly clean, Ramona surveyed the plushly made-up bed and the drawn shutters that stood between her and a return to communion with her view of the water.

"Come on in, sunshine!" Ramona spoke aloud as she flung the plantation shades wide open. She threw her arms open to match the shades and briefly closed her eyes to bask in the sounds of the gently crashing waves and the warmth of the sun through the window. The bed reminded her of a mound of marshmallows as it beckoned to her with promises of comfort.

"And I will see *you* later," said Ramona in the direction of the bed.

Back in the kitchen, she saw a basket of oranges on the counter and what looked like a note scribbled on a torn-out sheet of lined paper. She read the words silently to herself.

Dear Latrice,

I truly hope that you'll enjoy my cozy little home on the beach. I've left you some healthy snacks, oranges here on the counter, a few things in the fridge, and some vegan protein bars in the cabinet.

The grocery store is just down the street and there are plenty of restaurants at the Malibu pier and the Country Mart.

It's pretty quiet, but sometimes Jay has a fitness class down at the beach out back. If his music is too loud, just let him know. He's usually good about turning it down.

Feel free to use anything you need, including my shampoo, etc., in the bathroom.

Merry Christmas to you and thanks for letting me stay in your place.

Sincerely,
Chelsea Flint

Latrice? Ramona realized that Latrice must have made herself the primary reservation holder. Feeling a dart of concern, she pulled out her cell phone and scrolled to Latrice's number. Latrice picked up almost immediately.

"Hey, girl! Is everything okay? I almost called you like ten minutes ago. I'm over here straight-up pacing . . ." Latrice's flood of concern almost made Ramona forget that she was the one who made the call. "Are you settled in there?" Latrice continued. "How is it? What's it like?" And on she went with a barrage of questions until finally stopping for air.

"It's great—just that, Latrice, did you put my name on the reservation?"

"Girl, yes! I made the reservation, so I'm the primary name, but I added you. For sure, your name is on there. I figured, what difference would it make—it's not like it's a hotel or something, and Helena knows that you're the one actually staying."

For Ramona, someone exceedingly organized, this was disconcerting. "Helena? Who's Helena? I have a note here that says it's from Chelsea . . ." Ramona started to fidget with the paper, feeling a slight heat warming her face.

Latrice replied with no sign of dampened excitement. "Remember I told you the woman that owns the house has her artist goddaughter living there! That must be Chelsea. She left you a note?"

"Yeah, on a torn-out piece of notebook paper, but it's fine."

"Not the notebook paper, girl, really?"

"Yeah, next to a bowl of oranges. Jus' sayin', I prepped my place for two days—fully stocked."

Latrice laughed. "Ramona, in all the times I've been to your place, I've never even seen a pillow out of place. You have containers in your refrigerator for food that already comes in containers. I've never seen anyone else put a craft label on water. I wouldn't bet on anyone *not* failing the Ramona Tucker hospitality test. What's the rest of the place like?"

Ramona smiled. There wasn't really anything she could have said to make the observation untrue. In the way of hospitality, she was very much like her mother. She made a small survey of her surroundings to give Latrice her of-the-moment impression.

"Oranges aside, it's actually really nice. Girl, it's tiny, like the same size as my condo, but a cottage, right on the ocean. And that's almost all that matters, because when I tell you I'm right on the water, I'm on the water. Like, *in* the water. There's a deck outside, and it's like being on a boat. And you should see some of the houses around here. Next door is like something out of a magazine. I bet a famous person lives there."

"I heard Beyoncé lives out there, maybe she's your neighbor."

"I'd believe it. Out here, Latrice, it's magical. It seems like anything is possible . . ." Ramona hesitated with the next words; they were, after all, a little difficult to say. "And . . . thank you. I know I was being a little stubborn, but this is perfect."

"Moe, somebody had to save you from yourself and your web of *lies!*" Latrice broke into laughter.

Ramona's face warmed anew. The person Latrice was describing was such a departure from the person she'd always been—earnest, hardworking, honest, sensible—always saving for a rainy day. And now . . . this person. Someone who *escapes* the holidays with her family? Ramona loved Christmas. And the farther away she'd come from Chicago, all the way to what looked to her like the edge of the earth from Chelsea's living room windows, the more ridiculous her reason seemed.

"Latrice, it's not funny!" Ramona's body spit the words out as a physical rejection of her thoughts. "I . . . *had* to!" she protested, and then allowed herself a breath. "No matter how I got here, I'm here now. And I'm going to enjoy myself. A nice, calm, cozy Christmas in Malibu."

"You enjoy yourself, Ms. Malibu."

"Girl, you already know."

Ramona was halfway out of the sliding glass door leading to the deck by the time she actually said goodbye to Latrice. She wanted to waste no time descending the stairs to the beach below to sink her toes in the sand and feel some ocean water at least splash around her ankles.

She took her time walking down, feeling the grainy cushion of beach give way beneath her at each of her steps. Stopping briefly to take her shoes and socks off, she gave herself a moment to take it all in. Deep breaths of briny air teased through her nostrils, filling her lungs and releasing the weight of all she'd left behind in Chicago. Lifting her arms up to take in more of the sun, she smiled. *I'm free!* she thought. *I'm finally free!*

• ● •

As it turned out, freedom made an already hungry Ramona even hungrier, so just a couple of hours and two particularly juicy oranges later, her stomach insistently demanded something of richer substance. All she could think of was wild burgers or whatever it was that the driver had been telling her about. Just the idea made her mouth start to water. With her delivery app in hand, Ramona found the nearest Round and Out and made her order, as wild as possible, please. She added fries and debated on a milkshake but decided not to risk it based on the delivery time. According to her delivery app, Malibu wasn't close to much of anything other than the beach itself.

Forty-five minutes later, the notification sounded on her phone that her driver had arrived. In barely contained excitement, Ramona bounded out of the door, leaving it cracked behind her. When she returned with her bag of still-warm food, the door wasn't cracked any longer. It was closed shut.

Ramona had left her phone and keys on the kitchen counter. She felt the rise of panic in her throat and walked back to the road-facing side of the bungalow. She looked alongside the garage. There was a keypad on the frame, but she didn't have the code, only the access instructions for the exceptionally difficult lockbox. *Oh no*, she thought. She looked back at the lockbox but remembered with full certainty that she took the only set of keys that was in there. *Oh no, no no no.* In the build of panic, an image arrived in her memory of the wooden deck on the beach side of the bungalow and the slightly ajar sliding glass door that led into the living room. With no hesitation, she ran to the back and fumbled around toward the entry. By this time, it was nearly dark, and the ocean was much closer to the piles of the house foundation. The higher tide left a thin strip of sand, and the edge of the water lapped closer to her feet. With clumsy effort and dwindling light, she climbed the metal stairs up from the beach, up, up to the deck above and hoisted herself onto the wood. Quickly, she crossed the creaking wooden planks of the deck to reach the sole possible point of entry. Only when she finally gripped her hands around the handle could she breathe a large sigh of relief when it gave easily to her grasp.

"Thank God," she muttered aloud. She pulled the door open, admiring the pinks, oranges, and deepening purples of the sky as the sun completed its quick evening descent into the sea. Ramona took one more breath in, catching the hearty scent from the paper bag in her hand of cheeseburger beckoning to be eaten.

As it turned out, "wild style" could have been synonymous with "messy" and also "absolutely delicious." The tangy and creamy sauce dripped from her fingers each time she bit into the savory beef and a mouthful of pickles, mustard, and onion. Ramona thought she was tasting heaven every time her teeth broke into the toasted butter rim around the bun, with a satisfying crunch just like the lettuce. Oh, and the fries! They were crispy in a way that she'd only associated with potato chips, but these! These were so much more, even slightly cold, and stiff. Ramona made a mental note to go there in person for a do-over before she headed back to Chicago.

Consumed with sauce-laden fingers and a dwindling supply of ketchup-covered fries, Ramona barely noticed the doorbell when it rang. In fact, she did miss it the first time. The second ring startled her to look up. She wondered if the delivery person was lost and what help she could possibly offer to navigate this new planet she had only occupied for a few hours. Taking a quick moment to clean off her hands on a conveniently placed mound of napkins, with a mouth still full of delicious, she bounded quickly to the door. As it opened, and she was able to fully focus into the darkness of nighttime before her, she was surprised to see a uniformed man standing across the entryway. Right away, Ramona's body went cold, an automatic internal alarm perceiving a multitude of immediate threats. First, she was alone, very alone, and isolated in the cottage. A strange and uninvited man was in her doorway. Her mind processed this fact very quickly, looking for the black and white of a police cruiser, the thick belt of weapons, the official gold-tone badge shaped like a star. In the milliseconds of a first glance, nothing from the uniform, to the car out front, to the man himself looked quite like a police officer, but more like an imitation. What was absolutely certain was Ramona's pounding heart, her palms starting to sweat, and the enjoyment she'd felt earlier turning dry and acidic in her mouth.

"Can I help you?" she asked. She squinted for a second to look at the emblem beneath his shoulder lapel, to try to read it clearly. It looked like a police badge in color and shape, but with closer examination, she could read an unfamiliar name followed by *Sentry Safety Patrol Private Security Company*. She narrowed the door opening as she waited for a response.

"Um, ma'am, we received a call from a neighbor about a possible break-in here. Are you the owner?"

Ramona gave a sigh, irritated and wondering why she couldn't have just passed the evening with only the company of her last few fries sogging up back at the table.

"No, I'm not. I'm renting. And there's no break-in. I just left the key . . ." Logically, that explanation—plus Ramona standing there in her leisure clothes, shoes off, probably with the last bits of sauce she got to enjoy somewhere around her mouth—should have ended this situation, with *his* apology. But, of course, that is not what happened.

"I just need to see an ID and a confirmation to verify?" The man did not turn and leave, nor did he retreat from his position. Instead, he leaned forward as if he had a right to more from Ramona, more explanation, more of her time, more of her peace of mind, to his satisfaction, as if the interruption was not only justified, but somehow necessary.

At first, Ramona thought, *Hell no, I will not show you my ID, or anything else for that matter.* But in the effort to salvage her meal and her evening, she decided differently, as the anger and helplessness began to build inside her. She forced herself to remain calm but couldn't hide the fact her hands were shaking.

"Just a second, but you stay here." She debated whether she should close the door all the way as she turned her back to it, and then regretted that she didn't, taking a risk that this man wasn't some masquerading con artist. She walked over to her purse and fumbled through its contents to retrieve her ID. Clumsily, she scrambled to also find and then pull up the reservation on her phone. *Crap. It still says Latrice,* she thought, after a quick read of the confirmation message. And then, remembering Chelsea's note, she was thankful she'd called Latrice right away to clarify. Ramona had learned at some point in life that you could never be too sure of anything when you're deprived of the benefit of doubt. But then again, she didn't need to explain herself to private security. Technically, *he* was the one trespassing.

Returning to the door and opening it the same sliver of a crack as before, Ramona held up her phone first, which did show Latrice's name and hers farther down, and then her driver's license. He tried to grasp it, but she held on tightly.

"Uh-uh," Ramona countered firmly. "This stays with me. Do you need to see anything else?"

Following a bit of an awkward pause and hesitation, he seemed to back off. He pulled out something black from his utility belt. Ramona drew a sharp breath. To shoot her? Ah, no, a phone. Would he call the police now, although proven wrong? Would he escalate? And if he did, what more would that cost her? Already, the wonderful promise of the evening, of the place, of the trip even, had been ruined. There's no way that enjoying a burger should—beyond a risk of high cholesterol perhaps—lead to the feeling of a life-and-death experience. Ramona's heart thumped in her chest and echoed in her ears so loud she could barely hear the words of the patrolman when he began to speak again.

"If you just give me one second, I'm going to call the contact we have in our records." He walked off a bit with the phone up to his ear and then seemed to find himself engaged in a very vibrant conversation filled suddenly with a number of apologies on his end. He finally hung up and returned to speak through the remaining crack in the door that Ramona had left to see out of.

"Ma'am, my apologies. I spoke to the owner, and we're all set here. You enjoy your evening."

"Humph!" Ramona returned in a protesting tone, tired, *so tired*, annoyed and on edge, and still very much afraid. "No, you enjoy *your* evening," she said, as firmly as she could muster. And with that, she closed the door with a slam that rattled the walls. And then leaned her exhausted body against it with a thud. Her head landed against the door, her body slumped, releasing the tension, and the tears came on their own. Just as she fully released her deepest breath, her phone started ringing—a London-based caller. She quickly wiped the tears off her cheeks and composed herself to answer.

"Hello, hello—Ramona?" The voice on the other end had a distinctive, groggy British accent.

"Hi, yes, that's me." Ramona's voice was soft, small, and echoed bone-deep exhaustion.

"Ramona, this is Helena Covington. I'm aware of what just happened, and I'm calling to apologize. I am so *sincerely* sorry to have your stay interrupted by such a regretfully ridiculous visit. Please tell me that you're not thinking of leaving, are you? I trust it hasn't entirely ruined your evening?"

It *had*, in fact, ruined her evening. Yet, Ramona paused in answering, as she hadn't had the time to think about much, not about leaving, not about the threat of a patrolman, and not about the sad pile of wilted french fries she'd been looking forward to finishing. She was so angry now, she started shaking again. The phone in her hand trembled along with the rest of her.

"Leaving, um, I . . . I . . ."

"Oh dear," Helena continued with concern mounting even through her pristine formality. "This is completely and entirely our fault. I'll beg of you to, please, just consider completing your stay, and I'll do my best to make it up at the end? Perhaps a refund of a night?"

A night? Ramona tilted her head. She wasn't thinking of leaving, at least not yet. The logistics of solution finding were too complicated for a state of shock. Understandably numb to the totality of her feelings, she wasn't ready to concede anything, to agree or disagree. In fact, at this point, she wasn't even entirely sure what had happened, why it had happened, or just what exactly she was owed. Above all, she felt tired—so, so tired in her body, in her mind, and in her soul. Ramona was ready to stop talking altogether now, and eager to be alone, *at least* alone, *at least* to think. And miraculously, after everything, after all that had happened, in a mismatch for the circumstances, Ramona still couldn't help but be polite.

"Thank you, Helena," she said. "I'll consider it."

"Okay, dear, please do. I'm sorry, I'm in Europe and it's very late here, or early morning rather, but please just let me assure you that this will absolutely *not* happen again."

Ramona sighed. *If only Helena could make her words true,* she thought. "Surely," she said. "Good night to you."

Finishing her call, Ramona finally allowed the real tears to fall. There was no way to stop them from coming, in streaks down her cheeks. Perhaps she was mourning the loss of her enjoyment, or peace, or time, or the innocence she'd begun to feel. Perhaps in some small part, she mourned just the wasted delights, remnants that resembled nothing of her earlier meal. The tears from her eyes spilled onto her hand as she swept wrappers, papers, containers, all decorated with "wild sauce" and ketchup, into the trash.

Tomorrow, she thought. *Tomorrow, I'll know what to do.*

DECEMBER 20

•●•

CHELSEA ON A PARTICULARLY NOISY
MORNING ON CHICAGO'S GOLD COAST . . .

CHELSEA AWAKENED WITH A START TO BLARING HORNS AND THE chugging sound of construction. *City noise*, she reminded herself. The sounds of the city used to be welcome energy in her former life in Downtown LA. The area that became known as the Arts District was blocks of potential in abandoned spaces. Chelsea remembered that through art she and her friends managed to make the dingy and discarded come alive with color and welcome. They did art and ignored fear. They brushed aside inconvenience and held on to even the frayed edges of life itself. Not anymore though. After the softening that comes following years with the sea, this level of stimulation felt like disturbance rather than invigoration, and the city noise in Chicago made Jay's morning music sound more like a delicate symphony in comparison. With the rattling of her mind, she barely noticed her phone buzzing next to her announcing a caller and, evidently, four other missed calls from the same number.

"Hello, Helena," Chelsea croaked.

"Chelsea, I've been trying to reach you all morning!" Helena shrieked above the usual background buzz of her whereabouts.

"Helena, it *is* morning. I'm in Chicago. What's going on?"

Chelsea could barely imagine what could be *so* wrong *so* early, but if it meant an escape from the noise . . .

"Didn't you see any of my text messages?" The edge in Helena's voice was uncharacteristic. Chelsea straightened herself in the bed, putting the phone closer to her ear.

"No, Helena, I just woke up. Is there something wrong at the house? I know I made a mistake with the note I left, it said Latrice, but I realize I'm at Ramona Tucker's house and—"

"Oh, no, dear," Helena cut her off abruptly. "It's *much* worse than that. Would you have informed your neighbors about a guest staying?"

Chelsea squeezed her eyes as her head swiveled back and forth with one obvious thought. "Jooooan," she groaned, and Helena continued.

"Joan? Well, *Joan*, or another one of your, I would assume, overprotective neighbors sent the neighborhood patrol to visit your houseguest, Ramona, on her very first night on holiday. *Dreadful.*"

At first, Chelea was simply confused. "I'm not sure who it could be other than Joan next door, but I left a lockbox," she mused. "Why would she . . ." And then, the sharp gasp came. Chelsea's thoughts began to catch up in a slow realization. The pictures in Ramona's home—above the fireplace, on the side table next to the couch, neatly arranged on the walls. It was clear which of the people depicted was Ramona, and more important, that Ramona was . . . Black. "Oh God." Chelsea buried her face in her hands, dropping the phone with a thump on the bed.

When she picked the phone up again, Helena's voice continued in a steady stream of words. ". . . and in spite of the hour, I had to do my best to *try* to persuade her to stay, but I'm not quite certain that worked, so—"

"Helena," Chelsea interrupted. "Did you know that Ramona is . . . is . . . Black?"

Helena's end of the line was suddenly, momentarily silent. "Oh God," she finally managed.

"Yeaaah."

"Well, if it was this *Joan* . . . is she . . ."

At the mere thought, Chelsea felt instantly defensive. "Joan? Oh, no, no, no way. It must have been a mistake. I mean, she's nosy for sure, but not . . . not . . ."

"Hmph." In a very unusual circumstance, Helena sounded like she didn't quite know what to say. Neither did Chelsea.

"Well, what should I do?" Chelsea asked finally.

"I don't know, dear. I did my part. If you say your neighbor isn't . . . well, um . . . isn't prone to doing this sort of thing, then you'll have to be the one to make sure of it. I needn't remind you, if your guest leaves, you'll have to figure out another means to pay taxes. The *late* taxes. I'm turning the matter over to your very capable hands."

After the phone went silent, Chelsea scrolled through her text messages and saw that, aside from the barrage of insistent messages from Helena, there were also three from Joan. Chelsea clicked them open to read the first.

JOAN: Hey, are you expecting a guest? Call me.

Then, she opened the next message.

JOAN: Called the patrol, don't worry. Will call you if a problem.

Chelsea brought her palm up to her forehead as if she could press reality away. *Oh, Joan, why can't you mind your own business?* She took a deep breath before opening Joan's third and final message.

JOAN: OMG, so sorry! Didn't know you were doing BnB! Will take a welcome basket in the a.m.

Joan's words brought a pang to Chelsea's gut. This was not the welcome committee she envisioned for Ramona or any other guest. In fact, Chelsea hadn't put much thought into it at all, not even to tell Joan that she'd be gone. She never imagined that Joan would go so far as to call the patrol. And if she did it because Ramona was . . . No, no, she couldn't have. *At least she didn't call the police*, Chelsea thought with a grimace. She checked the time and let her fingers dance across the screen. She wasn't sure Joan was up, or what she was up to, but she wanted to stop that basket. She had to. With her house on the line, Chelsea wasn't willing to risk another brush with Joan's judgment.

> **CHELSEA:** Joan, please, no basket.

> **CHELSEA:** Ramona just wants to be left alone.

To Chelsea's surprise, three dots in a bubble popped up on Joan's side of the text thread. She held her breath, hoping, for the first time ever, Joan would take no for an answer. To her dismay, the dots disappeared.

JOAN FOX IN HER DOUBLE-LOT, TRIPLE-LEVEL, MULTIMILLION-DOLLAR PALACE BY THE SEA IN MALIBU . . .

JOAN FOX VOTED FOR OBAMA, *TWICE*. SHE'D REPEATED THIS FACT to herself approximately thirty-seven times since ten p.m. last night when she shuffled down her well-worn copy of Ina Garten's *The Barefoot Contessa Cookbook* and flipped to her tabbed page of the recipe for strawberry scones. Her expansive kitchen, equipped with essentially new appliances from Viking, Wolf, and Miele, looked like a disaster area, with remnants of flour, discarded baking sheets, and dough-graffitied mixing bowls, which filled her ceramic farmhouse sink to overflowing. The dishwasher was humming, the microwave was beeping, and her generous hood fan whirred above her head.

Throughout the night—from nearly the first moment she learned of her incredibly unfortunate faux pas until now—Joan had been baking. Out of the long wall of windows facing the sea, she could see the first rays of light change the midnight blue over the ocean to a peachy orange-and-lavender mix of early morning.

Baking was what Joan decided to do with all her nervous energy, the never-ending farmers market–sourced supply of strawberries that usually dotted her yogurt, and the three-quarters-of-a-pound of all-organic grass-fed butter that she'd used precisely chilled (not cold, and certainly *not* room temperature) in the mixer. Other than the Barefoot Contessa's signature recipe, she'd used her formerly spotless oven to produce four types of Christmas cookies, two of which had icing, and a loaf of her almost-famous banana bread that used the very last of her breakfast fruit.

Her doomsday thoughts of whether or not she'd proven herself to be the dreaded r-word (she could not, in fact, bring herself to think it, let alone say it) were almost drowned out by the impossibly meticulous attention to detail required by baking. It was four measured cups *plus* exactly one tablespoon leveled for the flour and five eggs beaten two ways, plus two types of sugar, one in particular for sprinkling on top when everything was finished. Joan needed to measure and mix, bake and pack, not think. Because if she thought, then she'd replay the events of the previous night over and over again, wondering how it was that she *wrongly* saw the circumstances of Ramona's reentry into Chelsea's house so clearly as a home invasion. Wouldn't anyone, seeing any unfamiliar person entering their neighbor's dark home, call a patrol of some sort? Wasn't that the neighborly thing to do? And wasn't it a virtue to be the keeper of her neighbor's property, the maintainer of the gates, the last defense between the high-tide line and the private property rights that were so expensive and well-earned? Malibu was small, a tiny community of people who'd made it so easy to determine who and what belonged there, and who and what did not. You just trusted your gut, and anything and anyone out of place just so happened to stick out like a sore thumb. And certainly, Ramona stuck out . . . but not because she was . . . well, different. Joan had her eye trained for anything unusual, and Ramona entering Chelsea's house was simply that—unusual.

And now that all was sorted, what was the harm? And what more to do than simply forgetting it and letting it go? Best to just move on . . . Joan's thoughts continued as she lined one of her spare gift baskets in the pantry with a fresh cloth that she just happened to also have. As she learned from frequent entertaining and being even more frequently entertained, you never knew when you'd need to bring a gift basket with you in a pinch, and who had time to head down to the Malibu Country Mart? Oh, and anyway, she'd only called the Sentry Patrol, the private security, not the police. So, was Chelsea's guest ever in any danger? What was her name again? Rolanda? Regina? Unable to recall, Joan resolved to text Chelsea again just to make sure she had it right, before she marched the fifty feet to next door armed with a basket full of treats and a welcome worthy of Queen Oprah herself, whom Joan had met, of course, several times.

As Joan fumbled around in the space underneath her sink for the basic cleaning supplies for her kitchen, a task usually handled by others without her involvement, she once again replayed the events. It was seven thirty p.m., already dark and with seemingly nobody on the stretch of beach sand behind hers and Chelsea's houses. So, it could have been anyone who was the shadowy figure lurking along Chelsea's deck space and who ultimately fumbled their way inside through an open door. Joan would swear it was impossible to tell even if it were a man or a woman, and in the twilight, of course, near impossible to see race—although she could see hair, lots of it. In a puff pulled up on top of the person's head. But again, how was Joan to know?

Joan looked down at her hands now immersed in warm suds in her sink. *Will this dish soap ruin my manicure?* she wondered. It was so infrequent that she washed dishes, especially not by hand. The unusual experience briefly recalled her childhood in Bakersfield, California, a place she'd much rather forget, when cleaning was *her* job, rather than someone else's. Standing back then in the tiny kitchen of a modest home, not much more than a stationary trailer, reaching barely over the rim of the dingy metal sink, little Joan was familiar with washing dishes. She was charged with cooking for herself and leaving a spotless kitchen before her waitress mother came home from the late shift most nights. When high school ended, Joan couldn't have run away fast enough from her very small town to come to Los Angeles. She rode the wave of what attention her beauty brought—small acting jobs at first, and then a series regular role on *Knots Landing*. And then, the grand coup of the time back then, a high-profile marriage to a television producer, *the* David Fox, which landed her right here, where she belonged, ensconced high on the social ladder of insular Malibu.

These days, in each of her homes, there was always someone to tend to the kitchen. But in Joan's childhood, it had been different. And the idea of a dirty kitchen still filled her core with dread. The need for spotlessness was etched as deeply in her subconscious as the memories of her once-threadbare existence that she couldn't shake. So, as her maid wouldn't arrive for hours yet, Joan was washing spatulas, spoons, and bowls and scraping the burnt remains of otherwise perfectly baked goods off their aluminum baking sheets. There was so much that little Joan wanted to leave behind that this Joan, divorcée Joan, wealthy Joan, Joan who got the beach house in Malibu and the Westside friends and half the residuals from not only one but two of her ex's very successful shows, this Joan did not do dishes and was certainly *not*, well, that dreadful r-word.

Joan had appearances to maintain, after all, truly, after *all* that had happened with her marriage, which was quite a bit. The whispers started long before David's assistant became pregnant and decided to stay that way. So, when the news broke it was only a matter of time before the functional façade of the marriage crumbled and divorce followed. By that time, two kids and three decades later, there was no career to restart—her highest-paying and most visible role had been David's loyal wife. But, as long as she maintained her social status, it wasn't the worst outcome to get the Malibu house, plus the Cabo house and a condo in Aspen, plus a generous chunk of David's residuals.

Joan did, however, take special care to maintain her status within her circle of friends. The embarrassment of David's long stretch of betrayals required her to keep appearances at all costs. There was nothing like a broken woman to leave a trail of blood in the water for a swift social death. So, Joan maintained the façade, and still hosted the most elaborate dinners, the after parties for the Emmy Awards, the midnight brunch that everyone attended after the illustrious *Vanity Fair* afterparty with a signature eggs Benedict that had even the industry's most sinewy-limbed action star exposing his appetite rather than his usual public-facing self-restraint.

And now, after all these years of surviving threats to her image, her reputation unscathed, she'd run the risk of one tiny mistake labeling her the most unthinkable thing. The one thing that would get her quietly uninvited to everything she'd fought so hard to maintain not just from the divorce, but in her whole life. Joan Fox belonged here, and she was going to make sure that it stayed that way.

With a clean kitchen and a filthy conscience, Joan loaded her arm up with a cornucopia of baked delights and made her way to formally introduce herself to the new neighbor next door. Joan was absolutely certain she was just one dollop of clotted cream on a fresh strawberry scone away from sweeping the events of the prior night perfectly under the rug.

CHELSEA IN CHICAGO . . .

IN THE ABSENCE OF A USUAL MORNING ROUTINE, CHELSEA USED her nervous energy to assemble the elements of a late-late-morning first pot of coffee. It wasn't difficult to find the necessary supplies in Ramona's kitchen—the mug was in the cabinet over her shoulder to the right, the spoon in the drawer to the left of the sink; the coffee itself was in the pantry, behind the only full-size door in the kitchen. And the filtered water was in the carefully labeled carafe in the refrigerator, written in neat white chalk handwriting on an erasable black panel. Where Chelsea had left her guest a note, Ramona had left Chelsea detailed notes upon notes of how to find everything from a fork to a hammer and an organizational system that was worthy of its own HGTV series.

As worried as she was about the future of the Malibu house and without access to her usual comforts, in particular her studio and wide assortment of painting supplies, Chelsea would have normally channeled manageable anxiety into productivity, perhaps some arranging at her temporary home. But Ramona's place was already spotless. There wasn't so much as a tastefully patterned accent pillow out of place on the sofa. Moreover, in the daylight, Ramona's clear sense of decorating logic spoke in silent volumes of beiges and cream neutrals, slight hints of soft, delicate, barely-there pink and warmed-up grays. She'd either made or inherited a lime-washed brick fireplace, and the blues and white in the area rug perfectly offset the windows that faced a frozen Lake Michigan. Chelsea imagined the view as lovely in the much warmer summer, and her touch of the glass let her know just how incredibly cold it was outside. She shuddered with the thought of it and wondered how it might work to stay within the modest confines of a single bedroom, bathroom, and living room for the entirety of the rest of the week.

And it was there, staring out of the windows at a dreary day in a frozen city with a frozen lake, drumming her fingers against the glass, that Chelsea heard a knock on the door. Expecting no one, she would have ignored it but for the subsequent sound of the lock turning and then the door handle moving, and the door creaking open.

She would have screamed—the noise was stuck right at the back of her throat—but for seeing the biggest, brightest smile that for a second actually took her literal breath away. In front of her was a tall man, six feet at least, of square frame with chocolate curls on the top of his tapered haircut. Thick eyebrows covered bright, friendly dark-brown eyes, whose long lashes nearly graced the top of stubbled cheeks with skin the color of a caramel latte. Remembering the sound of the key quelled some of the panic in Chelsea's body, and instead she stood in the room still silent with her mouth slightly agape, unable to find a single word to speak.

"My bad," the entrant said midstride with his hand still on the doorknob. "I knocked, but thought you might have run out real quick."

"I'm not Ramona," Chelsea said. It was ridiculous and also the only thing she could convince her mouth to say.

He laughed, and Chelsea felt herself smiling back. She wanted to be angry at the intrusion, but his smile was so friendly, disarming, and inexplicably familiar.

"I'm not Ramona either." The big smile smiled bigger. "I'm Carlos." He reached his hand toward Chelsea as if to shake it, extending his long, winter-insulated arm in a bundle of coat. And then he halted suddenly as if to change his mind. "My bad . . ." As he continued, his cheeks started to redden a bit. "I'm Ramona's play brother . . ." Seeing the immediate confusion in Chelsea's face, he searched for a different reference to describe their relationship. "Her . . . let's just say cousin? You know, brother from another?"

Chelsea shook her head slowly with recognition. She'd seen this man, Carlos, before. Now, with context, she recognized him from several of Ramona's pictures.

"I'm Chelsea. Ramona's guest, I guess? She's staying in my place in Malibu." It felt like the words were stumbling out of her mouth.

"Right. Her West Coast hideout. We're all accomplices. I'm taking care of her dog." He started to close the door behind him, completing his entrance, but hesitated and turned to Chelsea. "You mind if I step in and grab a few things, actually? For the pup?"

Chelsea nodded her consent. By now, the level of quite obviously unnecessary fear was settling into something that more resembled excitement and an unmistakable and quite unexpected current of attraction. She managed to take a staggered deep breath as Carlos first tapped then wiped his Timberlands against the thick macramé floor mat and finally continued his long strides toward the kitchen.

"She always keeps it so warm in here." Carlos zipped down the top half of his coat, loosened the tan-colored wool scarf that perfectly accented his complexion, and completed his short trip across the compact space to a position in the center of the kitchen. "I just stopped by to get some treats. Evidently it has to be the exact treats she gives him. He literally won't eat anything else and needs to be bribed to do everything." Carlos's words floated to Chelsea as an echo from the cabinet under the sink, as he was bent down rummaging through another of

Ramona's meticulously arranged spaces. Seeming to find what he was looking for, he popped back up with the energy of a kid who'd just won a prize, admiring the brightly colored plastic bag of dog treats he'd been looking for. He then turned to fully examine a still somewhat listless Chelsea.

"Sorry about the intrusion though. I'm sure you didn't expect anyone to come through the door. You good?" Carlos paused and raised an eyebrow, looking at her. Chelsea nodded, and then, seeming satisfied with that answer, he continued. "So you'll be here a week . . ." he said, with the consideration of a scientific discovery. "California time, that's right. You're probably still pre-coffee, right? You got anybody here in Chicago?"

"I don't know anybody here," she said quietly.

"Now you do." Carlos punctuated it with an even bigger smile. "Coming from the West Coast, you don't know about this Midwest winter. Got a warm coat?"

Chelsea remembered the Burning Man special she'd stuffed in her luggage at the last minute.

"I *guess* I do," she said. "It worked for me in the desert."

Carlos's face scrunched. And then he shook his head. That glorious head full of lush chocolate curls. He beckoned toward her with his fingertips.

"Let me see it."

"You want to see my coat?"

"Yeah, let me see it."

Chelsea hesitated but decided to comply. "One sec," she told Carlos and headed into the bedroom and returned with the coat. Somehow then, in Ramona's contemporary dream of a living room, it looked much more ratty and matted than it ever did within her own walls. She held the coat up between herself and Carlos. It resembled a dingy tan roadkill animal, if the roadkill animal was dripping small cascades of sand into tiny dunes on the wood-paneled portion of the floor beneath her.

"What is that?"

"My coat."

"It looks dead."

"It's faux. It was never alive. I don't wear dead animals."

"Now, that's some LA shit," Carlos said with another generous laugh, as if Chelsea had said the most ridiculous thing in the world. "This is *Chicago*. You wander around downtown wearing a roadkill robe dripping actual sand everywhere you go, and the *cops* are gonna pick you up, *for sure*."

Chelsea looked at the coat again. It truly had served her just fine in the desert. But Chicago was a different kind of cold, that much was made clear even in the brief moments of her exposure to it when she arrived. This kind of cold was far more intense, not like the desert at all. And so, although, she had no certain plans of *ever* leaving Ramona's place, Carlos had a point.

"You know where to go to get a coat?" His right eyebrow lifted as he waited for her to reply.

Chelsea knew absolutely nothing about Chicago. She didn't even remember exactly how she'd gotten to Ramona's condo the night before other than plugging an address into her rideshare app. She gave no answer, but pulled her arms up, crossing them in a tangle with the coat across the front of her body.

"Tomorrow, Cali girl, we go and get you a coat." Carlos gestured good-naturedly in her direction. "And some real coffee. That stuff Ramona keeps here, that ain't what you want."

Without waiting for a reply, he turned to the door, quickly doubling back on his path. Half out of the door, before closing it, he squeezed his head and shoulders back inside.

"Nice meeting you, Chelsea."

The door shut behind him, and Chelsea could still see his smile as if she'd just looked at a lightbulb. She realized that while she never agreed to needing a coat, already she found herself looking forward to tomorrow.

"Nice meeting you too," she said finally, while the remnants of Burning Man continued to build in tiny piles of sand on the ground beneath her feet.

RAMONA BURIED NECK-DEEP IN THE BEDCOVERS IN MALIBU . . .

RAMONA SPENT THE ENTIRETY OF HER FIRST NIGHT TOSSING and turning, reviewing events moment by moment like a long grocery receipt, leading up to the unthinkable tally of a patrolman confrontation at the door of her vacation rental. This, at minimum, was a development as inexplicable as seeing a ghost. There'd been no natural cause to connect to the series of events, thus creating the impossible puzzle that Ramona confronted—how could she find an explanation for what seemed to be the wrongdoing of simply being. Being somewhere, *somewhere*, being Malibu. Not that she'd thrown a loud party. There'd been no ruckus, no noise, not even an eventful entry, as she'd managed to retrieve the key with only minor pause and difficulty. And yet, nonetheless, she had to confront a patrolman. Why? Was it that she was Black? Or was it something else? Bad luck? Unfortunate timing? Circumstances beyond her control?

Ramona Tucker had no idea. So, without answers, she fretted. What demands the mind makes after trauma, requiring an explanation at least, an assurance that what felt dangerous won't happen again. *Shall I file this in the drawer labeled "unusual"?* the mind asks, begging for its return to safety. Ramona's mind did, certainly. But this kind of disturbance couldn't be labeled as unusual because it simply wasn't. And so, after all the consternation, without explanation, Ramona did what she did best—worked the numbers.

She counted the number of times that she'd been stopped by police. The number of times she felt afraid when she saw a uniform in front of her or the black-and-white pattern of a standard patrol car behind her. The seconds of panic she'd felt in her life hearing a siren or seeing lights flash, perhaps only to go around her in pursuit of someone else. How many times she'd double-checked the location of her driver's license and wallet in her car. The number of eyes that stared at her with suspicion when she was minding her own business. How much extra time she spent trying to be unbearably acceptable. She even calculated how much this rental, this time in Chelsea's cottage, was costing her by the minute and started to think about Helena's offer. Could she determine how much she was actually owed for this situation, this experience and all of its dissatisfaction? In the end, she basically figured that the numbers weren't adding up.

This was how she decided that she should depart this place. And this was how the day greeted her, as Ramona watched the sky change from midnight blue to royal blue with a hint of periwinkle, with the thought in her mind: *I should leave.* Lying in bed, Ramona blinked into the developing sunlight and contemplated closing the shutters. But, waking up to the ocean was still a glorious view, even with just the few winks of sleep that she'd managed.

Despite Ramona's thrashing, Chelsea's bed was still a comfortable mess of expensive down comforter, a generous king-size memory foam mattress, and stacks of pillows. In the last hour, Ramona's body had sunk into an exactly Ramona-size indentation. She needed the rest. With effort, as she turned away from the windows, rotating her body in the groove beneath her, Ramona's satin sleep bonnet made a whoosh of friction against the soft cotton pillowcase. Somehow, she'd managed to keep it on despite fitful tossing and turning, restless with the mental replay of her run-in with the Sentry Patrol. *Someone phoned a complaint*, she recalled him saying. *Nosy-assed people*, she thought to herself, feeling the acute sense of not belonging. It just seemed like, already, Malibu was going out of its way to be clear that she wasn't one of its own.

"I should just go back home," she said aloud to no one.

In reply, she heard the distant whoosh of the surf interrupted by the sudden start of the thump and high-pitched synth of electronic music that was much closer.

"Oh my God, it gets worse," Ramona mumbled, bringing her hands up to her temples and squeezing her eyes shut. She should leave, but couldn't leave, not without somewhere else to go, and a new plan. And so, the only thing she really could do was to call Latrice and hope that in this one instance, she would not be the voice of reason. One very deep breath later, she began fumbling around in the layers of bedding for her cell phone. Pulling up the screen for recent contacts, she dialed.

"Latrice, why did I let you convince me to do this?" Ramona could hear the sounds of the city in the background on the other end of the line.

"Girl, I'm about to get on the L," Latrice replied, sounding like she was also shivering. "Are you okay? It's cold as *shit* out here."

"I think I need to come home," Ramona said.

"What?"

"It was a mistake to come. I should have known."

"Known what—that someone would call the patrol on you? How would you?"

"Latrice, it's Malibu. We both should have known."

"Are you serious, Ramona?" Latrice sounded frustrated. Ramona saw her pinch the bridge of her nose with her gloved hand in the frame of the camera before the hand unfurled palm forward, taking up most of the view. "Hold up. Let me calm down." A very long exhale followed. "So, we're just supposed to stick to the boxes someone else has drawn? Just lie down flat, accept this simple bullshit that we know is bullshit? Because those people in Malibu don't want you there? Is that what you're saying, Moe?"

Ramona hesitated. "I mean . . . I might have said it differently, but—"

"But what? If you leave, period, point blank you've let them win. They win and you . . . lose. That's it. Have you ever searched the news for Malibu?"

"Didn't you when you picked this place?"

"Yeah, I did. And I still picked it because it's beautiful and affordable for your hardworking ass in the offseason, and you *deserve* it. Because it is damn *gorgeous*. And yes, it's a place where rich, white-minded people live, who've come to think the world revolves around them. Do I know what it means to have *so* much money and *so* much time that you'd spend it inventing ways to try to literally own the beach? No. Do I know what it means to design fences to cover walkways, or expand driveways and move dumpsters so people can't find walkways to enjoyment? Girl, I don't have the time. And neither do you."

"The ocean, the beach, the palm trees, Latrice, the weather even—it's all so beautiful here. So beautiful that I wouldn't even try to describe it—I just want you to see it for yourself. I wish that everyone could see it, be touched by it like I was. My first feeling was wanting to share. I guess that means no, I just don't understand."

"So, imagine thinking, for some reason, you have the right . . . or the duty even, to ruin all that beauty for someone else? What kind of person wakes up to that view, *miserable*?"

"Honestly . . . today? Me."

Latrice sighed aggressively. "Moe, you can't let whoever infect you with their unhappiness. That shit is contagious, for real . . ."

"Let's just say it worked," said Ramona, growing more irritated and frustrated all the same. And she didn't mean to take it out on Latrice. She didn't mean to take it out on anyone . . . other than herself. But the words were there, and they kept coming. "I was so close to happy, Latrice. So close . . . last night, I could feel it. Happiness, right there, peace, right there. Just one moment, to relax . . . to enjoy what I could provide for myself. I work so much, so hard . . ." Then, she had to stop talking. Because the moment that she spoke the word *hard*, she thought about it and how much she actually did work—the responsibility that she shouldered, what that took from her, and what she didn't and couldn't get back—the rest of the words caught in her throat. Now was the time for her tears again, and the weariness. She sniffled and then sobbed the rest of what she needed to say, everything that had been pent up from the night before, when she'd cried herself into the little bit of sleep she'd managed. "The enjoyment is *gone*. Now all I can think about is, *Who called the patrol? Why did they do that? Who else is going to come in the middle of the night?* I mean, Latrice, am I even safe? Why can't I just *be here*? Why?" Ramona wailed. It was as if the pain she felt had cracked through an opening and now could only pour out. Ramona wasn't even sure if the phone line was still connected, but she couldn't stop. She couldn't stop until it all came out.

"All I wanted to do was to come for a week, let Christmas pass, and go back with a little more time. That's all, Latrice. But then, when I got here, and felt the sun and the breeze, and my goodness . . . saw the great big ocean, I hadn't felt that good for so long. For one moment, I exhaled, like I spent good money for a good reason. That somehow, after everything, I needed *this*—that there was something here for me.

"And then, for absolutely no reason, when I'm where I'm *supposed* to be, some stranger comes in the dead of night trying to force his way in to snatch my ID? Like I owe him some kind of explanation? I don't have to explain anything. And I'm tired of pretending that I'm okay. Of taking polite phone calls and saying 'Hmmm, I'll consider it' when someone offers to pay me back a night. Seven hundred dollars for my troubles, right? So, then I guess I'm not hurt anymore? But I *am* hurt. When do I get to say something bad happened to me? And who do I say it to, Latrice, if not you?" Ramona had finally run out of words. She was breathing hard now, with tears streaming down her face, onto her hands, into the sheets and comforter below her, like rain on the surface of the sea.

For a moment, the line was silent on Latrice's end. Very uncharacteristic of Latrice, who always knew what to say, except when there was truly nothing to say. Because the pain that Ramona expressed deserved space, as well as acknowledgment. After a few seconds passed, Latrice did reply. In a much softer tone, she said, "I'm sorry that happened to you." And it was a tone that carried empathy, understanding, and the tacit commiseration of knowing exactly what had happened, exactly how she felt, because it was commonly experienced and, in another place and time, it had happened to her too.

In the silence between them, Ramona breathed. She gathered and soothed herself. She pulled sheets and comforter and her own arms around herself and hugged tightly. "Thank you," she said, wiping her tears. Then, as her body calmed and quieted, the outside noise assaulted her ears again, and she recounted the lesser ills of Malibu. "He also ruined what might have been the best burger I've had in ten years, and now some kind of thumping electro-house DJ has taken over my morning."

"Well, this gets better," Latrice said with a voice now full of intrigue. "Somebody's playing house music?"

"Girl, not Chicago house. Definitely *not* Chicago house. More like . . . New Jersey house. And I barely got any sleep, and the ocean is noisy, and—"

"Ramona . . ." Latrice let out another very loud and very long sigh. "I know this is hard. But I have to be honest with you. For real. Whatever it is that is there for you in Malibu, whether it is just to sit for five minutes in the sun, or wade into the ocean with your bare feet, or splash in some water up to your neck so you don't mess up your hair, you *need* this. And yes, before you say it, I'll say *this*. Look, you can come back to freezing-cold Chicago, but if you do, just remember, it's not going to be any easier. And now, Malibu owes you something. It's up to you to figure out what that is . . . and take it back. Because nobody ever offers you what you're worth."

Ramona covered her eyes again with her hands and vigorously rubbed the sides of her face. She needed to wake up.

"Latrice, I—" she began. Interrupting her reply was the sound of her doorbell. *Dinnnng . . . donnng*, it rang, as ominous as ever. *Not again*, she thought. As if pulled by an invisible wire, Ramona shot straight up to a seated position in the bed. Immediately, the jolt of panic arrived, deep in her gut. Heart rate increasing, she felt her breath come faster as she looked around for some reassurance of safety. But there was none, just Latrice on the phone. Other than the ocean outside and the music that continued to play, she was alone.

"Ramona . . ." Latrice echoed back.

"No, *not* Ramona. Someone's at the front door." This pronouncement Ramona whispered, even though she wasn't quite sure why she did. She began bunching the bedding around her, looking to find her way out of it. Preparations for whatever was about to happen.

"Is it the Sentry Patrol again?" Latrice sounded concerned.

"I have no idea, I'm in the bed." But, as Ramona spoke, she was making her way out of the bed, pulling the bunched covers off her brown legs, dropping her toes down to meet the rug covering the wooden floor planks. Shifting her weight slowly to standing, she strategized her next move.

"Don't you have a doorbell camera or something?" Latrice offered.

"This isn't my house, remember?"

"Right. Go see who's there, then. I'll stay on the phone with you."

Latrice's last words gave Ramona a sinking feeling. They brought reality all too close to bear. That here, in the presence of the sea and sand and witnessed by the majesty of the ocean herself, Ramona couldn't just be a guest in a house. That it must come traumatically, that she would have to find courage somewhere that didn't belong on vacation. "Why is this happening to me?" she whimpered. "Should I just stay here and hide?"

"You think they'll just go away?"

"Latrice, this is serious."

"I am being serious. Turn your camera around and at least go see who it is. I'll be your witness."

With a loud groan, enough to echo the near totality of all her frustrations, Ramona pushed herself to move. She shuffled her feet into her slippers and pulled a robe around her sleepwear.

"I can't believe I'm doing this . . . *again*," Ramona whispered into the phone. On the screen she could see Latrice leaning forward, seated on the train, silent but watching diligently. Ramona crept forward, tensing further with each step, stress rising through her body like steam. It wasn't a long distance from the bedroom in the back of Chelsea's house to the front door on the other side of the living room, but the thirty steps felt like an eternity for Ramona. Finally, she got close enough that she could see the outline of the figure of a woman, no longer ringing, but now physically rapping a staccato knock on the door with her knuckles.

"Don't answer," Latrice whispered. "I bet it's the neighbor who called the po-po on you."

Ramona took a step closer to get a better gauge. "It's a woman," she told Latrice.

"Does she have on a uniform?"

"It looks like she's holding a wicker basket."

"Are you sure it's not a gun?"

"A gun doesn't look like a basket."

"True dat. But still. And she's alone?"

"I *think* alone, from what I can see. Should I answer?" The knocking continued, and the bell rang once again.

"*Hell no* you shouldn't," Latrice said. "Back up from the door and just wait. If it's a basket, maybe she'll leave it and go the hell away."

Ramona peeped carefully around the corner of the sofa. She still saw the silhouette standing there, seemingly shifting the outline of a large loop-handled basket from one hand to the other. Finally, the basket fell out of her field of vision and a folded piece of paper slid under the door. The woman's silhouette reappeared, then started to shrink and, eventually, disappeared.

Ramona pulled the phone back up to eye level. Latrice was still sitting on the train with the phone's camera at an unnaturally close distance from her face, distorting her features.

"She's gone," Ramona said, turning the camera setting to face her again.

Latrice on her end leaned back into the seat and slouched with a loud exhale of relief.

"That was intense."

Ramona remained silent while she tiptoed to the door to take a closer look. The folded paper lay calmly next to the door, reduced now to just an artifact of Ramona's dread and the unwanted visit that caused it. The *second* unwanted visit.

"Should I read the note?"

"Do you even need to ask? Girl, read the note!"

Ramona bent down and reached for the carefully creased white paper on the ground in front of her. It was folded exactly in half, and the paper seemed to be one of those very fancy stationery types, with texture and unfinished edges. Ramona opened it to reveal a plain stamped monogram on top, FROM THE DESK OF JOAN FOX, and a swirl of signature on the bottom. Written in the middle in a mixture of elongated swoops and elegant lines was a note. Ramona read it out loud to Latrice.

> Dearest Ramona,
>   Chelsea told me that she'd have a guest for the week. Please accept these simple treats to welcome you to our community. I hope this will be the start to a wonderful time. There's so much to enjoy. Please do call me anytime. I'd love to treat you to lunch or dinner and would be thrilled to show you our little town by the sea.
>   Most sincerely,
>   Your next-door neighbor, Joan

Ramona looked up to see Latrice staring at her intently. "And then she left her number. Oh, and a 'P.S.' It says, 'The banana bread is gluten-free.'"

For a second, they both sat in silence, contemplating the developments. Of course, Joan was a suspect, but the note was so friendly and the situation so unfamiliar. If she knew Ramona was coming, why would she call the patrol? Perhaps Chelsea sent Joan? And would the same person who called the Sentry Patrol on an innocent Black woman care enough to make *gluten-free* banana bread? People do want to believe the best of things, as Ramona did, except that Blackness is a cynical teacher. You must question all, even smiling faces, and what might happen without warning. Nonetheless, Joan's disarming note—so full of friendliness and an invitation to the other side of Malibu, its welcoming side—did the work as intended. Finally, it was Latrice who spoke first.

"Well, the banana bread *is* gluten-free," she said haltingly. "*And* it said 'treats.' So maybe you should open the door and just see."

"What if she's waiting for me to open the door?"

"You really think she's ready to pounce?" Latrice laughed. "Ramona, c'mon. She's probably harmless."

"Or not," Ramona shot back. As much reluctance as she felt, already she was reaching for the door handle. Despite all the circumstances, curiosity had won. Ramona pulled the door open, looking around from left to right for any sign of her visitor. Seeing no one, she cautiously bent down to retrieve the basket. It was huge, at least one foot high and made of heavy woven reeds, lined with a beautiful gingham-printed fabric and filled to the brim with what looked and smelled like freshly baked goods. Ramona pulled herself and the basket inside, closed the door, and headed straight for the kitchen island. Placing the basket on the surface, she gave herself the opportunity to examine the contents more closely.

"There really is banana bread in here, Latrice."

"Girl, let me see."

Ramona held her phone over the top of the basket, letting the view fall over each item carefully nestled in place inside the generous cavity. She could smell the butter and sweetness of sugar and vanilla, strawberries, and of course the unmistakable perfume of banana and cinnamon. She had to admit that the room had been immediately filled with the smell of heaven, and she was having a hard time keeping herself from indulging in a bite.

"Are you going to try one?"

"I don't know." Ramona took a deep whiff. "Food from strangers and all . . . but it smells so good. When I moved into my place back home, the condo board didn't send me so much as a pizza."

"Maybe you're getting to see how the other side lives. But, double-check—do you see a teacup and a spoon in there?"

Ramona stifled a laugh but actually looked. "Nope, don't see either."

"Then it seems like you don't need to *get out*," Latrice pronounced.

"Goodbye, Latrice." Ramona maneuvered to end the call but hovered her hand over the screen.

"So, you're staying, then?" Latrice leaned forward again, face open and eager for Ramona's response.

"At least now I have enough carbs to fuel a wash day," Ramona replied begrudgingly.

As Ramona and Latrice discussed their plans for the rest of the day and Ramona eventually reached for a slice of the irresistible banana bread, little did she realize that Joan had positioned herself in her usual place on her deck, behind her usual sunglasses, underneath her usual hat, to wait.

JOAN BACK AT HOME
(NOT IN THE BUSHES) . . .

True that Joan did actually leave her basket of treats and her carefully crafted note. She was not lurking around any corners, especially since she could just as easily see nearly all of Ramona's goings-on from her perch at home. She felt satisfied with what she'd done, even as she walked away without Ramona answering the door. She had of course hoped that she would answer the door, having come bearing such a perfectly handcrafted welcome gift, but nonetheless left nothing to chance. *Maybe she was sleeping late,* Joan explained to herself and congratulated herself for leaving her number in the note.

She made it back to her own door just in time to look over, down at Chelsea's place, and caught her first daytime glimpse of Ramona Tucker as she collected the basket. Joan felt herself smile as she closed the door behind her. *Ramona Tucker,* she thought to herself. By now, after learning it from Chelsea, she'd committed Ramona's name to memory and had googled her twice. She saw that Ramona had graduated from DePaul (from LinkedIn) and that she'd evidently once won some kind of youth scholarship. She found her social media page, which was private, but she did see what she thought was a wedding registry? Strange, but she resolved to find out. Because she would most certainly meet Ramona. Looking at her cell phone, Joan thought, *any time now* and awaited the imminent ring or a ping of a message. When it didn't arrive right away, she resolved to keep her phone close by, because even if it took *all* day, Joan would make sure that Ramona Tucker knew that she was *welcome*, and that Joan Fox was *not* r—.

DECEMBER 21

· • ·

CHELSEA ON A RESTLESS MORNING IN
CHICAGO . . .

CHELSEA WAS UP SURPRISINGLY EARLY, ESPECIALLY FOR A SHOP-
ping trip to buy a barely affordable winter coat that she was
almost certain to never need again. She was dressed before
eight a.m. By nine a.m. she'd had two cups of Ramona's house
coffee blend that made her wish she'd heeded Carlos's warning.
His description of not "real coffee" for what those beans brewed
was surprisingly technically accurate. They'd made a dark, syrupy brew that was far too bitter to enjoy. But for the moment,
it was all she had to focus on while waiting for the time to drip
minute by minute before Carlos's arrival.

By ten a.m., Chelsea was in her third position on Ramona's
light-gray tufted microfiber couch. Her right knee bobbed up
and down as her heel tapped beneath her like a sewing needle
trying to affix her foot to the floor. For someone who previously
had no interest in seeing Chicago or freezing while doing it,
Chelsea found that she had plenty of interest in seeing Carlos
again. There was just something about him: his eyes perhaps,
or smile, or wit. Whatever it was lit something alive in Chelsea,
and that thing was beating in her chest, somewhere between
her heart and her stomach.

Relief jolted through her at approximately ten forty-five

(Carlos was fifteen minutes late) when she finally heard the knock on the door that she'd been waiting for.

"Coming!" Chelsea heard the words exit from her mouth so quickly in response to the sound that she wondered if she could be trusted with control of her own body. She scrambled her way off the sofa and toward the door in a very unglamorous movement that unveiled her eagerness, a state that Chelsea found both unfamiliar and uncomfortable. But yet, here she was, hand on the door, counting down five deep breaths before she turned the knob on the next part of her life.

Okay, Chelsea, breathe, she repeated calmly to herself. On the last deep exhale, she pulled the door open.

And there was the smile. Big, bright, better than yesterday for sure. Chelsea moved out of the way to let Carlos enter. With his insulated puffed-out coat, he needed the extra room.

"Whassup, Chelsea?" Carlos bellowed.

Chelsea's face betrayed her, breaking into a smile so wide it stretched her ears back.

"Hey. Good morning," she managed to say, preparing to fidget. But there wasn't time for self-consciousness to collect or for Chelsea to say much more, because there was another voice, a woman's this time, coming through the doorframe.

"Now, Chelsea, I told Carlos I'd just come up for a second to give a hello and a proper welcome. These kids these days—I can't believe Ramona didn't tell me you were coming. And Carlos said you didn't know anyone in Chicago and that is *not* how we do a Tucker family Christmas. Girl, if you are staying here, you're family, you hear?"

And suddenly, there in the doorway was a stunning African American woman, much browner than Carlos. She wore a scarf tied in the loose loops of European styling and a nearly breathtaking jewel-tone turquoise wrap coat made of wool, or was it cashmere? Atop her head of dark-colored barrel curls was a bright orange beret, a perfect match in color to the scarf, tilted just so, making an isosceles triangle on her head. Her makeup was tasteful and immaculate. She had the presence of a runway model but a warm openness demonstrated with a smile that matched Carlos's in radiance.

Still holding the door open, leaning on it a bit from a sense of overwhelming bewilderment, Chelsea turned to look at Carlos, who was now behind her in the apartment. His response was to shrug his shoulders, leaving Chelsea to navigate the circumstances in front of her with an attempt at an elusive deep breath. And then another, starting to resemble an actual fish out of water.

"Chelsea?"

Chelsea could only assume the woman speaking was Ramona's mother. Although, her face showed nowhere near the age to have a child who could afford a place like this. She seemed very concerned and stepped forward in an effort to again make an eye-level connection.

"I'm Melba Tucker, Ramona's mother? Are you all right?"

"Um-hum." The sound Chelsea managed to force out was accented by her nod of acknowledgment. She was still trying to self-regulate with the deep breaths she'd been taught, breaths that, despite her best efforts, were not yet flowing freely. She was also trying to hide it so as not to not alarm others without experience with her type of episodes.

Melba pulled back and placed her arm around Chelsea, guiding her to the sofa. Carlos appeared in her field of vision soon after, his handsome features reflecting an image of concern. A few moments passed, and with some concentration, Chelsea managed to avoid hyperventilating and was soon able to fill her lungs with air. Five breaths in, she found she could speak, and all she wanted to do was apologize.

"I'm so sorry," Chelsea said to the two sets of eyes studying her. "Sometimes I just . . . sometimes I have panic attacks. It's no one's fault or anything." She looked toward the ground, wishing that her introduction to people she barely knew could be something a little more normal and that she didn't have to go explaining the happenings in the dark corners of her mind. But the soft look in Melba's face at least quelled some of her shame. It was that unmistakable hovering motherly concern that Chelsea had seen from her friends' parents that she only sometimes wished for. She relaxed a bit more as Melba gently patted her arm.

"It's a lot to take in, I'm sure." Melba's voice was a soothing lullaby. It was one that Chelsea could listen to all day. "Being in a new place, in a new city. Carlos . . ."

As if on cue, Carlos perked up and took over for Melba. "I told Ma that you were here in Ramona's place and didn't really know anyone. And that I was going to take you to find a coat and some winter stuff so you could get around and see some things. Sorry for both of us to pop up on you unannounced, it's just that she offered to drive and . . ."

Carlos paused, interrupted by Melba, who seemed to be bubbling over with excitement about something or, as Chelsea surmised, might just actually be the happiest person she'd ever met.

"I offered to drive because I wanted to stop by and bring you a little welcome." Melba reached into her generous handbag adjacent to her on the sofa, pulled out a translucent waxed paper bag filled with popcorn, and held it out to Chelsea as if she'd won the door prize in a raffle. Seeing Chelsea's confusion, she shook the bag, rattling the kernels. "Chicago's finest, Garrett Mix, caramel corn and cheese. Salty and sweet. If you've never had it, you'll never forget when you first tried it." Melba beamed and held the bag out to Chelsea until she lifted her hand to take it from her with a quiet but sincere thanks.

"And the party, Ma," Carlos said.

"Yes, *and* the party," Melba continued. "The most important thing. Christmas Eve, you must join us for our family gala, we call it the Feast of the Six Continents." She waved her arms in the air as if she were a magician revealing her last act. "We do this every year—a celebration of cultures—dress up, have some good food, enjoy some great music, and everyone just drops by the house."

It had been years since Chelsea had given a single thought to Christmas, and she had no recollection of ever celebrating the eve of the holiday with something so elaborate. Maybe lately she'd allowed herself to sink too far into a shrinking world around her. She hated to be so far out of control of herself and to seem so easily rattled, so fragile. She used to be fearless. Her unbridled curiosity about the world informed her view as an artist. She tasted things, tried things, sampled life experiences, and breathed freely and deeply among people from all walks of life—at least, she used to. She hadn't meant to hesitate, but loss makes you careful in ways that she was still trying to understand. In her mind, at that moment, there wasn't a simple path to just saying yes like she really wanted to.

"You didn't make plans, did you?" Carlos's voice returned Chelsea's focus to the present. She had no plans. Her holiday in Chicago would be no different than Malibu—mope, helplessly lament what was past. Whatever it was that Melba described, it sounded better than staying inside, both physically and mentally, that was for sure. There was something magnetic about her, about Carlos; their presence drew her out. Their openness felt like an inherent invitation.

"Not even," Chelsea said. And then, most suddenly, the rest of the words finally came available. "I can come. It sounds great."

"Wonderful!" Melba stood up with hands clasped in excitement. "Just wonderful that you're hosting Ramona and Malik, and now we're hosting you. It's the spirit of the holidays. The most wonderful . . ."

Upon hearing the words "Ramona *and* Malik," Chelsea's

face scrunched in confusion. *Ramona and Malik? . . . Who's Malik? . . . Staying at my house?* The thoughts arrived in rapid succession.

"Who's Ma . . ."

Suddenly Carlos sprang up. "Me!" he said loudly, looking directly at Chelsea. "Just me as your tour guide today." He wrapped a long arm around Melba. "Ma just gave me a lift so she could invite you, right, Ma?" Carlos turned his megawatt attention to Melba, and once again, his big smile got bigger.

"Chelsea, is that what you were asking?" Melba turned to her skeptically.

Behind her, Carlos's face was distorting as if he needed to sneeze. So subtly, with the tiniest gesture, Carlos nodded his head up and down as if to say yes, the yes it seemed that Chelsea was supposed to deliver as a reply.

In the exactly three seconds of Chelsea's pause, tick, she looked at Melba—tick, then at Carlos, whose face instantly seemed to blanch of all color—tick, then back to Melba. She understood the assignment; there was something that Melba wasn't supposed to know.

"Umm . . . yeah . . . yes!" she said finally. Clearly, she'd just told a lie, and she wasn't sure why. She turned to Carlos in time to catch a wink; subtle, but there and just for her.

After the few minutes of small talk with Melba that followed and two important assurances from Chelsea—one, that she'd try the popcorn, and two, that she'd come to the Christmas Eve party—a satisfied Melba made her exit in an elegant swirl of jewel tones and hospitality.

Alone again with Carlos, Chelsea determined to uncover how she'd just become an accomplice. From what Helena said, there was only one occupant in her home and two people's names on the reservation. Neither of those was anything near "Malik."

"Who's Malik?" Chelsea directed the question casually toward Carlos, who looked like he was surprised to hear it. It took him a few moments of obvious contemplation before he seemed to relax and sink into the cushions of the sofa just inches away.

"Malik is Ramona's fiancé, and before you ask the next logical question, they broke up. Ramona doesn't want to tell anyone because she thinks they'll get back together, but most of all she doesn't want to disappoint her parents."

Chelsea considered his words as the entire scenario started to make a lot more sense, especially now that she'd met Melba. Clearly, no one in her near orbit escaped that kind of invitation. So, if Ramona didn't show up with Malik on Christmas Eve, there'd be nothing left to hide. If someone was trying to hide a breakup, especially from Melba, leaving town would be the only thing to do.

"Do *you* think they'll get back together?"

Carlos made a sound that wasn't quite a laugh, and his face contorted a bit into what wasn't quite a smirk but that hinted toward distaste, along with the shift in his body language. It was clear that whatever the relationship was, he was not a fan. "Honestly? I hope not," he said finally. He scrunched his face at Chelsea and scratched the side of his head. "Ramona's my sister, ya know? So, I think of her in a certain way, want the best for her. She always, always puts everyone else first. That's why when she asked if I could watch her dog while she went on this trip, I said yes." Carlos swept his hands together like he was clearing the air between them. "I wanted her to feel what it's like to get what she wants . . . even though I don't like dogs."

"You don't like dogs?" Chelsea hadn't meant to become an echo, but the disclosure was so surprising.

"Too clingy," he said simply. "Anyway, Ramona and Malik, I tried to tell her, he's not ready. I think deep down she knows that. So, let's just say, I'm glad she went to Cali." Carlos stood as if he were preparing to leave. "You ready to head out?"

For her part, Chelsea had a lot more questions, but she didn't want to push Carlos away. She took *clingy* as a warning.

But lately, she seemed like Velcro for other people's secrets. Now Ramona was hiding something too. She wondered about this, but decided to drop it, at least for the time being. Questions beget other questions, and Chelsea had her own secrets to keep. In some ways, even though she was staying in her home, the less she knew about Ramona, the better. That way, she wouldn't feel as guilty about promising Joan to stay quiet about her call to the patrol. She'd have nothing to feel terrible about, and nothing more to be responsible for. She needed Ramona to stay—and as long as Joan could manage to leave Ramona alone, barring any other misfortunes, everything should work out just fine. So, Chelsea was ready to head out, to change the subject, to change her environment, and first, that would require her to change her clothes.

She stood and turned to Carlos, arms in the air echoing her question. "You said I can't wear the coat I brought, so what am I supposed to wear?"

Carlos began to head for the door and pulled open the closet next to the entrance. Over his shoulder he said, "For now, just grab one of Ramona's coats. Do you have boots?"

Chelsea pointed down to the suede Uggs on her feet, a California staple. She supposed that the dense fur lining would at least keep her feet warm. She didn't expect to hear Carlos's laugh as his reaction.

"Those won't make it one block. Have you ever walked on a salted street?"

She shook her head no. Chelsea was a California girl through and through. She only understood road salt deductively, simply knowing that salt lowers the freezing temperature of water, and seeing the great expanse of frozen lake out of the window, she figured no one wanted to ice skate down the city streets by car or by foot.

"Let's take a rideshare, *Ms. Cali*," Carlos said. "We'll get back, you can change and then finally be ready for the weather."

He pulled out his phone and started poking at the screen. Chelsea walked over to the open front closet to find one more thing of Ramona's to borrow.

Almost exactly one hour later, Carlos and Chelsea had managed to whisk through a one-stop no-frills discount store, picking up a puffy coat with a hood because Chicago was far too cold to prioritize fashion over warmth. Chelsea also bought boots, a scarf, a knitted hat with mittens, all together for less than $200. Although the ensemble didn't quite match, it seemed like an unobjectionable combination. Chelsea couldn't afford to pay the property taxes, but she had enough money remaining from her share of sales proceeds to spend on comforts when necessary. Given her situation, she was happy enough that Carlos seemed more efficient with his spending decisions.

When he suggested lunch, Chelsea hoped she'd have a proper introduction to Chicago hot dogs or the Italian beef sandwich that had now become the star of a popular television show.

"Let's do Lou Malnati's," he said. When Chelsea registered confusion, he clarified. "Pizza. Original Chicago deep dish. It's not too far from here." As Chelsea nodded okay, even her small movements accentuated the biting cold outside that took advantage of every exposed place on her body. She felt herself shudder a bit, even though she was now well wrapped in a relatively inexpensive but still insulated bubble coat, with the pair of hot-pink knit mittens she found that looked a lot warmer than they really were. She squeezed her hands open and closed in front of her body to try to rev up the circulation to her fingertips.

"Here, take this," Carlos said. He pulled her hand into his and pushed a crackling plastic orange square packet into her palm.

Chelsea met his eyes for a second and let his hand linger against hers. She liked the feeling of it, not just his warmth, but his presence, and his touch, even through layers of clothing. When his eyes gestured down to their hands together, hers followed. When their eyes met again, Carlos answered just one of the silent questions she posed when looking at him.

"Hand warmers, Cali. It's only a few blocks' walk but even if we take the L, you'll need them for the train platform. This is real Midwestern cold, y'all don't know nothin' about that out West." And then, the smile came. That big, generous smile somehow managed to ignite a warmth in Chelsea's core, reaching places within her that the sunlight couldn't.

She reached out to take the hand warmers and ripped open the package, slapping the fabric-wrapped grains like two small bags of sand, and dropped one in the top of each of her mittens. Again, Carlos's hands met hers, pressed against them to help build the heat.

"It's working?"

Feeling a hit of much-needed warmth near her fingertips, Chelsea nodded. Carlos released her and turned to cross the street, gesturing for her to follow.

He walked quickly, his long legs making quick strides across the snow-and-salt-covered sidewalk, crunching along in rapid pace. Chelsea scrambled along behind him, taking in what sights she could of the city architecture to her left and right—a glance up the length of a high-rise here and, steps later, down to the window of a deli or a brief look at a passerby who was also fighting the elements.

Five thousand whole blocks later (or possibly it was actually only five), right at the point that Chelsea could take no more of the biting cold, Carlos made a quick turn between two buildings on Michigan Avenue, bringing them to an unexpected glass-door entrance with a miniature lightbulb marquee sign that read LOU MALNATI'S. She had never been happier or more relieved to reach a destination in her life. Even once inside, her body was still so frozen that she could do little more than stand there and wait for her brain to receive the signal of heat. Finally, she could rip off the scarf, and hat, and spools of clothes that had clearly been keeping her alive. It was unthinkable at home, in Malibu. Even at night when the temperature dropped, with the invisible cast of cool ocean air, she'd still never need this much attire. It was colder than skiing, than anything she knew, and even though they were inside, she still felt the chill in her bones as a reminder of where she'd just been.

While Carlos set off to secure a table for them from the hostess, still rubbing along her arms to warm up, Chelsea took a moment to survey her surroundings. Nostalgia throughout, black-and-white photos hung framed and tacked to redbrick walls. It must have been a popular place, because there were souvenirs ranging from T-shirts to a freezer full of pizza boxes with a sign that screamed, WE SHIP EVERYWHERE! Less interested in being a tourist, Chelsea hoped that she'd get a chance to learn more about Carlos. He seemed like the type of person who cared about other people and took the time to see more than just appearances. From Chelsea's perspective, she was a complete mess. But he'd offered to help way before her first display of anxiety. He was a tough read, caring but distant, confusing for sure. Other than his promise to get her something warm enough to brave the streets of a Chicago winter, she had no idea if she'd see him again before Melba's grand fête, even though she already knew she wanted to. He was the only person she knew in Chicago, but somehow, in a city full of strangers, that seemed like enough. There was nobody else she wanted to know.

Their table was called quickly. By the time they were seated in a spacious booth in the restaurant's basement dining room, Chelsea had almost reached room temperature. Across from her Carlos sat, explaining the menu enough that she knew to skip through the plethora of options and go straight for the pizza. It took very little convincing to split a delicious-sounding deep dish that had her mouth watering just from the description.

They had just crossed into conversation on the topic of work—Chelsea a painter, Carlos a photographer with odd jobs—

when a waiter brought a steaming round pizza pie to the edge of the table. As he dropped the black metal pan on the table between them, the rich aroma of garlic, tomatoes, butter, and sausage spices drifted to Chelsea's nose. The server scooped out a goopy wedge (definitely not slice) of flaky crust holding together what was barely identifiable as anything other than a sea of red sauce–topped melted cheese, now starting to cascade down along the sides of the triangle-shaped spatula.

"Chicago Classic," the waiter said. He glopped the slice down in front of Chelsea, immediately reactivating her salivary glands. Temporarily, she forgot about the fact that she had learned little more about Carlos to that point other than the fact that holding several jobs in the city supported his work as a photographer. They'd paused the conversation at her curiosity's peak.

"So, what do you like to photograph?" Chelsea asked, struggling to pull the webbing of cheese and meat to her mouth.

Carlos looked up at her, pausing his fork and knife in mid-movement.

"Landscapes . . . people . . . beauty," he said, ending after a noticeable pause.

Chelsea's face reddened immediately when he said "beauty," because his eyes were fixed on her and she wasn't sure if that was at all what he saw.

"You might want to use these." His eyes gestured down to his utensils. "Not like that flat pizza you have on the coasts."

Chelsea smiled back at Carlos, partially to hide her embarrassment. With the knife and fork she took a small cut from the tip of the pie slice and brought it to her mouth.

Chelsea couldn't hide her enjoyment of that first bite. The sound of "Mmm . . ." left her mouth, as her eyes closed of their own accord, shutting down one sense to savor the others. She tasted the salt of the cheese, and its creaminess. Then the slightly sweet-and-sour tang of the tomato sauce, the herbs of fennel, oregano, and basil in the sausage, plus its heavy bass note of unmistakable meaty richness that pulled it all together with the butter flavors in the small bit of gooey crust on her tongue. "Mmm," she found herself saying again. "This—" She pointed down to her plate with her fork. "This is *really* good. Dangerous, even."

Carlos, who was somehow already halfway through his own slice, laughed as if she was finally in on the joke.

"So," he said, cutting himself another bite of his rapidly disappearing first serving, "you said you're a painter? What do you paint?"

Chelsea took a deep breath. Carlos didn't realize it, but it was a loaded question. "Landscapes mostly . . . at least now. The sea sometimes . . . If I can find something that inspires me, I try it."

"Inspires you like what?" He leaned in more closely, chewing still, but waiting for Chelsea's answer. Her mouth dropped open a bit from a tinge of surprise. Because of nerves, she was blabbering a bit, slightly disconnected from what she was saying. She didn't expect him to pick up on the deepest thing and ask her to go deeper. There was most certainly a more official answer for this question—the one she gave most frequently to collectors, curators, in interviews sometimes, in the times before when these types of people cared enough to ask. But she got the sense that, coming from Carlos, what *he* wanted was the deeply held truth of it. But that part of her was guarded, and she had a hard time unlocking the door.

"What is this, an interview?" she teased.

He flinched, looked hurt. "No. You said it. I just want to know what you see."

Chelsea mustered the courage to look him squarely in his eyes. To not look away. And when she did, something activated within her, like at the catch of an engine or the last click of a gas starter before the flame. It was a feeling of sizzling anticipation, not to be wasted.

"Okay, the truth?"

"The truth."

Chelsea felt the solid angle of his knee tap the side of her leg beneath the table. It was like an electric shock. He was looking at her with such intensity that she started to sweat.

"The truth is . . . my best paintings are of what I'm most afraid to lose." Chelsea exhaled, making a deflated balloon of her upper body. She had no idea that she'd been holding her breath.

Carlos looked down for a moment and poked his fork at the remnants on his plate. His eyes met hers again. "People?"

"Yeah." Chelsea wanted to elaborate, to tell him about *Heartbreak*, to tell him about the memories she'd painted too, but it felt like too much, too heavy. He seemed to notice and cleared his throat.

"You selling anything?" he asked casually, shifting the energy before taking another bite.

The question surprised Chelsea. It was so direct, and she didn't have an answer she was proud to give. So, she decided to just be honest.

"Not really. My gallerist said my latest work was 'unsellable,' and that was her being nice."

"You have a gallery rep?"

"Yeah, in London. She's a friend of my parents . . . was . . . she *was* a friend of my parents."

Carlos's face scrunched a bit and then softened. He got it now, a quick study. Chelsea watched as his face revealed an understanding of everything else she hadn't said. She knew then she wasn't wrong about him. He saw a lot more than most.

"Me too," he said.

"You have a gallery rep?"

"No, lost parents."

"Oh." Chelsea felt the bump of Carlos's leg again, and she hoped the touch would linger. It did.

"Has it been long?" he asked softly, his voice low.

For some reason, he made Chelsea comfortable, relaxed. To a question whose answer was years of therapy, a lost career, and crumbling dreams, for Carlos, Chelsea found the most direct words she'd been able to say to anyone.

"It depends on what you mean by that. It happened seven years ago, but sometimes it feels like it just happened yesterday."

Carlos looked down at his plate and picked up the remaining crust strip with his hands. "Sorry. I didn't mean to bring somethin' like that up."

"It's okay," Chelsea said quickly. Within her, a door had been cracked open to a room that was filled with stale air. And for once she didn't feel completely terrified of what was inside of it. This time, she wasn't alone. "So," she continued, shifting forward on the vinyl seat beneath her, "the Tuckers, for you . . ."

Carlos answered before she could finish. "I was a little kid in overcrowded foster care. No one seemed to notice one less brown face at the dinner table. I followed Ramona home from school one day, same neighborhood, different door, but a real family on the other side. Ma, you see how she is. She's been feeding me ever since, I guess." He popped the last piece of crust in his mouth and reached for the spatula to dive in for another thick slice.

"Kinda like Helena for me."

"Helena?"

"Helena's my gallerist. Or maybe my landlord. Or maybe my family. I think anyone else would have given up on me a long time ago. But she keeps trying to find a way forward, even through the disappointments . . . She's been trying to help me find other ways of making money. I didn't expect to have to afford a house."

"Is that how you wound up in Chicago? Where Ramona's staying, don't you live there?"

"I did . . . I do. I just needed to rent it out, at least if I want to try to keep it. I live there . . . I own it, but . . . to afford it, I'd need to be selling big pieces." Chelsea moved her hands wide to show the size of her tableaux. "They take forever to do, and then, if they don't sell, which they haven't . . ." Lacking the rest of the words, the truth of what she was feeling, the feeling of *then what's the use*, of being ready to give up—she didn't say that. She couldn't. "After the accident, my parents left me the house and, as it turned out, a *bunch* of debt."

Carlos raised an eyebrow. Chelsea felt her face redden. Everyone thought her parents were so carefree, so glamorous, so bohemian. The myth of wealth without work, without obligation or responsibility, they lived that appearance in their trips and their zip code, but the reality was so far out of balance. They spent more than they had, and more than they earned, for years. It was a most embarrassing truth for her, about her family. But, in the moment, Carlos felt so disarming. With a deep breath, in a way that she'd never explained, and that only Helena knew, she decided to clarify.

"My parents, let's just say they enjoyed the life they lived but weren't quite the model of responsibility. Helena was their friend from uni. And she helped me, even when my paintings stopped selling. She tried to close the gaps and even advanced me payments for future work. It's been enough to live on because, honestly, I haven't been doing a lot of living. But now, taxes are due, and—"

"Nothing's selling," Carlos said softly. Studying her, he pulled the corner of his bottom lip between his teeth. At this casual gesture, Chelsea was riveted; there was something so honest about it—she drifted into imagining what kissing him would be like and had to physically shake her head to release that thought. It was the essence of distraction.

"Right. *Unsellable,* per Helena . . . *uninspired, boring.*" Chelsea sighed and stabbed at a floating chunk of sausage on her plate.

"There's nothing else you're scared to lose?" Carlos cocked

his head and looked at her with furrowed brow, almost as if this itself was of utmost concern.

"Not when I've already lost everything." Chelsea hadn't meant to say that, but it was truth that was overdue. And the air between them became heavy again with Chelsea's disclosure. She'd barely gotten the last word out before her vision blurred with a swell of water to her eyes. To say it made it acutely real. She looked up and blinked, praying her body would just absorb the tears before they fell. She hadn't meant to kill the mood. They were deep now into her pain and her truth, and she needed an off-ramp.

"So, what, you need some new inspiration?" Carlos gave the big smile again, and then it turned mischievous at the corners. "A nude model?" The big, big, straight-white-teeth, full-lipped smile that followed caused her breath to catch in her chest.

The brief thought of Carlos nude made Chelsea's face flush warm again. She dropped her eyes quickly to her plate.

"I don't come cheap, you know," he said.

Chelsea looked back up at him and instantly felt her cheeks mirror his face-wide grin. "Well, I am paying for lunch," she teased.

"Naw, I got this, Cali," he said, unflinching, his eyes still locked squarely with Chelsea's. "You'll start selling pieces again. And then it can be your treat."

The air between them started to fill with an unmistakable charge of energy. In fact, she felt more awake and in her body than she could recall. The cold outside, the heat inside; and the building heat within her started to crackle. A small fire was burning, and for once, Chelsea wanted to feed it. She wanted to feel it. She wanted to feel something, and she didn't want this, whatever it was, to end.

"You think you're warm enough now to go one more place?" Carlos said finally. "I want to show you something."

Anywhere, Chelsea thought, but verbalized that sentiment

as a casual "Sure," while her insides were positively boiling with want.

RAMONA IN THE MORNING IN MALIBU . . .

THE MUSIC OUTSIDE HAD BEEN THUMPING NOW FOR AN HOUR. Ramona stood in the bathroom mirror parting another section of her still damp and leave-in-conditioned hair for her styling routine. Escaping the somewhat monotonous nature of the task before her, and giving in to her body's urge to move, she let a small shake escape from her hips. A tiny twerk bounced her round ass beneath her favorite short heather-gray satin robe. With this motion, she smiled, happy to feel something familiar and in the groove.

This morning, Ramona was on hour three of her wash-day process. The same one that she intended to start the day before but that was thwarted by general fatigue and a sort of food coma induced by eating way too many of Joan's delicious (and still slightly suspicious) carbs. Especially given that her last foray for food items had resulted in a most unpleasant experience with the patrolman, in a natural response to traumatic events, Ramona felt less free to leave the confines of Chelsea's house. She was working up her nerve to venture out, to push past the feeling that was apathy at best, determined to reclaim at least some portion of the *maybe it's not so bad here after all* optimism that she'd started to feel while eating that burger. Plus, as La-trice said, Malibu did owe her—at least some sand between her toes and the good-for-you ions of fresh salted ocean air.

She'd already decided that she'd finish setting her very deeply deep-conditioned hair in twists that she'd leave in, rather than unravel. And that she'd also have another slice of banana bread for breakfast, completely ignore the still-folded note from Joan on her counter and definitely *not* call her, and take an unbothered walk on the beach to air-dry her hair, conveniently eliminating the banana bread calories as well.

As no respectable installation of long-lasting two-strand twists could possibly take less than one hour and three separate products to complete (leave-in, styler, and oil), by the time that Ramona reached the very last section of hair, smoothed and then entwined her curls down the inches of length, and finally felt the relief of coiling the last end in its small ringlet, the music had stopped. Observing her handiwork, she shook her head side to side so that she could enjoy the swaying of the heavy strands flowing back and forth against her shoulders like pendants of cascading onyx teardrops.

Ramona swapped her robe for a matching exercise set, grabbed a slice of banana bread from the kitchen plus her phone (and of course the key—can't afford to be carefree), and set out of the back of the house onto the sand. She found herself walking straight toward the ocean, and thus also heading directly toward a tall, bronze-brown, broad-shouldered man gathering sandy yoga mats into a pile. When he stopped to pull a loose tank top over his nicely defined abs, Ramona registered slight disappointment because they had been so nice to look at. His legs looked strong and well-defined, with calves that seemed like he could run for miles or balance on nearly anything. When he stood up and she was able to see his face, she was pleasantly surprised to find him so handsome, with silky, well-cut, mostly dark hair and generally unplaceable features. She didn't think he was Black, but he could have been, or mixed? Or North African perhaps? It was confusing, mostly—at the risk of being rude—not being able to determine whether she owed him a standard-practice acknowledgment, a tacit understanding between Black people in white spaces, an invisible social connection with deep-rooted meaning. Even if there were only two of you, and even as strangers, you were seen, and you weren't alone. When he looked up and did make eye contact, his face was full of general friendliness but lacked recognition. It was the answer she needed. Ramona smiled, but expected nothing, and spared herself the head nod that would have otherwise completed her greeting. All this assessment happened in a split second, and she was a little startled when he spoke to her unexpectedly.

"You here for the yoga class?" he asked, pulling his hand up to his eyes to squint at her against the sun.

"Since when does yoga happen to house music?" Ramona heard herself ask the question aloud, which was really meant to remain just a thought.

The man smiled at her and shifted his weight backward a bit. Clearly, she'd caught him a little off guard. He looked like the type of guy who might live in a converted van with his surf buddies, catching one wave to the next. As uptight as beachfront Malibu seemed, she wondered if he needed permits for his makeshift location on the beach, and how he'd managed to keep the vigilante locals off his back.

"Instructor's choice," he said. "It gets everyone moving."

He did have a point. Ramona remembered her little involuntary episode earlier in the bathroom.

"Maybe," she said, "but it's not my kind of house."

"Okay, I'll take the bait . . . then what is?"

"Green Velvet . . . Frankie Knuckles . . . Felix Da Housecat." Ramona started listing some of the names she had at top of her mind.

"Oh, what, you're from Chicago? It's time for the percolator?"

Ramona raised her eyebrows. Just the word *percolator* brought the familiar beat to her mind. Based on the music she heard the previous two mornings, she was surprised he had the reference available. It was hard not to bob her head as the song played in her head.

"Yeah, I'm here on vacation. Staying right there." Ramona pointed back to Chelsea's house. "Where I just happen to hear every minute of your class all morning. But at least I'm still two hours ahead."

"Oh, Chelsea's place," he said casually. "Nice to meet you, I'm Jay." He reached out his sandy hand to shake Ramona's. After her slight hesitation, he looked down at his palms and brushed the sand away against his biker shorts–clad thigh.

"How about a pound?" Ramona said, holding her fist forward for him to tap her back. "I'm Ramona, Ramona Tucker." The backs of their fingers collided efficiently, triggering a smile for both of them.

"Oh, we're doing full names . . ." Jay said with a teasing tone to his voice. "In that case, I'm Jay, like V."

"Jay-V like Jay-Z?" Without meaning to, Ramona scrunched her face.

"V, like Vijay Singh."

"Like Vijay Singh who beat Tiger Woods?"

"Impressive reference," Jay said. "It's a very successful name, what can I say. So, does that mean your people and my people can't get along?"

Ramona laughed, and let the smile spread to her cheeks and to her eyes. "I mean, it was a painful moment in Black history . . ." She was happy to see Jay smile too. "But I mean, your friends . . . my friends . . ."

"We can be friends?" He delivered the line perfectly. Ramona was intrigued, and the smile was infectious. "Look, I'm sorry about the music. I've tried almost everything other than silent disco. You down for a free class? Maybe I can make it up to you."

"Jay, I'm from Chicago," Ramona said, as if it were the answer to the final round of a trivia championship. "I'm used to all kinds of noise in the morning, and a little thump from your East Coast *techno* does not take away from the roar of the ocean and the beckoning of a glorious sunny day."

"That just might be the nicest complaint I've ever received," Jay replied. "So, you gonna come check us out?"

"Maybe I will." Ramona's reply sounded very much in tone like *I probably won't*. And that would have likely been her most honest answer, if not for trying to be polite.

"Life's too short for next time, I always say."

The words were impossible for Ramona to dismiss. "My vacation's just long enough to enjoy doing absolutely nothing."

"Recreation is re-creation. I think that's why they say 'Change is as good as rest.' But, whatever you decide, we'll be here. Same time tomorrow."

"Nice to meet you, Vijay. Whether I see you or not, I'm sure I'll hear you."

"It's time for the percolator," Jay said, exactly on beat. Ramona laughed, and he said it again, and then started to play the song out, sound effects and all. To this impromptu serenade, Ramona turned and danced her way down the beach away from him, twisting her feet in the sand. She threw her hand up in the air as farewell.

"Bye, Jay," she shouted over her shoulder.

"See you tomorrow, *Ramona*," he shouted back.

Continuing her walk, feeling the sun on her shoulders and the wind through her drying hair, Ramona smiled, knowing deep down that he was probably right.

CHELSEA IN THE AFTERNOON ON DAY 3 IN CHICAGO . . .

AS CHICAGO PASSED BY IN A BLUR THROUGH THE WINDOW, Chelsea could feel the rumble of the L train on its tracks through the seat beneath her. Carlos was absolutely right about needing hand warmers on the train platform. They only had a few minutes to wait, but in that time the chill managed to reach its grip around her legs and into her boots, making her wish she had foot warmers too. She'd never been so cold in her life, chilled literally to the bone, and yet the excitement of a new destination with Carlos made it feel like everything was exactly as it was supposed to be, cold and all.

Still, the temperature was stunningly low, and it took everyone a few minutes of stomping and shivering to settle into the thankfully warmed urban train cabin, with silver walls and hard plastic seats and metal poles overhead to hold on to. Five minutes into the ride, she felt like her mouth could finally move to speak, but when she turned to Carlos, he'd closed his eyes.

"Are you sleeping?" she whispered.

Carlos's mouth shifted, but his eyes stayed closed. To Chelsea, he looked like a gorgeous statue. "No," Carlos replied suddenly. "I'm not. Just resting my eyes. Worked an overnight shift last night."

"So, this morning, you came straight from work?"

Carlos opened his eyes and turned to look at her. "Have you never worked an overnight shift?"

Chelsea instantly felt like she was about to fail a quiz. Aside from promoting art events in LA with her classmates and lifeguarding one summer, she hadn't had a "real job" ever and certainly not one that required her to be somewhere overnight. With tight lips and reluctance, she shook her head no.

Carlos turned back around to face the windows and leaned his head back, closing his eyes again with a sigh. "I didn't think so, Cali. But nah, I had time to take a shower. I'm good. We got twenty minutes, so I'm gonna rest my eyes, and then you're about to see something great."

Chelsea wondered if she'd offended him, and hoped she hadn't. There were so many ways he could have interpreted her questions, but she had so many more to ask. It was curiosity that made her feel like in a million lifetimes she might never know as much about Carlos as she wanted to, especially with the personal walls he seemed to stand behind. In one moment, she'd felt closer to him, in the next, she'd felt him drift away, somewhere else, somewhere she couldn't follow. And as the train rumbled, screeching around its turns, she watched as the densely packed downtown buildings gave way to wider expanses of frozen landscape around them. Empty fields covered with patches of white snow bordered gated clusters of brick low-rises.

In Chicago, as Chelsea was discovering, the cold and the snow were so much a part of the winter city experience. The elements demanded attention, serving as their own exclamation point on the landscape. The presence of the snow made the stark contrast even more evident between the part of the city they left and where they were going. Each stop was marked by the trickling out of passengers until the car they occupied was nearly empty.

Six stops later Chelsea felt the stirring of Carlos next to her as he straightened his body and then lifted himself up from the seat to stretch and yawn. Bracing himself with a nearby pole, he leaned in toward Chelsea.

"You ready, Cali? It's about to get cold again. About a five-minute walk."

Carlos was telling the truth. After they stepped outside, the warmth Chelsea felt from the thirty minutes of train ride lasted about three minutes against the Chicago wintertime air. Carlos walked briskly with his hands stuffed in his pockets. Chelsea scrambled behind him, taking in the sights of a much-different area. There were bodegas on the corners and bars on some of the windows. People came in and out of a liquor store with faded color advertisements in its dingy window. They passed a clothing store that occupied a whole block with an entire fashion show of jeans-clad mannequins, winter coats, baseball jackets, and sports jerseys in the window. A barbershop was a revolving door of patrons across the street, and everyone had plenty of slush everywhere to wade through underneath their feet.

"Where are we?" she asked. It was a curious thing to be in

a place where nearly everyone else was brown of some shade or another. And what arrived was an unusual feeling of being self-conscious. Of wondering if she belonged in the unfamiliar place that she was in. And she wondered only briefly if this feeling was what Ramona was feeling in her time in Malibu, and if she too had questions in whatever she was doing then, of whether she was safe or in danger, or if she should have those feelings at all.

"We're in Bronzeville," Carlos shot back. "The hood, not too far from where me and Ramona grew up." Shivering a bit, the effort showed as he fought against the elements to push the words out toward Chelsea. "Got two more blocks. You all right?"

Chelsea had the exact same question. In this place, was she all right? It was something deep within her that caused her concern, but she also had access to her thinking logic, which quelled any rise of panic. She was with Carlos, who'd been nothing but kind, kinder than she deserved even, as she'd done nothing for him, and he'd asked nothing in return. Chelsea took a deep breath in, as deep as the cold would let it go, which wasn't far, and saw the white cloud of her breath billow out ahead of her as she exhaled. Chelsea picked up her pace, trying to keep up more closely with Carlos as they crossed a wide boulevard on the timing of a walk sign. On the next block, they slowed their speed, giving her time to observe, to absorb as much of the experience as she could. It was, after all, a visual feast. Her eyes scanned left and right—old beaten-up cars dotted the street in front of her, some new building facades mixed with abandoned lots picked up again in the combination of old and new, similar to what she'd known in her times in Downtown LA. Hope and despair. Abandoned and reclaimed. It was the same contrast that Chelsea felt inside now—it was how she saw herself. And the part of her that felt new, that definitely was Carlos's doing. Suddenly, walking in front of her, he slowed down further, dramatically, and then stopped.

They were in front of a brick building that looked refurbished. There was a modern glass entrance, plenty of burnished steel to offset the look of what was originally there. This was clearly someplace new out of the old. In the window display, she could see an elaborate design in a frame, broad strokes of paint, bright blue and purple and orange, bordered by a frame of gold filigree carved in swoops and volutes indicating its significance to warrant such care and splendor. Carlos had brought her to an art gallery.

"Gallery Guichard," Carlos said, holding his arm out to usher Chelsea through the door he held open.

She entered the lobby and looked around. Here, art covered every wall and sculptures shared the floor space. Next to her at the entrance stood a rendition of a disembodied jazz musician with his hands around a person-height floating saxophone. Chelsea tried to read the text on the placards as she passed by, noting artist names and the rich descriptions accompanying their work. Carlos led the way through another door into the expansive gallery space, all exposed-wood beams and white walls and chrome industrial piping overhead that created an urban rustic showplace for the explosion of art that was carefully positioned in every area. She could feel the energy of unabashed creativity, of audacity, of a heartbeat that she'd once had.

Overwhelmed with wonder, her eyes darted around, everywhere. Chelsea walked slowly, not wanting to miss anything, to see everything, but it was impossible to see *everything*. The art was abstract, some, and others were masterworks of mostly Black subjects and artifacts of culture depicted in mixed media, paint, cloth, collage, found items. Paintings reflected intricate, exquisite brushwork. It was all here, a world of wondrous design. If she'd had even just a few of these pieces in the downtown shows she produced in LA, they'd have sold for a small fortune. Everything was alive in its own way, breathing, beating, vibrating with intention and meaning.

"Here, this one is my favorite," Carlos called out, breaking the spell. She couldn't believe he'd been able to pick a favorite. It was a dramatic painting, of a woman painted nude from the waist up, monochromatic—royal blue skin and all, hair crinkly textured and set in a rounded shape. Her body was all angles and elegance. One arm hanging loosely, she wrapped the fingers of her other hand around its elbow. She faced away from the viewer, so you received only the back of her, against the color of a vibrant-red patterned background. It was breathtaking to behold, but captivating as a rare opening into Carlos's thoughts.

"What do you like about this one?" Chelsea asked.

Carlos stood squarely in front of the piece, looking comfortable and relaxed, like he'd stood in that exact same place a thousand times before. It was clear that he was savoring it even still, and there was a moment before he began to speak.

"She's blue but still beautiful," he said. "Regal. She looks like she's been through some things, but now she's got something to offer, if she decides to turn around. She looks like music. And her angles say she can dance, but on her own beat . . . not just the even or odd, but something in between. She has her own rhythm, and *her* rhythm is the dance. She looks like healing, like she's gathering herself, like it's temporary, but when she turns around . . . it will be magnificent."

"You . . . see all that?" Chelsea said, a bit breathlessly, because now he was looking at her.

"And more," he said, turning then to walk to another area. There were many other pieces of art yet to see.

Chelsea scrambled after him. "If you have a favorite, you must come here all the time . . . There's so much to take in. The work here, it's all magnificent. So . . ."

"Dope?" Carlos finished for her.

"Yeah, exactly," Chelsea mused. "You exhibit here?"

"I had a few photos in a show once. I've been trying to work up to a solo show. I need to get my weight up though. Build a little bit bigger portfolio, get my numbers up on social. I'm almost there. You ever do a solo show?"

"Yeah, I had one in LA back when things were hot for me. I had this one piece, and it got a really good review from this kinda asshole big-time art critic. Honestly, it wasn't even my best piece. Just . . . a memory. But it landed me a rep in LA and then in London with Helena."

"What was the piece?" The intensity of Carlos's attention, especially on this topic, made Chelsea want to dismiss it. How do you tell someone who was clearly sacrificing so much for his dream that you'd screwed up your big shot?

Chelsea fidgeted, pulled off her hat and tried to pat down her flame of hair. But Carlos didn't flinch or move, and there was nothing to do or say next but to answer. "It was a painting of two lovers kissing. It was the most passionate kiss I could remember back then, my best first kiss. And I called it *Heartbreak*."

"Another thing you lost, then."

"Another thing I lost . . ." Chelsea looked down and shook her head, as the replay of the blur of that time flashed through her mind. "And it doesn't matter anyway, because everyone said that my career was going to be *so* great. But eventually, the attention faded. *All* of it. No buzz, no more showings. It didn't matter what I painted, or the names I picked. I'm sure Helena still keeps me on now because of my parents. But it's just a favor."

Carlos studied Chelsea. She could see his eyes moving across her face. Her cheeks lit up with embarrassment.

Finally, after forever passed by, he spoke. "Do you still have it?" he asked.

"Still have what? The painting?" Chelsea asked, fighting the urge to look around her, to pat down her pockets. She shook her head no.

"The hunger," Carlos said. And the room became instantly still, with just the faded echo of his word in the air between them. Chelsea stood frozen as if the word *hunger*, like a magnet, could do the work of penetrating her, of searching her for what was like itself inside her. And all there was to do was to wait.

Chelsea, realizing at some point she'd stopped breathing, allowed herself a second to sharply fill her lungs with air. As she breathed in through her nose, again she felt the sting of tears in her eyes that threatened to fall. She wasn't ready to cry, she wasn't *that* girl, so instead she walked away from Carlos, into the next room.

In the next room, she reached another light-filled gallery space. ART THAT TOUCHES THE SOUL, the black print on the wall read. The pieces here were more abstract but just as exquisite, just as moving. Something *was* stirring in Chelsea's soul. It was waking up from its slumber. It was getting off the night shift.

Carlos followed her, his eyes glued to her face as he stepped around her in slow, deliberate paces. "It's still there," he said. "I can see it," he whispered in her ear as he crossed behind her, close enough that she felt the heat of his presence. "The only thing . . ." He stepped again, the heat reaching the side of her body. "An artist ever makes . . ." Carlos said over her shoulder, continuing his slow circle. "Is what she sees with her soul." And there, he stopped. Standing in front of her with those eyes, those dark-brown eyes holding such intensity, such clarity, he saw her. She knew it and felt naked. Entirely exposed, so raw, so tender. She couldn't hold on to it anymore. He caught her as she collapsed into his arms. He held her as she let the tears flow into the soft fabric of his sweater.

"I'm sorry, Chelsea," Carlos said over her head and sounded so intensely sincere that Chelsea felt like he was apologizing on behalf of the entire world, for its unfairness, for her pain, for her losses.

She wanted to cling to him, to bury herself in the freshness of his scent and feel the sturdiness of him against her. That was where she wanted to stay. But as her awareness returned, the soft part inside her that Carlos had touched was throbbing with life, with truth. Carlos was right. He had awakened her hunger, her desire, her wish for something more, maybe even a vision beyond the drifting that she'd been doing through the currents of her present life.

"Please, don't apologize." Chelsea sniffled and wiped her tears and nose with the back of her hand. With reluctance, she pulled herself farther back from Carlos and, despite embarrassment, pushed herself to look at him. All she saw staring back at her was concern. "You're right . . . thank you . . . for taking the time to show me this place." She meant the treasure house of art in which they were standing, and also somewhere else inside herself that she thought she'd never find again. Suddenly self-conscious, Chelsea turned again to their surroundings. "Are we here alone?" she asked. "Where's the gallerist?"

Carlos smiled again, his eyes dancing with light this time, lifting the energy in the room. "It's all good, we have some privacy. He'll come down and lock up when we leave."

"Thank goodness," Chelsea said, still arranging herself and regaining composure. "This is really embarrassing. I'm not used to—"

"What, showing that you care about something? Yeah, that's very not of the moment."

Chelsea laughed. "Or slobbering all over a stranger."

"We're still strangers?"

Chelsea smiled back at him, the light dancing in her eyes now. She took one more quick look all around them, the gorgeous paintings, the collages on the walls, the figures looking back at her, all witnessing the moment.

"Nah," Chelsea said. "Not anymore."

The two of them retraced their steps, back through the front of the gallery, back past the floating jazz player, and back down the salt-crusted sidewalk to the L-train platform. They rode back into the city core together, casually connected, seated side by side.

When Chelsea returned to Ramona's place, the sun had already started to set for the day, giving a gray-purple hue to part of the sky. Only then did she think of the sea again, and Malibu. She wondered if Ramona was enjoying herself, if she'd found anything of it to love. If the place had opened its arms to her, if she'd found a place to belong. And then, she thought of Joan, reminding Chelsea that here, sitting in Ramona's life, she was keeping two secrets, Ramona's and Joan's, and she didn't want either to ruin today, or any of her tomorrows, especially the ones she had left in Chicago.

Chelsea retrieved her phone and pulled up her text window to compose a message.

CHELSEA: Joan, please don't bother Ramona. Everything is fine.

Everything *was* fine. And it would be, as long as Joan left Ramona alone. But something told Chelsea that was the one thing she couldn't trust Joan to do.

JOAN PERCHED IN MALIBU . . .

BY THE TIME CHELSEA'S TEXT REACHED JOAN, JOAN WAS ALREADY pacing her "beach chic, but make it neutral tones" living room. She walked in slow steps along the long wall of windows showcasing her backyard expanse of ocean, sipping her "super-duper greens" juice concoction, strategizing exactly how she was going to engage with Ramona before the day's end.

After all the flour, butter, bananas, and baking, Joan expected at any moment a call or at minimum a text message to arrive from an unknown number, thanking her for all of her efforts. This was supposed to be the plan. And for Joan, everything always went according to plan, and schedule, and neatly ordered perfection. So, the fact that she hadn't heard from Ramona was driving Joan further to the very edge of reason, where she was in danger of falling off the cliff. To Joan, Ramona's refusal to contact her was proof of what she feared most, that Ramona suspected her of calling the Sentry Patrol. Of course, she had actually called the Sentry Patrol, and was the most obvious suspect, but that was really no matter. Joan believed strongly that her good deeds could absolutely make up for and deflect from her bad ones. She was certain that her good-personness was duly evinced in the hours of sifting, stirring, measuring, whisking, and sprinkling that made a delicious pastry basket. And why *wouldn't* just one taste of baked goodness—that contained the goodness of Joan's very soul—erase any awareness of what tiny little bad she'd done? Did she have doubts? Well, would most people ask themselves such uncomfortable questions? Of course not. *I'm a good person*, she reminded herself and set about making sure that was true in the most familiar of ways.

That morning, Joan had purposely stayed inconspicuously in the corner of her immaculate *Architectural Digest*–featured deck, a nautical-theme showplace for her celebrity exterior designer. Here she normally took her morning coffee, daily dose of sunshine, and surveillance post of the beach and its occupants. She felt good about herself in that way. She paid attention to what was happening, kept an eye out like she was supposed to do. No one had ever trained her specifically about what to look out for, she just followed her instincts about anything that looked or felt suspicious. She was a neighbor who looked out for other neighbors. And in her surveillance, she'd even endured what felt like Jay's extra-loud music on that day, the insufferable *thump-thump-thump* of his class that lasted well over an hour.

From the corner of her lower balcony, facing the ocean, Joan saw Ramona talking to Jay, all smiles between them, toes kicking the sand. Joan recognized it right away, the signs of flirtation, the good looks and charm that Jay had weaponized, keeping his classes full, and probably his bed also. She knew the type well, not much different from her ex-husband, David, *that snake*, who could have at least been much more careful, let alone discreet, during their marriage. She was also sure that Ramona had no idea what she was getting into, having walked right into the den of a likely wolf—she'd never so much as seen Jay with a consistent companion, only the regular orbiting of an assortment of waiflike girls who looked like perennial summer and youth. He probably wouldn't know what to do with a mature woman like Ramona, who Joan had already assumed was very much like her anyway and thus couldn't wait for their future conversations laughing over glasses of wine well past the sunset. Surely, befriending the woman would be the absolution she needed, perfect evidence of "no harm done."

So, Joan decided that, rather than waiting for the undesirable natural course of events to transpire, leaving nothing more to chance, she would make sure that she and Ramona met today instead.

And it was after this very firm decision that the notification pinged on Joan's phone, a message from Chelsea. And the message itself, before she read it, brought her brewing obsession to a rise because her worst fear was certainly that Ramona, or anyone else for that matter, had learned about her actions before she'd had a chance to rectify the matter. And what else would Chelsea be messaging about, other than a confirmation of her worst fear?

Joan, everything is fine. That's the message she saw, or at least the gist of the message, or moreover, the part that Joan actually decided to process as her takeaway. *Everything is fine, just fine,* Joan thought on an extra-long tension-releasing exhale. And it would be fine, perfectly, suitably, comfortably, wonderfully fine, just as soon as she made her way over to Chelsea's place next door and finally met Ramona.

RAMONA IN MALIBU, PRECISELY ONE HOUR AFTER CHELSEA'S TEXT ASKING JOAN *NOT* TO . . .

RAMONA WAS BUZZING FROM HER DAY OUT ON THE SAND. THE weather had turned perfect; after a long morning of overcast, the sun appeared as if a magic wand had been waved across the sky. Just suddenly, all the clouds dissipated, leaving an idyllic sunny day. She was amazed by her new tan lines, taking her caramel Chicago-winter brown to a much deeper rich choco-late brown with stark contrast lines along her shoulders where her spaghetti straps were. Fresh from a shower and wrapped in a towel, she pulled her bouffant plastic shower cap off her now sun-dried twists and began to contemplate how she'd spend her evening.

For the first time since "the incident," Ramona felt a sense of relaxation, of calm and a growing peace in her mind and spirit. Maybe this was a good idea after all. She decided to phone Latrice and update her, as the day had been not so bad. Maybe she'd stay, and maybe she'd find something more to enjoy.

Since it was officially five p.m. in Malibu, it was already seven p.m. in Chicago, meaning that she was at minimum one day closer to accomplishing her goal of avoiding a holiday di-saster, and if she were fully honest, the break from faux bridal planning was a welcome relief. When she and Malik had first gotten engaged, her parents' excitement about a true family wedding was unmatched. When her brother, Reggie, had got-ten married, her sister-in-law's mother had handled the bulk of the arrangements, the color picking and dress selection, the venues and the music, everything that Ramona's mother de-lighted in and anything her father quietly cared about. Anyone who'd ever been to a Christmas Eve at the Tuckers' house knew that it was all glamour and extravagance, the annual reward of frugality for the family. It meant so much to be able to spend with freedom, to not have to worry about what something cost as much as just deciding if you liked it. Ramona's father had taught her to save, to make pennies stretch into dimes and dollars, but he didn't seem to mind the splurge at Christmas. And he hadn't denied her a single request for the wedding she'd been planning.

There was only so much longer that Ramona could put off making final choices and decisions for a wedding, and only so many more dress-shopping excursions before the novelty wore off and her mother started to get suspicious. Still, for this small moment of respite, she wasn't worried about Malik and what he was or wasn't doing, she wasn't looking at old photographs, she wasn't feeling guilty about eating carbs, and she wasn't wearing her engagement ring. It was neatly tucked away in the bottom of her purse, resting comfortably in a corner of Chelsea's bedroom. For once, she felt free. Free of that ring, free of Malik, and even in that moment free of her bra. *Why wear one?* she thought, pulling on her casual T-shirt to match the shorts of her leisure set.

After heading into Chelsea's intimate living room space and admiring its priceless panoramic view of the Pacific Ocean, Ramona went to the kitchen to pour herself a glass of wine and to watch the sunset. Several slices of banana bread remained in the basket, and after trying to convince herself to turn away, she thought, *What the hell, it's vacation*, and grabbed one anyway. Unknowingly nibbling on the pride and joy of Joan's endeavors, Ramona pulled out her phone to call Latrice.

"Girl, shouldn't you be somewhere talking to a dolphin or something?" Latrice answered, sounding half-distracted.

"It's Friday night, I didn't think you'd even pick up," Ramona said, with a mouth still a little full of banana bread. She pulled the phone up closer to her ear, put the wineglass on a low table, and plopped herself in the chair in front of it so she could face the water.

"It's Friday night, and I'm still at work," Latrice said. "You better be having a good time for both of us."

Ramona instantly understood the weariness she heard reflected in her friend's voice. It was the Friday before Christmas, and while the holiday vacations should have already started, Latrice was stuck working on a project deadline. Thankfully, in the finance group, there were no such emergencies, especially not around public holidays.

"It's Friday afternoon, and I'm braless looking at the Pacific Ocean," Ramona mused.

"Ain't no worries when the titties are free," Latrice said, lightening up a bit with a tiny chuckle.

"Girl, so true," Ramona said, taking a gulp of wine and biting off another corner of her snack.

"What're you eating out there in California? Some salad? Tofu? Tofu salad?"

"Banana bread," Ramona said, mouth still full, turning her response into something more like "Bwa-wah-wah red."

"You're still eating that lady's pastries?"

Ramona forced down a swallow. "I can't help it," she admitted. "They're good, and other than some oranges and protein bars, it's the only food in the house. I've been eating scones for breakfast, banana bread for dinner."

"Have you spoken to her yet?"

"No, I thought about texting a thank-you to the number she left, but there's no way I'm going to call some strange white lady who clearly is trying to kill me with carbs."

"Yeah, highly suspicious. What do you think she wants?"

"I don't know, Latrice. I'm trying to avoid finding out. This is a weird-assed place. One neighbor calls the cops, another leaves a pastry basket."

"Both *so* inappropriate."

"It's been one actual *hell* of a welcome."

"You still want to come home?" Latrice sounded concerned, as if Ramona might say yes.

"And miss Surf Yoga tomorrow morning?" Ramona quipped, taking slight pleasure in demonstrating her newfound optimism.

"Now hold up," Latrice said. "Who's *this* I'm talking to? Is that what we doin' now, Malibu Barbie? You hanging out with Malibu Ken?"

"I did . . . meet a guy," Ramona admitted. "It's his headache music every morning that he calls *house*. I told him I'm from the Chi. We *know* house and *that* ain't it. Buuut, he did invite me to join his class on the beach."

"First thing, Chi-cah-go *invented* house," Latrice said. "But music tastes aside, as long as his name's not Malik, I support this development."

"This is hard to say, but . . . you were right, Latrice. Maybe I needed this. Even after what happened at first . . . I'm starting to see potential. I'd feel better if I knew for certain who it was . . . but, I'm not gonna lie. I'm looking forward to tomorrow. Malibu does owe me something . . . something good . . ." Ramona leaned back, put her feet up, and draped her newly melanated legs over the chair fabric.

"Ask and you shall receive," Latrice replied.

Almost as if on cue, the doorbell rang, a sound that both of them could hear.

"Dinner's arrived," Latrice remarked.

"No, not dinner. I didn't order anything," Ramona whispered, ducking down trying to avoid the line of sight from the front-door window.

"It's that lady coming back for her basket," Latrice teased. "This time, she's bringing the teacup."

Ramona sighed heavily in frustration. The last morsel of the banana bread she'd been eating was still in her hand, taunting her. It *was* good. She'd resolved to enjoy it in peace. But what harm was it to answer the door? "I'm going to answer," Ramona proclaimed. "If you don't hear from me in exactly twelve minutes, call search and rescue."

As she and Latrice said goodbye, Ramona looked at the remaining morsel of banana bread with disgust. She'd lost her appetite. She'd meant to enjoy that last bit just as she'd found her most comfortable position in the seat. Moving rather quickly, her breasts jostled against her, reminding her that she'd planned for privacy that evening and wasn't at all dressed for company. The doorbell rang again, this time with the top of a head full of highlights bobbing around the door window. *Nosy neighbors, intrusive neighbors . . . What is this place?* Ramona thought, approaching the source of the insistent bell.

She answered the door with a forceful swing open, then crossed her arms awkwardly across her chest. Across from her she saw a pencil-thin woman, no bigger than a ship plank, dressed smartly as a Ralph Lauren advertisement. The sleeves were rolled up rustically on her white linen shirt, exposing deeply tanned forearms freckled and sun spotted and exceptionally lean. Meeting her eyes, Ramona found them strikingly blue, under absolutely perfectly shaped and obviously dyed unnaturally brown eyebrows. The socket corners crinkled with the overwhelming intensity of the woman's smile, a mouth full of flawless teeth in a color white that could only come from the expertise of a very expensive cosmetic dentist.

"Hi," she said, reaching her hand forward. "I'm Joan." Her other hand reached up to press against her chest. "I left the basket?"

Ramona braced herself against the door, and extended her hand out, leaving the other hand to secure her chest into an uncomfortable uniboob. "Ramona," she said matter-of-factly. Everyone was still a suspect. But, remembering the banana bread that was probably still on her breath, Ramona figured there was no harm in at least thanking the woman and being done with it. "Um, thanks for the basket. It was a really nice welcome, especially after a not-so-nice welcome. I didn't expect . . . either."

"Oh? Did something happen?" Joan asked with a look of concern.

Ramona's eyes narrowed. "You didn't see the Sentry Patrol outside? Two nights ago? That was my welcome committee."

Joan blinked with surprise. "Ah . . . no . . ." she said. "I'd have probably come by sooner. Are you all right?"

"I wasn't . . . maybe I'm not, but I'm finding reasons to stick around." Ramona leaned against the door, narrowing its opening. She wanted to say thank you and move on with her evening. And, beyond that, she wasn't sure what Joan, still standing there smiling at her, was waiting for. "Oh, your basket!" Ramona remembered suddenly. Of course, the basket. It was huge, and so nice, quite durable. Certainly, with its sturdy wicker weaving, it was nice enough to reuse, and Ramona had no designs on keeping it. She pointed behind her from the door. "It's right in the kitchen, if you just give me a second, I can grab it for you."

Joan hesitated for only a second, looking briefly confused, but never losing a moment of cheer. "Oh, no," she said quickly. "Don't worry about that, not at all. I'll get it another time. And just know, I am *fully* committed to changing your impression of Malibu . . . for the better, of course. Chelsea said you'll be here for a week?"

Oh my, Ramona thought, overwhelmed by Joan's disarming display of charm. She felt cornered, like a small animal. Her instincts said, *Close the door,* but she told herself, *Give this woman the benefit of doubt* instead. Perhaps Joan did simply want to give a neighborly welcome and then, most important of all, be on her way back home. Sensing awkwardness in the air, Ramona decided to answer Joan's question, choosing the path of least resistance to resume comfortable nestling in the lounge chair.

"Um-hum," she said simply, with a closed-mouth smile and a hand on the door, while she positioned herself to move behind it and to close it imminently. She could see the end to this peculiar exchange approaching. It was in sight. All she had to do . . . was . . . say . . . "Okay, well, good ni—"

"How about dinner tomorrow?" Joan said quickly, peeking around the edge of the door.

"Dinner . . . tomorrow?" Ramona parroted.

"Dinner . . . tomorrow," repeated Joan, zeroing in on her closing pitch. "I'll show you classic Malibu, a great spot. Delicious and with the best sunset view. You'll love it. You don't have plans already, do you?"

The riptide of Joan's unrelenting hospitality was no match for an already exhausted Ramona. She didn't even know which question to answer. "No . . . I . . . don't," she said reluctantly.

"Fantastic!" Joan said, only thinly hiding her win. "We'll have the *best* time."

"Can't wait." Ramona forced the cheer in her voice. She hadn't exactly agreed, but what the hell, it would be just one night. After all, she did eat the woman's banana bread. *I should've left the basket outside,* she thought.

Joan turned to leave. And then turned back over her shoulder. "Anything comes up, you have my number," she said.

"Your number?"

"Yes, in the note. The note with the basket."

"Oh," Ramona said. "Well, I'm sure it's here, I'd never throw a note away." *As much as I'd want to,* Ramona thought.

Forcing a new smile, Ramona waved goodbye and closed the door.

DECEMBER 22

CHELSEA IN THE MIDMORNING OVERCAST
OF CHICAGO, RESTLESS . . .

Roaming about Ramona's condo, Chelsea was looking at the gray of winter outside but thinking very much in color. Every time she closed her eyes she saw the rich hues of the gallery, the deep browns, the regal blues, reds, and yellows, the abstract strokes, the canvas brush lines. And everything around her, she was starting to see it again as an artist would, how she'd been trained to do, to see the lines of definition, the shapes within the shapes, and the colors for dimension.

This morning she didn't just ignore the apple on the kitchen counter, she saw a fruit bowl, or better yet a woman eating the fruit, hand dripping with juice, her expression of surprise and delight reflected just so. A viewer could themselves taste the ripeness of it, the crispness of the skin, the exact moment of biting into the flesh, the slight bitterness of apple peel crashing cleanly into the ecstasy of sweetness within. And she knew exactly how to paint it. This morning, she felt so capable, so alive. On this morning, Chelsea Flint was awake.

On this trip, she brought no paints, no pencils, no supplies. She had nothing on hand to extract any of the colors swirling within her. To capture the stardust from a streak of inspiration, Chelsea didn't need much. A quick search on her phone showed an art supply store nearby. *Why not?* she thought. She could take a ten-minute rideshare, but for half the price, the map showed a direct route that required some walking and a two-stop ride on the Red Line L train. And besides, as she considered it, Chelsea was eager to reconnect to the heartbeat of the city. She wanted to walk, to bundle up in her coat, to feel the rumble beneath her on the train, to feel the cold even, just a bit of it, through her hot-pink mittens just before she stuffed her hands in the pockets of her coat. It was invigorating. She'd never need that coat in Malibu. There she couldn't feel the elements the same way; she couldn't feel much of anything. And starting today, that was no longer what she wanted—it was no longer enough.

Along the walk to the L train, the cold was so cold that it numbed her thinking brain, activated her survival instincts such that her mind had no room to wander. *Stay warm . . . walk faster . . . huddle closer*, her mind repeated. The wind ripped through the top of her hair, and she pulled her hat down lower and adjusted her hood. She reached the train platform minutes before she'd been just about ready to give up and look for a taxi. It wasn't a cold you could stand still in. Even the tears the wind whipped from your eyes could freeze in minutes. Chelsea shivered a bit on the train platform and shifted her weight from side to side, just to keep moving, crushing the salt and fresh snow beneath her feet. The overnight snowfall remained, as there'd still been no sun yet to melt it. But, even with the overcast, Chelsea glowed inside with the small fire that had been lit by Carlos in the gallery.

As the doors of the train closed behind her and her body started to thaw, Chelsea remembered sitting next to him on the long ride to the south part of the city, to Bronzeville where the gallery was. She wished for that trip again, and for another reason to see him. Maybe the dog would need something else or run out of food. Maybe she'd have a leak in the condo, or a lightbulb would need replacing. Maybe, maybe he'd miss her?

Maybe he'd find an excuse, any excuse, to see her before the twenty-fourth? Two days would be too long, she thought. A lifetime away.

Once through the doors of the art store, Chelsea felt instant familiarity. The inside of the store was almost exactly the same here as it was back home. Among the aisles of paint tubes, infinite types of papers for charcoals and watercolors, pre-stretched shrink-wrapped white canvases and some black ones also, pencils and brushes, she knew exactly where to go, what to ask for, how each of the tools could serve her. The art store was a wonderful invitation back to comfort, even in the heart of Chicago. A place where she could make all the same choices she usually made, with access to the same tubes of colors, the same brushes, the same canvases.

Would she paint, or would she draw? What colors would she need? The beauty of paint was, you could make almost any color with five simple pigments. Pencils, they didn't blend in the same way she was used to. Chelsea loved knowing that with paint, if she picked the exact right red, the right yellow, and the perfect blue, along with a base white and a carbon black, she could paint almost anything she saw in the world, and anyone as well. *Almost.* The key word was *almost.* And for Chelsea, walking through the store, what she most wanted to paint, who she saw the most clearly, was Carlos, and *almost* was not enough. She found herself thinking toward what made him who she saw. What was the brown of his skin? Was it just some yellow, red, and black, or would she need a touch of ultramarine blue, a dash of white? Should she start with burnt umber as a base or dark brown? And then what about his hair? Could the color theory she'd once mastered mix a perfect dark chestnut to capture the curls atop his head? And what about his eyes, how would she paint the depths she'd found there, the pain, the purpose, the drive, the kindness? What color was enough?

Chelsea pulled six inexpensive paint tubes. A cadmium red and yellow, an ultramarine blue she wasn't entirely satisfied with, the dark brown of burnt umber, and basic black and white. Since she had a full set of supplies back at home, and only a few more days in Chicago—this would do. Besides, she had so many images in her mind to pick from over the past few days—the view of the frozen lake, a delicious cheese-laden slice of pizza, a twirl of turquoise, her neon-pink mittens, even her own red hair—but the image that burned in her mind the most, the one that she could see no matter whether her eyes were open or closed, was Carlos. And she wanted to paint him in the way he saw her. The way he held her, how he didn't judge, didn't make her feel crazy even though she was being crazy. If she couldn't see him for days, she would paint him. This was how she'd hold him close whether he was there or not.

She added on practice paper, a medium canvas, brushes, some thinner, and a few other small items. In total, her entire purchase was under a hundred dollars but filled her with immense happiness. She barely remembered a time she'd been so excited to create. Finally, she had the desire again to paint something that was just for her.

Hours later, back at Ramona's condo, Chelsea had already laid the first layer of what she most wanted to render. She'd captured an image of Carlos that was indelibly imprinted in her mind, the face she saw, full of compassion in the moment she looked up at him in the gallery, her own face full of tears, just after he told her she wasn't wrong to hope.

RAMONA, MORNING IN MALIBU . . .

IT WASN'T THE THUMP OF MUSIC THAT WOKE RAMONA WITH A start, it was the feeling of apprehension. If she followed through with it, she had just one hour before she'd be standing in Jay's class, or worse, possibly falling down, in front of a bunch of super-toned, veggie-powered, sun-kissed self-described athletes who could probably each teach the class themselves. It wasn't that Ramona didn't love her body and its dimples and curves, she just didn't trust it to do certain things that were unfamiliar. In school, Ramona was more of a mathlete. She was never picked first in gym class and didn't quite dodge the ball when it came barreling in her direction with that painful pounce of a slap against her arm or leg. To think about now asking her limbs to contort with grace and coordination within the confines of a tiny rectangle on the sand might have been asking too much.

Still, she managed to get herself up and moving around the bedroom and over to the window to widen the blinds, noting the morning overcast, the low-slung clouds that covered most of the sun. She had learned already that a slight chill lingered until they burned off around eleven. She rooted around the well-organized contents of her suitcase for the second set of exercise attire she'd packed. Usually, at the end of vacations, her workout clothes were the only items that had gone unworn. But this time, for the first time, she was actually going to wear what she'd packed.

She secured her breasts into her sports bra, shifting one, then the next toward the center of her body and using the fabric to hold her in. It was in stark contrast to the freedom of the evening, at least the early part of it when she was undisturbed, not having to feel restricted, or even watched, and especially not to be appropriate—the ultimate constraint even more constricting than the bra was. She practiced a deep breath, feeling the sides of her rib cage push against the tight elastic fabric, insisting on its give. As the final touch, she pulled her twists into a compact ponytail and admired the result. She was ready.

"There." She said it aloud, to nobody at all, a pronouncement of her completed and extensive efforts, especially for what was starting to feel like a real vacation. Rather mummified in the contraption that was her workout gear, Ramona nonetheless congratulated herself for accomplishing the key feat of many a person's tropical holiday, simply getting the exercise clothes on. She had time to grab another slice of the dwindling banana bread and a swig of the fresh-squeezed orange juice that she managed to snag for almost ten dollars at the fancy local market. The banana bread of course reminded her of Joan, and then Ramona debated having an extra slice as some kind of compensation for not only the intrusion of the previous night, but also the dinner obligation later that she still didn't know how she'd manage.

Outside, it was brighter than Ramona expected. She squinted, walking out onto the beach, bringing her hand up to her eyes so she could survey clearly across the sand, all the way to the water. Chelsea's place backed up close enough that all she really had to do was come out of the back door, step across the deck, and down the steps. The house was clearly older, as if it had been there much longer than its neighboring homes, including the long and elaborate multilevel expanse of what Ramona surmised was Joan's place. Chelsea's cottage was quaint, cute, small, and in need of some updates and repairs, but still a location that must have been worth a fortune. Ramona made a mental note to congratulate Latrice on such a lucky find. She wondered why a Chelsea, or a Helena—whoever's home it was—would ever want to leave.

Down a bit on the beach, Ramona could see the group of people, mostly women, setting themselves up for Jay's class. There were a few shirtless men, one in spandex shorts, another with the body of a soccer star wearing what looked like too-warm striped track pants. But with a physique like his, who would notice? The women were all cropped tops and bikinis, short shorts and even bikini bottoms, lean lines, and confidence. The fitness Ramona did on sporadic occasion, these people seemed to live as a religion. Feeling far out of place, she started to turn around. And she would have, but for catching a glimpse out of the corner of her eye of Jay's wave beckoning for her to come closer. Her head shook gently from side to side as her body made a deep sigh of its own resignation.

The cool sand crunched under her feet, feeling a bit like a massage against her soles as the grains fell in between her toes, giving way against her steps. For more stability, she elongated her strides, reaching Jay in a matter of moments, as he adjusted one of the speakers facing the dozen or so early arrivals to his class. Where he stood, closer to the edge of the water, the sound of the rolling waves was much more insistent, a rhythmic roar in her ears that made her better understand why the music was so loud.

"Hey, you made it," Jay said, smiling at Ramona as if he was genuinely happy to see her, if not a bit surprised. He reached out for her hand and came in to kiss her cheek with a greeting she'd seen him give a few others as she walked over. On the other side of them, people seemed to be arranging their mats on the sand, claiming what appeared to be familiar places, likely the hard-core closer to the front to better show off their mastery of whatever the class had in store. "You need a mat?" he asked, leading Ramona to realize that the beach towel she'd brought from Chelsea's was making her look like an amateur.

"I do," she admitted, reaching for the rolled foam in Jay's hand. "Put it wherever?"

"Wherever you want," Jay replied. He had such a vibe to him, so cool and assured. When he smiled at her, his way was so easy and open, Ramona felt herself relax a bit. He was standing before her as the most inoffensive embodiment of *relax, I've got it all under control* that she'd ever experienced.

"Cool," Ramona said, smiling at him bigger than she wanted to, and then feeling embarrassed enough about it to turn quickly and shuffle with her new mat and old towel to an empty place on the sand within the loose pattern of other class attendees.

By the time the music started, that familiar *thump-thump-thump*, about forty people had shown up in total, clearly the equivalent of a fan club, with bright eyes and receptive dispositions, following along through the pronounced choreography of the warm-up sequence, seamlessly taking them up, down, and up again, on and off the mat. Ramona was familiar with some of the terms, her downward facing dog was a bit of a grunt as her boobs threatened to swing into her face, until she adjusted her positioning. And the plank down to a cobra position stretched her back and shoulders as she pushed her chin toward the sky and her upper body off the mat below her with palms against the shifting sand beneath.

"And ease into it . . ." Jay's voice said through the speaker. "Not too much, not too little. We want to push it just right, get into that stretch. Feeeeeel it in your body. Let your body say yes."

My body says yes . . . Ramona thought. She was enjoying the physicality of it. Parts of her body that were tense were releasing their tension. And the parts of her body that felt weak, Jay was giving constant permission to give them rest. The dance continued of stretch . . . tension . . . release . . . stretch . . . tension . . . release.

"Listen to your body," he said. "Push only as far as it wants to go. Hold that, push that, feel that . . . one . . . two . . . three."

Ramona heard Jay's commands, and her body obeyed.

"And now, we're going to move into warrior two position," Jay called out. In response, everyone took the stance of a surfer on their mats, facing the water, arms outstretched perpendicular to their bodies, reaching toward the sea. "Feel the sun . . . Feel the wind. Smell the salt of the ocean, absorb its energy . . ." Jay's voice said over the music. Even the music seemed to obey. It was less thumpy now, instead much more melodic, full of chimes and woodwinds, haunting and light, a beautiful soundtrack to the feeling of being embraced by the breeze. For the very first time, Ramona wondered what it must be like, being out there on the water, balanced like this on a real board in the turquoise surf, sliding along on a cresting white wave.

While the breeze caressed her along her exposed shoulders, the sun was managing to break its way through the clouds in an announcement of concentrated warmth. Ramona had the feeling of exhilarating joy, the high of movement and accomplishment and the peace of finding, but not crossing, one's limits.

"And . . . let's move to child's pose," Jay said, after completing several more seamless combinations of the up-and-down, flat-to-standing motions of a surfer on their board. Ramona was breathy, sweating, ready to be done now. It'd been an invigorating class. "And bring your legs around, to lie flat for Shavasana . . ." Ramona heard and complied, following the instructions of Jay's voice and the physical cues of the other class participants to find her way to lying flat on her back. "Bring yourself now . . . into the present," Jay instructed. "Right now, you are exactly where you're supposed to be . . . You're already doing everything you need to do . . . You're only responsible for what's happening on your own mat . . . one rectangle of space. If it's not going on here, it's not of your concern . . . Releeeasssse it."

Release it, Ramona repeated to herself, echoing Jay's lullaby. Letting her eyes close, she finally heard just the sounds of the ocean, the melody of the music, and felt the warm, warm caress of the sun, enough to drift out to sea, drift away, drift away, far away from everything.

"Ramona?" Jay's voice speaking her name directly brought Ramona to quick attention. She took a breath, filling her lungs with air as if she'd been underwater. But she hadn't been underwater. She'd been asleep. Evidently, for quite a while, as the beach where the class had taken place had all but completely cleared out now, save for a few stragglers still chatting with each other. The music had stopped, and Jay's previously bare torso had a shirt covering it with a faded logo of what looked like a shark to Ramona's still-blurry eyes.

"Shit," Ramona said, sitting up quickly. Instinctively, she moved to pull the towel around her as she gained her bearings. "How long was I sleeping?"

"Not that long." If it wasn't for the strong assurance in Jay's voice and its entire lack of judgment, Ramona wouldn't have believed a word. But rather than be embarrassed, she decided to be satisfied with what she'd been told. After all, she was only responsible for what was on her mat.

"You . . . are *good*," Ramona said, realizing the fullness of relaxation Jay had delivered. "You've got me out here dreaming of being a Black girl surfing." She laughed at the ridiculousness of it, thinking of her big brown body up on a surfboard, blowing her hair poof to oblivion, then of course falling with a splash into the freezing cold waters, deflating her hair and her pride just before she drowned.

"You can be," Jay said. "Why not?"

Ramona's face crinkled. Was it a rhetorical question? "Can you seriously imagine me? On a surfboard? I'm from the South Side of Chicago. We're a real commonsense type of people. It's nice to dream about though."

"How about tomorrow?" Jay said.

"Tomorrow what?"

"Tomorrow, surfing. *Real* surfing. It's my day off from class. I'll take you out on a board."

Ramona smiled but shook her head no. Definitely not.

"You're shaking your head no, but are you *saying* no?" Jay was unfazed.

Ramona actually had to contemplate what he was asking. Her head was shaking no. Because that's what she believed she should say. And just like everything else in her life, she was doing exactly what she thought she was supposed to do. Those kinds of decisions had landed her here. Hiding, lying, scared. That wasn't who she wanted to be, and she could feel the pull to take a step outside of the box, to try something else. To be someone else. Maybe, finally, herself. And now, on vacation, she had time. She had time to place between her normal reactions and new choices, to examine not just what she wanted, but why she wanted it . . . or didn't.

"I'm not saying yes either," she said. "What if . . ."

"No experience required . . . I promise," Jay said, anticipating the common objections.

"And you're a teacher?"

"I can teach *you*," he said firmly.

"Can teach me to do what?"

"Paddle out to a wave. Stand up on your board. Ride your first wave in. You can swim, right?"

Ramona gave him a look of disbelief. She already knew how to swim from summers at the community center in her childhood, but surfing? It sounded so far-fetched she wanted to challenge him on it.

"I can swim, but how far out do we have to go from the beach?"

"If you can swim, you'll be fine." Jay smiled at her so assuredly it looked like a wink. "We won't go far. But you'll love it."

"This is crazy." Ramona stabbed at the sand in front of her with her toe, mainly to avoid looking at him. If he looked at her again like that, with that smile, it was over.

"Your *this is crazy* sounds a lot like you *should* be saying yes," said Jay with an actual wink this time.

Was Jay flirting with her? Ramona couldn't tell. But she liked having his attention, and his instruction, and his assurances that allowed her to suspend her healthy and well-conditioned skepticism. It also didn't hurt that he was handsome and tall and so sturdy-looking. Already now, she believed that she was exactly where she was supposed to be, doing exactly what she was supposed to do. So why not float on just a little bit further out? She'd have something good to tell Latrice, Carlos would be proud, and, as long as she survived, there was no one else to worry because they would never know.

"Let's do it," Ramona said.

"Perfect," Jay said. "You know what I always say, life's too short to wait for next time."

And just then, Ramona understood exactly what he meant.

JOAN IN MALIBU, ON HER UPPER DECK, OF COURSE . . .

JOAN WATCHED EVERY MINUTE OF JAY'S CLASS THAT MORNING with great interest. From her perch, she saw Ramona walk out across the sand with her beach towel. From the corner of her upper deck, slouched down in a (very expensive) all-weather striped canvas sofa, hidden from view, she scrutinized the class as it unfolded, with Jay's faux-enlightened woo-woo ha-ha and platitudes, and even witnessed how he let Ramona (poor thing) lie there on the sand like a beached sea animal while everyone else scattered back into the rest of their lives.

A real shame, Joan thought, that Ramona would get caught up with someone like Jay so quickly. From Joan's perspective, men like Jay were common to the beach. She associated him with the stories that she heard from friends, stories so vibrant and cautionary that they seemed to suffice as a proper substitute for real-life interaction. Joan assigned no extra credit for the fact that he showed up faithfully on all his class days—she just knew that, based on the odds, he was up to no good, no good at all.

And because she didn't feel that she could trust Jay, Joan had *never* attended any of his classes on the sand. In fact, when her private yoga instructor arrived on Tuesdays and Thursdays, they'd both question the standard sequence of poses he'd announce. "West Hollywood yoga" is what they'd say and then exchange a knowing glance between them as if only they were in on the secret. Joan's yoga instructor was triple certified in Hatha yoga, Bikram yoga, and, of course, Ashtanga, because everyone knew that she had been the backup instructor to Madonna in the best days of her sinewy physique. Or maybe she was the backup backup, or the instructor to Gwyneth? Anyway, it was no matter. Joan paid her $400 an hour twice a week to help her use her body to still her mind and to feel good about the fact that her ex's alimony payments were being put to good use for her maintenance.

Now, partially satisfied at having set dinner plans with Ramona, Joan started to feel even more hopeful that the past could be bypassed, buried, and forgotten about. *Let's just move on*, Joan thought. Going forward, she'd take responsibility for Ramona and ensure she enjoyed herself. From now on (notwithstanding the events of that first night), Ramona would feel welcome *and accepted* in Malibu—Joan would see to it.

So, for Joan's absolution, all that was left was the matter of their friendly rapport to solidify. Yesterday, in their exchange, Joan could sense Ramona's lingering suspicion. Tonight, Geoffrey's stunning location and Joan's first-class treatment would provide the perfect anesthesia for remaining doubt. Joan could imagine the conversations that she and Ramona would have—facilitated by Joan's overwhelming kindness and generosity—laughing, sharing their dreams, confiding their embarrassments. The promise of it brought to mind Joan's own daughter and the closeness she still hoped for. But both of her children had moved so far away, so terribly far, too far from the reach of Joan's loving arms of protection and attentive care. Joan was thus left with plenty of extra room in her mind and time on her schedule to obsess over, but not examine, her other relationships, measured in what others thought of her but, mostly, what she thought of them.

Seeing Ramona talking with Jay was an unanticipated complication to carefully crafted plans. At first, she thought she was going to tear her hair out, follicle by precision-dyed follicle. She counted how long they lingered, the minutes passing by like eons. There were too many smiles, Joan thought. *What was he saying?* Joan wanted to know what made Ramona laugh like that, to set her at ease. Like Joan didn't realize with David when she'd just gotten started in her career, men in this town, they pluck you before you get your feet firmly set. Make you experience everything through their access. And when they wanted to move on, they did. You were left with the scraps, scrambling to hold on to a pedestal so high it made you forget that you'd been anybody before. *Jay's going to take advantage of her,* Joan told herself, just like he did with the rotation of women who came to his classes each week, there looking for something, buying his promise of being a good guy, his companionship, charm, and good looks. His pseudo-inspiration was soaking into their ears, burrowing into their brains, making them silly fools, flopping to his instructions with the boppity bop of that chaotic, loud music every day.

In her home, as the sun made its arc through the afternoon, Joan paced across lush hand-knotted silk-tufted area rugs. Deciding it was time to get ready, she headed into the suite of rooms comprising her personal quarters—a bedroom and two studio apartment–size closets, chandeliered and full of light and mirrors. One of those closets used to be David's. She'd since remodeled to remove all traces of his influence. Open French doors showcased a boutique's worth of clothing— shoes, scarves, and handbags of every designer in nearly every color, neatly organized in racks, rows of shelving, and a marble-covered center-island display case. Even though dinner was still hours away, Joan thought about what she'd wear—it was an important evening with important goals to accomplish. They'd go to Geoffrey's for the sunset, *of course*, where without a reservation she'd secure her usual table with the best view, facing due west. She was enough of a regular that there'd be no way they'd not accommodate her, even on a Saturday night. Ramona would feel truly special, and Joan would be happy to extend her privilege, *of course*. Joan imagined that they'd talk and share just like good girlfriends do, right at the peak hour of people-watching and drink-sipping, picking and pecking at her usual salad or the entrée special.

Beyond the scene at Geoffrey's, there was so much for Joan to show Ramona of Malibu—the Malibu Country Mart and all its boutiques where Joan was known by name, and the very private estates of a few close friends who'd happily open their clandestine gates to allow them access for the day. Joan smiled and felt giddy. Already there seemed to be a new layer of life in the small world to which she'd become accustomed. She envisioned clinking champagne glasses at Duke's and slurping sunset oysters at Moonshadows. Last night had been just a fluke. And today, Jay was just a blip. Hers were the much better options. Soon enough, Ramona would see that for herself. They'd become friends, and Joan would see to it that everything, absolutely everything, would be just fine.

RAMONA, IN THE AFTERNOON, IN MALIBU . . .

ABSOLUTELY BUZZING WITH EXCITEMENT AND A LITTLE BIT OF nerves, Ramona pulled out her phone to text not just Latrice but Carlos as well. She couldn't believe what she was about to experience.

RAMONA: Guess who's going surfing!

Ramona was happy enough to send the message twice, once to each of her closest confidants. She debated sending Malik a message as well, as if he'd care. She hadn't heard from him in weeks, not even to check on her or to say he missed her or to ask silly questions about life logistics that he was seemingly now handling on his own. But Ramona was here now, in what looked like the early stages of her "See, I'm thriving" era.

Plus, Ramona's excitement needed no response from others to build. In less than a full day, she'd be doing something she never imagined, breaking a barrier of an activity that was certainly not on the Black girl bingo card, one that combined open water, a floating piece of Styrofoam, and potential exposure to sharks, but she was here for it. There was something about Jay that made her feel relaxed, noticed, protected even, enough that she managed to doze off right on the beach. And no doubt that some of this was a result of being away from work and, in part, also being alone on this trip, keeping her own company. She had so much space to hear her own thoughts. And to slow down enough to feel—strangely, something she often did not allow, as she was usually desensitized to her fatigue, her pain, and even her pleasure. His words, about her not worrying about anything that wasn't in her immediate control—she was ready now to try extending them to all of Malibu. Ramona felt unusually free and happy for the moment, thinking grand thoughts of adventure, bolstered by the ocean breeze making its way through Chelsea's efficient space.

A noise on her phone signaled Latrice's message back.

LATRICE: Whhaaatt?! Get someone to take pictures!

And moments later, Carlos sent his own reply

CARLOS: Get your Nique Miller on, Moe! Proud of you!

Both comments made Ramona smile, as she was feeling proud of herself; one, for taking a risk, but also in that special way of breaking through a barrier holding Black people apart from joys they weren't welcome to experience. Yet, here she was, having somehow slipped through the gates.

On an explorer's high, she didn't even mind so much that she was preparing for a Saturday-night dinner with a woman she barely knew and rightly didn't trust, even though the banana bread hadn't killed her and was now nothing more than crumbs. The reluctance was not that Ramona was usually unfriendly, or even less than personable. She was easily cordial and could get along with almost anyone. But she knew instinctually when a certain person bore watching. It was an ability honed by years and years of climbing the ladder in corporate America—especially working in finance where the common culture of exacting number crunching and attention to detail superseded natural interactions. She knew how to smile and laugh at jokes that weren't that funny and even some that were borderline offensive. She was a pro at making small talk, about the news but not politics, culture but not race, holidays but not religion, which left mainly chatting about vacations, or Beyoncé, or the latest celebrity hookup or breakup, or the antics of the realest housewife franchise. And other than with Latrice, she knew to hold her trust tightly to her chest and keep the truest parts of herself covered.

Without the events of the Sentry Patrol when she first arrived, Ramona might have taken a different view of this dinner invitation. Had she been able to maintain her innocence, her positive expectation, her clean and fresh view of a new place, Ramona would not be left wondering in the back of her mind who it was nearby who viewed her as suspicious, enough to call an intruder of a different nature to her home. She wouldn't be left with concern about her neighbors, the great mystery that remained for her about who called, who was watching her, and how much of her enjoyment was subject to being patrolled. So, against this background, what was unknown and unexpected, Ramona's experience had shaped her expectation—and that was definitely not to have a great time. She expected to smile and bear it, look forward to surfing the next day, and wait out the rest of the week until she could go home to Chicago.

She'd barely had a chance to put the finishing touches on her makeup when she heard the doorbell ring twice at precisely four fifteen. Ramona slipped on her shoes and took a look out at the water through Chelsea's living room windows. The sun was starting to slip lower in the sky. Hopefully, the shortest day of the year would not turn into the longest night of her life.

Ramona opened the door to a smiling and effortlessly elegant Joan, dressed casually in a sleeveless black linen romper belted by a tan Hermès leather band around a very tiny waist. Her perma-tanned arms were enviably toned, with perfect contours, as if sculpted to be worn bare. *Joan should never wear sleeves*, Ramona thought with a tinge of awe. She could also see the hint of her perfectly made-up eyes behind tinted aviator shades underneath a black-banded wide-brim straw sunhat, placed carefully atop blond-streaked brown beach waves.

Joan looked fantastic, like a magazine spread come to life—windblown and yet still perfectly put together—an embodiment of how Malibu was supposed to look, if there was such a thing. Based on her experience so far, Ramona was sure there was.

"Ready?" Joan said. "The car's pulling up—" She gestured behind her to a spit-shined black Suburban, complete with livery decals on its bumper. The driver jumped out to circle around the vehicle, not at all in the casual wear of a typical rideshare host, but instead in black pants and a crisp white shirt, as if this was actually his main job, not a side hustle.

Ramona smiled widely as the door was pulled open. If only Latrice and Carlos could see her now. And her mother and father too, for that matter. A pang of guilt hit her gut as she remembered that in spite of the unbelievable turn of events so far, she was here under the falsest of pretenses. If her mother knew, she'd be hurt. Normally, at a new frontier, she'd bring her family with her somehow, her community, her friends. It was just normal for her, what she learned that you do, just as her mother shared her travels with all of the neighborhood, encouraged everyone to get a passport, no matter how much it cost.

"Wow, Joan, this is . . ." Ramona's lack of words said far more than any she might have found to say could have. It was the silence of awe, of being impressed. Ramona nearly skipped forward to the open car door. Joan crossed just in front of her, billowing a trail of the delicate headspace scent of white flowers. Gorgeous and subtle, the faint breeze of intoxicating aroma stopped Ramona briefly in her tracks, just so that she could take a deeper waft of it. *Joan smells amazing*, she thought, while settling into the soft, crinkling leather of a luxury ride.

Ramona and Joan's arrival at Geoffrey's was only minutes later, a short drive up the coast on the PCH, just past the point where the ocean view became obscured by the much larger estates and gated enclaves that claimed their monopoly on the shoreline. It wasn't until they decamped from the car and reached the restaurant's hostess desk that Ramona had her next glimpse of the water. It wasn't the same view as from Chelsea's windows. This time, they were higher up, on the rocks, looking out farther onto the seemingly endless carpeting of waves, alive and undulating with ripples and disappearing whitecaps of foam. The sun was getting much closer to the horizon line now, washing the sky with ombre peach tones and the blue parts slipping into lavender.

Joan's laugh from the hostess stand sharpened Ramona's focus. "But that's impossible," she said, laughing again. "I come here aaaaall the time. Everyone here knows that's my table."

"I'm so sorry, Ms. Fox," the very flustered hostess replied, starting to show desperation in her typing on the computer in front of her. "We have a very lovely table that's available now, just on the other side of the patio."

Joan's face reddened and her mouth opened, seemingly to protest. Then, suddenly she turned to Ramona. "It's not my usual table. But do you mind? We could wait, but then we'd miss the sunset. And honestly, why come here if not for the sunset?"

Ramona nodded, because of course she didn't mind and really couldn't understand the problem. There was nothing but an incredible view in nearly every inch of the restaurant, which was already packed with people. That they had a table at all seemed like a minor miracle. But ahead of her, following the hostess, Joan was all grumbles.

Almost as soon as they were seated, a server appeared with two glistening flutes of champagne. "Compliments of the manager, Ms. Fox. We're terribly sorry about the inconvenience."

What inconvenience? Ramona wondered. Already, she was impressed by Joan's influence. They were at a glorious table, right at the edge of the tiled patio area, with an unobstructed view of the water from there to eternity, as the sun was kissing the lip of the horizon. And the fact that her host had become accustomed to something even better, that somehow *this* was insufficient, baffled Ramona. She wondered what it was like to be Joan, with both a tinge of envy and a sense of relief. Taking a sip of the effervescent liquid apology, she inhaled the air and enjoyed the flawless coastline scenery.

That first drink for both Joan and Ramona was bubbles and small talk, the basics of making acquaintance that told Ramona nothing important about why she was sitting there at the edge of the world with someone like Joan, who had such a fabulous life. She learned that Joan was an empty nester, that she baked vegan paleo keto sugar-free cookies every Halloween for trick-or-treaters so their parents would approve, she raised money for Black Lives Matter, and her family had established a scholarship for writers at USC. Joan had managed to also make it evident that she knew almost everyone who was anyone who actually lived in Malibu. Also, according to Joan, all the celebrities went to Nobu, farther south, but here tonight was where the real Malibu glamorati gathered, to see and be seen. Otherwise, like rare animals in the zoo, they sheltered much more privately behind their gates and along their own patches of shoreline.

Ramona also learned that several of the television shows that she'd grown up watching, shows in syndication now, whose names everyone would know, were products of Joan's ex-husband's media kingdom, the fruits of which would be paying for their dinner. "So now his new child is the same age as a grandchild would be, but nobody's filming that—" Joan gave a tight smile and then punctuated it by finishing off the last swig of champagne that remained in her glass and waved her carefully manicured hand in the air to signal another round. Strangely, another round appeared near instantly. When Ramona told Joan that she was excited to go surfing, and that Jay had invited her for a lesson, Joan wasted no time telling Ramona about the nature of Jay's yoga classes and how they were always filled with women, the same women every day, dressed in their athletic wear, hoping for some extra attention. "But I can't speak to his *private* surf lessons," Joan said. "Who knows what happens when he gets women alone . . ."

Nothing's gonna happen with me, Ramona thought. She found it all interesting, but harmless because, after all, she was only recently (and perhaps temporarily) unengaged. With Jay, it had all happened so organically, naturally. And Joan had just appeared, crashing wave after wave of generosity upon

Ramona, overwhelming her with strange and seemingly unwarranted attention. For her part, Joan didn't just spend all the time talking. By dinner, she'd asked Ramona about herself and her family, her job, and if she was involved with anyone, questions that Ramona answered, and she reluctantly disclosed her breakup. And so in return, Ramona had a question of her own.

"You wouldn't have any idea who could have called the Sentry Patrol, would you? Any of the neighbors when I arrived?" she asked. "I just can't shake this feeling that I'm being watched."

It was hard to gauge any reaction from Joan other than a slight clearing of her throat before she sipped her flute of champagne. "Watched?" Joan said, as if Ramona had asked her about aliens. "You feel like you're being *watched*? By whom?"

Ramona shrugged. "Dunno. I'd just feel better if I knew who it was, I guess, so I can stop looking over my shoulder."

Joan reached over and patted her hand. "The only person in Malibu that you need to worry about is, what's his name, Jay?"

"Well, Vijay, but Jay."

"Right, *him*," Joan emphasized. I'm just saying . . . be careful."

But Ramona was already careful, as life had taught her to be. She would follow her gut about Jay and resolved that she might never know who'd originally called the patrol, who was a threat, or who strangely viewed her as one. But it was no matter now anyway.

Just before the sun set fully, Ramona took two pictures. One of the landscape to send to her mother. The other of just her, with her back to the ocean, looking delicious, draped in a sky of pastels, cranberry, and deepening violet, capturing the dance of the sun and the moon trading places.

"Perfect vacation photo," Joan said as she tapped the screen of Ramona's phone once again and then gingerly placed the phone back on the table.

Just perfect, Ramona thought. She smiled at Joan, thinking much less at that moment of how she'd originally been greeted by Malibu, how she'd originally felt, or how much she'd wanted to go home. She'd almost stopped wondering who it was that had called the patrol on her, stopped looking over her shoulder, and *almost* stopped feeling uninvited. She also quickly dismissed her own just very brief suspicion at Joan's clear disdain for Jay, or her insistence about planning their next outing, which Ramona skirted committing to. Now instead, she wondered how she'd become so lucky, how someone so great, so glamorous, and so open as Joan had found her interesting enough to befriend, and how, in the moment, the evening she'd dreaded was turning into a most wonderful time.

CHELSEA IN CHICAGO . . .

CHELSEA SPENT THE EARLY PART OF HER EVENING HAPPILY painting. *Happily*, because there was something new to paint and a feeling that had been sparked alive, especially when she was thinking of Carlos. And Chelsea's way of visualizing always started with what she noticed most, which meant she'd started the painting with his eyes. She'd taken care to spread scratch paper across Ramona's tasteful dining table now turned makeshift studio. She'd pulled her hair into a fiery swoop of ponytail and was deep in concentration over the making of something she'd call her own. A piece of someone, the part she could capture and hold on to. When her parents passed, she'd painted their portraits until she could no more. For every memory she wanted to keep, for every photograph she didn't have of every moment that now meant so much—because there would be no more of them—she painted it. When she ran out of things to paint, of times to remember, she started clinging to the house, trying to squeeze out of it all that it held, of maybe just one more drop of memory if she stayed long enough. For the first time in a long time, she desired to hold on to something new, something alive, someone else.

She picked up the small metal tube and squeezed a viscous dollop more of a rich, dark-brown pigment onto the plastic palette. It had been a good idea after all to make that splurge of just one more color—the burnt umber. She needed to match *this* brown—the brown of Carlos's eyes. They were the color of iced coffee in sunlight. The highlights were the tint of clouds in the sky after a rainstorm. She imagined him, holding the image of him in her mind from when he sat across from her the day prior, and especially when he held her. Yes, that was it. That moment. She wanted the exact second that he looked down at her when her eyes were still wet with tears. The moment that he had awakened a hunger within her and a desire that she feared might have faded. The desire was there, glowing now with its own energy, and she was deeply, deeply invested in capturing every single detail of how it had happened.

So engrossed was she in the fine brushstrokes of eyebrows over what was turning into a near-perfect rendering of Carlos's left eye, Chelsea almost missed the sound of her phone registering a text message from the actual Carlos.

CARLOS: Wanna step out?

Chelsea read it twice just to make sure it said what she thought it said. Of course she did, wherever, and she didn't hesitate to make that known. When he said he'd pick her up in twenty minutes, she rushed off to find something to wear, yank the rubber tie down the length of her hair, and scruff the top of it into a style.

On the ride over, Chelsea watched the lines of the city morph again, from brightly lit streets and tall buildings to lower-slung brick row houses, to warehouses, as they finally pulled up to their destination. It was cold, freezing, especially in the pitch dark of night, and just the short walk to the door ahead made Chelsea's fingertips feel stiff, even in the insulation of her hot-pink mittens. It was a nondescript building, long and low, made of brick and wood. A barn door marked the entrance for Chelsea to step inside and once again partake of warmth. Carlos guided her along, his hand on the small of her back, into a place that was a surprise of an open display of antiques, and furniture, and old signs with half of their marquee lights missing. Along the floor there was a trail of candles, marking a path through the mess of dusty items that covered nearly every inch of floor space.

"What is this?" she heard herself say aloud. She turned back to look at Carlos.

"You could just walk along to find out," he replied. "Or do you want me to tell you what's thirty feet ahead and ruin the surprise?" His smile was mischievous. He was testing her. Curiosity burned, so she turned around again to follow the trail of lights, now leading up a flight of steps, then another, and then finally opening into another very large room. In spite of herself Chelsea gasped.

There in the darkness, the path of candles had led to even more candles, a room of candles everywhere, just enough to lift the darkness. There was an arrangement of chairs, people seated in careful rows all facing a stage with instruments like those in a jazz quartet. Carlos ushered them to two open seats near an aisle as Chelsea turned to survey her surroundings, which she still couldn't believe.

"We're a little late," Carlos whispered coarsely. He sat down and pulled off his jacket.

Chelsea did the same, still wondering if he was going to tell her where they were and, perhaps more important to her now, why they were here. There was no good way for her to ask if this was a date, and if so, why he'd asked her so last minute, or if this was his notion of romance. Regardless, it was unmistakably romantic and became more so as the band started to play its opening notes.

"I'll be right back," Carlos said and asked her what she wanted to drink before disappearing to the bar along the back of the room. She let herself get carried away with a cover of José Feliciano's all-instrumental version of "Jingle Bells" that she'd never heard before but made her body sway in the seat nonetheless.

By the time Carlos returned, holding four plastic cups full of dark wine, a soloist was performing a rendition of "Silent Night" in both English and Spanish that brought tears into her eyes. There was an unmistakable tropical feeling to the music, and it was too gorgeous not to know what the performance was called. Chelsea decided to ask about that.

"Latin Christmas, by candlelight." Carlos grinned.

Chelsea memorized the look of his face, this time illuminated by a hundred tiny flames. She noted the new shadows, how the light reflected in his eyes looked like a night sky full of stars. Later, she would paint this too.

"The next song, we can dance if you want—" Sure enough, as the haunting ballad was ending, one of the band members announced their next number and encouraged the crowd to leave their seats in favor of a small dance floor in the corner.

"I can't dance," Chelsea admitted.

"I'll dance. You can just sway to the music." Carlos gave her a wink. Chelsea wondered if he'd seen her earlier. Had he been watching her from the bar? She looked into his eyes for an answer, but in the dark of the room all she saw was candlelight flickering there. She wanted to be closer to him, to know him more intimately. The thought of their bodies swaying together was the perfect ideal worth trying for. She nodded, and he took her hand, lifting her with a gentle tug. It was the first time she'd felt the direct warmth of his skin on hers; and the softness of his hands, that surprised her. He directed them to the compact dancing space that had started to fill with other couples. The others stepped together, turned, stepped apart, came in close, and some never touched at all. But with Carlos, Chelsea was close enough to breathe the heat of him emanating from his body pressed close to hers. To smell him in leather and evergreen scents, the mix she remembered from the gallery. She closed her eyes to inhale the intoxicating smell of him, to let herself sway with him, to release herself to him, following his synchronization with the music. She let his hips brush against her while his arms gently guided her where to go. While their feet barely moved, she felt so much closer to him, with the sounds of Christmas, the words *Feliz* and *Navidad*, making beats to dance to. She didn't understand all the lyrics, but she felt their meaning through Carlos. He sang along, and she experienced his joy, and quite deeply, her own.

Within a single night, there'd been the two drinks and then another each, the dancing, the gorgeous music, and the ethereal candlelight. In the car on the way back, Chelsea leaned into Carlos, and he allowed her to rest her hand on his thigh. His arm draped loosely over her other side. *That's not nothing*, she thought, while still wondering if there was enough attraction between them to act upon.

When the car stopped in front of Ramona's building and it was time for Chelsea and Carlos to part ways, Chelsea's brain was on overdrive thinking of how to avoid that conclusion to the evening. *Kiss me*, she willed. Tipsy, she leaned forward with eyes closed, running her tongue over her lips, biting the now-moistened lower one. Her heart was beating a mile a minute, and a hollow silence filled her ears. Her breathing staggered, and the energy of her desire filled the car of its own accord.

She imagined him gripping the back of her hair, the gentle tug at the nape of her neck pulling her head back so that he could reach her. So that he could put his lips on her neck, her face, her lips. And she felt the warmth of him draw closer, and then he was so close she could feel the moist heat of his breath on her ear. She couldn't take it anymore, and she turned her face to meet him there, with an audience, the car running, the ride unstopped. She didn't care who saw, whether it was the driver or anyone passing by. She was in the carelessness of want in the clutches of a desire beyond desire, one that had waited too long and was reckless now. She pushed against the generous softness of his lips together and then as they opened. She took his top lip in her mouth and then the bottom one with teeth and suction. When she felt his tongue push across her lips, she met him with her own, intertwining, *yes*, dancing like they had before, *yes*, softness, *yes*, the friction, *yes*, the smell of him. *Yes, please come upstairs with me*, Chelsea pleaded with everything but words.

"I could come up," he said, his voice low, seductive, his words slow and determined.

"Yes." Chelsea was so sure that this is what she wanted.

"But . . ." Carlos hesitated, looking genuinely pained. "Maybe it's not going to mean what you want it to mean."

"I don't want it to mean anything." Chelsea busied herself with his lips again. "I just don't want tonight to end here. Come upstairs."

In a rush of swirling feelings and frantic yearning, Chelsea and Carlos exited the car to the certain relief of the driver. But Chelsea didn't care so much about having an audience. It was easy to forget that anyone else was there. She didn't think about the drinks she'd had or how her emotions were elevated by the alcohol that also dulled any logical objections. In a few days, she'd be leaving. What difference did it make? And so what if she never saw him again? Did she need to see him again to have a good time tonight? Maybe she just needed *this*. Maybe she just needed him now, for this moment.

In the elevator, on the trip of twelve floors, they kissed. It was enough time to be pressed against the wall together, for hands to roam under clothes, weave through layers, to touch goose-bumped skin. It was enough time to for Chelsea to feel Carlos's leg between hers and to rub against it, awakening her body further and driving her deeper into pure unbridled want. Twelve floors were enough for Carlos's body to respond too. With her back at the wall, she felt his arousal pressed against her thigh, her pelvis, her stomach. Her body tingled along the line his lips traced down her neck.

"And you'll be fine if I can't stay?" he said, with his lips just a breath away from her collarbone.

"You mean like stay the night?" Chelsea really didn't want to waste time talking. Her body was past that. It felt too good to just let go. Nothing mattered—just what was now, right in front of her. She didn't care about anything else.

"Yes." Carlos pulled back, he stopped the kissing, the feeling, the exploring. He waited until Chelsea's eyes met his. There was meaning there. So much so that Chelsea briefly sobered.

"What, are you married or something?"

"Nah." Carlos's face scrunched briefly with pure confusion as if he couldn't believe the question. "Definitely *not* married. Tonight . . . I was supposed to be on a date. I just don't want you to think . . ." Chelsea understood immediately what he meant. Carlos didn't want her to think this night was intentional. He didn't want her to believe that it had been for her, about her. And anything that happened next wasn't about meaning, it was about the rush of lust, which they could both give in to if they so wished. An offer of his body for hers, but not his heart. He was giving her a choice.

Chelsea was too far past logic. She didn't want to think. She was feeling, finally. She was concentrated in the lower half of her body, throbbing with its own heartbeat now. "Let's go inside," she said.

When the door closed, there was nothing left to hold back. She couldn't pull his coat off fast enough, right there in the doorway. Her sweater hit the floor. His hands wrapped around the sides of her breasts with a soft squeeze and then his fingers gripped her bra, pulling it down in a swift motion, exposing her nipples and their sensitivity to the air in the room. His mouth was so much warmer. He suckled her and he bit her. It hurt and then it didn't hurt, and she wanted so much more. Her head was spinning, swirling, boozy, free, uninhibited. Her body was ready.

Moving in one mass together, arms around each other, hands exploring, groping, squeezing hard, soft, hard again. Chelsea felt Carlos's firm body flex against hers, and then the softness of the bed beneath her as she lay down underneath him. He pulled back.

"Turn over." He was instructing her to lie on her stomach, naked, almost fully naked, only her panties remaining. But she did as he said and turned over. There was nothing at first, just her breasts, so sensitive now, pressed into the sheets beneath her. The palms of her hands feeling the texture of the bedding, gripping it tightly. She channeled her nervous anticipation of what he would do; she couldn't see him other than as a shadow in the window in front of them, the outline of his body standing above her as she was exposed beneath him. Her breath was rapid, shallow as she waited for him to take what he was going to of her. By reflex her shoulder blades tensed, the tiny hairs on the back of her neck came to stand at attention, waiting . . . Suddenly, he was there, leaned down now over her; she felt the heat of him on her back. Kissing her down the length of her spine. Those same lips that she'd held in her mouth making a trail of hot and cold down her skin. Everywhere he'd been she could feel. His teeth caught the top of her underwear and pulled down. The fabric slid against her skin, past her butt cheeks, down the top of her thighs, pulling away from the crevice between her legs. She felt every millimeter of it. She was all feeling, all sensation, all arousal, all desire, all impatience. And then his hands slipped underneath her thighs, as he lifted her up to meet him, and Chelsea made no resistance to it, her body pleasured and loose. It was only her anticipation and curiosity that brought her the slightest feeling of trepidation, of danger of not knowing what would happen to her. What he would choose to do next.

But it was his mouth on her again, her softest part. His tongue where it was most sensitive. With deftness and precision, he delivered her to her first release, rich swirls and waves of the ocean inside her, the high tide cresting on the shoreline, she melted herself into him, into the bed, into the whole world.

DECEMBER 23

• •

CHELSEA IN CHICAGO

THE MORNING WAS A ROUGH START FOR CHELSEA. HER HEAD throbbed, and a foggy haze made every one of her thoughts arrive slowly through the thick, unorganized soup of her mind. She blinked at the light through the window and struggled to orient herself. *Where am I? Oh, that's right, Chicago. In a complete stranger's bed. No, technically my bed at a stranger's house.* She turned and patted to her right the rumpled sheets in complete disarray—a vestige of the prior evening's events. But she was here alone. She hadn't been alone though. Flashes of the night before arrived in quick succession. A memory of perfectly crisp awareness at the candlelight concert . . . then, dancing . . . then, more drinks . . . then . . . kissing. *Oh shit.* Then, there was more, so much more. Thoroughly naked Chelsea, wrapped in chaotic ruching of sheets, pulled her arm up above her head to drop her hand in a flop across her face.

She groaned an *ugph* . . . as she rolled over to bury her head in a pillow, which she tried to roll up over the sides of her face. Which pillow she also then tried to punch with the back of her head as if it was the one recounting to her harsh accusations of all that had happened the night before. But it was her slowly sharpening mind, running through what she said, what Carlos said, what she did—*Oh God, what did she do?* And then there was the matter of who put what where and when it all happened and another "*ugph* . . ." out loud again when she felt embarrassed about how many times she'd come and if it was loud or strange, or just how the person she'd just had sex with received her.

Last night, she didn't care, couldn't have cared at all if she wanted to, but this morning, how she worried. She wanted to pull the covers over her head and roll back into a peaceful sleep that would last her until her flight three days from now. Where the shame came from, she had no idea, as she used to be *that* girl, the exact one that everyone told you not to be. The old Chelsea had a sexual freedom to her, one that allowed her to experience a person physically as easily as she did in collaboration for an art project, or even sometimes as a type of conversation. When it was done it could be finished and she needed nothing more. The experience itself was the virtue that needed no justification.

But Chelsea had changed, admittedly so. She hadn't dated since she lost her parents, not really. On that day she spent in the gallery with Carlos, something had shifted in her. She could feel that now, even as unbelievable as it was. Was it possible that someone could speak just one morsel of truth so directly to you, so keenly, that it stirred your very soul?

Chelsea sat up in the bed with a start and pulled the sheets around her. Carlos said he wouldn't stay, she remembered. But then, there was something else. She'd forgotten about the painting she was doing, of him. Had she left it on the table?

Despite being alone, Chelsea suddenly felt very exposed. It was one thing for someone to see you naked on the outside. It was another for someone to see your raw thoughts, your stripped-down heart, your soul itself, removed of all its pretenses. She wrapped the bedding around her and made a rapid march into the living room. There on the table, she saw everything she'd laid out of her paint tubes, the palette still there covered in plastic, her brushes—cleaned and neatly laid in place. And the unfinished painting of Carlos lay in the center of the table. Surely, he'd seen it as he left, Chelsea thought to herself. And how would she explain it? How would anyone feel knowing they were the unwitting subject of an artist's inspiration, and that you were captured with such detail? Would it be flattering? And then, with Carlos's disclaimer before—of no strings, of not wanting to be connected past the night, not even to the morning—would he think her crazy? Fragile perhaps?

Chelsea closed the rest of the distance to the table and picked up the unfinished painting. To her, it was unmistakably Carlos, as it was meant to be. It was a reflection of her memory, the thing that she'd most wanted to preserve before it disappeared. Which led Chelsea to the biggest question of all: Had he now become something she was afraid to lose?

RAMONA IN MALIBU-YAAH . . .

RAMONA OPENED THE BEDROOM BLINDS ON THE FIRST QUIET morning she'd experienced in Malibu and started the day similarly to almost anyone else who'd had a prior evening of at least four glasses of champagne (but who was counting?), a light seafood dinner, and an earful of Joan Fox at her best. Her head was swirling as if she'd been on one hell of a ride. An aspirin and some orange juice would fix the mild hangover, but there was still the matter of Jay. According to Joan, she'd learn to surf and secondarily be seduced into his harem of lululemon-clad acolytes.

But Ramona was leaving in a few days and in no danger of getting carried away any more than she feared being swept away by the ocean. And the latter was in fact an actual fear.

The one person who would have been proudest of Ramona going surfing today was most certainly Melba Tucker, who encouraged both of her children to know as much of the world apart from Chicago as she had through her travels. Only that current circumstances were such that Ramona's very own mother was the one person she couldn't tell.

From Chelsea's kitchen she surveyed her view of the ocean. The day was still overcast, for now. The water was tame, and low tide had the edge of the Pacific grazing the sand as gently as you might pet a baby animal.

Ramona picked up her phone and selected Latrice from her list of Favorites, and within two rings heard her friend's familiar voice.

"Did you meet Jaws yet?" Latrice chided, without so much as a hello.

"Why can't it be Ariel, Latrice?" Ramona shot back, already smiling. "You have me getting eaten by a shark?"

"Just sayin' of the two movies, one is slightly more realistic than the other."

"I'm starting to regret making you my emergency contact," Ramona said.

"So, for real, when do you go?"

"In a couple hours."

"I swear, Ramona, surfing? You out there doing the whitest white shit possible. You can swim that well?"

Ramona laughed. "Of course I can swim. Can't you?"

For a second Latrice was quiet, and quickly, it occurred to Ramona that maybe swimming wasn't as common as she thought.

Latrice cleared her throat. "Nah, I can't."

"Latrice! You can't swim? Or you just don't swim? You didn't learn in school?"

"Moe, I'm serious. I can't. And you *know* I wasn't trying to mess up my hair in high school. I opted all the way out of swim class. When did you learn how to swim? Like, you can swim, swim?"

Ramona thought about it. "My dad took us to the Y when we were little. Me and my brother learned as kids. When there was a pool, we swam."

"Girrrlll . . ." Latrice said. "I'll dip my toes into Lake Michigan in the summertime . . ."

Ramona laughed and then she stopped abruptly. As they'd been talking, she was trying her best to visualize a Black surfer, or even competitive swimmer, for that matter. There wasn't much to reference. Her image of the water was overwhelmingly white, just as Latrice had said.

"Do you wonder why that is?" Ramona spoke her thought aloud.

Latrice stopped talking about cold weather to answer. "Why what is? In the summertime? Girl, do you know how cold it is right now?"

"Latrice, no. I meant, do you ever wonder why when we think of surfing . . . we can't see ourselves in mind?"

A loud sigh came from Latrice's end of the line. "You know what, Moe, I actually don't wonder."

"Because you already know," Ramona said resignedly.

"I *already* know," Latrice echoed. A brief silence passed between them. "What are you going to wear?" Latrice asked with shifted energy.

"Jay has a buddy with gear, a wetsuit, board, everything I need—"

"Except shark repellent."

"Latrice, I'm sure it'll be fine."

"So said everyone who was about to meet calamity."

"Girl, get you some optimism," Ramona said.

"*Optimism?* Who are you and what have you done with my friend Ramona?"

Ramona laughed. "It's the same me, but I have to admit, things are unfolding much better than I expected."

Ramona enabled her camera for Latrice so that she could see the view, the ocean, and the beach outside that still managed to look peaceful and inviting despite the sun's late arrival.

Latrice, who happened to be working on a Sunday, appreciated the glimpse into the world outside of her office.

When Ramona and Latrice ended their call, Ramona couldn't get it out of her head what Latrice said about surfing—that it was for white people. Most of all, it needled her that even though she'd met Jay, who wasn't white, and even though she'd be trying it herself, she still didn't feel in her heart that Latrice's words were untrue. *Were there spaces in the world, enjoyments especially, that weren't available to her still?* Searching within, she could find no examples to counter this strange segregation that persisted, which was especially alarming if its roots were held only in her own mind.

Hours later however, shivering on the beach in a bathing suit, Ramona started to wonder if perhaps Jay was actually the Pied Piper of Malibu and if he had very possibly charmed her into a spectacularly bad decision.

He was off to the side speaking with his friend, standing next to a dusty old VW Microbus in powder blue and white and corroded chrome. The faded writing on the side indicated that the vehicle also doubled as a surf-school headquarters. To his credit, in the payload was a wide assortment of boards and gear looking professional enough for someone whose "office" was once likely used for weed deliveries.

Just as Ramona was wrapping herself with a towel and shifting her weight again in her ongoing effort to generate some warmth against the ocean breeze, in her peripheral view, she saw Jay heading over. Across one arm he was holding out a limp black wetsuit. His own was pulled over his legs and unzipped above his waist, exposing his wondrously bare chest and rippled abdomen. Under the other arm was a long and large turquoise surfboard that Ramona assumed would be hers.

Extending one sinewy arm, he held Ramona's suit out to her and then with the other gently dropped the board lengthwise in front of her feet.

"We start on the sand. It'll be just like class 'cept you swap the board for the mat." Jay smiled like he was getting a kick out of Ramona's hesitation. And, of course, her mind filled each moment with a new reason why she shouldn't. One wave crest looked too big. *Wasn't that a riptide?* That person who fell out there in the surf, did they get back up? Ramona had already counted the lifeguard shacks along the shoreline, and there didn't seem to be enough.

Ramona watched Jay pull the top half of his wetsuit up and tug it over one arm and then the other like he was wrapping himself for preservation. "I'm supposed to put this thing on?" she said, her face crinkled with confusion. The suit Jay handed her looked like it might have been for someone much smaller. She had no idea where to even start—how to go about folding herself into the puzzle of a clothing item.

"Yep, hold it open, then one leg at a time. Putting a wetsuit on is all about small victories."

One at a time, Ramona thought to herself. She dropped one foot in the end hole and felt the seal of the suit shrink-wrap her calf. But there was still give in the suit, and she managed to pull it farther up her leg. When both sides were accomplished, with a fair amount of shimmying and grumbling on Ramona's part, she was winded but satisfied to finally have the suit at her waist. She copied Jay's gestures of putting one arm in and then the other, and all that was left was the torso-length zipper behind her.

As Ramona turned about from one side to the other to complete the exercise, Jay set in motion in her direction.

"Let me help you." At her back, he pulled the sides of the suit together. Romana felt the seal close around her with the satisfying sound of the zipper closing. Something about the finality of it spoke directly to Ramona's nerves.

"You know, there are a lot of people who'll be upset if anything happens to me." Ramona was only half kidding. She could only imagine how infuriated her mother would be if she'd somehow managed to get herself killed during a faux trip at the hands of a stranger she'd already been warned about.

Jay walked around to face Ramona, intently, and stepped close. He was near enough to touch her, and he did. He laid his bronze-brown hands on her shoulders. The warmth and weight of them resting on her lent a certain gravity to his words as well. "You," he said, "are in good hands." And the way he said it, so definitively, so carefully, with such confidence, Ramona believed him—she needed to. Latrice's words had stuck with her. *What if she really didn't belong?* Others in the water, who did not look like her, seemed to be enjoying this unfamiliar activity. *Why else would they be out there?* It was already so much work. Did she really need a wetsuit contraption? Perhaps she'd learn there was something inherently wrong about the water, or it would reject her somehow, or her it. And at the same time, even with all this doubt, she still felt looked after, as if somehow this man could and would help her, help keep her safe.

Jay moved to position himself on the other side of the board in front of Ramona with his back to the ocean. Behind him were the waves of the water, frothy white crests that advanced and disappeared into the sand at the end of their glory. She couldn't believe that in just moments she'd be out there, riding on the water. *There's no way*, she thought.

Like a skilled instructor Jay paced back and forth, delivering Ramona the rules of the waves. "Don't cross into another surfer's space," he said. He told her to never release the board, which she couldn't imagine happening with it tethered to her via the ankle strap currently lying along the sand. The board he'd selected for her was long, wide, and pretty thick—he assured her it was the right shape and size for beginners. "And it's got a textured top to help your foot grip," he said, referring to the soft dimpled top layer on the board. Even that was a reminder of what was to come. In the water, out there, she was supposed to somehow stand on this thing while it was moving. For Ramona, the entire idea was mind-blowing.

Jay was all business. "Okay, we're going to practice paddling out and then popping up," he said. He had Ramona lie on the board and show him her freestyle swimming stroke. He adjusted everything about it, from the way she bent her arms to the angle of her hand hitting the water. "Like a fin," he said, showing her with precision. "You want to push the water, not pull yourself . . . one arm at a time." He watched her intently as she practiced the stroke, studying her for corrections to make in each repetition. By the time he finally said, "Okay, now we're going to practice standing up," Ramona felt like she'd already swum across Lake Michigan.

Standing up on the board, and even practicing it, was going to require Ramona to push herself up from a lying position flat on her belly to crouching on her feet. Watching Jay demonstrate it for her made her feel nervous and self-conscious. Her arm strength was weak, and she was heavy, especially top-heavy. The thought of embarrassing herself made her cheeks burn, and instantly she reignited her regret. Next to her a couple of seagulls tittered, looking for food, and then flew away. She wished she could join them.

"See, it's just like yoga class," Jay said over the roar of the ocean, demonstrating the choreography again for standing up on the board. His movements were so fluid, so masterful. There was no way Ramona could do that herself, and frankly, she didn't want to try. "Your turn," Jay announced, gesturing to the board on the sand below. Ramona vigorously shook her head no.

"I don't think I can do that." She folded her arms and turned toward the sea. When the breeze blew the smell of the seawater into her nostrils, she took a deep, defiant breath and looked for the nearest way out. Maybe this really wasn't for her. Perhaps she wasn't meant to be here. But yet, here they were, just the two of them, only feet away from the water. The challenge itself beckoned to her; she'd come too far now to leave and not know.

"I saw you do it before," Jay said. "Only, in class it was *harder*." He smiled. "This is going to feel easy. We'll do it in steps. All you have to do right now is lie down, flat on the board."

Ramona hesitated, knowing that she was being managed. She hated the part of herself that liked it, appreciated it even. Jay was good, with confidence and information that exceeded her knowledge. What she felt was a tinge of regret, like she was out of her mind, filled with contradictions. She worried that he'd be able to convince her to do anything. To go past her limits. Maybe that was the reason for Joan's warning. *He's going to have me out here looking stupid*, she thought, remembering how she fell asleep. But then, she looked down, and Jay had taken her place instead. He was lying flat on the board, stomach down.

"Stomach down flat on the board," he said, seeming to pay no attention to Ramona's obstinance. "Chest lifts up . . . right toes stay stuck . . . Left knee comes up to kneeling position, right up to your chest." His actions were slow and easy to follow, just like the yoga class. To Ramona, the moves did look simple, easier than what she'd done before with a downward dog and surely easier than a plank position. "And then we stand up just by lifting our body with the back leg, bringing the knee off the ground and twisting the back foot so that it makes a *t* shape with the centerline of the board."

Ramona managed to drop her scowl, but she kept her arms folded.

"Okay, I'm going to do it again." Jay repeated the same sequence on the board in front of Ramona three times, before she actually started to feel silly for just standing there, and after the fourth time, she wanted to do it herself, if only to save him from another repetition. He never complained or goaded her, he just kept doing it, the same move over and over again.

Somehow, she was now more self-conscious for him than she'd previously been about herself.

"Okay, you win," she said. Ramona bent over the board, lowering herself onto it like she had with the paddling exercise. She put her hands on either side of her and pushed her upper body up, boobs and all, and was surprised how easily the position came to her. Repeating what Jay had shown her, she pulled her left leg forward into her chest, which was a little uncomfortable until she straightened her back, giving her much more room to breathe. And then, she was kneeling.

"That's it!" Jay clapped his hands together. "Okay, now . . ." He came over to place his hands lightly at her waist. Another reminder of support, that he was here. And Ramona registered a jolt of determination.

"I think I've got the rest." Ramona was feeling confident now, assured. Trusting her body for the last move, she pushed her right knee off the board just like Jay said, and there she was, standing. She made it up. She couldn't hide the widening smile on her face. She beamed with pride at a true accomplishment. "I did it!" she said and wanted to say it a thousand times more into the wind.

"Now it's time to get in the ocean." Jay showed Ramona how she'd carry her board into the water. How to find a wave that had already broken. "See, where the wave breaks, when it becomes white and foamy, see that froth? That's the whitewash," he explained. "With beginners, we usually start there and try to ride one in."

"Stand up? In the water?" Ramona said.

"That's kinda the point," Jay teased back. "The faster you're going, the easier it'll be. I can show you . . . better to do it than to just stand there and think about it." As Jay explained, all she had to do was to move into position, get on her board, paddle through, and stand up, just like they had on the beach.

Ramona held her look of skepticism. "Jay," she said, "why do I feel like some other man is saying the exact same thing to some other woman in equally questionable but totally different circumstances?"

"You don't believe me?"

Ramona groaned. "I'm here to try, so let's just try it," she said.

At her response, Jay broke out into a smile that looked almost goofy, like a kid with a new bike.

Twenty minutes later, wading into nearly waist-high water, Jay held Ramona's board for her while she pulled herself up to lie on top of it and start to paddle forward. They'd spotted a series of swells, the nearest of which had turned into the frothy crested wave just as Jay had described. Somehow, according to Jay, she'd ride one of these waves back to the shore. She paddled out beyond it, riding against and then with the swell of water. The passing wave lifted her up with such great power it focused all her senses in exactly the present. It had been enough to lift her up on the board, farther than she thought, and drop her down at least two feet, slapping against the water and jostling her posture. Ramona wiggled to realign herself to the center. On the other side of the wave, Jay helped her turn her board to the shore. And Ramona could feel the power of the ocean beneath her, even in the shallower water. She turned her head to see the water building behind her. Her wave was coming, building into a break. She was waiting, floating on her board, trying to stay calm and maintain her breath. And then the water started moving her forward.

"Torso up now," Jay called out to her with urgency. The rush of the moment filled her ears, along with the roar of the ocean surrounding them. She was moving much faster than she expected, as fast as a bike even, but riding smoothly on the surface of the water. She was within the grip of the forces of nature, and the raw power of the water beneath her was evident, palpable. Remembering her practice, she did as Jay said, holding on to the sides of the board, and with flat palms, she pushed herself into a cobra position, like she had on the sand. "Right foot anchors, left knee forward," Jay yelled out from behind her, sounding surprisingly distant. She performed the movement she remembered and suddenly she was kneeling on the board. The board that was moving on top of the water at speed toward the shore.

As she rushed forward along with the water, Ramona turned inward. She had a goal that she was determined to reach. *Just one more move, Ramona,* she thought to herself, steeling her focus and will for the last step.

Okay, now, quickly! Ramona's mind shouted at her. She remembered Jay's instructions. In the moment there seemed to be so little time to execute. "Pull your back leg forward, twist your foot perpendicular to the board," she repeated aloud.

Over the rumble of the waves, in the clutch of the ocean, Ramona felt powerful in her body as she never had before. She could and she did pull her leg forward and anchor her foot against the sticky top of the board as she'd been instructed. There in that moment, it was all her and the air, one with the board and the water beneath her, arms outstretched and into the wind. She was riding the wave. Ramona was surfing.

"Arms along the centerline!" Jay yelled, but it was too late. The board started to slow down, and then wobble. Ramona was surfing for exactly ten seconds, ten glorious seconds before her loss of balance tipped her too far to the left and she landed softly in the shallow turquoise water next to her. But for that brief time, that glimpse into what she'd been capable of, Ramona felt as if she'd won a championship. Every light within her was illuminated in full brilliance. The rush was unmistakable, the unbridled force of the ocean, the communion with nature herself, the ultimate mother. With her feet underneath her once again on solid ground, forgetting herself, she wrapped her arms around Jay with the fullness of her gratitude and joy.

"OhMyGod, I did it!" Ramona was all wet hair, water in her face and eyes, sand in places that had never seen sunlight, but she was all elation. "Thank you, thank you so much!" To her surprise, Jay wrapped his arm around her, returning her embrace. Amid the swell of feelings and Ramona's soaring delight, Jay's warmth around her became its own bit of electricity in her belly.

Jay looked so happy for her, like he knew all the while she could do it. "Nice dismount," he said, finally pulling away.

Ramona felt a small tinge of regret at him separating but recovered quickly as accomplishment continued to surge through her veins. She had surfed *and* she'd wiped out. "I wanna try it again," she said with a surprising eagerness. Ramona was surging with the rush of endorphins, the feeling of having broken the barrier of a new thing. She was bubbling with the excitement of possibilities and imagining being able to relive it all in every person she told. But the person she'd shared the experience with was Jay.

An hour later, Ramona had managed to stand up three more times with only one more wipeout and got in her longest ride of a full forty-five seconds before her board gracefully glided into the shallowest bit of water against the sand.

"So, this is what you do on your day off?" Ramona asked, when they were toweling off on the beach.

"Teach Midwesterners how to surf?"

"I meant . . . surf yourself."

"Sometimes. I go to different spots. As I'm sure you heard, surfing in Malibu is a little . . . complicated."

"Complicated?"

"It's not always welcoming. Some people feel like they own certain breaks, spots to surf . . . and . . . there aren't many brown folks in the water."

"But you do it." Ramona was confused. The rush she'd felt, it was indescribable. Like she'd just come alive. As if she'd been reborn in the ride, within the wave itself.

"I do it because I don't care whether or not I'm welcome." Jay's voice had a firmness to it, as if echoing a feeling beyond the moment, a frustration perhaps. "It wears on you though, feeling like an outsider, especially at first. But I found some different groups to surf with. And I got good enough that I feel like I can go out anywhere now, but there are still days I don't know what to expect—maybe a knucklehead or two, you never know. The thing about the ocean is that nobody owns her. And the minute you think you might have it figured out, she changes, something's different. Always different."

"A temperamental woman?"

"A temperamental woman makes the best kind of lover," Jay replied, holding eye contact with Ramona until she had to look away. She understood what he meant, having just left the sea, but couldn't help but wonder if he somehow meant her as well.

Jay's friend walked up and motioned to collect the suits and boards.

"See you tonight at Dockweiler?" he asked to no one, and thus to everyone within earshot.

"Dockweiler? Is that a bar?" Ramona asked.

Both Jay and his friend, who by then she'd learned was called Rip, laughed.

"Dockweiler is a beach. The only one nearby where you can have bonfires."

Ramona turned to Jay with a smile. "So, you *do* have other hobbies."

"I don't know if a bonfire is a hobby, but sure." He winked back at her playfully.

Rip lifted a deep golden arm up over his eyes. The sun had finally made its full appearance. "Hey, if you're into surfing, you should come. Some good people there, and there's nothing like seeing the firepits all lit up at night. And the ocean, it's like she has another personality."

"Ramona, if you want to go, I'll drive you," Jay said. "It's a little ways away from this beach."

"Yeah, Malibu is for surfing for sure. Dockweiler is for firepits," Rip said.

Ramona looked back and forth between the two men. There was absolutely nothing about them that signaled they couldn't be trusted. In fact, Rip and his dusty repurposed van, his sun-bleached curls and tanned extremities, looked far too relaxed to do any harm. Worst case, she'd be riding in a dingy VW with Jay for a bit.

"Okay," Ramona said after her deliberation. On the electric high of her first experience surfing, she would have agreed to nearly anything. And she couldn't wait to be back at the beach. *I'm sure it'll be fine*, she thought, just like she'd told Latrice.

CHELSEA IN CHICAGO
(DEFINITELY NOT SURFING . . .)

OTHER THAN MALIBU, THE MOST FAMILIAR PLACE IN THE WORLD for Chelsea was alone with her thoughts. Ordinarily she'd be comfortable there. Basic regret was manageable, or sorrow, even that was fine. But this day Chelsea's thoughts were driving her crazy with no place to go. Did Carlos see the painting? Did he think she was obsessed? A stalker? Would he want to see her again? Wait, why did she care? And so, for distraction and a bit of cheer, she decided to go to the most obvious place in town.

It gets dark so early in Chicago . . . This was Chelsea's thought as she glanced out of the window of the car she decided to take down to Michigan Avenue, the section best known as the Miracle Mile. There wasn't anything particularly miraculous about it until the holidays, when the avenue came alive with a million tiny lights strung along every branch of every tree along the street, a bonanza of Christmas decorations, Fifth Avenue–esque decorated shop windows, and a humongous Christmas tree sitting right at the base of the Wrigley Building. Roaming about almost like a single organism were the innumerable pedestrians, bundled up like waddling penguins trying to brave the temperatures, weaving back and forth between one another on the sidewalk and in and out of stores.

Earlier, in Ramona's condo, Chelsea spent the better part of the day working on another art piece, a charcoal pencil sketch from memory, trying to work the previous night out of her mind. She'd also paced the floor, listened to five podcast episodes, then scrolled all of her social media feeds until she started feeling insecure about her makeup, hair, body, career, and strangely not having a car or relationship, although none of this seemed to bother her as much before. Even without the digital FOMO, however, she felt very acutely the longing of wanting to be with someone, someone you could still feel against your body, who you could still smell on parts of you. Someone absent, but who you could still see every time you closed your eyes.

Chelsea had composed at least ten text messages to Carlos that she didn't send. "I hope you're having a great day!" she typed. And then deleted it, because of course she wasn't the type to put exclamation marks in text messages. "Wanna grab dinner?" was her most honest attempt, which she talked herself out of because wouldn't it be presumptuous to assume he didn't have a date lined up? After all, although they'd had an incredible night, it was only because an outing planned with someone else fell through. So, rather than obsess about what she couldn't control, she decided to channel all her insecurities into the most common solution she could think of—shopping. The next day was Mrs. Tucker's party, and as a small splurge she'd purchase the first dress she'd bought in years.

And this is how Chelsea wound up on Michigan Avenue back in front of the Wrigley Building, right next to the pizza restaurant where Carlos had first introduced her to deep dish. It was just approaching the end of the afternoon hours, and already the sun had all but disappeared during the very short dusk. The lights of the boulevard twinkled, casting a glow about the street and lending a festive air to the blocks ahead. The car headlights in the wide boulevard and the glinting decorations on the bordering trees, all sparkling in the spreading evening, made an amusing parade of the slow-moving vehicles and the bundled pedestrians costumed for winter warmth.

Remembering the trips that she used to take with her mother, Chelsea stopped in the fanciest department store that she saw, near the five-star hotels that dotted that portion of the double-lane avenue. There, she'd see if she could find anything special, sparkly, and *on sale*, worthy of the glamour that Mrs. Tucker had promised for the next evening's festivities. When Chelsea finally found a dress within her budget, it wasn't sparkles but instead something much more befitting of the theme, more representative of her, and something she couldn't wait to wear.

Satisfied with her relatively modest purchase and making her way down the escalator out of the store, Chelsea heard from above the rousing sounds of a caroling quartet singing a soulful a cappella of a Christmas song she'd never heard before but certainly wanted to hear again. "This Christmas will be a very special Christmas," echoed around her in harmonies and swells of melodic voices. She hoped that somehow, some way, it would be special—and not just a fleeting memory that she would scramble to paint before it disappeared . . . forever.

The lights on the trees inspired Chelsea to make a stop in one of the large drugstores she saw to pick up a few strings of lights and some candles, and upon returning to Ramona's condo with frozen fingertips and toes, she peeled off her hot-pink mittens and set about putting up some temporary decorations. Finally satisfied with the lights around the window and a smattering of a few stick-on bows, Chelsea snapped a photograph of it all and wrote a confident message to Carlos.

CHELSEA: It's beginning to look a lot like Christmas . . .

Simple and to the point, casual. So much easier than saying what she really felt or even asking for what she really wanted.

So, it came as a complete surprise when Carlos replied just one minute later. His text message was simple, but to Chelsea, it was everything she needed.

CARLOS: Wanna see some real lights?

RAMONA IN MALIBU . . .

WHEN RAMONA RETURNED TO CHELSEA'S BEACHSIDE COTTAGE, she was still wired with the buzzing energy flowing through her, bubbling like an effervescent glass of champagne. The feeling lasted even as she showered and rinsed out her hair, thankful that her twists had still held up in the seawater. Ramona's normal haircare routine was much removed from a simple "wash your hair in the shower" type of process. Her very thick type 4 curls were both fragile and obstinate, requiring care and patience to coax them into one of her customary styles, achieved like a chef's signature recipe. Usually, it took lots of love and even more conditioner (especially to detangle)—the kind that penetrated deeply and the kind that was left in to protect, and then a fixative—her favorite gel that smelled like the soft perfume of marshmallows. For Ramona, restyling her hair was her favorite "enjoy me today, tomorrow's wash day" T-shirt—a careful process that required hours of her focused time and attention. Each strand that grew from her head, and each millimeter of length thereupon, was an earned testament to growing hands and methods, intention, and sacrifice. Although the twists weren't her comfortable normal style, and the shrinkage she experienced as they dried brought her some disappointment, she was getting used to the look of them, finding the twisted strands of her hair to be less of an intermediate step and more of a style of its own, robust enough to weather the new climate of moisture-laden sea air.

Moisture brought changes to Ramona's hair that she couldn't always predict. But the twists, they held their shape. To dry, she pulled them tightly up to the top of her head and arranged them in a small-but-satisfying bun bundled at her crown. Her eyes delighted in the curves and bends of the textures twined around themselves, dark and lush and dancing with light. It looked rich and graceful, the style of a queen, fastened and affixed with care. "There," she said aloud, smiling at herself in the mirror. She saw a delighted Ramona, purely and simply happy, physically blooming, it seemed, spurred by a current of quiet confidence.

Ramona's stomach grumbled, an interruption reminding her that it had been some time since she'd last had a meal. The power of the sea, the weight of the surfboard, the resistance of the water, the sheer effort it required to focus all of her attention on a single point on that board—it had taken a toll. To stand up while being propelled on the surface of a rush of water had robbed her of whatever she'd last filled her body with to fuel it. Crossing into the kitchen, she rummaged for the sandwich she'd absentmindedly purchased on the way back from the beach.

Despite the intensity of her hunger and as she quelled it with her first bite, there was one thing that kept nagging at her. A place her mind kept asking her to go. To examine that feeling that she'd had in the water and how extreme was her exhilaration. Ramona knew then, for sure, that there was *no way* that this experience, this healing, this plugged-in connection to the raw power of nature was something that any group of people *just didn't do*. Because once you felt *this* feeling, it would be something you'd chase for the rest of your life. And you'd want others to chase it too because it was so pure, the purest of delights that when discovered; like a small child who discovers a delightful thing, the first impulse is to share. And so, she knew, she knew that there had to have been an intervening force. *Something had to have kept us from it*, she thought. *Something so big, powerful enough to suppress the soul itself.* And with this thought, the curiosity appeared within Ramona, white hot and burning. She had to find out what that something was.

When she searched "Black surfers" on the internet, what she quickly found was a history of struggles that played out on California's beaches and in the waves. It turned out that Latrice had made a great point about swimming, Ramona realized, as she read that Black people, who historically had little access to public pools, even in California couldn't escape segregated beaches until the 1960s. She read accounts of localism that ranged from name-calling to all-out violence and the acts of resistance like wade-outs and paddle-outs of people of color reclaiming their place in the water. She found the names of groups like the Black Surfing Association that formed in the seventies, the Black Surfers Collective, and then Color the Water, formed more recently in the name of increasing representation, plus Textured Waves, Black Girls Surf, and SurfearNEGRA, focused on Black and brown women. After coming across the award ceremony pictures in her search results, with smiling brown faces holding surfboards and trophies, she smiled back at the screen, wishing she'd been able to see A Great Day in the Stoke in person, beyond just the images that lived online documenting its historic competition, gathering Black surfers from around the world. It made Ramona wonder, if she kept at it, if she got good enough, could she compete, even for fun?

But where were all the professional competitors since Sharon Shaffer, like Nique Miller, who looked like her, to answer that question? There were not very many other names to be found. *Why was that?* Ramona wondered.

Between the articles she found, as she read voraciously and then searched some more, Ramona thought back to all that surfing might have required in the 1980s or later even, and especially for a Black woman—knowing how to swim, and having access to water, because as she read it, not even half of Black children or adults did. And even if she did, what would she do with her wet hair if she had to go to school or to work? A style like her versatile twists wasn't even fully protected from punishment until the CROWN Act from the repercussions of being deemed unprofessional or outside of a dress code. And if she decided to surf? Malibu was considered to have the best surfing beach in the world, but it was a place that had once been segregated by practice and now was made exclusionary through various weapons from simple hostility to actual physical aggression on the sand and in the water—the heartbreaking stories from the coastline were detailed in news archives and hard to read. "People are trying to own the actual beach!" Latrice had said. And now that Ramona found the articles, she learned for herself that, sadly, this was true.

Ramona read voraciously. One crumb of discovery led to another, word by word, article by article, narrative by narrative, each building together like a drumbeat, *thump-thump . . . thump-thump . . . thump-thump . . .* to a frantic crescendo. Her heart was racing, her mind thinking clearly, freely. Until it came to a point of stark realization, a breakthrough in understanding. The big *something . . .* was *violence.* Her people's right to recreation, to the enjoyment of leisure—the right that they had to their own bodies to do as they pleased, to their joy, to their time and clear thought—that right had been stolen by violence and intimidation, by privilege conferred on others.

Ramona savored then her experience of exploration and wildness, the purity of shaping her power through nature, reserving herself not for productivity and labor, but for re-creation. Rejuvenation, rebirth—these were freedoms too, bought and paid for by the salt of sorrow and tears that had now become one with the ocean itself. Her leisure, her communion, this time that she had taken for herself, it had allowed her to slow down, to examine her thoughts, to really listen to others and to herself, and to try a new way to reclaim her body, to reconnect to herself, to be free. This was her inheritance.

Too quickly, two hours passed with her phone in hand, consuming all that she could to help put rails of context around what she'd experienced earlier riding the ocean. Ramona was still on a high with a crackling energy that kept her buoyant.

She hit send on a message to Latrice, attaching the photo that Jay took of her in her wetsuit with the board. She only wished that, alongside that one, she had a photo of herself in the water, on even just one of the small whitecapped waves that she'd wrestled. That photo, if she had it, she'd frame it like a work of art, or a graduation certificate, a commemoration of its value—the induction into a new part of her life. She was now a wave rider, a watawoman, an enchantress of the surf. And without such a photo, without documentation or an image to refer to or just to proudly show others, she'd have to rely on her memory and her imaginings and what she was assured would be her longings to return. To Latrice's reply, telling her she looked "badass" and "legit," Ramona messaged that she'd call later—she'd hope to keep the spirit of the moment alive in its retelling. Without the photo, she'd use what the ancestors did, the story and the spoken word. For now, her rendezvous with Jay for the bonfire had arrived, and it was time to see another face of the Pacific, what it looked like up close in the nighttime.

When Jay pulled up, just a half hour after she'd finally set her phone to recharge, she wasn't sure it was him at all, although she could see him and the car he was driving from the window. She expected to see a dusty VW van like the ones littered around the beach parking lot with surfboards strapped along every free surface. Or an open-sided white Wrangler that she'd seen on television. Instead, Jay called out, "Are you ready?" from a very new, very matte, very expensive-looking, ultraluxury SUV. She never imagined that teaching yoga on the beach could be so lucrative.

As she stepped into the car, as much as she tried to assume a neutral countenance, she must have registered her confusion on her face.

One of Jay's hands was wrapped around the leather steering wheel, and another dropped down to adjust the complex-looking climate controls. He turned to face Ramona. "You were expecting something else?"

Ramona had to decide whether she was going to be honest. She certainly was expecting something else, but clearly now, her early assumptions about Jay's presence on the beach had been incorrect. "Perhaps . . . I should think about being a yoga instructor," she said.

Jay laughed. "I haven't always been a yoga instructor."

Ramona did a quick take around the opulent interior of the car. It was more than she'd imagine purchasing at this stage in her career, or even years from now. And for once, still carried by bliss, she cared little for measuring herself against comparative accomplishments, at least not professional ones. She was interested to know who he was, how he'd learned to surf, and if the story started here, she'd take the bait for an opening.

As Jay turned the car onto the PCH, its wheels crunched loudly, rolling upon coarse gravel. Jay was focused, looking over his shoulder for traffic. Ramona turned to him, pushing her body against the seat belt, and asked, "What did you do before?"

In the twilight, cars zoomed past them in a parade of headlights. Jay watched intently, looking for timing to join them. He turned into an opening, and as the shape of Chelsea's house shrank behind them and the wheels of the car began to hum against the road, Jay finally answered.

"I worked in finance. Deals mostly. Investment banking, some private equity." He turned to look at Ramona quickly, and then back to the road ahead. "Teaching yoga is my retirement job."

"Retirement?" Ramona looked at Jay more closely. Aside from the salt-and-pepper sprinkling in his hair at the temples, and in the curls at the top, he didn't look old enough to have retired, even from a lucrative finance job. His skin was smooth, bronze brown, and other than the fine crinkles at the corners of his eyes, he appeared to be a young man in his prime years.

Jay laughed. "Retirement as in I made enough money in my career, and I got out before it was too late. While it was still fun . . . and when I still had a grasp on any sense at all of having enough."

Now it was Ramona's turn to laugh. The concept of *enough* was a puzzling choice of words. *Enough of what for whom?* she wondered. "What's *enough* mean to you?" she asked.

Jay turned to look at her again with surprise registering in the shadows of his face this time. By now, the sun was beginning its approach toward the long curve of the ocean horizon. Soon it would be dark, and she'd miss the subtleties of his gestures. Their eyes met briefly, and then Jay turned slowly back to his driving while the corner of his mouth lifted in a hint of a smile, as if he was remembering a pleasant thing.

"My first time staying in California, I was in LA for work, from New York, on a deal. We had a lot of pressure to close, not a lot of time. For two weeks we worked like . . . sla—" Jay paused, looked at Ramona quickly, and then restarted. With closed lips, she smiled in amusement, knowing what he was about to say. He continued, "Like, around the clock. And the guys from the other side, they had no shame about telling us we needed to start our negotiation later in the morning 'cause they were gonna go surf. Can you imagine?" Ramona shook her head, for she most certainly absolutely could not. She'd never felt entitled to leisure, and certainly not so much so as to openly prioritize it over work obligations. *Never.*

"Uh-uh," Ramona said, her head still moving involuntarily back and forth as if even it independently held its own objections.

"Right?" Jay continued. "So, I worked that deal, and we closed it. And then I said to myself, *I'm* gonna go surf. I took a lesson, my very first time on a board, had never even thought to try it on vacation. And you know what? That feeling you felt? That first time on the water? I was hooked. I pushed back my return trip and stayed another week—taking lessons. And then, the first time I went out by myself, I decided I was going to the best beach, right? So, I came out to Malibu. Here I am, an awkward beginner and all, and I'm this brown dude, and there's nobody out there in the water who looks like me. *No one.* But I go anyway, you know?" He turned again to Ramona, but this time, it was dark now, so all she could see was the reflection of the interior lights of the car in his eyes and off his skin, and the passing illumination that came from lights on the other side of the road. She nodded yes though, and he turned again back to the road to continue his story.

"So, I got in the water, and I'm practicing, and there's a few guys in the water. They're looking at me but not really talking to me as we sit in the lineup."

Ramona felt her face scrunch, her eyebrows furrow. "What's a lineup?"

Jay laughed; she could see the perfect alignment of his very white teeth in the darkness of the car. "It's *the* lineup," he said as the car jostled beneath them over a rough patch of asphalt. "It's the calm place in the water out beyond the break where the surfers wait for the waves to come. You sit in the lineup and float and wait . . . just *wait* for that perfect wave."

"Wow . . ." Ramona said, not quite meaning to; but imagining it, so close to the time that she'd just been in the water, she couldn't help herself.

"Yeah," Jay continued. "So, then this wave comes. I have enough room to take it, and it seems like it should be mine. I'm a newbie, remember, so I could've had it wrong. And then the guy next to me comes up, drops in on the wave right after, snakes me . . . but with the timing, it might've looked like I snaked him." Jay turned to Ramona, seeming to intuit that she had no idea what he was talking about. "Snaked him . . . took his wave, cut him off . . . accidentally, *maybe*." Jay lifted his right hand off the steering wheel to raise a finger in the air to accentuate his point. "*Accidentally, maybe*. And you know what that guy said to me?"

Ramona shook her head no.

"He said, 'Dude, get the fuck out of the water. You don't have enough tax money for this spot. Go back down south.'"

"Down south?"

"Like to the more southern beaches. It's where Black people used to go . . . exclusively."

Ramona remembered the mentions of Inkwell Beach from her earlier research. During the period of practiced segregation, it was the only beach that Black people were "allowed" to visit without the overt threat of violence, far away from Malibu. "But you're not Black," Ramona said.

"Does that matter?" Jay turned to her quickly.

Ramona looked at him and then turned to her right, over her shoulder, to look out of the window. By now, this far down the PCH, she could see the ocean again, in its majestic midnight-blue robe. As a body, the Pacific had witnessed it all. The totality of humanity. And yet was still welcoming to all, held itself back from no one. The surface of the water looked like folds of satin, creasing and uncreasing in the moonlight. Yes, this water was mixed with tears of all sorts. Its body held the bodies of her ancestors. Its beauty was surely that of salt and sorrow, joy and pain . . . to ebb and flow, to surge and roar, reminding Ramona of her own resilience.

"Then what did you do?" Ramona asked, thinking of her first night in Malibu.

"I decided to see what *enough* really was," Jay said. "I got home, and I pulled up my accounts. That deal that closed, I made my bonus. I looked up the cost to live in Malibu and at the time, it was less than the cost of a two-bedroom apartment in Manhattan. So, I decided, why not me? I had enough, and I'd had enough. I was tired of working and having nothing to show for it, so here I am."

This intrigued Ramona, not because she also worked in finance, but also because she'd never heard anyone close to her age speak of *enough*. When you come from the South Side of Chicago, *enough* is a generational accomplishment. *Enough* didn't mean leisure, or a life in Malibu. It meant having enough, making enough from your earning years, with the labor of your mind and the requirements of your body to not be uncomfortable. It meant having enough to eat, to pay the bills, to have a little fun on the weekends maybe or a vacation. For her parents, *enough* meant sacrifice—turning a dime into a dollar to feed and clothe two kids, to scrimp and save so that the next generation could go to college and have a chance in the world. *A chance for what though?* Ramona thought, adjusting her shoulder against the seatback to contemplate what Jay had shared.

It wasn't lost on her that they were heading south now from Malibu. That they would pass the Inkwell in Santa Monica, or what remained of the location, along the rest of the way to Dockweiler. They rolled down the stretch of the Pacific Coast Highway that kept the ocean and the sunset on their right side. This day's sunset had already turned the sky into brilliant swaths of periwinkle and peach, colors that Ramona didn't see during the winter months in Chicago. In the darkness now with the windows down, the heavy ocean air blew in through the car and flapped the loose parts of their clothes. Ramona relaxed, finally allowing herself to sink deeply into the full comfort of the plush leather seat.

While they continued to talk along the half-hour drive, Ramona wondered about Jay's decisions. How differently enough was viewed between the two of them. Even that he'd been able to consider it and decide he had *enough*, what a luxury that was. Ramona spent most of her life chasing *more*, in a household with two kids plus Carlos and anyone else from the neighborhood who needed some extra love or a dinner plate—more, because it seemed like there was never enough. She'd worked her entire life just to have a small condo in the right area with the right view. She'd never gone surfing. She only knew how to swim because her father made sure she learned when she was young at the rec center. Otherwise, there was no pool. With few vacations, she took no time for herself, not really. She lived on the lake, and looked at it, but never went down to enjoy it, for recreation. And all this time she thought that she knew what joy would take, what true happiness would require, but never expected to feel it for free that day, the fullest and most unbounded joy she'd ever experienced, right on the water. So, then, what was *enough*?

By the time they reached Dockweiler Beach, much farther south, the stars had appeared in the sky's changeover to night. Airplanes soared up above with a roar into their flight paths, up and over the ocean into single dots of blinking light. Down on the beach below, the ocean was whispering its rhythmic whoosh, with a casual low tide that just gently graced the shoreline. But what filled Ramona with a swell of awe was seeing the active firepits dotted along the sand, blazing in the night, with fireflies of embers and smoke drifting up into the darkness. There must have been at least fifty, a sight that widened Ramona's eyes with wonder as she absorbed the culture of the western shore.

"You've probably already heard about Bruce's Beach," Jay said as they stepped down from the car in the parking lot. "It's down a bit farther in Manhattan Beach."

Ramona had heard about it, after public attention was focused on returning the land to the descendants of the Black family who established the resort in the 1920s. The news of it reached all the way to Chicago, but Ramona thought it was a singular circumstance. Instead, Jay told her that beyond just Inkwell, all of the city's southern beaches had been aspirational destinations for the Black residents of Los Angeles; but, during Jim Crow times, access was limited by city councils, by police, by practice, and by attacks.

"How do you know all this? "Ramona asked.

"I think it's important to know about where I live, don't you?" Jay said, eyebrow raised.

"I hadn't thought about it until today," Ramona said, bundling up further after a surprising gust of chilled evening air.

The two of them continued their walk from the parking lot to the beach, while Jay made sure Ramona understood the significance of where they were. All around the same time in the '20s, Jay explained, while Bruce's Beach was confiscated by eminent domain, and the Pacific Beach Club was a magnificent resort burned to embers by arson before it could open, Dockweiler Beach was a resort that was never built at all. Once white residents got wind of the plans of Los Angeles to lease the land to Titus Alexander, a Black entrepreneur, they petitioned local officials to rescind their offer of the lease.

"It was strange times back then," Jay said, "but I had to understand then to understand now."

Ramona thought back to her arrival in Malibu. She wanted to say something about it but, unsure of how, allowed Jay to conclude his story, even though she already suspected the ending—the project was abandoned. It was, and the city took over the land. Land that they stood upon now, that they would endeavor to enjoy now, perhaps as those who came before them wished they could then, but could not.

"Does knowing give you any comfort?" Ramona asked.

"No, not really," Jay replied.

"What, then?"

Jay paused for a second, eyes shifted upward. When his gaze returned to meet Ramona's inquisitiveness, there was an intensity present that she didn't expect. "It gives me reverence," he said.

Ramona wondered then about what it would come to mean for her, the history and the present of this place, what it would bring her and what it had taken. "I was met by the patrol when I got to Malibu," Ramona said after a beat, more as a musing to herself rather than to Jay, but aloud nonetheless.

"At Chelsea's?" Jay looked shocked and shifted his stance toward her, stopping his stride toward the firepits. "Who called the patrol on you?"

"Right now, it feels like the whole of Malibu did, like I'm not supposed to feel like I belong. Maybe it's always been meant to feel that way."

In response, Jay gestured to the water, still on their right side. "When you have a place like that . . . the best surf, the cleanest water," he said. "And only some people get to enjoy it . . . I guess you'd understand why it makes me happy to see brown folks out here, why I teach for free; maybe one person's not enough to make a difference, but at least I try."

Ramona sighed. It was such a beautiful night. But would her experience be an interruption of joy? That ever-present reminder that the fabric of this place, every place, had woven within it a haunting spirit, the malignant suspicion toward people who looked like her? What was the conditioning of such spite? The infection that turned a naturally occurring wish to share into one so primed to exclude, to keep things selfishly, but without awareness or questioning? As she did often, as many others she knew did often, Ramona took a deep, deep breath, releasing it out into the air to carry away the undercurrent of sadness, of knowing, of mourning, so that she could with some peace enjoy what the evening promised.

Jay's walk with Ramona down from the parking lot to the beach concluded when they reached the shoreline. The powdery grains poured defiantly into her shoes as the carpeting of sand gave way under each of her steps. They quickly closed the distance to the crowd gathered around the glowing fires. A loud "Hey, you made it!" from their right side caught Jay's attention, and it was Rip from earlier standing within a smaller group of people, some with foldable beach chairs, some sitting on coolers, and some on blankets. Then, in rapid fire, Ramona was introduced to so many people she couldn't retain all the names. There was flannel-shirt guy, and UCLA-sweatshirt girl next to him, another holding a beer can sitting on a cooler, and then someone called Lauren who looked like a volleyball player with her height and long limbs. Everyone was friendly, so friendly in fact that when the woman in the UCLA sweatshirt offered Ramona a can of beer, which Ramona didn't normally drink, she accepted and drank it anyway.

"Technically, you can't have alcohol on the beach, but quietly, we do the cans," she said. "And recycle." Sweatshirt pointed to a black garbage bag set up on the outskirts of the group.

The night felt special to Ramona, like she'd entered another world entirely—a surprisingly welcoming one. It could have felt unfamiliar—with the choices of attire, the shorts, beer-branded T-shirts, and the West Coast sports teams and colleges represented everywhere, or the fact that Ramona was (as, of course, she'd noticed) the only Black person in the group—but rather, there was an air of ease and relaxation, a sense of casual enjoyment that she was starting to enjoy.

"Cold?" Jay appeared at Ramona's elbow just as she'd made a small shudder, now understanding the stark difference in daytime versus nighttime air at the beach. This was a damp cool, one that could put a chill in your bones if you weren't carefully insulated. When Ramona nodded, admitting that she was, Jay directed the two of them closer to the fire.

"We can snag these for now," he said, pointing to two open chairs. Once they were seated, he turned to Ramona. She could see the fire reflected in his eyes and briefly wondered again if he was flirting. It was impossible not to recognize the flicker of hope that he was.

Jay leaned over, tapped her with his shoulder. "Surfing, bonfire, seems like you found your way to living the California dream. Is that what brought you out here?"

Ramona considered the question. *Why not tell the truth?* she thought. What difference did it make to confess to a person you'll never see again? Except *her* whole truth—the secret she'd been keeping, the sense of *maybe* that she'd been clinging to— that was too complex to explain to a stranger.

"A bad . . . breakup, screwed-up wedding," Ramona said. "Basically, I came here to hide out and avoid my parents' disappointment." Ramona shifted in her seat and clasped her clammy drink. She'd been as direct as she could, the gist of it. The words left her feeling stripped down and bare. After all, she'd taken every opportunity she could, with even the most remote rationale, to make something true because she was afraid of who she'd be without it. And perhaps, even worse, who she wouldn't be. Except that now, the truth felt clumsy and inconvenient.

"What, you're like a runaway bride?"

"Maybe more like a stowaway?" Ramona said, face scrunched with discomfort.

Jay laughed. "Ah, that's interesting. Parents do take the breakups pretty hard at this age," Jay said, leaning back to pull his beer to his mouth for a swig.

"Who're you telling!" Jay's response made it easier for Ramona to agree without elaborating. And then, he continued before she had a chance to correct him. At least, that's what she told herself.

"If it's any consolation, you just might be talking to the poster child for parental disappointment."

Ramona turned to look at him, puzzled. "You?"

Jay took another sip of his beer and then pointed the can at Ramona. "You came out here to avoid disappointing your parents . . . *temporarily*. My coming here was the end of my parents' dreams for me. Now, I'm just the son who's a beach bum."

Although Jay seemed like he meant his words sincerely, Ramona couldn't stop a small laugh from escaping. "Seems like you're doing all right for yourself," she said in conciliatory fashion, thinking of Jay's car and the enviable career he'd had.

"Let's just say my parents didn't come to the US for their kids to give up midstream."

"That sounds like my parents too. They sacrificed so much, wanted us to go further, have everything, all of what they couldn't."

"Yeah, but those dreams aren't free, and they definitely aren't of being free," Jay said. "Those dreams are just about having more, after coming from a place of having less."

To Ramona, just then, Jay sounded like a dreamer. And in a flash, she felt the urge to correct him, or to redirect what he was saying. But instead, she paused, and she thought about it. And she started to wonder where her dreams originated, the aspirations and ambitions for *more* rather than just *enough*. With the sound of the ocean behind them, rhythmic with the crash of whitewash into the shoreline, Ramona felt boundless, unconstrained. Like she had space to think, and to breathe, to breathe deeply as if her lungs could expand into all the space around her, as if something tight had been lifted.

"So now you have enough," she said. "And I . . . don't."

"What's missing?" Jay asked so sincerely, like he really wanted to know. Like the answer to the question mattered to him. When Ramona looked at him, she saw the movement of his eyes, intently searching her face for any clue.

"I just put myself in a situation I don't know how to get out of," Ramona said. "So maybe I don't have enough courage, I don't know . . ."

"I saw you in the water today. Getting out there . . . up on that board, you looked pretty courageous to me." Jay took another long swig from his beer can. "You're going to spend the rest of your life hiding?"

Ramona tried not to show it, but Jay had struck a nerve. "I'm only hiding this week," she said with quiet protest.

Jay smiled and shook his head. "Where I'm from, how you do one thing is how you do everything."

"Where'd you hear that?"

"Yoda said it, right after he said, 'There is no try.'"

Ramona laughed. "You know I've seen that movie—I have a dog named Wookiee. Yoda did not say that!" She landed a playful poke on his arm.

Caught, Jay raised his hands in surrender, and leaned back in. "Okay, he didn't. I heard it from my pops. It's what he always used to say." The fire crackled, releasing a trail of sparks into the sky as a log fell deeper into the pit. Both Jay and Ramona turned to observe it and then turned back to each other.

"What was he talking about?" Ramona was intrigued.

"He was talking about integrity." Ramona raised an eyebrow. Jay continued. "He'd say it all the time. When I wasn't giving my best in sports, when I wasn't getting great grades in school. When I didn't get the biggest bonus in my banking class. He meant was I coming up first. I realized I was spending my whole life trying to be *that*."

"And then what happened?"

Jay gave Ramona a grin. "I stopped trying in favor of doing."

"You're saying I should stop trying?"

"Do, or do not . . ." Jay began.

Both Jay and Ramona laughed, and this time they drank down to the suds from the cans they were holding. Ramona glanced at her left hand as she brought it back down to rest on her leg. And for the first time in a long time, the absence of her ring didn't feel like an absence at all, just natural, like she was exactly where she was supposed to be.

The moment felt to Ramona like being on the cusp of something perhaps worthwhile—something to run toward and away from all at the same time.

JOAN IN MALIBU, OF COURSE . . .

FROM HER WINDOW IN THE SITTING WING OF HER UPSTAIRS study, Joan watched every moment of Ramona's entry into Jay's car. She was upended by the make and model of his transportation and became all the more suspicious that he was in fact a wolf with identified prey.

For all of Jay's morning classes, and all the requests to lower the music even just a few decibels, Joan never had the occasion to speak to Jay about anything personal or to inquire how he was in any way different from the multitude of nomadic surfers lingering about trying to make a quick dollar. She did wonder how it was possible that he continued to show up day in and day out in front of her home, drawing people to the place where she coveted and enjoyed her privacy. Privacy was an important right—she did not want to be observed (only paid attention to), and she most certainly did not want to be disturbed.

Joan was not entirely satisfied with how the dinner went at Geoffrey's. She'd been thrown off by Ramona's insistence on reopening the issue of the patrol and was frankly a little bit thrown off by her lingering suspicions. In her further efforts toward self-absolution, this evening Joan had hoped to spend with Ramona, perhaps ushering her to the Malibu Country Mart for some light shopping and Italian at that cute restaurant in the back corner. Possibly even nails or, if they could, get a late appointment for facials. Well, a facial for Ramona only, because Joan's regular gal was elsewhere and there was no way she was going to let a stranger disturb any part of her expertly crafted face. Joan did not expect having to contend with the likes of Jay for Ramona's time. How a surfing lesson turned into an evening was guaranteed cause for unsettled concern. With Joan's self-absolution hanging in the balance, she realized she needed to up the ante. It wasn't just about casual social gatherings. It was about big, substantive, meaningful moments, a moment that Joan would need to create.

With a sigh, Joan slipped into her linen slacks and thick knit sweater, her perfect attire for the glass of wine that she'd sip on her deck to catch the sunset dip into the farthest point of the ocean. In her kitchen she pulled down a glass for her already-open bottle of an over-crisp Sauvignon Blanc that someone had sent in a holiday gift basket.

The stillness and quiet in her home were unbearable, upsetting even. Because her mind filled all the space and time with worry. *Where did Jay take her? Did she not tell me because she found out about the stupid guard from the Sentry Patrol? Does Chelsea know Ramona's with Jay? Did she warn her?* And when the thoughts would not still, Joan pulled out her phone. She would send messages to Chelsea:

JOAN: Did Ramona tell U she's spending time with Jay?

And to her children:

JOAN: Do you want cake or pie for Christmas dinner, or both?

And then another message to her children because thinking of dessert made her think of dinner and all of a sudden, she wondered:

> **JOAN:** Should we really have lamb this year?
> Or the roast like last year?

And, finally, frustrated because no one replied, Joan sent Chelsea a message just to be certain that she'd seen her last message:

> **JOAN:** ???

Then she sat frozen. *Of course,* she thought. *Christmas. Christmas dinner.* Her memorable moment would be having Ramona at her own Christmas table, right there with her kids. Seated like family. With a slow, satisfied smile, Joan wrapped herself in her favorite cashmere blanket in her favorite spot on the couch in front of the television and hit the remote on her fireplace. With a refilled glass and a deepening sense of satisfaction, she decided to skip the deck and watch whatever it was on the Food Channel until she heard the sound of Ramona's return.

CHELSEA IN CHICAGO . . .

BY THE TIME CHELSEA SAW JOAN'S TEXT MESSAGE (AND SHE DID see it), and the one that followed moments later, she was already in a rideshare with Carlos pulling up to what looked like a luxury high-rise hotel, right on Wacker Drive, next to the Chicago River.

As Chelsea read Joan's words and exhaled a hard and long sigh of complete exasperation, the door was being opened on her side and Carlos's simultaneously. One attendant seemed to recognize Carlos with a "Hey, man!" and a loud double hand smack and hug between them.

When asked why he'd come on his day off, Carlos said, "Just showing a friend how we do it in the Chi." Chelsea smiled, recognizing herself as the "friend," and thanked the attendant who held her car door open. She rejoined Carlos as they walked through revolving doors into a well-appointed luxury lobby space, with marbled walls and elegant neutral furniture, accented by fresh flower arrangements and the customary decorations of Christmas.

"You work here?"

Leading the way to the elevator bank, Carlos turned back to reply. "Second job of three. Art by any means. You understand, right?" Chelsea nodded. But she didn't understand or relate. Art to her had been a natural flow, something that she did when inspiration struck, and she would have done the same whether or not she was paid for it. It just so happened that she was paid for it, at one time handsomely. She looked at art now as less of a job and more as the one thing she knew how to do. She could never imagine working in multiple positions just to get the chance to paint.

"What's your job here?" she asked Carlos.

"You know . . . hospitality," he said. "Doorman sometimes, bellhop. Helping with bags is definitely the best tips, but we rotate." Because Chelsea had nothing to add and didn't want Carlos to think she wasn't worldly, or worse, was a sheltered dilettante, she said nothing, hoping he would elaborate or change the subject. When he didn't, she hoped she could change the subject herself.

Thinking about Joan's text mentioning Jay, as they waited for the elevator, Chelsea asked, "So, have you heard from Ramona? Is she having a good time?"

Carlos laughed. "Last I heard she was going surfing, taking yoga on the beach." He guided Chelsea to step into the elevator and tapped the button for the top floor.

"Glad to hear it." Even as she spoke, Chelsea felt her body relax. If Ramona was hanging out with Jay, that meant she wasn't with Joan. Even for Chelsea, Joan was best experienced in small doses. But now her involvement, her probing had gone too far, and Chelsea expressed that frustration to Carlos.

"I just got a text from my neighbor who was worried after the Sentry Patrol and everything whether Ramona was having a good time," she said.

Carlos's face wrinkled, and his head cocked to one side. "How'd the neighbor know?"

"Know what?" Chelsea asked, genuinely confused.

"About what happened . . . the Sentry Patrol."

Chelsea felt her breath catch in her throat. *Shit.* She'd need a quick recovery. "This . . . is a neighbor I spoke to about the incident." Chelsea tried to keep her voice even as she told a half-lie and a half-truth. Right away she felt guilty for not being honest. But it was just two more days to let this play out. Joan was harmless, really. And if Carlos knew that Chelsea had known this entire time who'd called the patrol on Ramona, that would be the end of everything. She just knew it, and selfishly, he wasn't another someone she was ready to let go of, not like this.

The elevator doors opened into an overwhelming hallway of entryways, releasing the air of silence between them. For the moment, Carlos seemed to have completely dropped his earlier line of questioning once he took her hand in his. Their palms touching instantly activated her base chemistry. That small fire that Carlos lit started to burn hotter. She was relieved that Carlos shifted his attention to the path ahead. Although each door ahead was numbered, it was impossible to tell them apart.

"This way," he said, leading her down the long hallway, and pulled out a plastic key card from his pocket. She wondered if they would relive the previous night in a new locale. A hotel room would be nice—sexy and glamorous. When they reached the door at the end of the hallway, Carlos opened it to a spacious and modern lounge. It was tastefully appointed, like a contemporary in-home library, if the home was a penthouse at the top of a major city, and if the single room was meant to seat a hundred people.

All of the walls were windows, from the ceiling to the floor. The sofas were plush caramel leather. The low-slung tables had drinks upon them, and the din of the room was clearly conversation between people who liked each other's company. Chelsea shifted her attention to the spectacular view and finally understood what Carlos wanted her to see. As they turned to the left, Chelsea could see the nighttime skyline of Chicago through the far window, the lights of the holiday, along the winding river, all the way to the inlet to Lake Michigan. She gasped and covered her mouth. It was beautiful, so overwhelmingly gorgeous to see, especially since Carlos was still holding her other hand. So inside, she was lit up, with joy as well as a growing feeling of apprehension. She was sure now—the painting she'd started of Carlos would be one of her best.

RAMONA AT DOCKWEILER BEACH . . .

When the warmth of the firepit started to dwindle, so did the crowd, winding down the festivities of the bonfire. Then, it was that awkward time of the night—still early enough to want just one more drink, and late enough that the options to fulfill that desire were slim. Ramona didn't want to go home, but with caution, she wondered how close she should get to Jay. They'd shared so much, and she felt so open. The two of them, Ramona and Jay, walked slowly back to the car, quietly and clearly in the space of not quite knowing what to say to each other. Neither wanted to speak their desire or knew what to do to be close without having the excuse of the chill, needing to be closer to the fire, or to have fingers graze one another handing off a fresh can of beer. But Ramona was quite used to being torn in this way. She was always in a battle between what she wanted and something else, whether unaware of it or simply used to letting go of the former. She was subscribed to doing what ought to be done, rather than following her feelings, like *these* feelings, and going the distance. While they walked, Ramona was certainly quiet because she couldn't summon the skill of saying what she wanted (or think of what to say to get it).

In the car, Jay hesitated at the ignition button. Just a few seconds' pause, but Ramona noticed.

"What?" she asked.

"Um . . . I was just thinking . . ." Jay said slowly, clearly searching for his own words.

"Okay, I'm in," Ramona said.

"But you don't know what I was going to say." Jay sounded confused. Blind trust is an unusual thing. But that's what was in Ramona's voice—she was agreeing. She wanted to go, somewhere, anywhere, else. Just one time to be free of the *oughts*.

"I didn't need to," she said.

"Okay, then." Jay started the car.

Ramona did want to ask where they were going, but she did not. She felt crazy, like she was doing something wrong. Whatever it was in Jay's mind would take her somewhere new. Wasn't that now what she wanted? All Ramona needed was a glimpse of another self that she could become, one she wouldn't dare imagine. But could she feel safe within that idea, as if a new path and the unknown didn't always lead to failure? Perhaps *that* was the opposite of what she'd always been taught.

The car retraced the path along the shoreline, on their left now. The moon had replaced the sun. It was an entirely new world they'd never been to, this nighttime place. Ramona recognized being on the Pacific Coast Highway again, but at this time, rather than the pastels of sunset, the moon shone a bright silver strip along a still midnight-blue expanse of glistening water. Even with the dotting of lights from homes along the coast and up the distant hillside, the ocean seemed endless. She felt as wild and free as the air that whirled in through the windows, lifting up everything in the car—the loose parts of her blouse, stray papers, her twists even—winding through her hair, whipping in and out, echoing the speed of the car as they passed through the curves of the road.

Although she'd only come that way a few times, Ramona recognized the point at which they were nearing the area of Chelsea's house on the PCH. It was after the ocean disappeared behind the beachfront homes, gates, and enclaves, when she could no longer see the water but for tiny glimpses in sparse and narrow open spaces in between. Jay's car started to slow down and then roll to a stop. Ramona could identify Chelsea's house just down the way, on the other side of Joan's. But why were they stopping here? It was just a garage, and next to it, a low retaining wall, so low she could actually see the ocean behind it. The wall was covered by foliage and seemed to be supporting an anemic palm tree that leaned against it as if the tree itself were tired.

"Where's this?" Ramona tried not to let panic swell in her body. She trusted Jay, she reminded herself.

"My house," Jay said.

"A garage?"

Jay laughed. "That's *the* garage." He turned to look at Ramona. The sincerity in his eyes disarmed her. "You want to come in? Have another beer?" Other than anger, there is only one thing stronger than fear—curiosity. And of the latter, Ramona's had been sufficiently piqued.

"So, you bought the house on the beach . . ." As Ramona spoke, she processed. The pieces of Jay's story began to connect for her.

"Yeah . . ." Jay turned to her with a look of relaxed confidence. The explanation was before her eyes. Knowing the background of it, inside, Ramona felt a rising swell of pride for Jay. A smile began to stretch across her face, thinking through the paces of what he'd done. And when she turned to look at the garage—or rather, the house—the meaning was reflected there, and momentarily, it became the most interesting house that she'd ever seen.

As it turned out, however, once they exited the car, the look of the place from the roadside was deceiving. The two of them entered a white shiplap door opening that had been hidden by the sagging tree. And behind the door were wooden stairs that ran alongside a hillside cottage attached to the garage.

"This is my rental unit, so not just *any* house on the beach. One that earns its own tax money." Jay pointed to the cottage. And then turning ahead, he said, "And *this* is my house."

At the landing of the stairs, ahead of them was a dark door, green perhaps, which was indeed in the middle of a long, single-story home. The door was opened by Jay to reveal a much larger version of Chelsea's living room, but with a freestanding Malm fireplace, with rustic wooden floors and wood slat ceilings with large support beams pulling your eye toward the only thing that truly mattered in that room in spite of its delights—the spectacular view of the moonlit ocean, majestic, dark, and dancing in the distance, rolling, sparkling, and duly hypnotic. Ramona was enchanted and speechless.

"Make yourself comfortable," Jay said, as he headed around the corner, leaving Ramona alone in the living area. "Bathroom is on the left," she heard him say through a wall. Having some more time with his space, it felt warm, but with a clear sense that he lived there without children, and without the vestiges of a feminine attention to detail. No accent pillows on the sofa, no family pictures around or on the walls, no small tables or items of décor that were more than functional, spare for a few large plants that actually looked pretty healthy. "Want to try something?" he called out from behind the wall to her right. He was clinking glasses, opening and closing cabinets and what sounded like a refrigerator door. Under regular circumstances, this would be normal. But Ramona's heart was racing. Not from fear, but with anticipation and the delicious taste of doing something wrong, something that felt forbidden. It was the rush of challenging herself, similar to what she felt on the water, but deeper this time, different, richer, more defiant.

"Sure," she said, and took his invitation as her cue to look around. She walked toward the windows and decided to go left. She crossed through a partially open sliding door into a small bedroom, but with its own wall of windows exposing the entire space to the ocean. The smell of lemongrass and the sparse décor made her feel like she'd entered a hotel suite. On the other side of the broad, king-size (and neatly made-up) bed was a bathroom of all wood and marble and glass, like a spa, but again few embellishments—no second toothbrush, no flowery shampoo.

Feeling somewhat relieved and still curious, she headed back into the living area and farther along the wall of windows to find Jay behind a divider in a small but fancy chef's kitchen. Beside a hulking cooking range and industrial broiler, he was popping open a cap on a large bottle.

"Here, smell this." Jay brought the bottle over to Ramona's nose, allowing her to inhale the fragrance of its headspace. It looked like wine, but she smelled cinnamon and coffee, and a dark mineral richness that wasn't of grapes. "It's an imperial porter stout," he said, smiling at her reaction. "Only made seasonally . . . for this time of year." He poured the dark syrupy liquid, revealing its effervescence, which Ramona did not expect. "Cheers." He handed her a glass and then brought his own up to tilt in her direction. "Happy Holidays."

"Happy Holidays." Ramona let the liquid, such a rich color in the moonlight, meet her lips. The first flavor that reached her tongue was cinnamon. And then coffee, that slightly bitter bite that she recognized from her morning routine, but that felt different in this elixir. She tasted a body that was syrupy like grapes perhaps, but more reminiscent of maple with a delicious finish of espresso. It was sumptuous. "This is a beer?" she asked with an air of surprise.

With his head still tilted down a bit toward his glass, a slow smile stretched across Jay's face. He seemed to appreciate Ramona's question and perked up slightly in answering it. "Technically, yes, but a sipping one. Think of it like wine but be careful . . ." Ramona raised an eyebrow at him. "It has the proof of a port or sherry. Too many of these and you'll sleep through Christmas."

"Sleeping through Christmas isn't the worst idea . . ." Ramona's mind was back in Chicago now, thinking of her mother and the Christmas Eve festivities that she'd come all the way to the end of the world to avoid. As she reflected, Jay ushered them to seats on the sofa facing the view of the ocean. Ramona sat and pulled herself back into the present, back to a focus on Jay. "So, someone snaked you in the water, and then you bought this." As she spoke, she turned her head to look all around at the surroundings, impressive for sure, just enough—an unmistakably gorgeous view of the ocean with its silver streak of moonlight and all of its changing moods. "It's really nice." She made it a point to meet his eyes, to show him her sincerity, and was surprised to find him so intently looking at her. In the space between them, Ramona's words sat in the still air, as her breathing became more shallow and her lips parted just slightly, not to speak, but to be met . . . with a kiss. It was what the energy of the moment called for, undeniably so. Carried by the sipping, savoring of tastes, both of them sitting with bronze-brown skin illuminated—sun-kissed from the day and moonlit in the evening—neither spoke for quite some while. It was a slowness uncommon to ordinary conversation. A magic of stillness, of time to consider, to think and to feel. Finally, Jay did break the silence.

"This is a great house," he said, seeming to still be considering his words and actions. "This place saved me." Jay lifted his free hand to run it across his head. His arm landed on the back of the sofa, near Ramona's shoulder. She began to wish it were closer, wanting to be touched by him, and so imagining it even as he continued with his story. "When I was harassed at that break, how that guy tried to take from me my right to be there, to think that he could intimidate me . . . my first inclination . . . was to buy the whole damn strip of houses. Every single one available." He seemed to have a small laugh to himself reflecting on it. Ramona shifted on the couch to fully face him as he continued, moving just a bit closer. She didn't want to miss a single one of his words. "But, on that trip," Jay continued, "I drove up the shore, found an outcropping of rocks, and just sat and looked out at the ocean—I looked for myself out there, my *true* self. What did *I* want? I tried to visualize what I dreamed my life to look like, my days to be, the choices I'd have, the things I'd explore or pursue. And so, I realized quickly that buying up land would have proved a point, but it wasn't the point. I'd still be owned if I did that, driven by someone else's impression of me. That was a choice that would force me to keep running, just to keep up." Jay lifted his head to look around. The arm that lay across the back of the sofa lifted in quick gestures. "So, I picked *this* house. This *particular* house. This was the house of having enough . . . for *me*." As he finished speaking, Jay brought his hand down again.

With Jay's body closer, Ramona listened to him even more intently. She wondered also what his experience would be like for someone else. Someone who could not just buy their way out of an insult or plant a house-size flag in the sand.

"And did buying the house make it easier to surf?" she asked.

Jay seemed startled to have been asked the question. Ramona could see the clouds of memories pass across his face in his expressions. Some seeming good, then seeming bad—the range of emotions read in his features as easily as the coming of rain, or a sunny day. She could see the pain and the triumph play out, even before he spoke. But then, he finally did.

"It's a process to surf. An hour just to arrange all my gear—wetsuit, board harnessed to the rack on my car, water in a bottle, supplies in a bag. There were days, with all that done, I'd pull up to park at the beach but then turn the ignition off and sit . . . just sit." Jay's gaze turned to the ocean, in front of them, deep and rolling in darkest blues now. "And I couldn't get out of the car—" Ramona felt the shift of energy, the moment before the rain falls, the heaviness in the air. But Jay swiped at his face quickly and pulled his glass forward to take a sip, lowering it again to sit on his leg. "And then, I'd think, Who am I? What am I doing out here? Guys like me don't surf—"

"That's what I thought too, about being Black," Ramona said.

"You shouldn't have to feel that way," Jay said, turning to look at her quickly, and then back to the ocean again as if to retrieve his thoughts from there. "There's only so much you can take, you know? To have to face nature—all *raw* power and energy . . . You don't know whether she'll be with you or against you that day. And then, to have *people*, who should be so full of joy . . . instead full of the purest energy of something opposite. Of anger, of violence. And *why?* Triggered just by my presence in the water 'cause I'm brown? Or 'cause I don't seem *familiar?* The idea of facing both . . . some days it was too much."

For Ramona, Jay's words might have been describing what it felt like for her to go to work, or to school when she was younger. Or to walk around sometimes in stores and be followed, or drive with concerns about being stopped, or harassed. Even to show up as her full self, with her big crinkly hair, or round features, or loud colors, and be misunderstood. To arrive in Malibu, on vacation, and to still be policed. It was why Ramona wanted to leave, to go back home, even though she needed to stay. Yes . . . it was all too much.

"I'd be there, ready to surf," Jay continued. "But I couldn't get over the feeling that I'd have to take my place. I'd have to actually *take my place* at that break. On that beach, in the lineup, on that wave. So, I started taking it. Pushing out the noise." He turned to look at Ramona, waiting until their eyes met before he continued. "It's made me a better surfer because I've had to be. I realized as long as I kept showing up, and as long as I got better—my skills and determination that came from that, they couldn't have. Because they didn't have to work so hard for it. And *that* . . . nobody can take away."

Nobody can take that away . . . Ramona's thoughts echoed Jay's words. The cinnamon elixir had relaxed her, and the ocean seduced her with its dance. The air was charged and full with the energy of Jay's transparency. Together they sat in the quiet space of a tender wound, one they both shared. In vulnerability, as it felt right, she reached for his hand and pulled it down to her. On the sofa, in the narrow space between them, their fingers connected, wove together, until they were holding hands, looking out at the sea. And as if on a raft, the two of them, Ramona and Vijay, floated in the ethereal silence. And there was no self-consciousness there, no second guessing, just the purest language of touch and the slow motion of their breathing. All else was understood.

"Can I see you tomorrow?" he asked.

Ramona answered yes.

DECEMBER 24

• ● ○

CHELSEA IN CHICAGO . . .

CHELSEA WOKE UP IN RAMONA'S BED AGAIN IN A MESS OF RUM-pled sheets, alone too, but this time that was really the least of her concerns. Last night, in the midst of everything she wanted to happen with Carlos, and perhaps more, she'd almost let her secret slip. And it wasn't even her secret, truly, it was Joan's. And it was working its way out of her like a splinter. When she finally checked her phone from the prior evening, because literally no one, not even Helena, should have been looking to get in touch, she saw the flurry of texts from Joan—obsessing over Ramona as if she'd lost her own child in a shopping mall. And for certain, it wasn't Ramona spending time with Jay that Chelsea was worried about.

By almost telling the truth, Chelsea had sampled the feel-ing of it, making it much harder to deny what was the right thing to do. Maybe she'd never meet Ramona, but the more involved she became with Carlos, the more entangled, the more intimate, the more exposed, naked even, the more she felt guilty about hiding from him what she knew. Ramona was like his sister; he'd said it often. And he'd want to protect his sister from someone who'd nearly ruined her trip, or worse. *If not for the laughable impotence of the neighborhood Sentry Patrol in Malibu,* Chelsea thought. *At least Joan didn't call the real cops.*

At some point in the night, after her view from the top of the town and the vibes that somehow led to kissing Carlos (again) and then a return to Ramona's bed, before she woke, as he said he would, Carlos slipped out. But this time, as Chelsea smiled, knowing he hadn't seen any more of her work in progress—the painting now so blatantly of him, there'd be no denying it. This time, she'd taken much care to put everything away, just in case. What else could make her eagerness so obvious, so predictable? She'd wanted to ask what the rule was about, why he made the declaration in the first place—that he wouldn't stay, like he was trying to push her away. Like he'd need to. With only two more days ahead in Chicago, she was leaving anyway. Perhaps it was his honesty that drew her to him. And perhaps it was her dishonesty that would finally pull him away—regardless, the guilt seemed to be getting progressively worse.

For certain, in that very moment, before she went out for the day, before she started her last true day with the city of Chicago, she could have copped to it and done the right thing. She could have pulled out her phone, called Carlos, and simply said, *Hey, I was wrong.* She could have explained, *It was Joan who called the Sentry Patrol on Ramona, Joan who wanted to cover it up, and me who agreed not to say anything.* But the truth comes with certain consequences that Chelsea was afraid of. Because now, the dwindling time remaining to spend with Carlos simply seemed to matter deeply. At minimum, she'd need to complete her painting, but there was some newly awakened part of herself that also felt very much unfinished.

At least she had no need to wonder when she'd be seeing Carlos again. This evening was the trip around the world that Mrs. Tucker promised for Christmas Eve, and Chelsea was looking forward to it more than she ever imagined that she would. She had only a few more preparations left to sort. As Chelsea made herself ready to head outside—black coat, hot-pink gloves, hat, and hand warmers—she realized how quickly she'd learned to bundle up appropriately for a Chicago winter. Cold weather would do that, make you learn quickly. And so, with only a few short hours remaining in the shopping day on Christmas Eve, Chelsea was out the door on a mission downtown. She mastered the Red Line on the L train, anticipating its screeching arrival and feeling its rumble underneath her seat as she rode it south to the stop right next to Millennium Park. She knew it best and only from television when it served as a world stage on a historic election night. And it was spectacular then, but the Christmas version was entirely different, especially in person.

It was as if the city itself were alive and whispering to her the sights and sounds of the season. Ramona's welcome note had said, *And if you like ice skating, you'll love the rink at Millennium Park. It's right next to the big sculpture.* The giant silver-pebble art piece was as big as the trees and visible from the sidewalk as Chelsea approached. Reflecting the lights of the decorations nearby, it was an irresistible setting and close enough to brave the cold just for a few pictures. Perhaps it too would be something she'd paint one day.

At the rink, Chelsea watched the ice skaters make their organized circles, watched those who were learning slip and fall. One person who noticed her waved her over with a gesture and shouted, "Come join us!" She smiled and waved back instead, and then snapped a few photos, including a somewhat silly selfie, that would suffice for a souvenir of the place.

She walked down Washington Street past the old Macy's, which took up an entire city block, all the way until she reached the twinkling lights at the edge of the bustling Christkindlmarket— a German reference to the entity who was meant to bring gifts to children on Christmas Eve. Chelsea had less than an hour to find a gift before the entire outdoor market closed for the season. That meant she couldn't be distracted by the smells of rich cinnamon and roasting nuts or the savory aroma of the German sausages cooking. In part because of the time, but also the cold, she walked briskly through the miniature village of wooden vendor booths resembling small Bavarian-style homes. Their red-and-white-striped gable roofs were decorated for the season with strung lights hanging at the edges like icicles. It was a perfect place for the theme of Mrs. Tucker's holiday party, bringing all the world straight to a single family's house on the city's South Side. With a shiver, Chelsea stopped at a stall to make a quick purchase of a ready-made hot chocolate, savoring the aroma and warmth in her hand. Moving again, en masse with the crowd, Chelsea sipped and browsed until she came across a carefully decorated beer stein that she chose as a gift. And as her contribution to the potluck, a few steps down, she purchased a bottle of spiced glühwein and tucked it in her bag.

All that was left was to make it back to Ramona's. She savored the last sips of her too-quickly-cooled hot chocolate and tossed it in the bin just as she felt the vibration of her phone in her pocket. She stuffed a gloved hand in to retrieve it, rooting around awkwardly like trying to grasp a slippery fish.

"Hi, Helena," she said, after stabbing at the screen to answer.

"Happy Christmas, Chelsea dear!" Helena's voice rang out spiritedly from the earpiece. It was almost contagious, the merriment she heard, and it was a welcome accompaniment on her return. "I trust the holiday is proceeding better than you thought."

Chelsea debated what she was going to tell Helena, as there was so much. With days left and a bit of hope, she wondered if this trip could make a difference in the circumstances that had brought her here. And so, she decided that she would share with Helena what was most important to Helena.

"It's going well. I'm painting again."

"Well, darling, that's fabulous! Do tell, is it another *Heartbreak*, perhaps?"

And Chelsea thought about that. Of course, Helena would wish for the lightning in a bottle. But the word itself did strike a pang in Chelsea's gut, a sharp stab of apprehension, remembering the feelings from heartbreak that she'd barely managed to bury, and how long it took such wounds, once cut, to heal. That she could once again lose something that mattered, perhaps that was the charm of it and the risk. Maybe this trip would lead to a heartbreak, one anew with Carlos. She'd have to leave soon and lose him in a million possible ways—to distance and broken promises to call and visit. Yes, perhaps, yes, another heartbreak.

"I could . . . see that," she said. "I'll be at my best again, I think . . . very soon."

"That's perfect, then." The quiet on Helena's end of the call sounded like hesitation. In the silence, Chelsea could hear the unsaid, what Helena seemed unsure of asking. "And . . . you're . . . all right?" she said finally, hopefully, softly, a true question being asked in earnest.

Chelsea inhaled sharply; the cold air stung its way through her nostrils and down her throat, all the way into her lungs. She was awake, aware, and present. Because in that moment, with all the promise of the evening ahead, the answer was obvious.

"Everything's wonderful," she replied and continued her walk underneath the darkening skies.

JOAN IN MALIBU . . .

JOAN RARELY USED THE TRIPOD-MOUNTED BINOCULARS IN HER upper living room. Like the bronze nautical scope in the far corner, the large binocular apparatus situated against the windows was meant for more decorative purposes—to highlight the proximity to the ocean. Inside her house, anywhere facing west, you'd be looking at the majestic expanse of the Pacific—by design. At high tide, when the water swept in to cover the concrete piles beneath her home, the sea became her backyard. The scope was helpful then, to watch the sailboats in the distance, or the birds—to tell the difference between a brown pelican and a double-crested cormorant perhaps, or to turn it upward at nighttime to figure out whether she was viewing a star or a planet as a glowing orb in the sky. But this day, Joan dragged the heavy rig across her custom sixteen-foot Pasargad rug and placed it in the opposite corner of the room, incidentally next to the fireplace, and specifically pointed directly at Chelsea's place next door.

She'd frustrated herself the night prior by falling asleep on her sofa, too sleepy from the wine she drank to properly wait up for Ramona's return. This left the execution of her newly hatched plan to secure Ramona's presence at Christmas hanging in the balance. Already it was Christmas Eve, and there was no time to waste. Fully alert and espresso-caffeinated, she waited to ensure she caught a glimpse of her new neighbor. Now, if you asked in that moment, *What in the hell are you doing, Joan?*—for example, as a regular observer might at least think to say—she would tell you that she just felt . . . responsible. She felt responsible for Ramona. She wouldn't be able to tell you why, however, not even with any of the words of her extensive vocabulary. Instead, she'd see flashes in her mind of moments past, like her mother in her youth, speaking with the other neighborhood mothers about "those people" and whether they'd be moving in. And she'd think of the moment she moved in here in Malibu and was given the number of the private patrol, told to call if she saw or heard anything unusual or suspicious. *Anything.* And that made her feel safe. Safety was so important; concern was as much a personal virtue as vigilance was. And vigilance . . . required observation and surveillance.

Chelsea's home was less than a third of the size of Joan's, without a lot of options for where a person inside there could be. From her elevated position through her scopes, Joan had a full view of the next-door deck and side window of Chelsea's primary bedroom that happened to face Joan's house. If the bedroom blinds were closed, as they usually were when Chelsea was there, Joan couldn't see a thing on the inside. But Ramona as a resident seemed to enjoy more of the morning sunlight. The opening in the blinds didn't show Joan much, but she could see movement that would tell her Ramona was there, and *not* with Jay.

As soon as she saw a glimpse of what she was looking for, or rather whom, Joan was ready to spring into action, but this time, much differently than the inauspicious start to Ramona's stay. This morning, her plan was to make it to Ramona before Jay did, invite her to brunch today, and at the perfect moment, invite her to Christmas tomorrow. It'd be official then, having Ramona share a table with her and her kids, eating the lamb Joan prepared (or, still, possibly the roast?), just like part of the family, fully accepted, because Joan most surely accepted all, loved all people no matter what they looked like, or who they loved, or how they identified—except Jay. She did not love Jay (never did), or her ex-husband, David, for that matter (not anymore), and most certainly not that reprehensible woman-child that David married.

Joan had committed to standing there as long as it took, binoculars against the window, waiting for any sign to pounce. At least, until she got distracted. Her phone rang, confirming a pickup for one of the gifts she ordered, and while dealing with the minor hassle of it all, she realized that, more than anything, she really needed a second cup of coffee. The second cup of coffee led to her remembering she needed to brush her teeth again to preserve her whitening job, but then the closet was open next to the bathroom, beckoning for her attention. In her closet there was the matter of locating her Chanel snow boots for her January trip to Aspen, which she found just as she remembered *again* that she was meant to be checking on Ramona. And having missed the opportunity with her spyglass—

now all but entirely forgotten on her upper level—she decided that she would just head over next door and ring the bell.

Joan walked the twenty-five feet down her driveway, out of her gate, and into the quaint white pickets of the entrance to Chelsea's little beach cottage. When she rang the doorbell and waited, she heard shuffling on the inside, which she was sure was Ramona. And she hoped to goodness (for Ramona's sake, of course) she was alone.

"One second!" She heard the words in Ramona's voice called out from behind the door. And then a minute later it opened, pulled by a sleepy-looking Ramona leaning against the frame in a bedtime shorts set, crossing her arms around her chest. *She must be so relieved to see a friendly face,* Joan thought. And she figured, such relief likely rendered Ramona so happy that she was speechless, which was the explanation she provided herself for Ramona's lack of enthusiasm, or even a proper greeting. Of course, Joan could have alternatively thought that perhaps this woman, standing across from her, who she barely knew, was annoyed. That she was sleepy and irritated by yet another unannounced caller at her door. But Joan only created explanations that made her feel better, not worse. And so, accepting her preferred version of reality, she smoothed down the perfectly set waves along the sides of her middle part and adjusted her sunglasses with a smile.

"Good morning!" Joan threw the greeting at Ramona like a party popper, meant to explode the space between them with virtual cheer. When Ramona barely moved, Joan continued, shifting her gear up one notch. "I just wanted to drop by and invite you to brunch over at the Malibu Pier." Still nothing from Ramona, no sign of response, so Joan continued, knowing she needed to put a bit more fuel on the fire. "It's a tradition I used to have with my kids, but you know, they're in San Diego until tomorrow, so I thought it could be something to share with *you.*" It was just a tiny lie about her kids—they never did Christmas Eve brunch, but Joan felt like Ramona was on the verge of saying no. Most important, the *you* that Joan meant was the ultimate invitation—*You,* my new friend, Ramona. *You,* a person I've decided belongs here. *You,* who are so welcome you don't even know how welcome you are.

"Umm . . . now?" Ramona said after a long pause.

"Now." Joan smiled, trying her best to reach maximum hospitality. "Or in a bit, whichever works best for you, in case you need time to get ready." Joan smiled so big she felt her face stretch.

"Is it . . . fancy?" Ramona wiped her eyes and brought her hand up to her hair, patting . . . her . . . braids? Were those braids?

She'll probably want to tidy up, Joan thought. "Oh, no, dear, not fancy at all." Joan thought of the night at Geoffrey's when the two of them first dined together. What Joan had in mind was very different, café style, relaxed. Easier to talk, to open up. "Totally, totally casual," she said, and then couldn't believe she forgot to add the most important part. "And . . ." Joan could barely contain her excitement to share, "the owner is a Black woman!"

"Oh, how great," Ramona said flatly, squinting at Joan—the sun was coming up behind her from the east and making a rare winter appearance before the early afternoon. "I was up late, so kinda planned to sleep in."

Joan felt instantly deflated. And she chose to let it show. The same approach usually worked like a charm with her kids. "Oh . . . of course . . . I just thought that you might want to see Malibu Pier, and I definitely didn't mean to disturb your—"

"I . . . I can go—" Ramona replied, cutting her off. "Can you give me, like, an hour?"

Joan felt a sense of decisive victory. It was already an auspicious day. No sign of Jay, and Christmas would be hers.

•●°

ONE HOUR AND THIRTY MINUTES LATER, THE CAFÉ AT THE MALIBU
Pier was bustling with people and the extra twinkle of Christmas Eve morning. It was full of tourists (to Joan at least), and
very few of the regulars she recognized. But she managed to
snag a table by the water's edge, and she and Ramona waited
for their food orders that would replace the plastic number flag
planted upon the painted wooden slats of their tabletop.

"This is nice that you used to do this with your kids," Ramona said, settling into her seat on the white wooden bench.
The ocean behind them was relatively calm, lapping gently
against the weathered-white poles of the pier. The breeze was
light and refreshing, and the air smelled like the brine of the
sea. Even the sun was cooperating, lighting the day as perfectly
as any day of the summertime, having already burned off most
of the clouds from the sky. That was what Joan focused on,
rather than Ramona repeating the tiny little lie she told earlier,
or the fact that she'd now have to double down on it for the sake
of conversation.

"Christmas traditions are the best," Joan said. Now *that*,
that was true and a perfect setup as well. She didn't intend to
waste time getting to the point. "Do you have any traditions
with your family in Chicago?"

"Just my mother's Christmas Eve party," Ramona said.
"She always wanted to bring the entire world to our neighborhood, to remind us that we're all a part of something, of somewhere so much bigger."

"That sounds so . . . festive," Joan managed. But it was the
opening she'd hoped for. In a spur-of-the-moment decision,
picking up on Ramona's mention of Christmas Eve, thinking
of the risk of Jay and his greedy need for attention, she decided
to hedge her bets, leave nothing to chance, and invite Ramona

to her plans for the evening and then for Christmas as well. "I'm sure it wouldn't compare, but I'd love for you to come to my house, *tonight*. We could do a Christmas Eve at the water. Sit on the deck, watch the sunset . . . have some wine and chat—"

"I'm so sorry," Ramona cut her off. "I . . . already made plans."

Joan was shocked. "Oh?" And then her worst fears started to cloud her mind like a gray rainstorm over the sea. "With that *guy*, Jay?" She couldn't help herself.

To Joan, Ramona looked surprised. But *of course*, Joan knew. It was how men like Jay operated. Meet women on the beach, at work, strike up something under the guise of friendliness, and next thing she knows, she's taken advantage of and left for the next conquest. Something like this could ruin Ramona's trip. Her whole life even. But most important, it could ruin Joan's plan.

"Um-hum," Ramona said, only partially penetrating Joan's cascading thoughts.

"You know, Ramona, men like that . . . they . . . come to the beach for . . . *opportunities*. You wouldn't want to be one of those opportunities. You know what I'm saying?"

Ramona laughed. "Hardly," she said, chuckling through the entire word.

Ramona doesn't realize the threat, Joan thought. The danger of people like Jay; they could seep into your psyche, make you make decisions you'll regret later.

"Regrets can last a lifetime, that's what I would say to my daughter." Joan moved her hand so the server could set down her salad. She picked up her fork and held it like a pitchfork. "Not everyone can be trusted."

"That's for sure," Ramona said. "My first thought was that he might have been the person who called the patrol on me when I first got here. That's ridiculous, right? How would he? It could have been literally *anyone*. But then I realized that since it happened, I'd been wondering that about everyone. And if I kept doing that . . . well, I can't let that shape my entire trip, right? Imagine, looking at *everyone* like a suspect . . ."

Joan hesitated and felt her eyes widening behind her sunglasses. An accusation had just whizzed past her like a bullet, a narrow miss. Her breath caught in her throat. The mistaken identity and the call she'd made, the tiny little quite-harmless goof. It was almost impossible to imagine that the experience still bothered Ramona at all. *Why can't she just let this go?* Joan wondered silently. She seemed to be having such a wonderful time. But it wasn't an opportunity to waste.

"And you're sure he isn't?" Joan said, quickly gathering herself and channeling her best attempt at pure curiosity.

"I'm as sure about him as I am about you," Ramona said, laughing.

Joan thanked God for Botox, as she hoped her face registered no sign of a tell. She smiled quickly. *Ramona thought it was someone else.* Realizing this, Joan laughed too—just as someone would who was in on the joke.

"How much do you know about him?" Joan asked. And if someone perhaps asked, *Aren't you being a little nosy, Joan?* she would say that at the moment she was acting as a concerned friend. Because caring was concern, and concern required questions.

Ramona's eyebrows furrowed, as if she was confused. Joan continued to crunch upon her salad as if nothing at all was out of the ordinary. Finally, Ramona replied, "He's your neighbor, don't you know him?"

"He lives on the beach?" Joan almost spit out her arugula.

"Yeah, four houses down from you. You didn't know?"

Joan had absolutely no idea. And it was so confounding to her, perhaps the absolute last piece of information she'd expected to receive. *How?* and *Why?* and of course, the question of *Where did his money come from?* flooded her mind all at once.

But most of all, she didn't want to seem like a bad neighbor, or a person who didn't see people, or who couldn't see people correctly. But when she opened her mouth, there was nothing that would come out. And she tried again to the same effect. So, she did what she knew best to do, she got straight to the point of getting what she wanted.

"Well, then, it seems you're busy this evening, but what about Christmas, dear? You'll join us for dinner?"

Ramona looked confused. But that, Joan had anticipated. All that mattered now was whether she'd say yes. And in the seconds of Ramona's hesitation, Joan decided two things: that she would make the lamb *and* the roast, and that Jay had turned out to be a much more formidable opponent than she'd expected.

CHELSEA IN CHICAGO . . .

CHELSEA WATCHED THE CITYSCAPE OF CHICAGO PASS BY HER IN a blur. Just days ago, it was a completely unfamiliar place. Now, she almost felt like she knew where she was going. And in some way she did. She was headed to the Bronzeville area again, on Chicago's South Side, just like what Carlos said, close to the gallery they'd visited together.

Making an adjustment to the skirt of her dress, Chelsea watched the progress of her trip on the phone that rested in her lap. Melba Tucker's house was on East Forty-Eighth Place, east of the city's MLK Boulevard and just north of Washington Park. As Chelsea got closer, the neighborhood changed in wild swings, from carefully tended blocks to those that looked as if they'd been abandoned years ago. There seemed to be so much history reflected in the architecture, some preserved, some virtually ignored. The artist in her searched for the meaning in it. From time to time, when the car stopped for traffic, she pulled out her phone to take pictures of both the beauty and the blight.

When they finally came to a full stop, having arrived at the Tucker home, she was greeted by a stately greystone, narrow and elegant, with a façade of rough-cut large bricks. The door and accents on the bay window frame were black, and at the top of the three stories was a gable roof. Beyond an iron gate, the railing of the stairs leading up to the front door was woven with holiday lights, and large candles glowed in the first-story windows. Chelsea could see others walking up and could hear the sounds of merriment before she even managed to step out of the car onto the sidewalk.

"Have a great time," her driver called out. "I'm jealous." Chelsea smiled and thanked him as she shut the door. The air was brisk outside. Freezing. She adjusted her coat and the package containing her gift from the Christmas market and her glühwein potluck contribution. Two people in fur coats were entering ahead of her, reminding her of how far she'd also come from the ratty coat contraption she'd traveled with that would likely never stop dripping sand.

"Come in! Come in!" Chelsea heard Mrs. Tucker say, as the door in front of her opened. Chelsea walked forward quickly, crunching on snow and salt, in part because she was just so, so cold, and also so she wouldn't have to make a solo entrance. Melba greeted all her guests by name, including, "Chelsea, you made it!" in a version of genuine joy that made Chelsea feel immediately welcome. In the entryway, directly in front of her were a set of stairs along an exposed-brick wall, and to her left a room of all exposed-brick and wood, carved built-ins, and a fireplace that spoke of the original era of the house. There was so much charm in the décor, all warmth and family. All over the walls and on tables were pictures of people she'd seen in decorations at Ramona's place—Ramona and a younger Carlos; her brother; Ramona and her parents; Mrs. Tucker on her travels, in uniform and out, in pictures with her family and what seemed to be her colleagues.

Melba swirled Chelsea out of her coat, and someone swept it away before she could notice where it was going. But it made a momentous reveal—she was clad strikingly in a long strapless tartan-plaid dress with a serious poof in the skirt. The tartan was fitting for her own Scottish roots and happened to scream "Christmas" with its crisscrossing colors—traditionally red for the myrrh, the green for frankincense, and yellow was symbolic of gold.

"Don't you look pretty!" Melba pulled out a portion of Chelsea's skirt between them. "This is just gorgeous, just gorgeous!"

Chelsea's face stretched into a wide smile that reached all the way to her eyes. "Thank you—I tried to stay on theme," she said, relieved she didn't go with sparkles.

"Girl . . . you understood the assignment." Melba laughed, and Chelsea savored the words like music. "Come, make yourself at home. Drinks are on the table just here." Melba pointed to a long table to her left. "And appetizers and food are here on this table." Chelsea's attention was directed to a long table farther back in the room, surprising her by how deep the narrow-looking house actually was. Chelsea offered up her gift and alcohol contribution, which was again swept away by someone wearing a catering uniform. "My cousin," Melba said, smiling. "She's in culinary school, so I guess that makes me her biggest client so far . . . but not for long." Melba was beaming with the pride of an elder, which you could easily tell contributed a great deal to a person's well-being. Her spirit of mothering was expansive, room filling. Chelsea wanted to breathe it in like an intoxicating fragrance. Melba thanked her with a hug and then shooed her toward the other guests.

As Chelsea walked forward, she became increasingly conscious of being a stranger here, and that Melba Tucker was the only person she knew in the room. There weren't many people there, and Carlos wasn't due until after his overtime shift.

Chelsea, looking around for anyone else familiar, for anyone else with whom she might have something in common, perceived that she was the only white person in the room, a feeling she'd dealt with before, in Bronzeville with Carlos. Again here, everyone else was a brown of some sort, but *so what?* Chelsea thought and resolved to be comfortable. She reminded herself that she liked her tartan dress, and found delight in appreciating the gorgeous bursts of color around her. She wasn't alone, or isolated either, but rather surrounded by other people and the rousing sounds of their merriment. Taking a deep breath, similar to the ones that calmed her nerves, she started to look for what more there was in common. The exercise brought immediate relaxation and interest. Some had on elaborate and colorful African attire, big and formfitting. There was a woman wearing a sari and another in a Hawaiian-style dress. She felt a bit of a kinship with a darker-skinned man in a bright-red plaid suit jacket and matching red suede shoes.

The drinks table was its own marvel. There were bottles of French Bordeaux and Spanish Riojas and Tempranillos, and to Chelsea's surprise she hadn't brought the only bottle of glühwein—there were at least two more. There were beers from everywhere, ranging from Mexico to Austria to Michigan. There was vodka and liqueurs, Italian aperitivos like Montenegro and Aperol. And Ethiopian honey wine alongside sake and a bottle of what looked like peppermint schnapps. It was a world tour right on that table and a perfect place to start for Chelsea. She poured herself a basic concoction of vodka and cranberry and turned in the direction of a "nice dress" compliment that seemed to come from behind her. There was a woman in a dress of gorgeous Ankara cloth, bright and fitted around her curves. Thankful for an opening to socialize, Chelsea returned the compliment and asked enough questions to start a conversation.

Unfortunately, however, as much as she wanted to, she couldn't entirely focus. Not on what the woman next to her was saying, nor the exact words she was using to say it. Every time the door opened, her attention went there and there alone, looking for Carlos. When he did finally appear in the doorway, Chelsea, who had been enjoying perfectly interesting banter, felt like her whole world had lit up, a Christmas tree with the lights on, bringing a glow to the entire room.

"Heeeyyy!" Carlos walked into the room with his arms up as if he owned the place. "Merry Christmas, y'all!" His gloved hands held bottles and bags, and he moved quickly through the same entry ritual as Chelsea had. Watching him, her heart rate started to increase, her breathing became that of excitement, anticipation. When his eyes met hers, finally, she could relax. Away from everything she knew, everyone familiar, she felt at home.

RAMONA IN MALIBU . . .

IN THE FIRST YEAR EVER THAT SHE'D MISS HER MOTHER'S CHRIST-mas Eve party, Ramona instead looked out upon the ocean from Chelsea's windows, preparing for a new type of adventure. It was the third day in a row that she'd spend with Jay, a detail that was not lost upon her. Thankfully, in the way that their plans seemed to continually evolve, it was simply a matter of saying yes. It was always just yes, simply yes. Any denial of the building attraction she felt was becoming increasingly difficult, especially since it was more like a natural side effect of a string of delightful interactions.

Given Ramona's reasons for this trip, companionship was unexpected. Usually for Ramona, physical attraction came first, as it had for her and Malik. But that had ended, hadn't it? This new awakening of feelings, of interest sparked by Jay, left Ramona feeling slightly conflicted. True, she hadn't heard from Malik in weeks, a detail that she used to care about, or rather obsess about. Only now, in a matter of days, she'd essentially stopped thinking about him. When she thought toward her future, she envisioned her own dreams. And lately, there was no Malik in anything she imagined. She'd even stopped dreaming about her wedding. These days, she was thinking about surfing and wondering what else she could do with her body if she took more possession of it, even if that meant just to rest.

And while Ramona—the daughter of two working-class South Side parents, who made her way to the Gold Coast—was never one to give up on a dream, or a person, or anything really, it was almost impossible to deny that the version of life involving her and Malik together seemed to have run its course. And what made her smile, just a bit, and then fill with dread, was that she didn't want to deny it any longer. But then, on the other side of letting Malik go were the questions, both big and small, that Ramona feared the most. Like, *How could a person choose and then un-choose her?* And *How could he want to get married and then walk away so easily?* And *Did he want the ring back?* Or even, *Did she want to give it back?* Most of all, perhaps the deepest concern, she wondered whether she'd ever find love again because *What if, somehow, it was all her fault?*

Ramona sighed and settled deeper into the seat. *Tonight,* she reminded herself, *Chicago is a world away.* Her mother had already sent pictures of the party—the decoration in progress. *Look at the lights!!* she wrote in her text, attaching an image of the fully decorated Christmas tree and the candles she always placed in the front windows. She sent pictures of feast preparations, the salmon going into the oven and the pounds of crab legs set to boil—a true annual splurge. She sent pictures of the early guests, and Ramona caught a glimpse of a single white person among a growing sea of brown faces, someone she'd seen before, with unmistakable bright red hair and this time wearing a long plaid dress. It was the same person she'd seen in paintings around the house here. *Cute,* she thought, recognizing Chelsea. And then realizing with mounting panic that was *Chelsea* . . . at her mother's house. What was she doing there? And what if she let something slip about her being in Malibu alone? Ramona quickly texted a message to Carlos.

RAMONA: What's Chelsea doing at Ma's party? Can you make sure she doesn't say anything about me here alone?

Ramona waited, relieved to see the three dots appear.

CARLOS: Merry Christmas to you too.

And then three dots again and another message from Carlos.

CARLOS: All good, don't worry. I'm on my way there had to get that double time pay.

RAMONA: You play too much.

And then her finger hovered over the send button. Realizing she'd been holding her breath, she let out a long exhale and added:

RAMONA: Merry Christmas.

She finally hit send. She never expected that Chelsea as a houseguest would weave her way into a Tucker Christmas Eve, but her mother was good at finding anyone who needed the warmth of family. If she could help it, she'd never let so much as a stranger spend the holidays alone. And someone staying at Ramona's house? Never. If her mother caught wind, it'd be like they were family all along.

Ramona imagined Melba just stopping by to see if Chelsea had plans. To make sure that even a stranger felt welcome and anything but alone in Chicago at Christmas. *Maybe Joan was like that as well,* Ramona thought, remembering her invitation made over lunch. "You'll join us for dinner?" Joan asked at the pier. Ramona felt guilty for not giving a commitment, and still felt somewhat guilty now. Put simply, something about Joan made Ramona uneasy. For all the attention, and hospitality, for all the baked goods and fancy invitations, something just didn't feel . . . genuine. And because Ramona couldn't make sense of it, she'd purposely held herself back. Just maybe besides, a small part of her wanted to see Jay instead. So, with great difficulty, she'd asked Joan if she could let her know tomorrow for certain. But now, thinking of her mother, Ramona decided she'd make it a point to go. And why not? Joan had taken such care, just like Ramona's mother would, to invite her out, to make her feel welcome. Now, after all that had happened, with only the evening and one day left in her trip, Ramona was making an effort to put the early incident of her arrival behind her. At least, she was trying to forget about it, as if it hadn't happened—except, it had.

Ramona was enjoying her trip, but every time she left Chelsea's house, she still checked the door three times just to make sure she could get back in. She made sure she had the reservation confirmation available and had added Helena—the rental contact—to her Favorites list, just in case. She kept the key in the top back pocket of her purse and reached her fingers for it before she left, every time. And, despite what she'd said to Joan, even as she tried not to, she still looked at everyone she encountered with just that tiny residual bit of suspicion that kept her disconnected in a way that perhaps she was already too used to. Like nowhere in the world belonged to her, that every place was somewhere she didn't belong. That there was nowhere she could be free—except on the water. On the waves, in that surf, on the board. The ocean met her as it did anyone else, and that was an experience that she did not get to have on land.

•

JAY'S ARRIVAL WAS A KNOCK ON THE DOOR, WHICH RAMONA didn't expect, nor did she expect him to rush in with a "Mind if I use the restroom?" only to pass by in a blur.

"It's on the righ . . ." But before Ramona finished, he'd already disappeared around the corner after a seeming mental coin toss over which direction to turn in the already efficient space. When he finally reappeared, wiping his hands on his slim-fit dark washed denim, Ramona expressed her confusion about why he was in such a rush coming from four houses away.

"I didn't come from home . . . errands," Jay explained. "On Christmas Eve, everything closes early, almost nothing's open tomorrow."

Noting the time, Ramona wondered aloud how in just a few hours she and Jay would find any magic at all on this Christmas Eve, especially when the sun was shining over what looked like just another ordinary day in Southern California.

"Never underestimate a determined man with good intentions," Jay said, ushering the two of them out the door.

And then the two of them were whipping their way down the PCH again, water on the right, sun overhead, and Ramona was glad she'd managed to maintain her twists, pulled into a half-up and half-down style today that let the top explode festively in a spiky cascade of corded tendrils. Her hair could blow and not be unruly—a lesson she learned from the sea air on the night of the bonfire. *Next time, braids* . . . The thought crossed her mind for what must have been the fifteenth time that week. One way or another, a Black girl on vacation travels with her hair as an often temperamental plus-one.

"So, you said you always have fish on Christmas Eve . . ." Jay said after turning down the radio. Still, the wind made its way through the open widows, flapping their clothes like applause, making it hard to compete for the loudest sound. When he turned to Ramona, Jay was nearly yelling. "There's only one true way to have fish in LA . . ." he said, voice at full volume.

After just ten minutes on the road, they pulled into a place with a sign that said, DUKE'S MALIBU, and that looked like a large tavern restaurant straight out of a surfer movie. They walked into an interior that resembled a mix of a tiki bar and a beachside hut, if the beachside hut was absolutely full of bustling dining booths and tables. Based on the size of the crowd, Ramona wondered if they'd manage to get seated before closing time. But of course, there came Jay, smiling his goofy kind of smile with the Hawaiian shirt–clad hostess following closely behind and holding two menus.

"She comes to my classes sometimes," Jay leaned across the table to say, once they were settled. They'd been placed in a booth with a great view of the Pacific, showing off its ribbons of exquisite turquoise at low tide. Ramona lowered her menu to look at him. "And I don't charge her sometimes," Jay added with a shrug of his shoulders. "I don't do it for the money, anyway." Ramona watched a mischievous look cross his face. "You mind?" He placed his hand on top of her menu, prepared to pull it away. Ramona felt the sense of challenge fill her, the instinct to grip the menu tighter. They tugged over it for a moment, and then Ramona decided to go with the adventure of it and let it go.

Jay seemed thrilled to have the responsibility, to be in charge of the experience. He clearly enjoyed having her trust. And perhaps for Ramona that was her greatest and most elusive gift. When the waitress arrived, he ordered fish tacos for them both and two beers that Ramona had never heard of.

"*Fried* fish?" Ramona asked, thinking about the reputation of the "healthy" Californian lifestyle. "What about grilled?"

"*Never*," Jay said. "Everyone knows the only respectable fish taco is fried."

When the food came, Ramona understood what he meant. Battered fish was cradled in a tortilla under cabbage slaw, pico de gallo of tomatoes, cilantro, and onions, plus a creamy dressing with the tang of fresh limes. Ramona lost herself in the crunch and taste of it, the combination of flavors, the freshness of the fish. Her mouth awakened, and the satisfaction of her senses tickled its way through her body, so much so that she closed her eyes to relish in the delight. Maybe it wasn't the assortment of fishes her mother would serve, but just this one was perfect in this way, another reward of trusting what was to come.

CHELSEA, SOUTH SIDE, CHICAGO . . .

CHELSEA WAS SURPRISED AT HOW QUICKLY THE FIRST FLOOR OF the Tuckers' greystone filled after Carlos's arrival. The din of the conversation blending with the music, blending with the drinks she'd helped herself to, made for a delightful energy within the evening. She wasn't feeling as self-conscious, and Carlos was there now, engaged with her and others in conversation near the heavily ornamented tree. He'd introduced her to a creamy concoction he called coquito, which she'd never heard of before, but it was delicious—like cream, or coconut, or coconut cream and spices, cinnamon for sure, and then definitely some alcohol, rum perhaps—that felt appropriately festive, but certainly strong. She made it a point to slow down, although she could have easily had as many glasses as were in the entire container.

She'd had enough, however, to turn her head into a delightfully boozy, comfortable blur. She was smiling, and Carlos was talking, saying something, and people were laughing, she was laughing, and then his face looked suddenly like he'd seen a ghost.

"Oh shit!" he said, and then covered his mouth. Everyone turned to him and then to the door. Someone was walking in. And just then, Chelsea felt like she might be in danger, that they all might be—perhaps an intruder had come who wasn't supposed to be there. She felt the quick strike of anxiety below her ribs, the shot of adrenaline through her system that set her heart to racing and triggered her hands into shaking a bit. The woozy warmth was exchanged for a crisp sharpness, an over-awareness of her surroundings. She gasped without knowing why exactly she was gasping, other than this sense that something bad was happening or about to happen, and it was that apprehension that her body processed even despite her happy buzz of just a few moments prior.

But then "Malik!" is what she heard Mrs. Tucker say with a sound of . . . was it surprise? Cheer? And then Chelsea recognized the name from that first day with Carlos, who, by the way, now looked like an actual ghost to her right, his usually brown face entirely ashen. All of a sudden Chelsea felt dizzy and needed to sit down. "What . . . wh . . . where's Ramona? You're back early?" Chelsea heard Mrs. Tucker continue, and it sounded like words in a tunnel.

"Excuse me," Carlos moved by in a blur; his presence became nothing more than a rustle in her ear of his clothes as he passed. In four paces he was over there at the door talking in a hushed tone to Ramona's mother and to the newly entered Malik. This was a reunion of sorts, one of obvious confusion as the conversation moved from one person to the next with Carlos doing most of the talking. In an almost admirable seamlessness, he moved all three of them toward the back of the room and then they disappeared as a group into the kitchen, followed closely by a man who Chelsea recognized from the family photos and surmised to be Ramona's father.

RAMONA IN MALIBU . . .

AT THE EXACT MOMENT RAMONA'S PHONE BATTERY DIED, SHE was at Jay's house laughing at the fact that they'd actually seen snow that evening in Southern California. Earlier, at Duke's over lunch, when she wistfully mentioned snow in the middle of a gorgeous day of Malibu sunshine, the last thing she expected was a response from Jay. She was explaining that in the frigid temperatures of Chicago, off the lake in the relatively flat areas of the Midwest, it was common to have snow at Christmastime, and this was another reason that holidays just weren't made for the West Coast. In reality, she was teasing, giddy from a great meal and starting to feel like the company she was keeping couldn't hardly be bad at all with such great taste.

He'd guided her through yoga, taught her to surf, introduced her to beers she normally wouldn't have touched, and finally showed her that there was a much more elevated experience of fish and it was in the center of a taco, fried of course. Her feeling of elation was rapidly building into a measure of trust, not just of Jay, but also of her experience and decision to come, believing now that nothing more could go wrong. She even started thinking about that first misfortune, the one with the patrol, as perhaps just the cost of being Black, perhaps of having locked herself out, or perhaps just the usual breaks and maybe the only setback she'd suffer. Even so, when she whimsically said, "But there's no snow," she hadn't expected Jay's response of treating it like a wish to be granted. And all of this unfolding as it did contributed to Ramona letting her guard down at precisely the wrong moment.

From Duke's, Ramona and Jay hopped in his car, whipping along the PCH with the Pacific on their right, all the way down until it turned into a freeway, which turned into streets which, eventually after a lot of traffic, turned into a parking structure at someplace called The Grove. As the daylight was dwindling and the hour approached for all of the shops to close—early in the observance of the holiday—Jay rushed them along through a faux Christmas village worthy of a movie set. A trolley rolled past a perfectly ornamented red-and-white chalet for Santa, and in the background, stores beckoned with as many decorations in the windows as goods for sale. In the town square center of it all was a fountain that seemed to dance along in synchronization with the piped-in music that played from everywhere around them. To Ramona, she'd entered a magical place, one with bows and tinsel tied around palm trees, and lights that somehow found their way to almost every available surface. It smelled like peppermint and sounded like children's laughter when they got everything they wanted from their list of toys, no matter whether they'd been naughty or nice.

In the middle of it all, as Ramona turned to take everything in, sure enough as the sun had shone earlier, from above her indeed it did start to snow. It was snow, lots of it, fluffy and white and falling everywhere, to the delight of all the people around them—the last snow of the day, in the closing hour. They'd made it in time. Ramona turned her face up with delight. This was the best moment, the one she didn't expect, that brought with it the lifting excitement of surprise. The drifting white snowflakes canvased the night sky, making a contrast against the palm trees above, filling the space around Ramona and Jay with magic. The music started to play again, and Andy Williams's classic voice confirmed—with an orchestra of strings and a chorus to back him up—that it was, in fact, the most wonderful time of the year.

A wave of elation carried Ramona all the way back to Malibu, zipping up the PCH again, this time with the water on the left, all the way around the bend where she knew to soon expect Chelsea's small little cottage by the sea. But why go there and sit by herself? It was evening for certain, but the evening wasn't over yet.

"Do you have any more of that cinnamon beer?" She turned to Jay in the driver's seat. It was good timing, as they were just about to pass his place. He wasted no time saying that he did, bottles of it, part of his errands that day. And that's how they wound up at his house again, with Ramona's focus on the wonderful time she was having—satisfied with Carlos's assurance that he'd take care of everything that could have gone wrong in Chicago, which was going *very* wrong by now. So, this was how it happened that, at the worst possible time, Ramona's phone sat in her bag, running through the last flimsy bits of its battery until the screen went entirely black.

CHELSEA, SOUTH SIDE, CHICAGO . . .

BY THE TIME CARLOS RETURNED TO THE DWINDLING PARTY, Chelsea's nervous energy had wound up and then wound back down again. Over the time of his absence, as more and more people trickled out, Chelsea ran out of conversation. She sat, nursing a plastic cup of some Austrian beer that someone said she should try. From the look on Carlos's face upon his reentry, and that of the person walking beside him called Malik, plus Melba trailing and Ramona's father too, the party was over. It wasn't quite Christmas, not at all, and Chelsea wasn't sure if the cheer would return anytime soon to the Tucker household.

"Hey, you ready to go? I can take you back to Ramona's." Carlos appeared at her elbow, his voice registering unmistakable exhaustion. Malik said his goodbyes to Ramona's parents and disappeared out the door into the night, the way he came. Melba and her husband split ways to speak to the last guests, clearly forcing the appearance of hospitality. It had been a long time that they'd been in the kitchen in the back. Bottles were empty, food trays nearly cleaned out.

"Is everything all right?" was all Chelsea could think of to ask Carlos, even as it clearly was not.

"It will be," Carlos said distractedly. "But it won't be tonight." His phone was in his hand, and he was typing aggressively and sighed when his finger drifted over to the right side of the phone, Chelsea presumed to hit send. "Ramona's not answering her phone. It's going straight to voicemail," he said. "And she's not replying to texts."

Chelsea bit her lip. She could always send a message to Joan to check on Ramona, but she wanted to leave Joan out of it. "Maybe she's sleeping?" Chelsea offered to Carlos's back. He hadn't heard her, and she let him go anyway to retrieve her coat from wherever it had been taken, along with his. All the merriment of earlier had been drained out of his demeanor. His shoulders slumped, dragging at least an inch or two off of his impressive height.

He returned with two coats on his arm. "Let's go," he said tersely, handing Chelsea her coat with the unmistakable pink mittens still tucked in the sleeve. She finished the rest of the beer in her hand with one gulp and held up a finger mid-swallow to signal that she was going to make her goodbye to Mrs. Tucker. Even despite the turn of events, the evening had been one of unforgettable colors, tastes, and experiences. Melba Tucker had indeed brought a sampling of the whole world to Chicago, to a greystone on the South Side. Chelsea felt enormous gratitude for being included.

She found Melba in the back, straightening up the bottles on the drinks table, looking as if she didn't quite know what else to do with her hands, or herself, for that matter.

"I just wanted to say thank you," Chelsea called out. Melba looked up, distraction showing in her face. She looked pained, worried.

"Of course, dear," she said. Her voice missed the sparkle Chelsea had come to expect. "Carlos is going to see you home?"

Chelsea assured her that he would.

"Okay . . . then," Melba said.

Chelsea hoped that she wouldn't see the woman cry. And she hoped that this wasn't how they'd say goodbye. Not like this. But it wasn't something she could fix. Almost by instinct, Chelsea lurched forward and wrapped her arms around Melba and held her, inhaled her, remembered for a moment what it was once like to hold her own mother and be held by her. And recalling the pain of seeing her mother sad, she felt the helplessness of a child. So, this hug, that was all she could do, for now.

"Okay," Chelsea echoed, wishing that there was more to say. She released Melba before the tears came to her own eyes and turned toward the exit. She did not dare look back.

Carlos was already at the door, holding it open. The rideshare car had arrived to take them back to Ramona's. And Chelsea hoped that this car ride wouldn't be her goodbye to Carlos either, but it felt like a distance had somehow developed between them, as if they were traveling together in the backseat of a car but growing further apart each minute that passed. Carlos did not look up from his phone.

"Still nothing from Ramona?" she asked.

"Nah, nothing." Carlos turned to her. "I'm starting to worry for real. I mean, who turns their phone off on Christmas Eve? Maybe something happened to her, or someone called the cops again, or . . ."

"It was just the patrol." Chelsea tried to quickly redirect his thinking, ease his worry. "They're harmless." Behind him the lights of the city whizzed by as the car headed north toward the shoreline of Lake Michigan. The car hadn't fully warmed her yet, and so Chelsea, thinking the matter settled, with a shudder of chill, huddled herself closer to Carlos to warm up and to shake off the moment.

"It's never *just* the patrol," Carlos said, backing away from her. "You wouldn't understand." And he turned to look back at his phone. There was nothing for Chelsea to protest. She didn't understand. What was harmless to her was maybe life and death or at least felt like it to someone who the world treated differently. She was shielded from knowing that. And as much as she wanted Carlos to feel better, the only thing she could offer then was the truth.

"Carlos, it was a one-time thing." She said it low and slow, fully aware of what she was doing, and what she was saying. Carlos looked up at her, eyes narrowed.

"What, exactly, was a one-time thing?"

"The patrol, Carlos. It was that neighbor . . . the woman next door, Joan. She . . ." That was all that Chelsea could get out before Carlos turned away. His eyes closed and his head slumped, turning side to side as if to escape what she said and the knowing that it created.

"So, you knew . . . and you *lied.*" As he spoke, the air in the car stilled, became stifling.

Chelsea scrambled for an answer. "I promised Joan I wouldn't say anything. She made a mistake. I asked her to leave Ramona alone. To let her enjoy her time. I'm so sorry, I didn't think for a second that Ramona wouldn't be safe."

"But I *asked* you . . ." Carlos's jaw twitched. He took a breath in through his nose, keeping his mouth closed tight. Chelsea could see his body tense, clenched. He pulled his hand up behind his head and gripped the back of his own neck, still saying not a single word.

"I know, but I just didn't want to ruin . . . I'm sorry. Are you . . ." Chelsea couldn't quite find the words to address something so wrong that she'd done or find the courage to ask if Carlos was mad or if she'd lost him. Because in her heart, she already knew.

"I'm choosing my response to you," Carlos said, his voice quiet and controlled. To Chelsea it felt like an ending, a goodbye. One that she didn't intend but couldn't prevent. Finally, he turned to her just as Chelsea felt the car roll to a stop. They were in front of Ramona's place. "Chelsea," he said. "I just thought you were . . . different . . . and that you knew. For some people, mistakes *are* life and death. And if you can't understand that . . . then, I don't know what else to say."

Chelsea moved to open the door. *It wasn't me that called the patrol,* she thought. Still, something about the circumstances made her feel as if she was responsible. As if there was something she was supposed to do but that she couldn't quite grasp. And she didn't understand, but she wanted to. So badly, she wanted to.

"Is this something we can talk about?" she asked so eagerly it was almost begging. She wanted to plead with him, *Please come upstairs.* She wanted to say, *Please let me fix this.* But there was nothing more she could offer.

"Not tonight," Carlos said. His voice was flat, empty. Chelsea stepped out of the car. "Merry Christmas," Carlos said.

"Merry Christmas." Chelsea said it back to by instinct, but it wasn't true. It wasn't true at all. She turned to walk into Ramona's building and didn't hear the car drive off until she reached the entry and was halfway inside. Carlos was gone.

Chelsea went upstairs, exhausted and spent. She took off the dress and lay on the bed in full makeup in her underwear. Phone in her hand, she pulled it to her face. She opened a message and typed to Joan.

CHELSEA: Where is Ramona?

RAMONA IN MALIBU . . .

IF IGNORANCE IS BLISS, THEN IN THIS TIME WITH JAY, RAMONA was in seventh heaven. In his living room, after some minor effort of arranging cut logs in the drum of the Malm fireplace and tending to slightly uncooperative kindling, he managed to light the fire, which filled the entire space with a crackling glow of both warmth and character. He delivered a well-timed joke about having few decorations for the holiday, causing Ramona to remember that Christmas was ubiquitous, but not a day of any particular import to everyone and not to people of his faith. Still, for guests and general nostalgia, a very small tree sat in the corner on a side table, one that seemed to be pre-fabricated with both ornaments and lights. He plugged that in with a somewhat satisfied "There, now it's Christmas," and grinned at Ramona as if he'd done something great, which he had, just for her, adding considerable charm. Here with him, she felt twinkly too, like a shiny thing of light, and tinsel, and bows.

Ramona was happily curled up on his sofa, comfortable enough to not only take her shoes off, but to also bring her legs up and rest her feet on the overstuffed cushion underneath her. She inhaled the cinnamon-and-coffee-laced fragrance of what was quickly becoming one of her favorite drinks and lifted her gaze to the view of the ocean that was still the commanding focus of the room. Its character at night was serene, feminine, calm, dark, and mysterious.

"Some music?" Jay called out as he fiddled with a complex-looking set of electronics beneath the television mounted on the wall. Ramona nodded to him as he looked up at her. "Christmas or something else?"

"Let's try Christmas," Ramona said. And in response, Jay reached for a tablet screen near his blinking arrangement of technology gear, swiping and tapping with his finger.

"Do you know there are like, five hundred versions of 'The Christmas Song'?" He turned to her as if he expected a response.

"Well, just pick one," Ramona replied.

"Okay, Sinatra or Nat King Cole?"

Ramona's brow furrowed. "Um, you know I'm going to say Cole . . ."

"Then let's start with that." Jay smiled and turned back to his tablet. "Nat King Cole it is . . ." And suddenly the room filled with the sounds of violin strings and a deep velvet voice singing about chestnuts.

Jay joined Ramona on the sofa, not too close so as to be touching, but close enough that she could feel the additional heat of him, the presence of him nearby. Near enough that she instantly remembered the night before and felt the want of that again. There was a draw she felt, one that she couldn't explain. Any lingering guilt had already drained from her, somewhere around the time of his manifestation of snow. But truly, this new and expanding version of herself, one that had been birthed in just a moment of freedom, wasn't ready to reenter the shell sized by her previous life. She no longer wanted to feel obligated or confused. Because finally now, she wasn't confused at all. The desire that had been building inside her was sharpening to a point, an ache in the direction of Jay. And with that feeling, she only wanted to be wanted in return—by him.

The air between them was awkward and filled with the crackling energy and expectation of romance. Like a room full of ignition fuel primed for one simple little spark. The two of them were a gear cranked all the way forward, a tension spring ready to snap. And all Ramona needed was a single excuse, because it had been months, months since she'd been touched, caressed, and made to feel the hunger of her body. That craving inside her was buried so shallowly, just one touch, one light caress could surface it uncontrollably.

All insecurities about her shape, her size, her hips, ass, and thighs, whether her breasts were too large or too small, or whether her hair was cute, or makeup was right, whether her lashes were on or off, nails done perfectly—all the things she'd become accustomed to relying upon, her checklist of confidence—none of it mattered. Jay was right, the only thing stronger than fear was curiosity. And Ramona was terrified. Scared of being rejected, scared of being misunderstood, scared of making a mistake, but now, in *this* moment, right now, she was most afraid of wasting time.

Ramona looked at Jay, trying to slow her breathing, deciding what to say. Her skin was tingling electric, aching to be touched by him. He was beautiful in the lighting—his profile, the strong lines of his silhouette—the glow of him was bronze.

"Why are we here?" Ramona finally spoke, slicing into the magic of the music, which had magically transitioned to a melodic Mariah Carey rendition of "O Holy Night."

Jay turned his gaze away from the water and to Ramona. "Isn't that the kind of question you ask *yourself*?" He smiled at her, leaning toward her, closer now. "Where do you want to be?"

Ramona took in a sharp breath. The truth was obvious. "Here," she said. "Where do you want to be?"

Jay met her eyes with his and held her gaze. "With you." As he spoke his hand crossed over the remaining space between them. He reached for her hand and took it in his. He brought it slowly to his lips and finally she felt them, softly, sweetly, as they brushed against her skin. And all she could think about then was kissing him, of meeting his lips.

Tonight, she would tell the truth. She was curious, and curiosity was stronger than fear.

She was falling there, caring less, letting go.

And so it was Ramona who then kissed him back. It happened without thinking—her hand leaving his and reaching around him to the back of his neck and feeling him respond. Then, her lips met his in softness, just softness at first and a gentle exploration between the two of them. Jay's response escalated quickly. He reached back for her, wrapping his hands around her body, squeezing a release into each part he touched. Her arms, her shoulders, the upper part of her back. As they kissed, and the desire in Ramona built, the tension released in other places, and along with it the limitations and restraint.

She felt lifted and carried on a wave of yearning, of hot and hungry want, of a deep need to be touched. She relished the feeling of cool air in the room in contrast to Jay's hands that unbuttoned her blouse and delivered their bare warmth against her breasts. Those hands took in progressively more of her to caress and release. His hands were an instrument expressing his own hungry desire, beyond his lips that continued to cover her with their softness. His lips brushed against her neck and where it met her shoulders, her clavicle, the top of her breast while his hands found the outside of her bra. It had been so long . . . so long since . . . since being wanted, since feeling like the object of pure and shameless desire, and since her own arousal pushed her far beyond the borders of concern. Jay's eagerness for Ramona seemed to match her own for him—his interest in exploring her, even the ripples, the round places that she worried about; too round, she'd think at other times, but tonight, he wanted them too. He held them, squeezed here and there and kissed her harder, more intensely, through it.

By this time, after minutes or hours of this, Ramona had no idea, when Jay finally pulled back from her, she was naked from the waist up, her pants open, with her most personal parts exposed. He too was naked from the waist up, with nothing to be unsure about. When she'd placed her hand between his legs earlier, felt him hardened and met the sturdy thickness of him, she realized that he had nothing there to be ashamed of either. And when he stood up in front of her, pants open at his waist, exposing the hard lines of his lower abdomen, the parts she had seen to some degree on the beach, but closer now, she wanted to touch him, to feel that part of him, the ripples of him beneath her hand. She wished to slide her palm over his skin and feel his firmness that contrasted so much with her softness. The intoxication of it overwhelmed her.

"Let's go." Jay reached his arms down toward her to take her hands; the sinewy muscles of his biceps and forearms flexed in response to her attaching to him. He pulled her up from the sofa cushion to stand against him, kissing her again, squeezing more of her that he could reach. Her breasts, all of her breasts this time. Her ass, he gripped, pulling her to him. Inside her, arousal activated, as it had been before, but more intensely now; the most intimate places began to swell. Her lips were bruised with kissing, engorged now fully, and the lower lips mirrored this engorgement as if they too would be touched very soon.

Ramona knew the way to his bedroom already, and he wrapped himself behind her, his arms around her, hands still touching, touching everywhere, as he ushered them together to his bed under the illumination of the moonlight. Ramona's thoughts swirled, but mostly she allowed herself to be wanted, to be consumed with and met with desire until she and Jay, with the moon as their only witness, became the undulations of the ocean together, rolling as waves and crashing, building an ebb and flow of their movements like the tide. Jay's release Ramona could feel like a torrent, all power and force. His noise was satisfying to her, a low and long groan, and then in her ear he actually whispered, "Thank you . . . thank you . . . thank you . . ." as he kissed her again softly, softly and sweetly on her neck, her face, her ears, all the places his mouth could reach as he lifted himself away.

But Ramona was aroused still because she had not climaxed. She often did not and had lost the expectation of it. So, she breathed deeply and was surprised to feel his hand again between her legs, in the soft place there, so very slippery still. He felt and tickled a bit.

"Did you—"

"No," Ramona whispered, the honesty breaking through her as easily as her longing did.

"Can I—" Jay's fingers completed the rest of his question. He used them as brushes, featherlight strokes against her most sensitive part, brushing, brushing, steady and slow, across and across again, one after another as the feeling built in Ramona.

"Yes, yes, that . . . that feels—" Ramona bit her lip to stifle the escaping moan. The strokes he was making, the overwhelming nature of it, the gentle rush built into something greater within her. It became no longer peaceful in her body as the cresting wave crashed through her, all through her in a disaster of pleasure, gripping her body in thrashes, and she did finally release it all, leaving nothing other than peace, quiet peace, and the silent witness of the ocean from the window.

In Jay's bed, Ramona lay next to him, breathing deeply, aware of the presence of his body, the smells of the sheets, and the unmistakable salt air of the ocean that filled the place with a certain electricity. By now the high tide had pulled the sea under the house, to become one with it, and it was almost as if they were floating, floating on an island of just the two of them. It was her Shavasana, and in this peace, she drifted into sleep as the living room music kept playing the sounds of a jazz trio and the soulful melody of H.E.R. singing a sultry promise that *Christmastime is here . . .*

JOAN IN MALIBU (SHE RARELY LEAVES) . . .

JOAN FOX HAD NO IDEA WHERE RAMONA WAS. WHEN SHE RECEIVED Chelsea's text asking after her whereabouts, she was in her lower living room, sitting in a pile of her own creation, shoulder-deep in wrapping paper drinking Chablis (definitely *not* Chardonnay). "Where's Ramona?" she read aloud. In response, from built-in speakers in the ceiling above Joan's head, Bing Crosby sang about glistening treetops. She pulled out her phone and typed back to Chelsea.

JOAN: How would I know??? Isn't she with Jay?

Joan looked out through her huge glass windows to check the sea. The strip of narrow beach outside had disappeared now—the high tide meant that it was close to eleven in Chicago. She looked back at her phone, confirming the time but focused now on the three little dots in her message box that kept appearing and disappearing.

"Dammit, Chelsea, what?" Joan said to the phone, irritated. Here she was, just trying to enjoy what was left of Christmas Eve, *alone*, as she hadn't planned to be. But if she was, in fact, going to be spending Christmas Eve with just the sounds of recorded cheer, she wanted to do so *in peace*. If Ramona had just accepted her plans, Joan's plans, she wouldn't be in whatever mess had been caused.

With a little chime, two new lines of text appeared on Joan's phone from Chelsea.

The first was:

CHELSEA: Her phone is going straight to v/m

The second was:

CHELSEA: I had to say you called patrol but wouldn't do it again.

"Fuck!" Joan yelled, entirely without meaning to. Hearing herself curse was jarring, and despite being alone, she looked around for someone who'd heard. But there was only the sea outside. She hadn't used such language since her days back in Bakersfield, long before she leaned into her new role in Los Angeles of actress turned high-powered plus-one. Cursing was unbecoming, what her mother did after late nights in the diner. She was far past that now. It was unexpected of pretty and charming girls, and Joan was Joan Fox now, *still*, in a four-thousand-square-foot place by the sea.

She had half a mind to walk over to Chelsea's place and bang on the door, demand an audience to explain herself, her point of view. To deliver all the justifications and reasons why in the situation, the action she took, as controversial as it was perhaps, was truly, deeply, seriously her only option. It was her right to feel safe, after all. And what was so wrong with that? She stood up, walked over to the window, but she couldn't see much from her lower level. So, up her majestic circular staircase she climbed to her upper living area, toward her binoculars that she still hadn't moved. The lights were out next door. There was no motion from the bedroom window, nothing on the deck. Ramona wasn't home. Ah, but *maybe she was at Jay's?* Joan experienced the minor glimmer of hope that she could just march down there then, wherever *there* was, bang on *that* door, and demand the return of Ramona. Ramona was hers, her new friend for Christmas. Now that she knew she was a person . . . or rather, knew *who she was* as a person. Same thing really, right? Joan was filled with the sudden surge of knowing exactly what she'd do. She'd save Ramona once and for all from the clutches of Jay, because that was her mission now. He lived down a few houses, as she recalled hearing. But in which direction? How many houses? Joan realized then that she had no idea at all where Jay lived. He was just the man on the beach with the loud music. The womanizer who taught classes to take advantage of women. She hadn't thought of him as a neighbor, or realized for even a second that the beach was also his. And so there Joan was left, floating in indecision, waiting for her next best idea. Because there was no way she was going to lose now.

DECEMBER 25

•●

RAMONA IN MALIBU . . .

FOR THE FIRST TIME IN A VERY LONG TIME, OR PERHAPS EVER, Ramona woke up in a bed that she didn't quite recognize. At least here, the first thing that she smelled was coffee. In the midst of rumpled sheets, she looked over to her left. She was alone with just the gently sloshing sounds of the ocean outside the window. It could have easily been Chelsea's bed, but the view was different . . . and, also, the coffee. She made quick work of collecting the pieces of her whereabouts. Malibu . . . last night, she was with Jay, snow . . . oh yes, there was snow . . . and then drinks and music and the fireplace . . . oh and those hands, yes, those hands of his led to . . . here, the bed she was in quite comfortably.

She draped the loosened top sheet around herself—creating a plain and inartful ruched white dress—and waddled in a tight shuffle in the direction of the smells. It was easy to follow Jay's own wall of windows. Out of the bedroom, on the opposite side of the living room behind the far wall, Ramona found Jay in the kitchen, stirring the contents of a French press.

"She is risen," he said, as if cause for celebration. "Merry Christmas."

"What is that, like a holiday mash-up?" Ramona bantered back with a smile.

"I'm just commemorating your interesting choice of attire."
Jay turned away from his stirring briefly to wink at her.

Ramona laughed. "Touché . . ."

She watched as he pushed the plunger down in the glass
cylinder and, after a beat, poured the dark liquid into a mug he
handed to her.

She waited until he'd poured his own mug and then made a
gesture toward him. "Merry Christmas to me, then." The mugs
clinked. Sipping the steaming coffee, unsweetened and black, reminded her of work, which reminded her of Chicago. And that by
now her family would be sending a cascade of texted greetings if
not calls, which she was surprised not to have heard already. "My
purse," she mumbled clumsily, rustling in her sheet-dress back
toward the living room. There weren't many places to look, and
she found her bag neatly nestled into the sofa near where she'd
been the evening prior. And of course, fishing into her pocket-
book produced a completely dead phone, black screen and all.

Jay offered her a charger, and within five minutes the device
came to life with such continual insistence of noise that Ramona
returned to it, expecting messages from her parents, and perhaps
her brother, and of course Carlos and Latrice. Instead, there were
about twenty messages from her mother, from Carlos, her father
even, and all of them saying effectively the same thing: *Where
are you, Ramona?* And there was, for the first time in weeks, a
message from Malik. *What was it about men?* she thought. They
all seemed to smell the moment that you've moved on. Except,
Malik's message was not about getting back together. It read:

MALIK: You didn't tell your parents we broke up?

How did he know? And then she started scrolling and
reading, opening message by message, as fast as she could as
within her the cold panic rose to the point that even the toga

was nearly suffocating. Carlos told her that Malik had shown up. And then he asked if she was with a person named Jay. And then just now, a message from her mother.

MA: Ramona are YOU awake? Are you there? ARE YOU OK? Did you get THIS MESSAGE?

"Hey, is everything okay?" Jay appeared behind her, his hand on her waist. It was a gesture that would have been so welcome last night, but she was wound up, so overwhelmed, it was a stimulus she recoiled from. His face registered confusion, and Ramona's first instinct was to apologize. But all she could do was shake her head. *No. No, it's not okay. No, no, no, this can't be happening.* No, she only had one more day. In the very real-time play-by-play of frantic text messages, her worst-case scenario was unfolding. Her family knew *everything*. And worst of all, her mother, her mother who'd enjoyed so much the wedding dress shopping, and the planning, the guest listing, the dreams of her daughter starting her own family, now knew it was all a lie, and worse, thought she'd been abducted. With her face in her hands, Ramona groaned.

"What can I do to help?" Jay offered.

She made her way toward the door to his deck. "I just . . . need some air." It was all she could manage to say. She shuffled her way outside to the deck, holding her phone. Deep breaths in . . . and out . . . she tried to take, but standing squarely at the convergence of all your bad decisions, there's no effective way to calm down. She couldn't tell Jay what had happened. How would that even sound? *My family just found out that I'd been pretending to still be engaged.* She could call Latrice, or Carlos. Who had the most information? Or she could reply to that text from her mother, rather than risk a search-and-rescue effort that would make this officially the worst possible day of her life.

She started typing a message to her mother and hit send.

> **RAMONA:** I'm [very] safe. I'll call you in a bit.

Immediately the three dots appeared. It was clear that her mother had been sitting by the phone. It wasn't the way that she'd wish for anyone to be spending Christmas, not on her account. Next, was a call to Carlos. He answered on the first ring. She needed to fix this, and quickly.

"Moe, where are you? For real, all night I've been calling you."

"I'm fine. My phone died."

"Yoooo, Malik showed up last night at Ma's party. It was some shit. But you know I handled business. And Chelsea said some woman named Joan was the one who called the po-po on you."

"*Joan?*" Ramona spat out her disbelief. "Jooooaaaan? Are you sure?"

"Yeah, Joan, that's what Chelsea said. You *with* her?"

She was shocked, positively stunned. But Joan's lies were the least of her problems for now. Immediately, Ramona had to address the aftermath of her *own* dishonesty. "No, I'm with . . ." She paused and looked around her. Jay was indoors. "I'm with another neighbor," she whispered heavily. "Jay."

"Oh shit, Ramona!" Carlos sounded almost giddy. "She did say you might be with a guy named Jay. And I was like, naah, not Moe. For real? In Malibu? And with Malik there checkin' for you last night?"

"Well . . . it's a little late for that . . ." Ramona thought back to the previous evening with Jay.

"I'm not even gonna ask. 'Cuz last week you were sure planning a wedding."

Ramona's face burned hot in the cheeks. "I know, Carlos, but sometimes . . . things . . . change—"

"Very quickly, damn!"

Ramona shook her head and sighed deeply. Carlos was the last person she needed to explain herself to. Reaching deep for composure, slowly, again, she started speaking. "Let it go, Carlos," Ramona warned. "Before I call Ma, what else do I need to know?"

True to their relationship, Carlos dropped the chiding and filled Ramona in quickly. The details of Malik's reappearance, the conversation that followed, and exactly how deep the shit was that Ramona was wading in. He explained that when Chelsea had finally told the truth and revealed that Joan was "the caller," as it was, she tried to assure everyone that Ramona was safe. But the panic caused by Ramona's unavailability didn't de-escalate until later when Chelsea informed Carlos— via text by the way, because by now he'd stopped speaking to her—that Ramona's whereabouts (per Joan) were likely with someone else.

"Is she mad?" Ramona asked her last but most important question. The real one, the one she dreaded most. Everything else was secondary. Because in this moment, it was clearer than it'd ever been that the only thing she'd wanted to do, even by coming across the country and hiding in a place called Malibu, was to avoid being a disappointment, or a waste, or worst of all a failure.

Carlos told Ramona that her parents were noticeably shaken to discover the lengths she had gone to conceal her breakup with Malik, especially finding out in the middle of a Christmas party. "But Ma seemed relieved to hear that you were likely somewhere you wanted to be," Carlos said. "You know *her* though. She's not going to rest until she hears from you yourself. Maybe she's not mad, just hurt. Either way, you need to call her. You'll find out."

"Wow," Ramona said, registering honest bewilderment. "Absolutely nothing in what you just said was reassuring, and yet, I get the sense that you're trying to comfort me. Thanks, Carlos."

"Aye. It is what it is, Moe. Oh, and Merry Christmas."

The irony forced a reflexive laugh and a flat "Right . . . Merry Christmas" from Ramona before she ended the call with Carlos. After a last deep, exhausted sigh, she leaned on the deck railing still wrapped in a sheet, gazing across the Pacific searching beyond the horizon for tomorrow, even though she had no choice other than to figure out what to do *today*.

CHELSEA IN CHICAGO . . .

THE LAST THING THAT CHELSEA REMEMBERED FROM THE NIGHT before was sending a message to Carlos. Or maybe it had been more than one message. Perhaps she sent five, or six, or ten. She couldn't quite recall and was scared to look at her phone. For a while, the entire universe of people she knew in Chicago believed that one of their beloveds was missing. So, Chelsea did what she could to give them comfort, even if that meant squeezing out the secret she'd tried so desperately to hold. And she hoped that telling Carlos what Joan said, that Ramona was likely with Jay, had provided some comfort. But she had no idea, because last she checked, Carlos still hadn't replied. In the silence, achingly honest now, Chelsea realized that it wasn't just out of obligation to Joan that she managed to keep what she knew undisclosed for so long. It was to her own benefit as well. Chelsea had needed Ramona to stay, and if Ramona knew that the person next door was the person who . . . well . . . did what Joan did, she would have left. Who wouldn't have? And while she hoped that the rest of the trip would have in some way made up for that horrible beginning, it was obvious to Chelsea now that she'd under-accounted for its effects on Ramona.

Perhaps it was this self-centeredness, rather than the secret she kept, that had frustrated Carlos. It stung when he told her that she'd missed the point about the patrol, but not because she immediately understood what he meant. She heard him, even in the haze of the evening's prior merriment. She could feel his pain when he spoke about how nothing about being "patrolled" could be considered "harmless," and that it wasn't ever, ever experienced that way. That the stress of the threat was itself a harm—the life-and-death idea of what could happen, carried day in and day out, reinforced by what *has* happened and keeps happening, so many, many times. To that, she couldn't relate. Because she hadn't felt it, not like Carlos did, or Ramona did. And Chelsea realized then, when the pricking of tears came and the room blurred before her, the thought in her mind had struck a vein of deep-buried truth, that in thinking *only* about what the patrol meant to her, she actually had missed the point.

So, in her time alone, curled up on Ramona's sofa as she hugged her arms around her shins and dropped her chin upon her knees, Chelsea searched herself for a memory, or an image, anything that could connect her again with Carlos. Across from the window that overlooked the frozen lake, she saw not through the tears in her eyes, or even through the glass outside. She viewed with her mind's eye, backward through her memories, trying to imagine a time when she'd felt less than safe, and what had made her feel that way.

All that came to mind, again and again, were times when she lived downtown—when she and friends were too silly or too drunk to fully absorb the risk—and felt young and wild, but never felt totally free. As women, at night, the downtown spaces often felt like places they wanted to claim and enjoy but didn't belong to entirely, because no one would or could protect them there, not fully. It was not safe the way she felt in Malibu, a place that was hers. And that was the point, wasn't it, that for Chelsea, there was a Malibu. And it was safe all the time and welcoming all the time to her—but it hadn't been to Ramona. And that's why Ramona wanted to leave.

And that's why Chelsea *didn't*.

That was why she'd gotten stuck there; yes, she was stuck, she could acknowledge this now. Because after losing everything, and the entire base of one's stability, so suddenly as with her parents and then her career, she had also lost the gumption to dream, to be silly, to be wrong, to be fearless. She'd clung to a rare privilege of safety—a bird whose fall from the nest focused its hope on getting back onto the branch rather than taking to the sky.

Inside of Ramona's condo twelve floors above the city, you could almost forget it was Christmas—if you hid away your phone (as Chelsea had) and turned the television off (she only watched streaming anyway), and didn't look out the window, although it was quiet outside and the lake was frozen and still. Chelsea rubbed her temples; her sleep-matted hair was a fireball, and her head was throbbing to the beat of a song she did not care to know. It was a rough morning. Chelsea looked like she'd been on the losing end of a battle, and in some way, she was. She'd endured the moment when your heart's broken open by a force so subtle, so unintentional even, that it slips right past all of your defenses. When had it happened? For Chelsea, it was impossible to tell, only that something was quite different. She was different, and people that she'd never met before all of a sudden felt like those who she couldn't bear living without. This was heartbreak, and this was also love.

Chelsea felt like she was *without* Carlos. It was an event to her—certainly not nothing, or *what does it matter anyway, I'm leaving tomorrow*. A catastrophe instead. A loss, something to mourn, or fix, or cling to like the string of a balloon in the wind. What if this person was the rest of her? The door to her future self? The key that unlocked the prison where she had caged herself since the day of her parents' passing? So, without word from him, not yet at least, to her last message of *Can we please talk, I'm sorry*—words wrenched from the clutches of pride—she decided to do what she'd been accustomed to doing, to hold on to that string, to prevent the memories from fading. To stop the love from leaving fully, she painted it. Or in this case, she resumed painting him.

Chelsea rummaged until she exhumed the canvas she'd tucked into the back of a closet following the close call after her first night with Carlos. She'd only managed to render one eye to completion but had sketched the rest of his face in the scene that she wanted to depict, the full moment she wanted to capture, that one in the gallery, when he confronted her with her own truth.

She resumed her mix of paints from the colors she'd purchased. Red and yellow to make the oranges, plus a touch of blue for certain browns. Of course, she had the burnt umber as a base for the eyes, to match that specific color of iced coffee in the sunlight. The beautiful browns of Carlos, the brightness of his countenance, she meant to capture it, so she could never forget. The bristles of her brush swirled in the paint, dipped in the water, ran in colors, left textures and marks on the canvas, built up dimension, shadows and light, contour and shading, lines of foreground and background. She was painting again, she was creating, doing art, going to that place she hadn't been in so long, the one within her that was as wide as the ocean and deep, a pool of inspiration connected to everyone and everything. In every brushstroke she was painting the whole world.

All day, Chelsea painted and cried sometimes, happy tears and sad tears, remembering and reliving times of this week past and the distant past. She needed to mourn who she'd been, what she'd lost. There'd been so much loss, as she knew so well. But there was now something new, a rebirth she was painting. She was confident again, felt the remembering in her hands, her arms, the control, the vision, the execution of a masterpiece.

It was dark outside when she finished. She admired the painting, seeing the subtle changes in the colors as it dried, as was inevitable. Nothing ever stays the same. For an artist, nothing is ever done, no story is ever complete. But it was settled and time to stop, to release it. She pulled out her phone again, finally, from where she'd placed it. And she decided to send one last photograph, her Christmas gift, to Carlos. It was her message after *I'm sorry*. It said everything she'd ever had to say. It was painted in there, mixed with tears of joy, and of pain, and . . . of love—for his eyes to see. She snapped a single photo, placed it into a message, and hit send.

RAMONA IN MALIBU . . .

FOR AS LONG AS RAMONA RESTED ON THE RAILING OF JAY'S DECK, just doors down from Chelsea's place, as hard as she thought about it and willed another solution to arrive, there was no other thing to do. She would face her family. She would have to speak the words, the truth. And she would have to face the consequences. She'd come so far from that day at the office, holding a coffee mug then, staring at the real snow falling outside and wishing she was elsewhere. Despite so much that had happened since then, the quandary she faced was the exact same. She'd tried running to the farthest reaches of the land, but even here she couldn't run far enough away from the truth.

Grateful for the space that Jay gave her, she exchanged her sheet for her regular clothes and gathered her belongings to return to Chelsea's place. Jay dropped her off, leaving reluctantly, with a concerned look and a promise to check on her later. Although she liked Jay very much, still, she wasn't sure she wanted to be checked on, or frankly, if she even deserved it. Leaving now, she could avoid telling him the truth. She didn't owe anything more to anyone. Not to Jay and certainly not to

Joan. Imagining Joan's blue eyes somewhere nearby, surveilling her every move, Ramona hurried into Chelsea's house with an uneasy feeling of being watched. Suddenly, she couldn't wait to leave Malibu, even if that meant going back to Chicago.

Latrice had gotten her into this calamity of a situation, or at least had been her prime enabler. So it was Latrice who she dialed first and who thankfully answered, sounding like she'd heard about none of the prior evening's drama.

"Oh my god, please tell your mom I'm sorry I had to miss the party," Latrice said, upon answering. "Even though you never did forward that invite, I still had to work," she continued. *So, for sure she hadn't heard*, thought Ramona, because Latrice hadn't been there.

"Malik showed up," Ramona grumbled.

Of course, Latrice was surprised. "Whaaattt? He had the nerve to show up to your mother's house? He got invited, and I didn't?"

"Latrice, you were invited. My mother just didn't have your number."

"Oh damn, but she had Malik's."

"And she didn't know we broke up, so . . . he was still on the group text. I guess he thought it was all good."

"But, Moe, he just came to hang out? Who does that? Not even some grand gesture or big apology? No dramatic scene, no 'I'm coming to get my wife,' with all the tears and shit?"

"Knowing Malik, he just came to eat. But everyone knows *everything* now. And, of course, my phone died in the worst part of it." When Latrice asked how everyone found out, Ramona had a chance to explain about Joan, "the pastry lady," as Latrice called her.

"And she never once told me she was the one who called the patrol," Ramona added. "Not once. So she was just spying on me the whole time?"

"How *sneaky*," Latrice said. "That's some terrible shit, Moe, pure *trash*."

"I don't want it, send it back," Ramona replied begrudgingly.

Latrice laughed, and in spite of the circumstances, after a beat, Ramona did too. Because, when it all falls apart, most of it your own fault, what do you do? You can laugh or you can cry. Ramona chose to laugh until her own tears came, because that was the only thing that felt good then, that was light, and allowed her to breathe.

"Girl, let it be the start of an era," Latrice said. "Your *send it back* season. And your mom?"

"Calling her next." Ramona sighed heavily. "Any suggestions?"

"Well, there's only one thing you haven't tried at this point. You could tell the truth . . . the *whole* truth." Latrice left a pause of silence, which Ramona presumed was for effect. There was honestly nothing for Ramona to protest. The truth was the only way forward, the way back to Chicago, out of this sleepy town of Malibu, where everyone seemed to be lying, or hiding, or tending the gates. Ramona, wanting to be nothing like Joan, decided that she should of course come clean, including to her mother, her father, Malik, Jay even, and most importantly to herself. But she didn't know the right time for any of those conversations.

After a few more words of encouragement, interspersed with Latrice's admonishments directed to her young nieces and her nephew who Ramona could hear clearly running wild in the background, Ramona and Latrice ended their call.

Nothing more stood between Ramona and her most important thing to do—call her mother and father, but really her mother, and finally tell the whole story.

In sum, the call did not get off to a great start.

"Ramona, where are you?" Ramona's mother, who had only recently learned to use the video feature on her smartphone, insisted on a video call, which was understandable, but unexpected. Melba was certainly not looking at the camera, and most definitely not even squarely at the screen, which completely distorted her head in Ramona's frame, making her mother's forehead look much larger than the rest of her face. But all of her was bobbing and weaving back and forth, one eye to the next, as if the view of Ramona in her phone wasn't dependent solely on how Ramona was holding the camera.

"I'm in Malibu . . . Malibu, California. Ma, look." Ramona flipped the view on her device to show her mother all around the compact living room area of Chelsea's house. In one quick sweep, she showed the living area, dining and kitchen areas, and then back around to the view, of course the view, out of Chelsea's wall of windows to the Pacific Ocean past the deck.

"Is that . . . That's the ocean? Right there? Look, Phillip . . ." Ramona's mother in the screen of Ramona's phone switched to her father, whose glasses and balding hazelnut of a forehead then bobbed in the same choreography as her mother.

"Hold it back some, Melba," her father said. And Ramona watched as the phone image of him zoomed back a bit, shaking her head because by this point her parents should have been more familiar with technology. "Well now, would you look at that . . ." Her father sounded stunned, but recovered quickly in the way that old-school Black men from the Midwest were wont to do when it came to maintaining a particularly stoic equilibrium. But his reaction made Ramona cognizant of the actual splendor of her view and wish that she'd been able to share it under different circumstances than these. After another sweep, which took a few moments, she turned the camera view back to her.

"Hi, Daddy." Seeing her father there, Ramona pushed back her own tears, imagining how upset he must have been, just thinking that something had happened to his baby girl. It was concern she never wanted to cause. He looked serious. With furrowed brow, he leaned into the screen.

"You all right, baby girl?"

"I'm fine, Daddy," Ramona said, hearing the little girl reply in her own voice.

"Okay, then," he said. "See you when you get back. Merry Christmas." And in his red checkered shirt and Christmas suspenders, he got up from wherever he was sitting—which looked like the couch in her parents' sitting room upstairs— and started to walk away.

"Phillip!" Ramona's mother called after him, "You don't have anything else to say?"

"She said she's fine, Melba," Ramona heard him say from far away and outside of the frame of the screen. "I'll see her when she gets back. Let her enjoy the rest of that trip."

Ramona's mother turned back to Ramona with a look on her face of mild annoyance, but it seemed not to be directed at her.

"Ramona, I'm just so sorry you . . . felt like you couldn't tell us . . . and, well, I'm just glad to know that you're okay . . . and . . . well, somewhere safe."

Ramona's guilt swelled. She'd fully expected that her parents would be upset, enraged even. But she hadn't anticipated how much they'd be palpably hurt. And with that realization, a mixture of relief and also regret swirled in her. And she knew then, especially, that she was going to cry. She would cry on the phone now, because she couldn't help it. But she would sob later. And as the first tear welled from her, from the back of her throat to the corners of her eyes, the worry on her mother's face blurred.

"Ma, I'm so sorry." And Ramona meant it for everything. In the way she'd apologized when she'd had her bike stolen when she was eleven, when she'd lost the spelling bee, or when she'd gotten her freshly pressed hairstyle wet when caught in the rain, she apologized now, because it hurt her the most to hurt anyone else, even when she was the one who needed the tending.

"Ramona . . ." In just one word, the name of her daughter, Melba incanted the hopes and the dreams of a mother—that the world would treat her daughter well, that she would find a place in it as she desired. That she would be free and happy, so happy, that the smiles of her childhood would be with her always, even when they were apart. And deep down somewhere, Ramona heard this.

"I know," Ramona replied softly.

"I've always wanted more for you than anything I've ever had. That your dreams would be bigger than mine, that your world would be beyond my imagination. And that would be worth anything to me. Do you understand?"

Ramona sniffled. With a staggered breath, she did reply. "I understand."

"Good." Melba shifted on the screen in front of Ramona, and then her face crinkled into an expression of concern. "So, you'll be spending Christmas alone?" Her mother sounded genuinely worried.

Ramona exhaled deeply. She thought of Joan's invitation, which wasn't something she could even consider. But to say as much would have caused her mother even more concern. Then she thought to Jay, and she looked out at the water, remembering that she'd found a new part of herself out there, and how that'd come to be.

"I've actually made some new friends," she said, and then considered her words. In speaking of Jay and the ocean, Ramona wondered, with the time she had left, if this would come to be true.

CHELSEA IN CHICAGO . . .

CHELSEA SEEMED TO KNOW THAT THE IMAGE SHE SENT CARLOS, the one of him through her eyes, those of a lover, would spark his response. There is a language of artists beyond words that reaches the heart directly. This, Chelsea was aware of and drew upon most urgently in her painting. But this language costs for its use. It requires all of one's energy to access. After doing so, Chelsea was spent. She'd fallen asleep on the sofa in the living room, in the silence of the evening with no sound from the extinguished television on the wall or the quiet, frozen lake below. Everyone else was making their holiday merriment sheltered indoors from the cold, with the ones that they loved or makeshift versions so as not to be alone on Christmas.

So, although she knew she would hear from him, she was startled to hear Carlos at the door, knocking. But it *was* him, it had to be. She knew it before she answered. She had *hoped* for him to come. Hearing the knock, she awakened, half groggy from a nap of complete exhaustion, and didn't even bother to ask "Who is it?" Chelsea was certainly going to answer the door.

Seeing him on the other side of the door when she pulled it open, her body flooded with the force of relief. Carlos, in the splendor of all his beautiful browns, was standing before her. This time, again his eyes held kindness and connection in them and all of the warmth that she remembered. Time and her apology, perhaps, her acknowledgments of what he explained and the work of understanding—it had made an opening for them, one to talk.

She only realized she'd been holding her breath when he walked through the threshold as if he was going to stay for a while. Only then did her body finally relax. Her shoulders lost a half an inch of their height, as she subconsciously braced herself for some kind of disappointment, any kind. While Chelsea had become used to losing things lately, it was much more uncommon to find them again. Like she'd been finding herself, recovering that portion that Carlos awakened that day in the gallery.

"Ma sent me," Carlos said. "No way she'd let you stay here alone. Not on Christmas." In his hands he held a plate wrapped in foil. "I brought this for you." Carlos lifted his arm up, the one with the plate. "And this." He brought up his other hand, holding a small, nondescript brown bag, folded across the top like it could contain a sandwich or a treasure, although for Chelea his presence was miracle enough.

"Thank you." Chelsea reached out to take the bag and the still-warm plate. Even with delicious smells drifting upward, she hesitated, unsure of what to do next. Right then, she was holding all the possibilities of what each of these could be, delight and disappointment, elation and something far worse. Gifts also came with an obligation, to demonstrate at least some kind of liking for them. Given the fragility of their reunion, this was a game of gift and giver that Chelsea did not want to lose.

Carlos took the plate from her hand. "Okay for me to come in?" Chelsea nodded, and Carlos headed toward the kitchen with the plate and deposited it on the top of the island counter. "I'm telling you, there's some good stuff in here. I hope you're hungry." He walked back over to Chelsea and pointed down to the bag she was still holding in a bit of stunned immobility. "Open it," he said.

Reanimated, she very slowly unrolled the folded top of the bag in her hand and reached in to circle her fingers around its contents. A tube? A small tube of something? She pulled it out of the bag and saw a tube of paint. A blue color, PB86, an unfamiliar shade whose name she did not know.

"It's super rare," Carlos explained. "The first new blue in years."

"Blue, a new blue?" Immediately, Chelsea thought back to the gallery, the painting that Carlos showed her, the one that was his favorite.

Carlos nodded. "You can do a lot with blue. And this one's special. A new color for a fresh perspective."

"How'd you get this?" Chelsea asked. She knew the rarities of special paints. Elusive colors could cost a hundred dollars a tube or more, and then be sold out indefinitely. Something like this, something new and rare, would have been difficult to procure. It felt like she held gold in her hand, and for an artist, the right color could be. An open door, a fresh perspective, the difference between work that sells and doesn't sell in a market of arbitrary prices based on how inspired one is to pay.

Carlos smiled. "I know a guy."

And then Chelsea laughed, and as that laughter rippled through her, she felt such a release, a fresh buoyancy lightening her entire body. She could talk to Carlos about anything, she knew this now. Well, almost anything. There were things she still dared not ask, not for fear that he wouldn't answer, but for fear that he would. But for now, he was here, lost and found, and Chelsea hoped not to lose him again.

RAMONA, BLUE IN MALIBU . . .

RAMONA EXPECTED RELIEF TO FEEL MUCH BETTER. CURLED UP she was, in Chelsea's bed, with the shutters partially closed out of concern about snooping Joan next door. Chelsea's bed was particularly well-made for moping, as it was plush and deep in pillows and bedding also. A person could stay buried there for days. Ramona, however, only needed to make it through twenty-four hours. Although the ocean called her from outside the window, and the sun still shone, and it was still Christmas, Ramona was wrapped in her feelings as much as she was the comforter and sheets.

She pulled the sheet up over her head and kicked her feet against the bed beneath her. She wasn't usually one for dramatics, but she was alone. Really alone, in Malibu, single for sure now, facing weeks ahead of actually unraveling wedding plans, confronting the reality of starting over, at least personally. And wasn't this her biggest fear, facing a life of unforeseen circumstances? And now, only one possibility remained, the one that Ramona had been trying to outrun—that Malik was possibly not the person for her, and never was. That maybe the love they'd fallen into was more like a groove of habit. That the proposal he offered was more about "knowing a good woman when I see one," and less about knowing anything specific about her. And that maybe getting married had been more about the *getting* than the *being*.

The ocean was noisy outside, the waves and the seagulls. Inside the small bedroom, with the windows covered, Ramona was starting to feel suffocated by the weight of not just her thoughts but the piles of bedding she'd burrowed beneath. Even this, this moment wasn't what she wanted. She imagined that she'd spend her last day basking in the sunshine, smelling the briny sea air, walking at the edge of the water, or going swimming in it, doing her best to bottle that feeling of freedom within her so she could take that back to Chicago. So that she could pour that out into her life, for whatever came next. She wanted to keep feeling like she was a person who rode on water, who could find balance anywhere, even on top of a rolling wave.

"Get up, Ramona," she heard herself speak aloud. It was the same thing she'd said to herself each time she fell days prior, when she lost her balance and slipped into the sand-filled shallow water beneath the frothy whitewash. And each time was the same, her feet found the ground below and she was ready to stand, and to try again. This was who she was.

By noon, true to his word, Jay had left a message for her.

JAY: Wanna go for a ride?

And Ramona did, for sure, but the answer wasn't so simple. She'd have to tell Jay something that brought her a sense of deep shame. But she owed him the truth and needed to be elsewhere, away from the eyes of Joan, her insistent and unpredictable visits. With this last escape, in the sun, feeling the breeze, she'd find a way to tell Jay the truth.

Soon after, she was in Jay's car again, just on the other side of saying yes. They were headed down the PCH, wind whipping in the windows with the ocean on their right side.

When they stopped, parked, and walked, she did not expect that "ride" would mean standing on the pier, the Santa Monica Pier, looking up at the giant Ferris wheel that had until now just been lights in the distance along the shoreline.

"Now you can't say I didn't get you a gift." Jay handed Ramona a wristband, which she managed to put on as he did the same with his own.

"When you said go for a ride, this isn't exactly what I had in mind," she said, maneuvering the plastic bracelet. "But thank you." Ramona couldn't help herself then and smiled her first real smile of the day.

Jay snapped the clasp of his band closed. "One of the few places open on Christmas. Good place to forget about things, have some fun." He turned out toward the water. All around them, kids were laughing, giddy, joyful. Parents hauled cotton candy and stuffed animal toys, following along in the merriment.

Ramona and Jay entered the Ferris wheel cabin together, and the ride began to lift them slowly up along its ascent path. They sat together, their legs comfortably touched on the bench. Jay's arm draped casually around Ramona on the backrest. She released all of her breath and relaxed into the crook of his arm as they surveyed an incredible view of the Pacific shoreline from a hundred feet in the air.

At the very top, Jay reached his other hand over to hers and held it. She turned to look at him, and he met her gaze. She left her hand there with his, to inhale the beach air and to remember that moment up there in the sky, like she belonged there. Like she could float on air. It was the right time to tell him, she wanted to, but *just a little while longer,* she told herself. It wasn't at all how she wanted to say goodbye.

Later, after the sun slipped into the ocean and the lights came on at the pier, after a day of long rides and short ones, a roller coaster and a pirate ship, Jay asked Ramona if she was ready to go. "Not back to Chelsea's," she said. So, with the wind whipping against them, carrying the moisture-heavy night air of the sea on their left, up the PCH they went back to Jay's place.

Ramona nestled into the cushions of the sofa in Jay's living room. Through the windows the moon hung high and full in the night sky and draped a wedge of silver along the gently rippling surface of the ocean. In the quiet, she recalled the surge of power she encountered in the water that belied all that stillness. Ramona had experienced her own power too, out there, as if strength was drawn from her to match the rhythm of the wave.

"Beautiful, no?" Jay's voice entered from the opposite side of the room, floating from around the corner just before he appeared holding two glasses filled with that same dark elixir. Ramona could already taste the rich cinnamon.

And while she was looking at the water, he was looking at her, and continued to do so as he transferred a glass to her hand, through a toast, and over the rim of his first sip. Outside, Ramona responded with the signs of flirtation. Inside, her body responded with the indications of attraction. She was both tense and relaxed, aroused and serene, desirous and lax. She lowered the rim of the glass from her lips and raised a finger there, not quite intending to trace her lower lip as she did. But the warmth inside her wasn't just the drink anymore. It was a brewing of something, something that if given more time would be special, she just knew it.

"What?" Jay asked his simple question and smiled at her. Ramona raised an eyebrow. "Just that, you're smiling. I wanna know why, that's all."

"My mother was worried that I'd be spending Christmas alone. I was just thinking how I'm not, not at all."

"That's an important thing to you?"

"To my family, of course. Togetherness means that you're loved."

"And what does being alone mean?"

Ramona met his eyes with her own look of confusion. She'd never considered the question. And perhaps that was what explained her predicament. What she'd return to in the shambles of a failed engagement. Starting over, alone.

"I guess I'm about to find out."

Jay reached over and placed his hand over hers that lay in her lap. "But not tonight."

She sighed and sipped again. "Not tonight," she repeated.

Jay maneuvered to meet Ramona's eyes. "You know, I'm often alone. It has its benefits—growth, introspection, life revealing all of its mysteries—"

"Like?"

Jay laughed. "Like joy, like peace, like pleasures . . ." While he let those words draw out slowly from his mouth, the moonlight's reflection made the brown of his skin look like satin. She remembered touching him. His hands touching her.

"Is that how you learned . . . last night . . . how you . . ." Ramona felt herself blush.

"Satisfied you?"

She looked down. Jay squeezed her leg. She felt wild all over again, as if she'd burst at the seams. Still-raw desire boiled hot inside her, for so much that she didn't ask for, but that had its own demand. It was everything that swirled beneath the surface of who she was; the calm of how she appeared wasn't calm at all, especially now.

"Yes," Ramona whispered.

"Most women don't climax from penetration. That's not a

secret of life though. Just some anatomy reading . . . and some practice—"

"So, what was—"

"*Pleasure* . . . is what you seek. What you ask for. When you don't accept less than what fulfills you. You demand more, and more comes, Ramona. Until you're satisfied." Remembering the night before, the heat built in Ramona. The current of arousal that flowed was enough to sharpen her senses and her awareness. Her sensitivity was a dial turned up to its max.

"What about *enough*, then?" She could barely push words beyond a whisper.

"A place to stop, yes . . . but, Ramona, I have a feeling you aren't even close."

While Jay sounded sincere, for a moment Ramona felt a flash of anger. She had accomplished so much, in her education, her career, her life even. Didn't he see that? She came from the South Side to the Gold Coast, in one generation, she'd done that. So, what did he mean she didn't come close to enough? What *did* he mean? And as soon as that stab of anger came, like a flicker of lightning, charging her, striking her in her core, she was ready to lash out. To defend herself. But from what? *What did he mean?* her thoughts insisted. Ramona bit down to keep her mouth shut. The twitch of tension reached her jaw. The question surfaced again in her mind, pulling with it this time a series of quick images—her early days in school of wanting to study art, but picking something safer. Of admiring Latrice and her building designs. Of hiding her disappointments away like acorns. And then, she did start to understand. Perhaps, yes, she was far from enough. Too far to settle and too close not to ask for more.

Ramona brought the glass to her lips again, tasting sweetness, some bitterness, and then the overwhelming essence of cinnamon and spices that she'd come to love so much. It warmed her going down, loosening her again, releasing the tightness, the resistance, leaving her open to desires, to pleasures, to joy.

"So, you're saying that I should ask for more?" She turned to look at Jay, and in her eyes provided flirtatious challenge.

In return, Jay gave her a very slow, very definite, *yes*. He leaned in toward her. His breath warmed her face and carried with it the same smell as her drink. She wanted to taste his lips again too, but something more pressing called for her focus. She needed to tell him the rest of her story.

"Jay . . . I . . . need to . . . well, there was something more to why I came to Malibu." Ramona turned to him. She was unsure of exactly how to say what needed to be voiced and apprehensive about how Jay might think of her after.

"Is this where you tell me you're not who I think you are?"

"I hope not . . ." Ramona's eyes scanned Jay's face for the depth of expression she could make out in the moonlight. "I just didn't expect that this would be more than . . ."

"More than what?"

"More than just one night. More than just acting on a feeling . . ." She wanted to reach out and touch him, to hold his hand. Not tenderly, but for reassurance, for something to grasp in case he pulled away from her. She didn't want to let him go. She was a saver, she didn't want to let anything go, not her relationship with Malik, not the version of herself that she'd envisioned once married. But her meaning now was more than who she dated, what man claimed her, or didn't. She'd gotten a taste of being her own, belonging to herself. Wondering what all she could do, what her body could do, and what her life could be if she just focused on her pleasures.

"Why does this feel like a breakup speech?" Jay's brow furrowed, but he smiled also. Ramona understood, she was confused too. "Like a terrible spoiler alert. I already know what's coming. You're leaving, going back to Chicago."

"You deserve to know the truth . . . which is, when I *left* Chicago, I still had my engagement ring on." Ramona's eyes darted to his as he sat there on the sofa. It was a place that was starting to feel so familiar, so comfortable. And now it seemed like she was messing it all up. But she had to. She didn't want anyone to feel the way that Joan had made her feel. And she wasn't keen on keeping any more secrets.

"So . . . you're . . . *still* engaged?"

"Well, it depends who you ask."

"I'm asking you."

Ramona shifted against the seat beneath her. Her insides were crashing against each other. "I'm saying that I wanted to be . . . still engaged. I came here so that I wouldn't have to tell my family that my relationship ended, that the wedding we'd been planning wasn't going to happen. And I didn't tell them because I didn't want that to be true." Ramona took a sharp breath in. It was the first time she'd heard the truth herself, an admission in her own words. And as bad as it sounded, it felt far worse.

"So, what are you saying? That you don't want to be still engaged?"

"This is the first time . . . I've felt free from it. Except, I'm not free from it—not yet. But right now . . . all I want is for you to not think I'm crazy."

"Then I don't know if this is off to a good start—" To Ramona's alarm, Jay sounded like he was losing some of his patience.

"I . . . was engaged," Ramona responded quickly, trying to catch up to the words that were spilling out of her now. "We were planning a wedding. My dad spent nonrefundable money. And my mom . . . she just loved everything about planning so much. I felt like I was disappointing them. To not see it through . . . And, um, we did . . . we broke up. And I kept planning the wedding. Just like nothing ever happened. After a while, it just seemed like the right thing to do. At least, I convinced myself of that. Because we could always get back together. And if nobody knew we broke up and we got back together . . . then everything would be all right in the end . . ."

"So, you thought you'd come to Malibu, have a little fling. And I'm the fling. Is that right?"

"Not a fling, not like cheating!" Ramona slapped her hand on the sofa next to her. "I don't think that he and I will . . . I mean . . ." She set the glass on the floor next to her and immediately folded her head down into her hands. "Jay, this is an *impossible* situation," she said finally. "Either I admit I'm crazy, or I'm a cheater, right? And . . . I don't know which one I am right now."

Ramona sat back up to look at Jay, hoping for some sympathy. An off-ramp perhaps. But the look she found on his face crushed her. In his eyes was hurt, she could see it even in the moonlight.

"Before anything else happens, between you and me," he said, "I need you to figure that out. Because I'm a lot of things, but I'm not a cheater. How you do one thing . . . remember? And I'm not playing that game with you."

"What do you mean?" Ramona was just as surprised by Jay's reaction. "You have women around you all the time. And I heard . . . well, Joan said—"

"I don't know Joan, and Joan certainly doesn't know me. Joan said what to you? Because she's never said more than five words to me, not ever."

"She just said that you're popular . . . with women."

"So now you think I volunteered myself to be your one-night stand? Your local distraction?"

"What's the difference between a one-night stand and something more?" Ramona asked, pulling away from Jay. "Maybe . . ." Ramona hesitated, sure of what she wanted to know, but unsure of what she was about to ask.

"Something more, like what?" Jay asked.

"Maybe . . ." Ramona thought back to the beginning of her trip. To her excitement when she first arrived. And everything she thought she'd experience—how it'd been altered. Because rather than just a traveler fumbling her way through a new place, the innocence of discovery turned into something traumatic. That first night, she was ready to leave, planning to. But, she didn't because . . . "I stayed here," Ramona said, "because of *you*." She spoke the words as she experienced the realization they were meant to convey. The truth rolled in for her, washed over her, and she had no choice but to surrender to it.

"What do you mean?" Understandably, Jay posed the question. His head shook as if Ramona had thrown him a curveball in conversation. But for her, it was no puzzle, just the beginning of an unfurling honesty she wished she'd always had the courage to use.

"When Joan called the patrol, when that strange man came in the middle of the night, I felt . . . so . . . *violated*. I wanted to go home. And I was planning to leave. But your music . . . You know I hated your music?" A smile broke through on Ramona's face. "And then you invited me to your class, and that was my first real invitation here, my first welcome. You helped me find comfort and peace again. And that's why I stayed . . . why I *could* stay."

When Ramona smiled, Jay did too, because it was contagious. And his expression quickly shifted from one matching Ramona's memory to a serious one that matched the mood of the present.

"So, why are we here . . . *now*?" he asked her, earnestly. His eyes softened, seeming to plead independently for an answer, showing his own vulnerability.

"Because, Jay . . . you turned this place into somewhere I wanted to be . . . You made somewhere I couldn't stay a place where I could find myself again. That's not a fling. That's anything but a fling." The scene before Ramona became blurry on the other side of the tears that filled her eyes. She hadn't expected to feel so deeply moved. "Only an incredible surprise that—" she managed to say, and just then a tear spilled, wiped quickly from her cheek with her hand. "I've had the most wonderful time."

Jay's hand came to meet hers, touching her face. Holding her cheek. Coming closer to her. Closer, until the space between them was tiny and then disappeared where their lips met. And after a soft kiss, Jay pulled back.

"Something more, like anything, is on the other side of decisions you make," he said. Then, he kissed her deeply this time, more deeply than he ever had. She returned his kiss, not wanting it to end, but knowing that these were the last moments of the most wonderful time of her life.

JOAN IN MALIBU . . .

JOAN HAD NO EASY TIME ACCEPTING THE OBVIOUS, THAT Ramona was not going to make an appearance on Christmas Day. In fact, dinner had already finished, with just her children in attendance—the seat reserved for Ramona remained empty. And just after they dined and opened gifts, the kids, or the adults they'd become, set off to the guest rooms to settle in for the night. Joan was alone again, not like she planned, with only her thoughts and the feral self-accusations of her mind.

When Joan received Chelsea's message the night before, the one about ratting her out, she'd all but finished wrapping her cornucopia of gifts, mostly for her children and those who provided her multitude of very regular services—a bottle of great wine for her hairdresser, an expensive scarf for the gal who did her facials. Never a gift card, or worse, an envelope of cash. To her that reminded her of the tips her mother used to count at the kitchen table, so impersonal, so unfestive. No, Joan was very much a gift giver and considered herself a very generous one at that.

The message about Ramona being "missing" and her return message to Chelsea about Jay confirmed Joan's original concerns about the man and exactly what she'd feared. That he'd taken Ramona out of character, taken advantage of her.

That she was just another one of his conquests at the beach, a casualty of his ego and libido. He didn't care about Ramona—how could he? He didn't know her, not like Joan did. After all, look at how much effort she'd made.

So, seeing the lights still out next door, the shades drawn, the place quiet and motionless, even when she succumbed (only briefly!) to the urge to take just one more peek with her mounted binoculars, she was infuriated by helplessness and determined still to find a way to make the case for her virtue. Without the ability to rescue, Joan did the only other thing she knew best how to do. She gifted. Heading back downstairs, she pulled out the bright orange scarf box with the horse on top and decided then and there that this one would be Ramona's, her own square of Joan's life, her very own symbol of belonging. She pulled the folded card out from under the ribbon that held it in place, picked up her pen, and started to scribble a note.

Other than her gifts, her invitations, and her (very generous) donations, she had nothing else to show for the fact that she loved and accepted all people. Her children were woefully ordinary, her regular friends embarrassingly homogenous. So, what else was there to evince her kindhearted, open-minded goodness if she couldn't make friends with people like Ramona? And now, having entirely ignored her dinner invitation, Ramona must be thinking the worst of her; of course, not that she was r—, but that, perhaps even worse, she was, God forbid, fake.

So, Joan decided that she would walk over to Chelsea's and leave Ramona her gift and the note that accompanied it. That square orange box with the horse atop, and her words of friendship, this would be the repair solution for *everything*. Joan climbed down her external staircase, the wrought iron spiral that spanned through all of her home levels down to the beach below. She walked along the narrow strip of sand that remained before the tide came back in, all the way over to Chelsea's house. She climbed up the spiral staircase there, similar to how Ramona had when she first arrived in Malibu. And on the wooden deck, Joan searched around in the dark for the best place to leave Ramona's gift without it being ruined in the night hours by sea air or ocean spray. And for just a brief second, with Ramona's gift, on Chelsea's back deck, Joan thought about where she'd *first* seen her. Right here, where Ramona was doing then almost the exact same thing as Joan now. And just briefly she wondered if there was someone who'd do what she did then, call the patrol on *her*. And then she thought, *That's silly*, because there was no one there to see her, and moreover for anyone who could, she was so obviously Joan, who belonged there, who belonged in Malibu. Joan, who belonged there . . . and Ramona, who . . . did not?

And then Joan froze. She froze still on the deck, standing on the gently creaking wood and the piles adjusting with the rising of the tide. She realized with such clarity in just that moment what she had done. She had one spectacular moment of seeing everything in a single flash of brilliance, how fascinatingly unintentional it all was—how preexisting conceptions of someone can shape your assessment of them, of the threat they pose, or the value they have, or of their belonging in a circumstance. And how that same split-second assessment determines the decision you make of what to do—whether the patrol is called, or not. Whether a hello is extended, or a helping hand, or an open door rather than a closed one.

But the awareness was brief, fleeting, too uncomfortable to sit with, an equation too difficult to solve. And rather than examining it, finding its roots, and pulling them out like she did with the unwanted hairs on her chin, or the tufts of ugly crabgrass in her garden, she left it there, with Ramona's gift and the card attached, to sit on the deck in the darkness.

DECEMBER 26

RAMONA LAY NEXT TO JAY, SPENT AGAIN, EXHAUSTED, AND catching her breath. Her body tingled still from lingering arousal. She fidgeted her toes to release some of the energy. Jay was next to her, lying on his side, propped up on an elbow. She could feel him looking at her, even though her eyes remained closed. As her body had been exhausted with Jay—rolling, rocking, rubbing together—the exertion of them physically, the way he made her insist on her satisfaction until she was *fully* satisfied, which was twice this time (a second time she didn't even know was possible), lasting until there was nothing more for her body to do. This left her mind free to wander, and where she returned was to the ocean. The water, the waves, the rush of power, of momentum, and the thrill of accomplishing something with her own self that was for her enjoyment alone. The use of her own body for her very own pleasures and delights, the reclamation of her internal and external spaces, this is what she thought of now. She thought of what was required for her healing, what would bring her back to wholeness. What she would claim of what remained of this trip to set her even. And there was only one thing, not to be given, but to be taken.

"What are you thinking about?" Jay's voice was soft and crooning. The only other sound now was the quiet of midnight. Ramona considered his question, and the answer came.

"Leaving . . ." she said. "I'm thinking about leaving you, the ocean . . . and how I wish I could bottle it up, bottle everything up and take it back. And I wish I could see what I looked like, out there, on the water. What my face looked like, what position my body was in, just right at that moment when I stood up on a wave. Jay, *that* moment, I had everything . . . It was all *me*, just me . . . *being* enough. I felt it . . . I'm just . . . I'm afraid I'll lose it. That when I go back, I'll forget."

Jay rolled over from his elbow to his back. He folded his arms underneath his head and turned again to look at Ramona. This time she was looking at him and he was smiling, they both were. The moonlight from the window was a silver twinkle in his eyes.

"What?" Ramona asked. In response, Jay smiled bigger, until his lips parted across his teeth and then he was laughing. Without quite knowing why, she was laughing too. "What?" she asked again.

"It wouldn't be like your lesson, but I have a board and a wetsuit that I keep for my rental unit. I won't be able to help you if you want me to take a photo—you'll have to go out yourself. But if you'd like to try again, we can try to catch an early surf before your flight."

Ramona was smiling now, big smiling, with her full face and eyes, with her mouth and her heart.

"So, you'll take the picture?"

Jay nodded.

And Ramona realized from there that the rest would be up to her.

At daybreak, the sunlight reached its fingertips through the window to dance on Ramona's face. She blinked, coming to. She'd been having a dream just then, of the ocean, of communion with her. Ramona had been swimming in her depths among the corals and large rocks at the sandy bottom. All around was a world of turquoise blue. And within that world was a voice, so calming and peaceful and serene, almost like a song through a wind chime. *Relax . . . Your healing is here*, the ocean said to her. *The water . . . is your inheritance . . . Come home . . .* the wind-chime voice intoned. As she lifted into wakefulness, Ramona struggled to hold on to that voice, to its invitation, to the feeling of peace that it imparted. The voice was all around her in her dream state and then gradually it wasn't, fading like a distance was growing, until, as Ramona blinked her eyes into the sun, all that remained was an echo in her mind and the sound of the waves from outside the window in her ears.

Then, there was not much time to spare. As quickly as she awakened, right at the alarm that she and Jay agreed to set, Ramona sprung up, arranged herself, and roused him. At seven o'clock in the morning, it was just dawn. By the time they retrieved the surfboard and the wetsuit from Jay's back-of-house cottage and walked down to the beach, the sun had clearly decided to participate in Ramona's goodbye to Malibu.

As she had in her lesson, Ramona began to peel the suit on, starting by dipping her feet toes-first into the narrow-bunched tubes of neoprene legs. Feeling Jay's eyes on her, she remembered the instruction when she'd first done this days ago, sorting the thick fabric around her with tiny pulls and stretching.

She pulled upward, focusing first on her calves, then knees, then up across her thighs. With the suit at her waist, she dipped her arms in as Jay had shown her and finished her enrobing. As she wriggled with the zipper in the back, Jay came over to pull it up to the top. She was ready for the water.

This time, Jay was positioned on the beach, with just his ankles barely beyond the shoreline for risk of losing the precious phone he held to capture evidence of Ramona's triumph. At least, her planned triumph—it was indeed a clumsy start. Wading out alone, Ramona fumbled and tripped at one point, managing the board for the first time without help. But, determined as ever, despite nearly falling in the calf-deep water, she continued.

Where the water was waist-deep, sloshing up against her wetsuit, it came time to steady the board so that she could lay her body on top of it, horizontal and flat. She put her hands on either side of the board, where Jay had told her to, took a deep breath in, and lurched herself forward to flop unevenly on the surface. On the first attempt, she slid off, back to where she'd stood, as the board tilted to one side, lifting up from the water. Ramona sighed. She turned back to look at Jay. He was standing there, at the edge of the surf, looking worried, but dutifully holding the phone in his hand, camera pointed in her direction. Seeing what she needed to see, and reminded of her mission, Ramona turned around to once again face the horizon.

"If I'm supposed to be here, then you have to help me," she whispered to the water below her. She placed her hands again on either side of the board, watching the whitewash of the waves break ahead of her. The flow of the water in toward the shoreline lifted the board up some, bobbing it up and down in her hands in rhythm. She took a deep breath, bent her knees, and launched up again, pushing past the grip of gravity, the pull of the water, and put enough air between her and the surface below to land with a satisfying splat of the neoprene suit against the top of the board. She'd landed somewhat diagonally, but still landed . . . enough to steady herself, which she scooted over to do, to find the centerline and align with it. She was floating now, on the top of the water. But she had farther to go.

With one arm on each side of the board, her hands dipped into the salt water beneath her, pushing along, alternating sides stroke after stroke, with a frantic freestyle out ahead. It was exhausting, and she quickly became winded. As she moved farther out, the waves began to lift her up and push her backward, erasing her progress. But onward Ramona paddled. She had to reach the calm, the space of the lineup. The place where the waves began to break, where she would try to catch her ride.

She paddled to the strip of calm sea, reaching it with much relief, and pulled herself up to a seated position straddling the board, just to catch her breath. She was breathing hard by now, panting almost, with the exertion of the swim bolstered by the urgency of the occasion. As she sat out behind the break of the waves, floating alone with only a speckling of other surfers down the shoreline from her, she breathed in the air. She took in everything she wanted to remember. The birds flying overhead in the blue sky. The rising sun. The feeling of her feet in the water, the gentle lifting and dipping of the rocking of the ocean. She closed her eyes for a moment and tried to hear that voice again, the one from her dream, the wind chime in the breeze. The voice telling her that she belonged, that this place was for her too, that the water in her body came from this place. That she could bring her pain here, her uncertainty, her mistakes, her fear, and exchange it all in a baptismal experience. She would claim her joy here, her confidence, her faith in the new thing her life would become. This was the time.

Opening her eyes now, Ramona could see her wave approaching along the horizon. Very deliberately, she began to lower her torso to the board, positioning it toward the shore. Her belly tightened with anxiety, knowing that the moment would be fast approaching. When the wave came to meet her, she'd be lifted up into the arms of the ocean, hoping to be received with kindness. She began to paddle fervently forward, toward the shore, picking up surprising speed. But it wasn't her speed, was it? No, it was the water rushing beneath her, with its power and grace. She was ahead of it now, the roar was behind her, the rushing of the waves, the froth of the breaking wave; this was the time to stand, to stand up and, for whatever moment she could, find her footing and balance. She pulled herself up on her knees, on all fours, ready to pull her left foot forward, balancing on the centerline of the board. The speed and the rush of the water reminded her that it was time now, now, Ramona. Now!

She pulled her foot forward, seeking the centerline of the board, crouching, riding; she felt the breeze in her hair, on her face, all around her as she moved with momentum toward the shore. With another breath, deep and held in her lungs, she took the final push in her body to stand. To stand in her lunge, to try to balance, to wobble, wobble, to tip, tip, but then try in milliseconds to correct herself, to find her footing again, so desperately trying to stay upright. But too far to the right now . . . as the wobbling increased and became unsteady, Ramona fell into a rumble of the waves beneath her.

CHELSEA IN CHICAGO

ON THE MORNING OF HER DEPARTURE, CHELSEA AWOKE TO THE surprise of Carlos still sleeping snugly in the bed with her. When he finally rose, groggy and rubbing his eyes, she'd already completed most of her packing. She was so relieved that Carlos had decided to stay. She'd passed some threshold with him, she thought, to some kind of mattering possibly, and maybe that she wasn't like all of the other girls—the ones he invited places, like he'd invited Chelsea, but maybe had not seen them the same way. She found it impossible to believe that he could have seen her so clearly without knowing her, and then spoken to her in that same language that artists speak, found the truth that sparked a flame in her heart. She was burning now, with a fire of ideas—what she wanted to paint, not just landscapes or animals this time, but people, bustling life, the city and all of its lights.

When he greeted her, she couldn't resist asking, "But, I thought you said you wouldn't stay?"

Carlos, still in the throes of sleepiness, seemed to perk up at this. "I usually don't," he said.

"Why not?"

"I don't do attachments. A good time, but not a long time, you know? You stay the night and then expectations come. I can only be what I am—not somebody's boyfriend, or brunch date, or valet, or cook, even. I'm an *artist*. I work three jobs, take extra shifts, to save for my exhibition. I can't compromise that, not for anyone."

"Then why last night?"

"Because it's different with you. You want what I want. And it seems like you have even less to give than I do."

"Christmas Eve . . . what made you—"

"I think you know."

"The painting?"

"You *finished* the painting. That first night . . . it was on the table. You'd just started it."

"Just an eye," Chelsea said. "Did you know it was of you?"

"Yeah, I did. But what does it mean when it's just a sketch of an eye? You know as well as I do that people find inspiration anywhere. A start is just a sketch, an idea. You could have left it there and never come back to it again. I saw how you finished it. That's what made it meaningful. That's when I understood . . . you were letting me go."

"So last night . . . is you letting me go . . ."

Carlos smiled. "Maybe, I wanted just once, to see what you look like, first thing in the morning."

"Will you take a picture of me?" Chelsea asked. "Just to have." She added that last part quickly, as if it excused her request.

"Like this?" He gestured to her. Her hair was a mess, all unruly and flaming bramble of tangles, not unlike the night they just spent together.

"Like this." As she spoke, she started to slide off the strap of her bra and then the other and pulled her arms behind her back to unhook the clasps that held it together. And then she stood up and pulled down the sides of her leisure shorts, hooking into the band of her underwear, that she pulled down along with it so that she was fully naked. She didn't know what part of her he'd want to capture, so she turned for him, unashamed, to the right and to the left, the full front of her and behind to let him choose. It was the ultimate practice of vulnerability, but also she did not want him to forget her. She wanted him to remember her lips and her breasts, her hips and the curve of her ass, her lines, her tones, the colors of her as well, like she had memorized his. She hoped that he would care to capture it in his form of art. After all, she had placed him in her own.

Carlos lifted himself from the bed and reached for his phone. Chelsea observed the rippling of the muscles underneath his skin the color of custard, doing their obvious work of moving his body, his abs and arms, toned and sinewy, themselves a luxury to look at. Trying not to move from her pose, Chelsea watched as he moved toward her, as the sheets fell away, uncovering him, the dark hair on his thighs, the lines of his quads and the power in them. She saw his masculinity hang between his legs, what he'd used to pleasure her in the night, swinging casually against his thigh, forgotten for now, just an appendage as was his arm reaching for his phone—his focus was elsewhere. And she wondered if she aroused him, if he thought her beautiful, or just interesting. If he'd wanted her body as something available, or if he'd wanted her. She posed some more, trying different things—making her chest concave, and then lifting it by pulling her shoulders back, so that her nipples would stand up high in the air, their pinkness perking perfectly—to see if it mattered.

As she moved, he moved around with her, around on the bed. He was naked, as was she, exposed, vulnerable, and in conversation somehow. Two artists, a call and response of physicality, one trying to touch the heart and the other trying to capture an idea. Chelsea pulled her arm across her face to pull her hair up, and then, deciding to leave it there, hair pulled atop her head like a flower, hand resting to hold it there, she tried to figure out what to do with the other hand, where to put it.

"Bring your other arm up," Carlos said. "Bend it and rest your fingers there, the tips right on your collarbone." He snapped again, tapping the screen of his phone. Chelsea wondered if she was doing what he wanted. If finally, he'd seen what he wanted to see. She felt her breast compressed against her forearm and was stimulated as the lower part of her wrist grazed its sensitive parts. She was alive now and released of fear. Carlos crossed the bed to her and left the phone somewhere in the tangle of sheets between them. He reached for her, and she reached back, arms intertwined and then lips. And then their bodies were locked together again like they'd been before, and all of him was present to pleasure her. But this time she felt connected to him and like none of those other girls. She'd made him see her, something of herself she gave him more than her body, more than her pain and longing. She'd let him see her fire, her freedom, her true self.

RAMONA AT THE BOTTOM OF THE PACIFIC
OCEAN . . .

RAMONA'S BODY TWIRLED AROUND ITSELF IN A BALL AS SHE bounced off the sandy ocean bottom. The air that was in her lungs pressed its way out of her mouth, and a rage of desperation flashed through her as she hovered on the edge of panic. That stream of thoughts cascaded into *oh no*, she'd gone too far. She feared now that she didn't belong, and what everyone warned about—why you didn't go into the water, why the ocean wasn't hers, or home—was true. But, below the water, as the energy of the surf started to dissipate, Ramona heard the word from her dream. *Relax* . . . The sound of the wind chimes reminded her. *Relax*, she thought. *Relax*. She let her feet drop, unballing herself. And she found that she was closer to the bottom than she realized. With her soles on the ocean floor and her knees bent, Ramona stretched herself upward, in the direction of the sun, and burst through the surface of the water.

The tug on her leg brought her attention to her surroundings. She was standing in the shallows now but being pulled aggressively by the board leash connected to her ankle.

"Grab the board!" Jay shouted in her direction, splashing toward her. "Pull the leash line, quick!"

Spitting the last salty seawater out of her mouth, Ramona focused quickly, bending down and grabbing the thick black plastic cable and pulling it against the force of the current, until she could feel the board moving back in her direction. It was heavy, even in the water, large and still unwieldy. But she managed to get it into her hands and then pushed herself heavy step by heavy step back toward the shoreline.

"Are you okay?" Jay asked, reaching her quickly. All Ramona could think of was one thing.

"Did you get it?" She was out of breath, panting from the exertion of it all. But she was safe now. She had succeeded. And she was no longer afraid.

Jay smiled. "I got the whole thing . . ." he said.

"I stood up, right? You saw that?"

Jay put his free hand behind Ramona's back as the two of them walked together out of the water, clearing themselves past the damp sand. He reached his hand still holding the phone toward her and scrolled to a video.

"Here, right here." Jay hit the pause button, and Ramona pulled his hand toward her so that she could see more of the screen. It was her, frozen in time, for just one glorious moment when she was riding on the water, in her stance, balanced and looking forward. The moment just before she fell, but she had it now. This was *enough*.

CHELSEA ON A PLANE HEADING WEST, SOMEWHERE OVER KANSAS . . .

DURING THE HOURS THAT CHELSEA SAT IN HER PLANE SEAT, buckled in on the return to California, she thought of Carlos. She remembered him as he looked dropping her off at the airport terminal. She smelled him still as she smelled him then, pulling her bags through the sliding doors, in a whoosh of the last of the Chicago winter wind to whip its way around her, making its own icy farewell. As the plane took off, she sat in her seat by the window and watched as the snow-covered plains retreated from her. The frozen lake got smaller and smaller, until there were only the clouds and the sky to see. Once she lowered the flap of the window and closed her eyes, the images she'd captured played like highlights across a screen. She saw two people, in a restaurant, one with flaming red hair and another with eyes the color of sunlit iced coffee, smiling and laughing, eating a pizza between them with tendrils of melted cheese hanging about. Their mouths were open and hands up with fingers splayed in front of their faces. Imagining this, she felt the sides of her face rise, goofy looking probably to others. But Chelsea didn't care. She didn't care anymore. She was flying now. She was going home.

RAMONA ON A FLIGHT BACK TO CHICAGO, TURNING EAST HIGH OVER THE PACIFIC . . .

SOMETHING FELT RIGHT ABOUT LEAVING MALIBU. AS HER PLANE lifted up, up, out over the sea, Ramona felt an unmistakable sense of lifting in her body, of weightlessness, of freedom. And when, already thousands of feet above the country, the metallic wings turned for a gigantic loop around, becoming a boomerang headed back east, Ramona sighed heavily. Her engagement ring was still solidly tucked away in her bag. Already, her exposure to the sun had caused enough of her melanin to conceal the shadow of it on her finger. She'd said goodbye to Jay, and to the ocean, and to Malibu itself in a way that left her with this deep sense of accomplishment. Perhaps it was only the simple act of leaving with a new version of herself, to have created a catalyst for something, for anything, for the rest of what her life could be.

This feeling of resolve, mixed with a bit of longing, stayed with Ramona until her car pulled up in front of the unmistakably familiar greystone, right there on East Forty-Eighth Place, where her bedroom used to be, and her childhood was spent, and where her parents still were waiting for her to return. This time, the view of what was so familiar filled her with apprehension. She understood what kind of a scene she'd likely caused there, what kind of fear and angst she'd created for her parents, how upset they must still be. And all of that brought her feet to the ground, setting them firmly in the snow. She crunched her way through salt and ice up the walkway to her parents' door.

They were expecting her, Melba and Phillip, who'd done so much together, who'd stayed together through good times and lean times, through the challenges of raising two children on Chicago's South Side, where there wasn't ever quite enough of anything other than love and good discipline. Together, they opened the door for Ramona. Facing them now in person, Ramona couldn't help but think of her childhood when her brother or Carlos might warn her, "Oooh, you in trouble." But she wasn't in trouble, she was *grown*. She was grown and could face the consequences. She was grown and could make decisions. She was grown and, therefore, could tell the truth. Ramona took a deep breath and walked forward, to close the door behind her. She continued into their outstretched arms, which quickly came around her, arms from both her mother and her father, encircling her. All of them connected, six arms together, hugging one another very tight.

Melba pulled herself back from Ramona and looked at her. It was a mother's inspection of close concern, a survey starting at the top of her daughter's hair, worn now in a makeshift poof, to her clothes and how they fit—whether she'd lost weight from not having enough to eat.

"You hungry?" Melba said, seemingly satisfied with what she saw.

Ramona was starving and nodded yes, observing her mother turn from the doorway toward the kitchen. This left Ramona on the landing with her father, and the understanding that the universal words for forgiveness had been spoken—her mother's "You hungry?" did mean just that. Between them, at least, all was forgiven for now, to be talked about later perhaps, but hard feelings would not linger.

"Come over here, baby girl, let's talk for a minute." Her father guided her gently toward the sofa in the living room. It was a place where he'd talked to her once about what not to do on prom night, and where he promised that she could always come home—no matter what—when she left for college.

"Okay, Daddy," Ramona replied softly, and followed the short distance. She sat on the sofa next to him, sank into the cushions and waited for what he was going to say.

Her father released a long sigh, his charcoal wool cardigan rounded at the shoulders a bit more. It was a pronounced reminder that time had also weathered him into much softer lines than the rough edges of his younger days. "Ramona, that young man, Malik, he came to the house the other night and said you weren't together anymore. Is that true?"

Ramona was surprised that her father was still allowing for the possibility that somehow, even after all that had happened, *she* believed they were. But his unshakable faith in her wasn't the right shelter for now, or an excuse to use. The time had come for Ramona to tell the truth, all of it.

"Yes, Daddy, it's true." It physically pained Ramona to admit this, but she continued. She owed this much. "We broke up. We broke up months ago. We started fighting during counseling . . . there was so much we'd never talked about. It started to feel like we had nothing in common. When he moved out, I just thought he'd come back and we'd work it out like you and Ma do. I really thought we might get back together . . . That we'd go ahead and get married—"

The words poured out of Ramona. The feeling of tears was there, the pressure behind her eyes at the corners. But she wanted to say what needed to be said first. She wanted to look her father in the eyes and apologize.

"I thought he just needed a little more time, and maybe I did too. I—"

Ramona's father stopped her. "You don't need to explain all that," he said, and put his arm around his daughter. His time-weathered hand, he placed over her still smaller one. "That ain't the point."

She looked at him, eyes glistening now. The water of tears had gathered, ready to fall. "I'm sorry, Daddy." It was all she could manage before she sobbed, into the charcoal-gray wool of his shoulder, into the embrace of his arms around her. And there she released the rest of it—the expectations, the guilt—as she mourned the version of herself she once believed she was supposed to become.

Ramona's father let her cry. He let her weep and shudder, but he did not let her hang her head. When she pulled away, her father positioned his fingers just under her chin and pushed her head up. He wiped her tears, and then the new ones. He dabbed the corners of his eyes behind his glasses.

"Do you still want to have your wedding?"

Ramona blinked and looked at her father, confused. "What do you mean? I just don't want you and Ma to lose money. There's so much that you've paid for, that—"

Her father looked pained. "Ramona, I'm not rich, but I've got money." He paused, long enough for the words he said with his whole chest to complete their reverberating journey. "For you, when it comes to you . . . I'll pay for that. If you don't want to see this wedding through, worst case we'll throw another party. But no child of mine will ever be stuck anywhere they don't want to be on account of me."

"Daddy, I—"

"*Never,*" her father said. "Never on account of me."

Like her family, Ramona was a saver. Her parents, she and her brother, and Carlos too had learned to make the most of a little, to focus on what mattered. And the little things, they stayed little. They didn't always have everything, but they had love and a good amount of healthy discipline. And Ramona realized her father was saying that forgiveness was a part of love, and she already had all she needed, and beyond that, all that he had to give.

DECEMBER 27

RAMONA IN CHICAGO . . .

RAMONA'S RETURN TO HER CONDO, FOR SOMEPLACE SO FAMILIAR, felt strange to say the least. Barely a day back, and the place was eerily quiet despite the sounds of the city below. What was missing was not just the sound of the ocean that she'd grown accustomed to as a background noise, but the presence of Wookiee, who was thankfully being imminently returned by Carlos.

Ramona knew by instinct at the sound of the door opening that Carlos had arrived, and before the door had even opened a sliver, a blur of fluff shot through the narrow wedge and raced toward Ramona on the sofa, catapulting himself onto her lap in a flurry of licks and panting.

"I missed you too, Wookiee!" Ramona could barely keep up with the frenetic excitement of her dog, who jumped from the sofa cushion to her lap, down to the floor to race around the kitchen looking for his usual things in their usual places.

"And what about me?" Carlos stood with his big smile in the entryway, with long arms full of dog bed, and bags, and necessities. He kicked his foot backward to shut the door and moved toward the kitchen to set everything down near the island.

"I missed you too, Carlos!" Ramona's smile spread across her face, and she stood to walk over to Carlos, navigating the path through the zigzagging of a still overexcited Wookiee. When she reached him, as the two of them hugged, she wondered briefly what all had happened in her home in her absence, and whether she really wanted to know.

Finally, she pulled back, processing all that was still unsaid. Ramona couldn't help but acknowledge a surge of appreciation for Carlos, new respect for a not-so-little brother. He'd stepped in capably, covered for her, and even when difficult, protected her still.

"Chelsea . . . what was she like?" Ramona asked, after a beat.

"I don't get to ask you first who's Jay?" Carlos volleyed back. Ramona smiled.

"Jay wasn't staying at my house . . . or a guest at Ma's party, Carlos . . ." Ramona poked him in the shoulder playfully, but firmly enough to get his attention.

"Chelsea Flint . . . you should look her up, Moe. She's a really dope artist." Ramona raised an eyebrow. As Carlos met her eyes, a flush came to his face. He was blushing. Ramona found it curious. Carlos usually wasn't prone to self-consciousness.

"Did you—" Ramona cut herself off even though curiosity burned within her.

"Did you?" Carlos tilted his head toward her as if he expected an answer.

Ramona felt her face light up with heat as a flood of images from her time with Jay rushed to mind all at once. She hoped the answer wasn't as obvious as it seemed. Suddenly, that big smile erupted again on Carlos's face.

"I hope so," he said. With that, some of the tension released from Ramona's body.

"What else about her, then?"

"She said she paints best what she's most afraid to lose."

"Did she paint you?" It was an obvious question to Ramona. But standing there with Carlos in the kitchen, him with his coat still on even, she didn't expect to see him so moved. The answer to her question was reflected in his face. He reached into his pocket and pulled out his phone, tapping and scrolling until he turned the screen to her.

"See for yourself." He held the screen closer to her so that she could see it. Ramona's breath caught in her chest. The image of Carlos on the screen was as if he were captured inside there, so viscerally and raw that she almost forgot the real version of him was standing right next to her. The richness of the colors of him, the contours, the depth reflected in his eyes, it was almost as if she were having a conversation with someone about Carlos who knew him as well as she did, who saw him how she saw him and, even more, as the man he'd become— and who loved him. Ramona was transfixed and could barely pull her eyes away.

"She . . . painted *this*?"

"Yeah, while she was here."

"Where is it?" Ramona looked around the apartment.

"She gave it to me."

"She gave you *that*?"

Carlos nodded and Ramona released a soft "wow" under her breath.

CHELSEA IN MALIBU . . .

CHELSEA STARED DOWN AT HER HANDS, HOLDING THE SQUARE orange box with the horse atop, found outside on her deck in plain view. Once discovered, she'd brought it inside and proceeded to drop it on the counter of her compact kitchen island. The cardboard had become slightly warped from the moisture in the sea air, but thankfully the contents, as she inspected them now, were untouched. And the note, the note placed inside was important, because without it, this box would be a complete mystery to Chelsea. But instead, the note was its own sort of time capsule, containing a message from Joan to Ramona and identifying the intended recipient of the gift.

Chelsea felt a little like a voyeur, inspecting its contents, or paying attention more than the bare minimum to the note's scribbled handwriting, signed by Joan. So, she quickly packed it all away and left it to sit again in its place on the counter until she could return it. And quite frankly, she had other things to do rather than to obsess about a box, or Joan, for that matter. She had images in her mind, swimming and swirling, over-flowing from here to there taking up all of the space. She'd been cracked open, and her imagination was overflowing like a boil-ing pot. Today she'd work on the image in the pizzeria. Tomor-row, perhaps the room of candlelight and perhaps the next day, the frozen lake. Her canvas was already prepped and ready even before the day's overcast managed to burn away. She mixed her colors, trying Carlos's new blue in as many ways as she could imagine—mixed in grays and browns, and purples, even some of her versions of white. And maybe it was just the fact that she was still activated by him, still looking for him in everything, everywhere, that she did see the colors become brighter. She did see that perhaps she'd create gold again, that something would or could sell. But more than creating something she loved—she was using the language that artists used. This was in her heart.

Chelsea was so deeply involved in this that she barely no-ticed the music that started outside, not until it became dis-tracting. She was so impatient to finish today's work that she decided to ask Jay if he could possibly turn the sound down a bit, so that she could concentrate. And by concentrate, she really meant reliving the experiences that inspired her.

Chelsea slid open the door and walked out to her deck and descended her stairs leading down to the beach. "Hey! Would ya mind?" she shouted over the noise. When Jay looked up, Chelsea gestured to the speaker. His class participants milled about in their expensive gear, all tight and tailored spandex, tank tops, and belly buttons. Some arranged their yoga mats in carefully spaced rows on the sand. Others practiced poses that looked more like performance art than a stretching activity. When his attention turned to Chelsea, Jay looked as if he remembered something, and turned to make an adjustment on his phone. Immediately the noise level of the music lowered, leaving the dominance of the wind and waves.

"Ah, I forgot! I'd gotten used to—"

Chelsea finished for him. "Ramona?"

Jay lifted his hand to his eyes. The wind whipped the longer parts of his hair around. "Yeah . . . she was . . . hmm, she's *missed*."

Chelsea, thinking of Carlos, understood Jay's response. What it meant. He'd spent time with her, gotten to know her. And now, she's gone, and also *missed*. That spoke volumes. Chelsea missed Carlos. And Jay, evidently, *missed* Ramona. She wondered what a person like Jay did with those kinds of feelings, like Chelsea painted hers.

"I'm glad she stayed . . ." Jay said, and smiled, but his eyes did not look at Chelsea this time. She could see he was looking elsewhere, in his mind, remembering like she was.

"You going to see her again?"

Jay opened his mouth to speak, but was tapped by one of his class attendees, whose hair bounced to the right and left in a ponytail as she bounded up to him. Chelsea couldn't hear their conversation, but noted when Jay gave her a pointed wave and turned around. *What does he do with feelings like that?* Chelsea wondered again. Feelings that swell up inside that make you want to fight to hold on past the changing of circumstances? Chelsea wondered what Jay would have answered, what she would have answered, and what fate would answer for them both.

DECEMBER 28

EACH YEAR, RAMONA ACCOMPANIED LATRICE AS SHE INSISTED
on doing her Christmas shopping *after* Christmas. According
to Latrice, this shopping was actually her duty, as she felt obligated to return each one of the Christmas presents that she
did not like or want, in favor of purchasing what she did want.
This theme of exchanging what you do not want for what you
do want was perfect on this particular year for the two friends,
as this was exactly Ramona's circumstance.

"Girl, you know you need to talk to Malik, right?" Latrice
pulled the door open for Ramona at one of their favorite fast-
fashion temples, a humongous storefront on Michigan Avenue
with windows filled with headless mannequins wearing sleek
designs. The interior of the store pumped some kind of nondescript techno beat, thumping, thumping as the soundtrack
to the inextinguishable consumption that permeated the store.

"And tell him what, Latrice? That I secretly kept planning
our wedding, ran off to California to hide it, slept with a surfing
yoga instructor, and now don't want him back?"

Latrice raised an eyebrow and then lifted a perfect forest-
green sweater on a hanger. "Well, since you put it *that* way . . .
Do you think this would look good on me?" Ramona shook her
head no. Latrice turned the sweater to look at it again, returned

it to the rack, and narrowed her eyes at Ramona. "I know you're just being petty, but I'm looking for something else anyway." Latrice turned to walk ten paces to another rack.

"Latrice." Ramona sighed in frustration.

Latrice turned from her rack raking to look at her. "The real question is what are you going to do about what's his name, Jay? You've been broken up with Malik for months. Any mourning you have left is about a wedding, not your relationship. And now you've already moved on! So, what you really need to decide is . . . not what are you going to tell Malik, but what are you gonna do about the rest of your life?"

"Maybe some things are meant to just be what they were." Ramona sighed again, dramatically.

"Well, let me ask you this . . . if you never saw him again . . ."

"I don't know. I think I've just learned not to hope."

"And if he never saw you again?"

"What's the difference between a one-night stand and the love of your life?"

"The rest of your life?"

"I wasn't asking you, Latrice. It's what I asked him."

"And what did he say?"

"He said it was on the other side of decisions."

"Yours or his?"

"Mine, I think. Although I didn't ask him . . . I don't know. He seemed pretty annoyed that I didn't tell him about Malik earlier."

"Girl, this is so tragic." Latrice shook her head.

Frustrated, Ramona threw her arms in the air. "Let's just face it! This is where everyone goes back to their original lives because nothing big enough happened to make a difference!"

Latrice froze in the midst of searching, of sliding hangers across the metal rod. Her hand rested on the last thing she touched. Her head whipped to face Ramona, eyes narrowed again with ferocity. "What do you mean, *nothing* happened? *You* happened, Ramona. *You happened.* When do you *finally* realize that *you're* the *big thing*?

"You, *Ramona*, who spends her whole life saving for something without even knowing why or what for. Who hides how she really feels, what she *really* needs from everyone else just to spare *their* feelings . . . like *you* don't have any. You take what life hands to you, and you keep it because for some reason, you think it's what you deserve. You, *Ramona*, who spent months, *months*, continuing to plan a wedding so that your mother could still have fun dress shopping. Meanwhile, the biggest events of your life so far happened in one week in California."

"It wasn't just a *wedding*, Latrice," Ramona replied, defeated.

Latrice raised an eyebrow in response and released a huff.

Ramona wanted more than anything to be understood. No, it wasn't really about a wedding. So, she tried again, beginning to speak haltingly, but finding more courage with each word to say the unsayable. "What if . . . what if there's never someone who chooses me again?"

Latrice looked as surprised as if she'd been struck. Her mouth dropped open, with a shock she seemed to need to shake off. She lurched forward suddenly and wrapped her arms around her friend, so tightly it was almost uncomfortable.

"*Girl, what are you saying?* Someone already chose you—we all have. Again, and again, and again. The people that happen to us, the experiences we share, they are not just coincidences. They're all *choices*. And the most important choices now . . . are *yours*."

"Not everyone gets a happy ending, Latrice." Ramona pulled herself back to look her friend in her eyes. Between them now stood the essence of her fears and her doubts, all very inconveniently shared over the thump of music and under the harsh fluorescent lighting of the least intimate place they could be. But it didn't matter, because the moment was urgent, as were the feelings.

"And maybe you're not the person who gets a happy ending because you don't ask for one." With a sigh of frustration, Latrice seemed to turn her attention back to the clothing rack. But then, after just a slight hesitation, she turned back to Ramona as if she'd forgotten something important. "Prime example . . . what did you get for Christmas?"

"I don't know, some clothes, a few gift cards. Some books. Why?"

"Anything you wanted?"

"Not particularly, but I didn't really ask—"

"Exactly. And are you going to return anything?"

"It's a gift!"

"If it's a gift you don't want, it's a liability in the back of your closet. Deadweight taking up space. Something you held on to so that someone else would never truly know you, right? So they can continue to believe you're someone you're not. So you don't hurt *their* feelings?" Latrice's words made tiny pokes into Ramona's gut, felt as acutely as if actually prodded by a finger. "You can't keep saving everyone else from themselves."

Ramona knew then that the words from Latrice would stick like gum to the bottom of her shoe. *You can't keep saving everyone else from themselves*, her mind echoed. And then, she thought of all the times she'd done exactly that. She opened her mouth several times to protest, then to reply, but there wasn't anything else she could find to say. Thankfully, Latrice saved her from having to. She was busy returning her unsatisfactory selections to the rack. When she finished, she ushered both of them toward the exit.

"Ramona, this should be your *send it back* era. If you don't want it, don't keep it. Let's go. I've got two more stores and then five hundred bucks in gift cards from Tar-jheh . . . from the people who really know my heart." Latrice smiled at Ramona. Ramona smiled back, because one of those gift cards had been from her.

DECEMBER 29

RAMONA IN CHICAGO . . .

RAMONA'S ARM BUZZED ALONG WITH THE HAND VACUUM AS SHE ran it across the fabric of her sofa cushion for the fourth time that day. Her hand chased the path of the nozzle and she brushed away remaining debris, although there wasn't any. Cleaning was simply a perfect channel for nervous energy. Since her conversation with Latrice, Ramona had built up the nerve to reply to Malik and do what she needed to, which was establish a time to speak. This would be the first time in months that he'd return to her place. Now overlooking this season's frozen lake, in warmer times it used to be the home they shared.

It was midafternoon, but the sun had already started to set, darkening the sky over Chicago, too quickly stripping one valuable weekend day that stood between Ramona and a return to work. A return to the same thing, the same grind, the same office and view, but this time, without even so much as an illusion to look forward to. It was jarring, to have felt so free, to be fed a diet of hope and happiness in some other place, only to return home and feel now like the best of things had already happened. What Latrice said, about asking for a happy ending, haunted her still. She wondered even now what that meant with someone like Malik.

In happier times between the two of them, the weekend meant the ease of him bringing her a coffee from his early rise and trip to the gym. It meant her cooking breakfast for them—the sizzle of eggs in olive oil—her remembering to season them just the way he liked. It meant conversations about what they'd watch. And then, being nestled up on the sofa together, navigating the stream of content that provided innumerable ways to be entertained, or educated, or provoked. And at times they made plans: she'd work a stable job in finance, one she could tolerate—this one wasn't so bad—and save for retirement. He'd build his career as a personal trainer, get more clients, make more money so they could afford a home together, a fixer-upper maybe.

He never noticed and she hadn't shared her penchant for decorating, or the fact that she'd picked the specific finance department of a specific architectural firm because it placed her just close enough to what was being created, even though once her condo was complete, she wasn't creating anything more herself. But she had listened to Malik's dreams and his proclamations. She'd lain under him and decided to enjoy what she could of that also. She made do with what life had given her, the best to expect with him and the lives around them—the examples that formed what she believed, even now. In all the time before Malibu, Ramona was still looking for what she deserved. And if nothing else, she learned that one week wasn't enough, not enough to twirl around in for a few moments, a tasting menu of joyful times and some terrible ones. As it always does, reality came in too quickly, pruning the sprouting parts of her that blossomed with the idea that maybe, just maybe, she could get away with expecting more.

Malik's arrival was Ramona's appointment with the last reckoning of her escape attempt. His arrival was announced with a knock. Ramona wondered why he didn't use the key he still had, or if he'd kept it, or if you're supposed to return it, like a ring that is no longer a promise. Her ring, now held in her hand, shone brightly in its velvet housing until she closed the cover with a satisfying snap. She left the box on the table just out of sight. As she walked back to the door, she straightened herself, her dress, smoothed her hair, still wanting to be memorable. She pulled the door open, revealing the man she hadn't seen in months beyond his images in photographs.

"It's been a long time." Malik's deep voice, his words, carrying the energy of him, took Ramona by surprise with this sudden proximity. Her face flushed with a rush of embarrassment, of what he knew now that he wasn't supposed to know. This arrival wasn't the return she'd been hoping for. What at first seemed like such a good idea a week ago, to escape and pretend, how silly that was, how ridiculous it felt standing in front of the one person who knew as much of the truth as she did.

But Ramona managed her breath and widened the door opening. She opened her arms, letting him take her into a hug. "It's good to see you." She exhaled the words into his neck, catching a whiff of his familiar scent. Breaking the spell of habit, Ramona pulled herself away, took his heavy coat, and invited him in. It was challenging not to do the dance of his arrival, what they were accustomed to doing when he was last there. *Where should he sit now? Where would she sit? How close? And what to do with her hands?* Wookiee rushed over to him, familiar and panting happily, like nothing had ever happened. Malik bent down to pet him, asking if he was missed. Ramona wondered if she was.

While Malik was preoccupied with Wookiee and his tufts of fur, Ramona went to the kitchen and poured herself a drink. She'd found a specialty shop, Binny's in the South Loop, where she could get just one bottle of that rich, cinnamon porter that she'd enjoyed so much on her trip. She offered Malik a glass.

"So, you drink beer now?" He seemed surprised and waved off the offer.

"I'm trying a few different things," Ramona replied.

Malik shifted on the sofa. "Like planning our wedding as if we hadn't agreed—"

"Malik—" Ramona held her hand up as if to protect herself from the truth.

Malik persisted. "We agreed it was better to call it done, Ramona. We did the counseling and the conversations and everything but the work . . ."

"The work takes time. I thought I was giving you time," Ramona said.

"Not on a deadline." Malik sat forward, further animated. "We can't try to make a relationship work just to save a wedding date."

Ramona cringed but quickly regained her composure. "I thought we made something good—"

"*You* made something good." Malik turned all around him, taking in Ramona's living space. "Your life is together, on course. Mine is all dreams. All dreams still. And it—"

"We could make those dreams together . . . *Could have*, could . . . have . . . made . . ." Ramona corrected herself.

"Not every dream is a team sport, Ramona." Malik slid closer to her across the cushions beneath them, took her hands in his, and met her eyes straight on. "Do you wonder why I never asked for the ring back?"

She shook her head no, although Ramona had held on to that ring as a symbol of hope. That he hadn't asked for it back to her was the possibility that he'd return. He'd have to, she'd thought.

"Because I do *owe you*." Malik squeezed her hands held in his. "I owe you for your inspiration, Ramona. I owe you for believing in me. I owe you for making a home for me, for us. For slowing down the race you've been running and inviting me to catch up. I owe you for the appreciation in your eyes almost every single time you've looked at me. And Imma be real with you, if it takes me showing up at a wedding to repay you for everything you've done for me, and to say vows and to walk back down that aisle into something I know that neither of us are ready for, I will. I will do it. But tell me, Ramona, tell me that that is *not* what you want."

"There was someone . . ." Ramona had no idea why she said it in that way, but, *who did Malik think she was? That she was that desperate?* She hadn't wanted a fake wedding. The feelings were supposed to be real. Something in her snapped against a moment so strange and so unnecessarily selfless that she couldn't stand it any longer.

Malik's eyebrows raised. A vacuum of silence activated between them, stilling the room. As the seconds passed, with each tick . . . tick . . . tick, for Ramona, anticipation was thick. She watched the subtle changes in his face—he bit his lower lip, a tell. His chest rose with a deep inhale. He brought his hand up and rubbed the lower portion of his cleanly lined fade. A muscle twitched along his jaw. Ramona realized she was holding her breath, as was he.

At last, Malik let out a long sigh. His shoulders deflated, and his head shook as if denying himself the next thought. "I don't get to ask you who," he said finally.

With relief, Ramona sat in the pause of wordlessness that followed. As she exhaled herself, it became clear. And she nodded her head gently, *yes*, as if allowing herself her own next thought. "And I don't get to ask you," she said. She understood now. It was over, long over.

For the first moment in the presence of Malik, Ramona thought of Jay. She thought of him freely, without the hesitation of before. It seemed like the right time now to close the door that was left open. She didn't need uncertainty anymore.

"The ring . . . let me—" Ramona turned to retrieve it from where she'd placed it.

Malik caught her hand as she turned, pulling her back to face him. "I don't want it back, Ramona."

"Why not?"

"Because I gave it to you. I want you to keep it."

Ramona's jaw dropped. As she looked at Malik, Latrice's words returned to her mind, bouncing around like an echo.

People don't know you if you don't return the gift, she'd said. Ramona loved Malik still, perhaps always would in some way, but that didn't mean she knew him, or that he knew her—especially if she hadn't let him. She felt quite complete in that moment as herself, *enough* without him, or the ring, or anything it once represented. It was time for him to know her truthfully, who she was *now*.

"Malik, one second." Ramona turned away from him, stood up, and walked over to where she'd placed the velvet box that held the tiny disco ball. She picked it up, brought it over to the sofa, and held it out between them. "I don't want this," she said.

Malik looked shocked. "But I . . . I bought it for you. And . . ."

Ramona reached down to take his hand, pulled it toward her, and pressed the box into his palm, wrapping his fingers around it with hers. "Malik . . . I appreciate you, but this is a gift that *I* don't want. I *don't want* it. And so, I am giving it back." Ramona didn't need any reminders of who she'd been before, living far from satisfied. It was time for a new era, especially now that she had every intention to ask for more.

CHELSEA IN MALIBU . . .

THE ORANGE BOX INTENDED FOR RAMONA SAT ON CHELSEA'S counter forgotten about for days. Chelsea was absorbed in other colors, the colors of Chicago, that she was frantically mixing from memories and painting in strokes on her canvas. It wasn't until she started an image of the *View of the Frozen Lake from the Window*—a description she thought of as a working title for the piece—that she thought of Ramona, and consequently what she might owe her other than a debt of gratitude. She'd borrowed her home, her bed, her coat for one day, ostensibly her life, in a manner of thinking about it, most certainly her wonderful family . . . and Carlos. But Carlos was not borrowed.

No, Carlos was a gift, the best part of the trip. And to him, her gift was to want for him what he wanted for himself.

Thinking about her gift, which was Carlos of course and the glorious experience of Chicago—she remembered that Ramona had a gift from Joan, one that she had no reason or desire to borrow, and that should at least be returned so that Joan could pass it along herself. Presumably, most people would likely want what was in such a fancy box.

The tide was out, but Joan was nowhere to be found on any of her outside deck levels. Chelsea decided to take the box on a short walk outside of her front door, fifty feet to the right, up the walkway next door, all the way to the double doors on the side of her neighbor's long garage. Joan's house was built with an extra level of living space and an entrance into a grand foyer, with a view straight out to the sea. When the door opened, it was Joan, squarely in the center of that majestic ocean view behind her, looking as if she wasn't particularly happy to have company.

Chelsea held up the orange box. "Is this a bad time?"

Joan's face instantly changed to a look of surprise. "Where'd you—"

"It was on my deck, saw it when I got back."

"Did you . . . read the note?"

"I saw it said 'Ramona.'"

"Then, you'll see it gets to her?" Joan made no move to open the door wider. Usually, she invited Chelsea in.

"It's not my gift. It's *yours*." Chelsea held out the box to Joan, a slice through the icy atmosphere, leaving her arm outstretched between them. She was not going to allow Joan to shift one more thing into her court.

Joan snatched the box, and as she did, a white piece of paper floated down to the ground between their feet. Joan bent down to pick it up. "What's this?"

"Ramona's address." Chelsea turned back to head down the walkway, but then remembered something and turned back to

Joan. "You know, she has the most amazing life . . . but I still have no idea what it's like to walk in her shoes. I wondered how that box landed on my deck. I hope that nobody called the patrol on *you*."

Before she turned to head back down the walkway, Chelsea saw Joan's face contort, like her mouth was ready to drop. She was satisfied that Joan would know exactly what she meant without another word. And perhaps it would be uncomfortable between the two of them, a bit icy between neighbors, for a little while. *But Joan should feel a little uncomfortable*, Chelsea thought. The luxury of comfort is just an illusion, one that keeps us from truly knowing one another, stuck in a box of fear. And Chelsea had had enough of being afraid, of being stuck, of hiding ensconced in this small world and its trappings and its limited colors. An idea was brewing for Chelsea, one that started a warmth in her belly and a smile to spread across her face. *It's time*, she thought. *It's time.*

JOAN IN MALIBU . . .

WITH ONE HAND, JOAN CLOSED THE MASSIVE DOUBLE DOORS TO her home. With the other, she held the square orange box that she'd delicately prepared and designated for Ramona, with the same card attached, folded over, all slightly warped now for having sat for some time exposed to the elements. Joan undid the ribbon and inspected the contents. Thankfully moisture had not reached the interior, at least as far as she could tell.

Her mouth was pursed, tight with distaste. It wasn't anything she'd eaten, because Joan faithfully practiced intermittent fasting and, other than a daily green juice, did not eat before noon. Rather, she was perturbed by her encounter with Chelsea. Not that Chelsea had been rude, but Joan felt . . . judged. She thought about it as she carried the box toward the dramatic spiral turngree to descend from her upper living area to the lower one, the much more informal one, heading to her personal suite. On the way, she dropped the box on her kitchen island corner, leaving it and its contents and the note alone so that she could continue with her thoughts where it suited her best.

In front of her mirror, in the extreme privacy of her personal suite, in her bathroom where the most personal of her private activities took place, Joan took a deep, long look at herself. She looked at her forehead, smooth enough, frozen even, as the injections there ensured. And down, below permanently dyed brown eyebrows, to her blue eyes, still crystal blue, mostly, and the sunbaked crinkles around her eye sockets that were stubborn enough to resist the intensive attention in appointment after appointment of treatments with her facialist. She searched the reflection of herself to see if she could find any hint of what she'd done, whether she wore it like a stain. The decision she'd made—she wondered, was it somewhere, and did it make her a term so objectionable she'd dare not even think it?

Imagining how other people might view her, Joan's mind wandered to the moment days ago, standing outside on Chelsea's deck. She was so sure that no one would ever suspect her of not belonging, even though it was not her home, even though she had not been invited or particularly welcome, even at night. And only now she wondered what it might be like to have no bit of the benefit of doubt, no share of a presumption of belonging, of innocence, of a right to be there or somewhere else and what it might feel like. But that feeling, even just imagining it, for Joan was uncomfortable. It placed her on both sides of a door in her mind labeled *The Past*—a door with a lock on it and a double bolt because she'd come so far from there, and *no, no, no,* she thought, no need to consider it.

She *belonged* in Malibu, with her friends and acquaintances, in seats at their tables and together at the Club, buckled into their private planes and invited, always invited to their soirées. She had the house and the clothes and the car and the well-known last name to prove it. She'd made a mistake, one simple little mistake that *anyone* would make . . . well, anyone in the position to make it of course. But in turn, she'd made Ramona feel so *welcome*, hadn't she? And thus, what harm in the end? Because without Joan, what would Ramona's trip have been? Without dinner at Geoffrey's or the Malibu Pier? Without her welcome basket of pastries? And she would have succeeded in the ultimate pièce de résistance, both the lamb and the roast, and Ramona's seat at the table on Christmas no less—but there had been that objectionable Jay who'd stolen her time. Jay who'd made her miss the gift that Joan had carefully placed, a final gesture to make all amends.

Jay, Joan thought, as her self-inspection continued. She brought her carefully manicured nail, gel polish only of course, to her face, and traced along the new vertical lines in her recently acid-polished cheeks. Small, fine lines that looked dangerously close to wrinkles. She was cracking, aging, perhaps, just like her ex-husband had witnessed. It drove him to something younger, richer in beauty, maybe a wiser investment. A man like him, and weren't all men like him? Jay too, roaming her beach, or was it *their* beach? Didn't Ramona say that he lived down the narrow strip of sand from her? Thinking of Jay as her neighbor made her think of him differently, almost instantly. Perhaps, because he lived there, he might belong there. If he belonged there, his classes might then be a service to the community, and then possibly his diligence and consistency of showing up every day meant that he could be trusted. Maybe he wasn't traveling along the sand, shacking up in house after house of his students. Perhaps she would join one of his classes one day, her neighbor Jay, and he would be useful, as Ramona's friend, for a last item of unfinished business.

Is that gray hair? Joan's inspection traveled upward, back up from the creasing she'd discovered while frowning, past the chiseled nose that turned slightly upward a bit further when she smiled. Up, up, her gaze traveled, back across the creasing alongside the blue eyes that sat under brown eyebrows, to the perfect highlights that framed her face. At the top of the golden-toned, honey-blond highlights overlaid on a Cindy Crawford–brown, there was a very clear narrow (but visible!) strip of gray. A strip of gray that extended from her scalp to the edge of all that hair-color perfection. A strip that screamed the truths about Joan that she *truly* dared not confront. Joan actually yelped, a cry for help that nobody would hear. A cry that would translate into a text message to her stylist. *An emergency!* she wrote. And that was as much thinking as she would do on that day, and perhaps ever, on the topic of Ramona . . . other than the one little detail that remained. The one that she would handle the same way she handled everything else in her life— she would ask someone else to do it.

JAY IN MALIBU . . .

AT THE END OF HIS CLASS, PERHAPS THE LAST PERSON JAY WOULD expect to see walking toward him, down on the sand, was Joan Fox. Not that he didn't expect Joan on the sand. To the contrary, she walked often, with similarly clad friends, similarly waiflike, sun visors sometimes, or other measures more drastic, as if the overall elements were more of an enemy than an enjoyment. More typically she shouted *at* him—although said nothing *to* him—from her perch on high behind the glass-enclosed deck space of her palace by the sea. So, now, to see her walking quite intentionally in his direction, holding something that looked very much like an orange box, was a puzzle until she lifted her hand up like a blade to cover her eyes, looked at him, and for once actually spoke *to* him.

"Hey, I need you to get this to Ramona." Joan lifted a wiry arm holding a box in her hand. Jay recognized it well. The contents in a box like that were expensive, and also quite popular with the women and some of the men he'd come to know in Malibu.

Jay did not know what to make of this. But Joan was far from the most challenging personality he'd encountered. Especially considering his prior life on the East Coast. Once, at work, he'd been screamed at by a principal on an M&A deal and then had a stack of papers thrown at his head. Perfect aim, considering his boss never moved his spit-shined leather tie-ups from their perch on his mahogany office desk. "That's interesting," he said to Joan casually. "Why me? Seems like it's your gift?"

"Isn't she your friend?" Joan asked, seeming genuinely confused.

"Isn't she *your* friend?" Jay shot back.

Joan, quite befuddled now, stammered for a few beats before responding. "I left it for her . . . on Christmas night. I presume she was . . . *with you.*"

Jay watched as Joan's lips formed into a tight line, pursed almost, unamused. Jay merely blinked at her, deciding what to say next. True, Ramona had been with him on Christmas night, and the morning before she left. But what did that have to do with Joan, who'd caused the initial mess of Ramona's arrival?

"And how do you know she didn't leave it on purpose?" Jay asked her.

"Who would leave Hermès?" Joan said with a puzzled look. "Why wouldn't you just send it?"

"Because I figured you might need a reason."

"A reason for what?" Jay widened his stance in the sand.

Joan blinked. "Oh, I don't know. A reason to be in touch, perhaps."

She stood and looked at him as if he were slow to the punch line, the one who had missed the point, while the shoreline wind whipped her hair like a *Baywatch* promo. It made absolutely no sense, that this woman would spend a small fortune on a gift, find out that it had been left behind, and then ask a virtual stranger to send it along, when she could full well do it herself. But then again, Jay also knew this type. Joan was of the tribe that did nothing herself, from her cleaning, to her hair color, to her nails, to her childcare, to the maintenance of her grounds, to making the money that sustained her opulent lifestyle. And of course, did not apologize. Why apologize when you can send a gift, pay an expensive merchant to say the three most expensive words in the entire English language—*I was wrong*—on your behalf? So, *Makes sense*, he thought. Why wouldn't she walk up and, in the first words she'd ever spoken directly to him, effectively demand his cooperation.

Not that Jay needed a reason to reach out to Ramona, or even to do something for her. In fact, he adored doing things for Ramona and wished there were more things for him to do for her. More places to take her, to see her smile erupt that each time felt as rare and as special as a meteor streaking across the sky—a thing to wish upon. Or to hear her loud laughter, when she was really amused, when she forgot herself and let it roll from her like the sound of the purest of fun. No, it wasn't a problem of doing something for Ramona, it was the issue of doing something for Joan.

And then, Jay called out to her, words that escaped from him, erupted almost, because his irritation was on delay. The audacity of it, of Joan, of people like her who'd maybe never own up to anything.

"Why don't you just apologize?" he said.

To see Joan react was like watching the clouds cross the sky for a storm. The blanching of her face, the flinch of terror that passed just as quickly as a bird's shadow on the beach. Her mouth dropped open, as if she were shocked to be asked the most appalling thing. And in the silence between the two of them, the ocean continued its noise, lapping at the sand like quiet applause. The seagulls circled the sky above them, searching . . . down below. But it took only seconds of stillness for Joan's composure to return. The impenetrable defense activated as it had innumerable times before. With her free hand, she pushed her hair to the side, out of her face . . . as if she had nothing to hide. And then, in a slow ripple of relaxation, the smooth and carefree countenance returned just as quickly as it had disappeared. And Joan smiled and tilted her head to the left.

"Apologize? For what?" she said with cheer, smiling, as if nothing had ever been wrong. She outstretched her arm farther, reducing the distance between Jay and the box she still held.

And now Jay, looking at Joan, was stunned, bewildered, but not surprised. After all, it was Malibu, a place where people came for the sun and the surf, and to enjoy but not necessarily to confront themselves. Not like Ramona had, like she had to. But Joan did not have to. And chose not to. So, there was no hope for Joan, no use in challenging. She was not going to change.

"You know what, you're right," he said, shaking his head. "You're right."

"Hmm." Joan's straight line of a mouth turned up ever so slightly, and it almost looked like she was going to smile. But she held out the box and pushed it at him with insistence. When he did take the box from her, as soon as it left her hand, "Very well, then," she said, and turned abruptly back in the direction of her house. She walked forward, with Pilates-honed posture, gliding all the way to the base of the staircase. And up she climbed, never once looking back.

The box, now in Jay's hands, was made of thin cardboard and wrapped with a decorated brown ribbon. Between his fingers and the box bottom, there was something sliding, a scrap of paper. He pulled the paper from under his fingers and opened it. It had an address, one he presumed was Ramona's, on Lake Shore Drive, in Chicago.

DECEMBER 30

• ● •

CHELSEA IN MALIBU . . .

CHELSEA WAS SO THRILLED WITH HER LATEST PAINTING, SHE DEcided to give it a name as grand as *Heartbreak*—she called it *Goodbye*. She pulled out her phone, angled the camera just right, and snapped a photo. Without thinking much more about it, she pulled up a message to Helena, dropped the name of the work, attached its image, and hit send. In the message window, on her sender's side, even at the size of the thumbnail preview, Chelsea could see the pop of the colors, the hot pink of the gloves on the seat next to the girl with the flame of red hair. The ruby bits of pepperoni on the square pizza on the mahogany table. The flash of white teeth from two people laughing, and the eyes of the girl's dining companion, the brown of iced coffee in sunshine, glistening with depth as if the whole world could be seen in there. When she saw the bubble appear, the three dots on the bottom left side of her screen, Chelsea knew that Helena had seen it. And as any artist does, she felt a tiny panic as one's art goes for its first time to be seen and experienced and to be judged by someone else.

HELENA: You've been quite busy!

The message appeared just seconds later. Chelsea was flooded with relief and a sense of accomplishment of sorts.

Because Chelsea already knew. She knew that she'd been working differently, that her color palette had changed. Not just that she'd integrated the color that Carlos had given her physically, but those others that she'd gained from experience. She'd been reawakened, with just a taste of family, of structure, of being incorporated somewhere, of having meaning to someone. She remembered what heartbreak was like before the breaking. The joy that the pain was worth, and what had been missing all this while.

Her phone rang. Chelsea answered, realizing that if Helena called, especially while on holiday, that this was more than just an acknowledgment of Chelsea working again.

"Chels-saah." Helena's staccato pronunciation carried itself through the earpiece of her phone. The distinctness of her accent, more formal now, let Chelsea know that she was likely with clients, and thus this call was as much business and opportunity as it was personal. Accordingly, Chelsea decided that she'd speak to Helena as if they spoke every day and took the cue to sound as interesting as anyone would expect of an artist, and as excited about her work as she would be during a show opening or at a gallery event.

"I take it you liked the piece," Chelsea bubbled.

"Much more than liked it, da-ahr-ling! I was just telling my dearest friend, who's with me here on holiday, that Los Angeles is the newest center for contemporary, which is certainly quite true, and then you sent this incredible item that I presume hasn't been seen by *anyone*, correct?"

"No other eyes, Helena, just yours." Chelsea played along, knowing precisely where the conversation was going and that the call was for an audience.

"And the inspiration? Is this Chicago?"

Again, Chelsea knew this drill. No different from the floor of an art gallery, a common question from collectors. They always wanted to know the inspiration, to hear flowery language, strange vocabulary around something so very basic, something that should be true for any artist, that was true for Chelsea now, she just painted what was in her heart.

"It captures the nostalgia of something past, of the fleeting nature of shared moments, of too little time that we get to spend with the people we love. That this particular moment is captured, just something so basic—that *is* its importance. It's meaningful just in itself, because it won't last. So, like the fondest memory, the most special one, there is particular attention given to the precision of the colors, the specificity of them, and the detailing of the brushstrokes. The carefulness given to the casual as if it were a grand portrait of nobility, that is the importance of this moment, a great meeting of two minds—they could be falling in love, or they could be saving the world. It's everything and nothing, but it matters . . . because it matters that it will end."

Chelsea had spoken to Helena the truth of her and Carlos, what she'd come to realize since returning. And she missed him, but held on to him still, in this way. One that could serve them both.

"And it's an original?" Helena's voice drifted back through the phone.

"It's one of one," Chelsea said.

It was a painting that Chelsea in fact very much did not want to sell. For her, it was a memory. It was something that she had left of what was no more. It was one of the kindest moments of her life, when someone tried to keep her warm in a world that was colder than she anticipated. Someone who cared enough to make sure she wasn't alone, even though she was a stranger. Who didn't care who she was or who she wasn't, just that she was there, and that was enough. That was the magic she'd painted that no collector would ever see, or would ever know. It was what made the art more valuable to her than to whomever she sold it to, at whatever price. But for now, she needed the money.

Chelsea could hear Helena speaking away from the microphone of the phone. There was another voice with hers, the voice of a man, muffled and unintelligible. And there was Helena's reduced to only a rhythm of speaking, but a rhythm that Chelsea knew. One that worked miracles, that whipped up a frenzy and made stars and millionaires out of struggling unknowns, that created urgency and amplified desire, that matched the art that was birthed to the place that would become its home. And while this alchemy worked, Chelsea stood, holding the phone, until Helena returned.

"Chels-saah, consider that piece sold. Show it to no one else. We'll confirm the wire of the funds. I trust the price will be suitable." A "suitable" price by Helena's standards was a guarantee of at least five figures, for certain. Chelsea tried to keep her cool.

"Great," she said, as casually as she could. "I'll hold it."

The call ended, and Chelsea immediately felt the sides of her mouth stretching toward her ears. And on her now-smiling cheeks the water from her eyes had a place to land, to slide down, to be wiped by her hand away from her jawline. It wasn't the painting she didn't want to let go of, it was the moment, it was the feeling of that moment. But it was money she needed, welcome income, already earmarked for what she wanted most.

RAMONA IN CHICAGO . . .

RAMONA PERUSED THE COLORFUL DISPLAY OF GLOSSY MAGAZINE covers and block lettering highlighting the celebrities du jour, just a couple that Ramona fully recognized and others she presumed were from somewhere in the world of the internet, made famous by an audience or simply being made famous by having their face plastered on these mini paper billboards.

"And, girl, get a home magazine . . ." Ramona was on the phone with Latrice, her virtual companion on this outing, as they were collaborating on their intended New Year's Eve activity of vision boarding, because next year *for sure* was going to be their year, and they would not be leaving this one unprepared. They were both of the age that, dateless for the evening, it was entirely too cold to go out looking for one, or even out trying to have a good time like it was a different night than any other night in wintery Chicago.

"I've already got two," Ramona replied. "Plus *Essence, Oprah, Vogue, Elle, Cosmo, Women's Fitness* . . . does it seem to you that there are a lot less magazines to pick from?"

"Yeah . . . because people like me and you are literally only buying magazines to cut them up. They need to do a magazine called *Vision* and fill it with just photos of shit we can't afford."

"Can't afford *yet* . . . and wasn't that always the point of magazines?"

"Truuuue." Latrice made a sharp inhale that could be heard through the phone. Ramona braced herself for what was coming. "You picking up a bridal mag?"

"On that note, nah. If I don't see another dress, another place setting for a long time, I'll be fine. Next time, I'll elope. You?"

"You know I still have dreams of walking down the aisle in my white tux . . ."

"Hugo Boss, custom tailored . . ."

"Stupid fresh, with the Loubie Louis Junior Spiked Low Lows I still got in the box. Gotta have my flat-bottomed red bottoms!" Latrice was so entirely particular about her fashion. Ramona laughed. Latrice laughed too, until she stopped, and the air went briefly quiet over the line. "You all right though?"

Ramona shifted; the phone at her ear felt heavy suddenly with the weight of the magazines in her arm and the awkwardness of a white poster board folded and pinched to her body with her elbow.

"I'm all right." Ramona was telling the truth. If you lose something, a dream, a person, a wedding, or a marriage even, you also lose the person you thought you were going to become. But Ramona was creating something else, in all those stacks of new dreams and inspiration, a new idea for herself—of what she could become. She would eventually fill the void of loss with hope, but in the meantime, she'd do it with cut-out images from about five hundred combined magazines. "None of this turned out how I expected," she said. "But—"

Ramona's phone beeped with a text message. "Hold on one sec." She pulled the phone away from her ear to check the sender. Jay's name, who she'd stored as *Malibu Jay*, popped up, and she read it, while Latrice held the line.

MALIBU JAY: You left something.

Ramona ran through in her mind what it could be. With one free hand, she typed back.

RAMONA: Too bad you can't just run it down to me. What'd I leave?"

MALIBU JAY: A gift.

RAMONA: You shouldn't have.

MALIBU JAY: I didn't.

RAMONA: Um, okay. You have my address? Chicago, not Malibu.

MALIBU JAY: Yeah, I'm going to drop it off.

RAMONA: Haha, ok. I'll be on the lookout.

"Helloooo!" Latrice's voice sounded small and from a faraway place coming through the receiver. Ramona snapped back to attention, realizing she'd been smiling, hard, her fingers hovering over the phone. Not seeing any more dots, and now looking forward to receiving a gift from Jay, Ramona returned to her call with Latrice.

"Girl, I'm so sorry!"

"I know they can't be texting you from the office."

"Nah, we're off. That was Jay, said he's sending me a gift."

"Now, that sounds promising." Latrice's voice perked up over the phone receiver. But Ramona wasn't similarly enthused. Jay was on the other side of the world.

"Not promising. Not anything. Just a moment that happened somewhere faaar away." Ramona sighed. She missed him, the text confirmed that. And the only thing that made it bearable really was that she had no hope whatsoever attached to him in any way. They'd had what they had—he taught her to surf, showed her a good time, a great time really, a wonderful time actually—and now she was back in Chicago, picking up pictures of other people's lives so that she could get half a clue about what she wanted for her own.

"He must not have hit it right . . ." Latrice laughed, but Latrice was wrong.

Ramona felt her face flush. "I cannot confirm that statement."

"Okay, surfboard . . ." Latrice teased, adopting the cadence of Beyoncé singing about lovemaking and intoxication.

And Ramona did think about the surfboard, the real one, standing on top of it, feet planted so firmly, balanced, assured, riding the waves, the wind, the moment, unafraid and ready to fall and to try again. She knew the feeling of freedom, she'd tasted it, and she was drinking it here now, in her life in Chicago. And for the first time since she'd returned, she felt the sense of real hope, of real possibility that life was as much of an unwritten road as the poster board tucked under her arm, and that, somehow, the best was still very much yet to come.

"Girl, I gotta go. I need to pick up a photo I had printed. And I still have to get collard greens—"

"And black-eyed peas too, right? You know they're gonna be sold out. Your mom doesn't make some?" Latrice asked.

"She does, but this year, I need my own luck. You cooking?"

"Girl, naw, but you know to call me if you need a taste tester. I'm going to sit in my bonnet, do this vision board, drink a glass of champagne, and hopefully be in bed asleep before the fireworks are over." The fireworks, over Lake Michigan, Ramona could see from the window of her condo. They launched from Navy Pier at the stroke of midnight each year. She imagined Latrice in her bonnet, asleep before midnight, and somehow the idea didn't seem half bad.

Ramona laughed, and then she and Latrice ended their call, so Ramona could jet around to find an area supermarket that still had two of the most popular items for New Year's, the staples cooked by Black families from Jacksonville to Portland, from Syracuse to Santa Fe, the collard greens for the money and the hoppin' john for luck. Especially this year, she'd love a double serving of both.

JAY IN MALIBU . . .

JAY SAT ON HIS SOFA WARMED BY THE CRACKLING OF THE FIRE IN his fireplace, sipping his well-poured IPA, and entirely ignored the roaring sounds of the Pacific just outside, and for that matter the view as well. Instead of looking at the seductions of the moonlit ocean, or the dancing fireplace, or any of the recorded people on television, he looked at his phone, at his last messages from Ramona. He scrolled down yet another time, as if reading them again—as opposed to the last fifteen other times—would provide some new information or clue hidden within the correspondence. *This is how you go crazy,* he thought to himself. How easy it would be to just ask her what she meant when she said she'd be looking out for him. *Did she really want to see him again?* he wondered. Except, to clarify would mean losing the excitement of possibility—the rich feeling of hope that he was using to fill the gap of uncertainty—and confronting a looming fear—the fear of rejection.

Jay's life was an uncomplicated one by design. He had no concerns for money. In New York, he'd already learned the mechanisms of multiplying one's wealth. He had accumulated enough of a nest egg after savings and bonuses and some very well-timed cryptocurrency investments, such that he could have what he wanted, materially at least. In the life that he built in Southern California, and in Malibu in particular, he'd managed to become quite good at hiding the fact that by forty, he'd already acquired far beyond all of his needs. He let very few people visit his home and had a second car, one built ten years prior that he used to get around the city. Had Ramona checked the odometer in his ultraluxe SUV, she would have seen miles that were exceedingly low, less than twenty thousand of them—the rides that Jay had taken literally just for joy, just to remind himself that he had enough, and that there was no one else he needed to make happy other than himself—not even his family, especially not his parents.

This fact about the two cars, Jay didn't share with Ramona, even as much as he'd let her know him. She was also unaware that of the few people who'd been to his house, none had been after just one day of knowing him. Because as calm and collected as he seemed, what he'd alluded to was true— Jay was petrified of being pushed into wanting or needing more than what he had. He'd witnessed his former classmates and colleagues, burnt out in one way or another, dependent on alcohol breaks between meetings downstairs at the local bar near Wall Street, or a line or two on a desk or in the bathroom, which was used far more often for that sort of thing than it was for biological relief. The ones who were married often exercised some sort of fetish hidden behind curtains of alibis of working late and other bullshit that hid expensive distractions of escalating risk. In his life in New York City, there'd been no such thing as enough, or anywhere close to it. You couldn't have enough when the scoreboard was lit with dollar signs and net worth was calculated in numbers of commas. Jay was tired of using his bank account to measure his self-esteem. For now, it only bought him freedom and choice.

Malibu became like a foreign country where the exchange rate allowed him to buy far more than he ever anticipated, including an actual life, along with his compact cottage at the sea, plus rental unit, of course. And here he could have enough, could be enough, even if that meant being alone. Because so many of the women he met were looking for the least of what he could offer—his ability to work hard. But usually, as he opened more of his life to someone, they'd start to push ideals on him of what he could be to them, provide for them, commit to them, and Jay wasn't about to drift into deeper waters. But he hadn't expected Ramona.

How would she know that in his messages that day, he was testing out an idea, one that he was far too fearful of proposing in real life. That idea of taking action—when you have that unmistakable yearning of missing someone, actually wishing they were here or you were there—for sure, it likely happens to everyone. But then, most people would toy with the thought, enjoy the idea of it a bit, a fantasy as some quick off-ramp of relief from the longing. Perhaps he could try, by diving into a memory of time spent, the sparkle of Ramona's laughter, or the moment he fell for her. The moment she fell in the water and stood up, soaking wet and a bit stunned, scared too, but with so much determination to get back on that board, to learn something new.

Or the version of her that fell asleep in his class. He knew that kind of exhaustion. He'd felt it, in countless nights in the office, shouldering too much responsibility with his family, trying too hard to meet an objective with a moving goalpost. He recognized Ramona because he'd been Ramona. And he appreciated Ramona because Ramona appreciated him. So, in the uniqueness of it all and how deeply he'd been moved, he couldn't think of her enough to fill the hole that her absence created.

So, as the memory of her wasn't quite sufficient, here he sat, with an orange box on his left side, near where Ramona had once sat, and his phone in his hand. His eyes were rereading her words "Too bad you can't just run it down to me . . ." But the fact was, with time that was his and a bank account that was fully sufficient, he *actually could.* It wasn't as easy as walking down the sand or driving. It would take more than a few drops of gas, some hours, or just some intentionality. But it was a decision he could make. *And this is how you go crazy . . . for a girl,* he thought, pulling up a website for flights, just to see, of course. It was New Year's, and he had no plans. Some people with no plans do nothing, and some people fly to New York, or Paris, or Jakarta, or Bali, just to be in the exact place they wanted to be when the sun comes up over a new year. Earlier, to Ramona, he had typed, *I'll bring it to you.* Was it a joke? Had he been joking? He'd been speaking wistfully for both of them, but what if? Why not? And how interesting that there was a flight in the afternoon. So, his fingers started entering his information, because they were connected to his heart and its desires, the tapping and the beating, the beating of his heart on his computer screen. Jay continued until all the blank spaces were filled. *So what if I don't go?* he thought. It felt good to try, to go through the motions.

So, Jay bought a plane ticket. And then, playing it all out in his head, because he'd surely gone mad by this point, he just started making a series of decisions because each one felt good to make. These were small risks, placing small bets that just happened to keep getting bigger. Each step made the next one seem possible and the next one seem to make sense—the next logical step. *Was there even a hotel room available?* he wondered. *What was the date?* It'd be New Year's Eve. *People made significance of that date,* Jay thought. Couples booked rooms together, created fantasies of just one night or two; friends booked suites only to wake up somewhere they'd forgotten how they reached. Perhaps there'd be nothing available in a city filled with visitors, and dreamers, everyone looking to make something feel different about life, to mark a new beginning.

Seeing one room available, and really not needing to worry about the price—*it's just a day or two,* he told himself, feeling great now about making these decisions—Jay booked a hotel room. And then what? The box, he'd just drop it off, he'd just drop this orange box off, because it was expensive and he'd have had to ship it with insurance anyway. *Why not just take it and leave it?* He'd delivered a pizza once, to a girl he liked in high school. But now he was imagining Ramona, and what he'd do if she answered the door, but would she answer? Well, yes, he'd get there, and he'd go to his hotel, and of course, she might be out or have plans for the evening, or maybe she'd even be there with that guy she'd supposedly ended things with. *She had ended things, right?* What if she hadn't? But Jay was wild now, wild with his imagination, in his thoughts, chasing the good feeling of making small decisions, of doing what he wanted to do. It did not matter *what if.* What if he got into a fight? What if the guy punched him? What if Ramona was home? What if she smiled? What if he saw her face and they kissed? What if they made love . . . again?

And with a ticket, a hotel room, and an orange box, Jay finally put down his phone. For once entirely satisfied. He could also do nothing, he realized. He could not go. He could forget the ticket. He could send the box. These were all choices he'd have to make . . . tomorrow.

DECEMBER 31

• ● ●

RAMONA IN CHICAGO . . .

THE INSIDE OF RAMONA'S CONDO SMELLED LIKE SAVORY GARLIC, onions, vinegar, and the earthy delights of collard greens and black-eyed peas cooking with smoked meat. The steam from the boiling pots filled up all thousand square feet of her home from the kitchen to the living room. It wafted all the way down the hallway, through the bedroom, and into the en suite where Ramona stood at the mirror and fiddled with her hair, deciding if it was worth a full wash day tomorrow or if she could get away with a high-placed poof until the next weekend. These were dreadful back-to-work decisions, when the New Year's holiday didn't fall on a Friday. Having just one day off would certainly not carry her far enough into the week, through what already promised to be a healthy measure of oh-hell-no-they-did-not bullshit waiting at the office. It was already evening enough, and it gave Ramona great comfort to pull her satin bonnet over her hair and head into her bedroom to put on her pajamas. It was the ultimate act of defiance, in fact, to practice for once the act of not caring—especially not about the fact that she wasn't doing something photoworthy on #baecation or flaunting some kind of materialistic demonstration of love on social media. In fact, her best photo, the one that Jay took of her surfing, was already printed and framed, placed in her bag to take to the office.

It was New Year's Eve, and the very best thing Ramona had in mind to do was practice her mother's recipes from the foods she had every year, the customs of luck passed down across generations from the cooking mothers of Alabama and Mississippi and their iron kettles making alchemy, learning how to transform the food scraps they were given into literal magic in your mouth, the best thing you ever tasted. This was what Ramona had also resolved to do with her life. This new year would be a new start, a new attitude, something new and wonderful that she just believed was going to happen.

"I just cut out a picture of this sista on a surfboard from the fitness mag, who knew it was so good for the abs?" Ramona was comfortable in her pajamas now, on a video call with Latrice, who was sitting in her own bonnet, at her place, and also cutting through her own magazines for her vision board.

"I just cut out that new Tom Ford cashmere pullover," Latrice said.

"Is that vision board worthy?"

"I can't afford it on my current salary, so it is to me."

"Ah, I get it. After that project that had you working through Christmas, shouldn't you be up for a promotion?"

"Good point. On behalf of the Grinch, let me also clip this photo of the Burj Al Arab from the *Robb Report*, and I need to find the letters somewhere for P-R-O-M-O-T-I-O-N."

"I'm looking for L-O-V-E."

"Let me tell you, the—" Latrice's voice continued, but Ramona didn't hear her over the sound of her doorbell, definitely the sound of her doorbell, and she turned her head away from the phone. "Is that your doorbell? Did you order something?" Latrice said. The phone came back into focus for Ramona.

"I didn't. Maybe it's Carlos." With some effort, Ramona stood up, untangling herself from the cross-legged pretzel she'd been seated in on the floor. The middle of her living room was a sea of magazines and paper scraps, a mess that her dog would exponentially multiply if left unattended. "C'mon, Wookiee." She slapped twice against her leg and all of a sudden, a fluff of fur brushed against her calf. She walked over to the door with trepidation, a feeling of minor alarm building in her gut, quelled by her self-reassurance that it was probably Carlos, stopping by for a plate, knowing she was cooking and trying to eat now rather than waiting for tomorrow at her mother's house.

"Oh right, Carlos has a super sense when it comes to the smell of cooking . . ."

"I know, ri—" Ramona never finished her sentence. She pulled open the door, and the first thing she saw was an orange box. A man holding an orange box. A man who looked like Jay, standing in her doorway, uncannily like Jay but who obviously couldn't be him because for it to be him, well, that was impossible. So, she just stood there with her mouth open.

"Girl, are you okay? Do I need to come over there? You know what? I *am* over there. I am right downstairs, and I have my piece, you know what I mean! You need me to call someone?" By this point Latrice was yelling, her voice carrying up Ramona's limp arm and drifting between Ramona and the Jay impersonator that she still wasn't at all convinced could be the actual person because there was no way. On every level there was *no way*. What a man would have to do to go that far out of his way, Ramona didn't believe a man would do *for her*. Or the speed with which the wish that left her lips that couldn't have possibly been fulfilled by the universe, Ramona didn't believe in that either, so for now, she just stood in the limbo of unbelieving despite what her eyes certainly were telling her was true.

And then the Jay impersonator was moving, lifting his arm up, holding out the box between them, in the doorway. And then he spoke. "I, um . . . I brought this for you." And the Jay impersonator was using Jay's voice, and it was such a strange delivery, and was it God's sense of humor or someone else's?

"Jay?" Ramona heard her own voice come out of her mouth now. It was full of shock, and surprise, and that high pitch at the end when you literally cannot fucking believe what is happening, like all of a sudden, you've turned into Minnie Riperton.

And then Jay's voice came out of the Jay . . . well, came out of *actual* Jay, standing right in front of her. "Hi," he said. And Ramona blinked as if blinking were some kind of Morse code, but nonsensical still, because she had no words.

"Ramona, girl, are you okay?" Latrice's voice was coming out of the phone, evincing escalating concern, but Ramona could not lift her hand whatsoever, or think, really, because of the short-circuiting that was happening in her own brain. The cross of wires, the intersection of disbelief and what must be reality, and actual Jay who was standing before her and all that that would have to mean. So, still, Ramona's mouth was just wide open, and the door was cracked open and she was standing there in her bonnet without the proper instructions to provide to her mouth or to the rest of her body because she had absolutely no idea what was happening and thus what she should do.

Ramona managed the simple task of returning the greeting. The greeting from *actual* Jay standing in front of her. The Jay who should be in Malibu or elsewhere. Jay with most certainly more important things to do. "Hi," she said breathlessly.

"Look, I know this is weird." Actual Jay started speaking again. "And I feel kind of ridiculous like I might have made a huge mistake, but I'm here. And for sure, there's a different version of this moment, right? Where I didn't get on the plane, you know? Where I told myself a million times how ridiculous this was, or maybe just one more time I let it play out in my mind how upset you'd be, or how crazy you'd think I was. There's definitely a version too where maybe you'd call the cops or tell me that I'd gone too far, and you never wanted to see me again. Or, even worse, that you pretended just as long as you had to that this was a good idea and then as soon as you could, blocked me, deleted my number from your phone and me from your life, labeled me something that I could never overcome—"

"What is *happeninnnng*?" Latrice's voice was loud enough to shoot through the air with an energy of its own. It stopped Jay from his nervous babbling, and it snapped Ramona out of a hypnotic daze. She was listening now, to the words of *this* Jay, of *actual* Jay who got on a plane *to see her*. And she managed to pull her arm up, to bring her hand holding the phone to her face, and to see herself on the screen, still in a bonnet with eyes big and mouth agape, alongside Latrice, now with her coat on putting a large kitchen knife into her purse.

Ramona seemed to reanimate then and snatched the bonnet off. "Wait, wait, Latrice, stop. It's Jay . . . from Malibu. He came . . ."

"Whhaaat in the . . ." Ramona watched the screen as Latrice stopped in her tracks. "Jaaayyyy? Are you telling me that you said . . . and then . . . the door . . . and now . . . whhhooaaa . . . I need to cut out some more pictures . . ." Latrice brought her free hand to her head and held the side of her palm to the fabric of her bonnet, as if that would somehow speed up the rate of her processing. "Girl, let me see." Ramona complied and tapped the button to flip the camera view to the direction of Jay. "Well, *damn*," Latrice said. "I'm . . . I mean . . . y'all doin' New Year's Eve surprises and shit? Look, send mine to iii—"

Ramona quickly flipped the camera back to her. "I need to call you back . . . One sec—" And then she ended the call with Latrice because the air was too heavy here, and she still wasn't quite sure it was real. "Sorry," she said to Jay and hoped he would continue.

Jay shifted on his feet. He pulled up his arm to scratch the top of his head, leaving his hair a little messy in that place. He seemed to notice that and smoothed his palm slowly down his hairline, down his face, and covering his mouth for a second, but then released his hold on his jaw, to start again. "I was just saying . . . in all these other scenarios, I mean everything I ran through in my mind, every little reason not to come—the plane was delayed, and I couldn't find my TSA number, and I mean the line was so long, long enough to think that I'm a complete idiot, especially taking off my shoes, but still—the *worst* consequence in *every* case, *every* scenario that I could imagine, was only that I'd never see you again, which is what I was most afraid of in the first place. So, I honestly just came to drop this off—" He lifted up the orange box to her again and held it out between them in the doorway. "That's what I said I would do. I can hand you this box, and leave. I can go back to my very nice hotel, and order room service, and figure out why in the *hell* I didn't think to pack a coat. Or—"

"Jay, you hungry?" Ramona looked at him and said the one thing that meant everything. Because food came from the heart and soul, and quite honestly, she already knew she'd *put her foot* in those greens.

From the moment that Ramona shut the door to Jay sitting at the table was fifteen minutes. From ending the call with Latrice to the time she stopped texting was twenty. From the table to the sofa for Ramona and Jay was another thirty. By the time an hour had passed, Ramona and Jay had made it past awkwardness and the shock of audacity to realize that this had, in fact, been a good thing to happen, however unlikely. And finally, they remembered that he had come this entire way purportedly to deliver a box, and that regardless of the fact that it was from Joan—Ramona had half a mind to throw it away, except that you do not throw away Hermès—she ought to open it. And so, she did open the square orange box with the horse atop. She undid the decorative brown ribbon and slid it away. She pulled off the slightly warped, thin cardboard cover. She lifted the transparent white tissue paper, delicately folded, layer by layer, like petals of a blooming flower. What was revealed was a beautiful scarf, folded at the bottom of the box, with a gorgeous pattern of understated jewel tone colors, in elegant combination, from what Ramona could see. But she couldn't see all of it, because on top of the scarf sat a small white envelope with her name written on it.

Ramona lifted the envelope and looked at it. She put it next to the box and tapped the top of it with her fingers. She had half a mind not to open it. To take the scarf and wear it well. To keep it just because she liked it. It would be *Joan* that she'd give back. She would forget about Joan as best she could and erase what she needed to from the scars of the start of her trip to Malibu and the lies that came after. Because it wasn't the scarf that would remind Ramona when and where others felt she didn't belong. And it wouldn't just end with Joan's erasure. It would still be everywhere all the time—every day in the office, in restaurants, on other trips. Everywhere but home, she'd still be an *other*. So, she'd keep just what was good from Malibu— what she wanted to remember, what she loved, who she loved, and who loved her. And as she'd learned there, she'd have to carry home in her heart, to make peace for herself anywhere and always. Nobody could take *that* belonging away from her, not ever again.

Emboldened, she picked up the envelope and pulled the top out. She slid the folded notecard out and flipped it open. There in black ink were the long strokes of elegant handwriting, the careful cursive of considered thought and intentionally selected words.

> *Dearest Ramona,*
>   *For wonderful times, when the wind blows—for the chill, for car trips with the top down and dinner with friends. May it be part of fond memories.*
>   *From your Malibu neighbor,*
>   *Joan*

Ramona read the written words out loud. And then she paused, deciding if she'd read the rest. The rest that was scribbled a little less carefully, in blue ink this time, obviously not even the same pen.

"That's it?" Jay was looking now, waiting, clearly, on her.

Ramona decided to be honest. "No, that's not it."

"What's the rest?"

"There's this last part, I guess she added it before she gave it to you. It says, *"I was wrong . . . about Jay."*

Jay's eyebrows rose.

"Don't even ask." Ramona held her hand up. And then the two of them shared a laugh, as she moved the box aside, stood up, and walked over to drop the card and its envelope in the recycling bin.

At the stroke of midnight, a couple of hours later, in Ramona's apartment, she stood with a glass of champagne looking out at the frozen lake. The fireworks show started at Navy Pier, and the sky lit up with explosions of color and smoke. The rim of her glass met the rim of Jay's glass as they toasted to a new year of beginnings . . . and to their night together, whatever that would come to mean.

JANUARY 1

• ● •

CHELSEA IN MALIBU, FOR NOW . . .

IN THE EARLY HOURS OF THE MORNING, CHELSEA WAS UP AND awake and putting the finishing touches on *View of the Frozen Lake from the Window*, which she decided to change to *Summertime* as the formal title of the painting. She'd painted what she remembered of that frozen lake, which was so different than the undulating body of water outside her window that continued into forever. Salt water versus fresh water, one was unchanging, seasonless, predictable to the rise and fall of the tides. The other was mutable, changing in shape and nature, of what possibilities it held—the lake in the summer months could be a time of sparkling enjoyment, while in winter a period of stillness, of quiet, perhaps of waiting for its better times. Chelsea hoped that she'd captured all of that in the image— what the lake had become in the winter as she experienced it and, below the surface, what the lake had been in the summer and would be again, as she imagined it. The lake was Chelsea, and her summer was on its way.

After the instant sale of *Goodbye*, Helena asked Chelsea for absolutely everything she had in the so-called Chicago series, which had not at all been a series before, either by intention or execution. But upon Helena's strong suggestion, Chelsea realized that she should work toward the idea at least.

Circumstances had changed for her, and for once, change was actually a good thing. Moreover, the five-figure funds had already hit her account in the wire of Chelsea's personal portion of the sale price for her artwork. It was the amount that she and Helena agreed upon after a deduction for the overdue, but now fully satisfied, tax payment, and some portion toward the expenses of the house. A house that held nothing more for Chelsea to discover; a house that provided a view that no longer inspired.

Since her return from Chicago, Chelsea and Carlos had been in touch in a regular way. Sending a joke here, or a meme there. Chelsea sent him a photo of her view of the sky washed in orange sherbet and lavender at sunset from her outside deck. He sent her a photo of a unique vertical perspective of an office building looking all the way up into an unusually sunny wintertime sky. She sent a photo of *Goodbye* and typed to Carlos:

CHELSEA: Sold it.

CARLOS: Already? That one is amazing. The fire is back!

Chelsea's hand hovered over the keyboard. A thought arrived of what she ought to do. It was the kind of thought that most people would ignore, an impulse or idea to be brushed away, one that was nice, perhaps, but too nice. A gesture beyond their character in the moment, a trusting of intuition beyond the seeming authority of the still-so-quiet voice within. But as an artist, when being an artist, sometimes it is only you and that voice; your art depends upon it. And Chelsea, being an artist, being more of an artist now than she had been in years, had a hankering to listen to that voice, to follow that idea, to see where it led.

CHELSEA: I'd like to buy the image that you took of me.

CARLOS: What image?

CHELSEA: At Ramona's.

CARLOS: It's already on your phone. I took it for you. I sent it to you. It's yours.

CHELSEA: Not yet. It's still yours. You took it. I want to buy it.

CARLOS: Girl, u crazy.

Chelsea smiled and then let out a laugh. *Carlos,* she thought to herself, allowing herself the swell of feelings. Over the phone screen, her fingers hovered and then set out again with quick tapping.

CHELSEA: How much is your show?

Immediately she saw the three bubbles. A message appeared with the sound effect for its arrival.

CARLOS: What show?

CHELSEA: Your show at the gallery. How much do you need for your show?

CARLOS: Dunno, I'm trying to save like $1200.

CHELSEA: Then, I'll buy the photo for $600. Deal?

The dots again. *Come on, Carlos*, Chelsea thought. It was the one thing she wanted to do, that she needed to do. It was the follow-through on the feeling of truly connecting to someone, of loving them—when you want what they want. Chelsea's wish was for Carlos. What she wanted most was what he wanted for himself. And she hoped that with what she sold, he'd allow her to do what she wished with the money.

CARLOS: I'm not trying to take your money.

CHELSEA: I'm not trying to take your work.

CARLOS: Send it back then! Haha.

CHELSEA: Carlos, please. It's important to me.

Please. Chelsea pleaded with him silently, watching the three dots appear and then disappear in their message thread.

CARLOS: OK

Chelsea let her eyelids fall and let her breath release. She would love Carlos, and she would let him go. And perhaps they would have cause to meet again.

For now, it was done. Chelsea put her phone down and crossed back through her living room and its wall of windows. In her bedroom, she opened the blinds to let in the rising sun. It was something to appreciate now, having been away from it, and knowing that she'd be away again soon—writing another note to a new renter, maybe making an exchange, heading somewhere else, somewhere new and unknown, with all its colors to discover.

On the first day of the new year, for the first time in a long time, from her window, Chelsea Flint looked out upon the ocean with wonder, excited about where she'd go next.

ACKNOWLEDGMENTS

IT'S HARD TO BELIEVE THAT THIS IS MY FOURTH NOVEL, ESPECIALLY since I was once convinced that novelists and authors were people other than me, those sprinkled with fairy dust, ordained and predetermined to do this magical art of creating worlds and people and personae that generate real emotion, while teaching us all something about the world we live in, whether directly or incidentally.

It's been such an honor to have readers who entrust me with their time and attention, and it's been the pleasure of my life to find the courage and skill to deliver a work of art worthy of this endowment. So thank you for making this all so worthwhile.

I began this journey as a team of one, and my, how the team has grown! I couldn't be more grateful to the travelers who have joined me along this road, starting with my agent, Lucinda Halpern. When the vision is young and fragile, when the time has been short to bring what's only in your mind into the world beyond, it is rare that someone can understand what you see simply by seeing you. That is what Lucinda did in 2020 with *Black Girls Must Die Exhausted*, and that is what she continues to do with each project that I excitedly share, like this one. Thank you also to the Lucinda Literary team, who support me in so many ways. You are all appreciated. Thank you also to Joe Veltre and the Gersh team for supporting the transition of my work to the screen. One down, many more to go!

Writing *The Most Wonderful Time* was truly, truly, as an artist and author, the absolute most wonderful time, and this is very much because of my incredible editor, Amy Baker. Amy, you have supported and believed from the very beginning, and to have the opportunity to collaborate on this particular story was an invigorating delight. And beyond the simple fun of it, your fearlessness and your depth of spirit, your intelligence and compassion helped evolve this story and its remarkable characters into people we can't help but to know. People we meet within the pages and continue to consider well after the last page has been read. Thank you for the many powerful conversations that helped to find the soul of this project. I believe it was worth it.

Thank you to the tireless team at Harper Perennial—and Heather, Megan, and Jackie, you are so appreciated. Robin, you find new ways to inspire me each time with your gorgeous cover designs. And to each and every member of the incredible HarperCollins sales team who have helped to place my books in the hands of readers, especially this one, thank you so much.

Thank you to Ashley Bernardi and the Nardi Media team; to Dawn Hardy, the Literary Lobbyist; and Bookstagram; BookTok; the Target team; local libraries; and all the bookstores of every size and in every location that regularly feature my books, that have supported this book, and that are instrumental in helping match readers with those of my books they might enjoy. Thank you also to the book clubs with whom I've already met, and those with whom I'll meet for this and future projects—your conversations have truly helped me hone my ability to write, and it is of immeasurable value to spend time with you.

I also want to extend a special thank-you to the Black and brown surfing community who so graciously embraced me during my research for this book. Thank you to Nate Fluellen, who generously agreed to be interviewed and then extended the invitation of a lifetime to attend A Great Day in the Stoke, which I hope I'll never miss for any of its upcoming years. Thank you to Rick Blocker, a surfing pioneer and legend whom I'm so thrilled to have come to know. Thank you to those I've met and who helped me navigate a very new-to-me world of surfing: Greg and Marie Rachal of the Black Surfers Collective; Tony Corley, founder of the Black Surfing Association; David Mesfin and the *Wade in the Water* documentary team (what a gorgeous must-see film); Color the Water; and so many others. I am forever inspired and couldn't be happier that this book required me to take my first surf lesson, which undoubtedly won't be my last.

Finally, but not least, thank you to my "home team" of friends and family! Thank you to my first readers, Mom and Kerry Ann, for taking the time to read that "book in a binder" I hastily sent you and for the encouraging feedback that helped me get through the last edits. Thanks to my dad for being my strategist in chief and making sure I know that I can always come home. And thank you to my love, Jeff, for putting up with late nights and early mornings, for letting me go off into these strange worlds, and for always holding my hand while still letting me type.

I love and appreciate you all.

ABOUT THE AUTHOR

JAYNE ALLEN is a writer, producer, entrepreneur, and forever-recovering lawyer. She is a proud native of Detroit and graduate of Duke University and Harvard Law School. Purposeful in centering and celebrating Black women's societal contributions, Allen crafts transcultural stories exploring contemporary issues such as modern relationships, workplace and career dynamics, and the complexities of race. Her common themes include mental and physical health and highlight the importance of self-love and self-care—all with a healthy dose of warmth and humor. Allen is also the author of the bestselling Black Girls Must Die Exhausted trilogy, currently being adapted for television. She lives in Los Angeles.

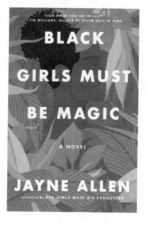
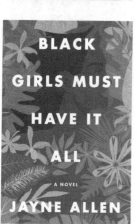